J

The Life and Correspondence of Charles Lord Metcalfe

Vol. I

SALZWASSER VERLAG

John William Kaye

The Life and Correspondence of Charles Lord Metcalfe

Vol. I

Reprint of the original, first published in 1858.

1st Edition 2023 | ISBN: 978-3-37513-456-3

Verlag (Publisher): Salzwasser Verlag GmbH, Zeilweg 44, 60439 Frankfurt, Deutschland
Vertretungsberechtigt (Authorized to represent): E. Roepke, Zeilweg 44, 60439 Frankfurt, Deutschland
Druck (Print): Books on Demand GmbH, In de Tarpen 42, 22848 Norderstedt, Deutschland

THE

LIFE AND CORRESPONDENCE

CHARLES, LORD METCALFE,

BY

JOHN WILLIAM KAYE,

AUTHOR OF "THE LIFE OF SIR JOHN MALCOLM," "HISTORY OF THE WAR IN AFGHANISTAN," ETC.

A NEW AND REVISED EDITION.

IN TWO VOLUMES.

VOL. I.

LONDON:

SMITH, ELDER AND CO., 65, CORNHILL.

1858.

TO

WILLIAM BUTTERWORTH BAYLEY,

ONE OF THE EARLIEST AND THE LATEST, ONE OF THE MOST LOVED AND MOST RESPECTED

OF

CHARLES METCALFE'S FRIENDS,

THESE VOLUMES

ARE

AFFECTIONATELY INSCRIBED.

Engraved by J. C. Armytage from a Bust by E. H. Baily R.A.

PREFACE TO NEW EDITION.

A FEW lines will suffice to explain in what respects this edition of the "Life of Lord Metcalfe" differs from the work as originally published.

The earlier part of the work is considerably compressed. This has been effected, without detriment to the completeness of the biography, by the omission of some passages of explanatory history and of some letters discussing the events narrated in those passages. As Metcalfe at that period—I mean, at the time of the first Mahratta war—held only a subordinate position, it is possible that in the original work those events were too much elaborated, and Metcalfe's opinions respecting them too minutely illustrated in his correspondence. At all events, this was the opinion of some friendly critics—in spite of my anticipatory protest in the preface to the first edition; and, as I have since gone over much of the same ground, and with better justification, in the "Life of Sir John Malcolm," who was really *pars magna* of the first Mahratta war, I willingly defer to the judgment of others, and send forth the early chapters of the biography in their present condensed shape.

But I have expanded another part of the work; and in stating this I must make another confession of error. I confess that I was one of those who believed that Metcalfe's repeated allusions to the insecurity of our Indian empire, and to the probabilities of some sudden and disastrous outbreak, were not in accordance with the general sagacity and the sound good sense of the man. His friends, I know, used to smile at this as his weak point; and in the original edition of this work, I did not speak of it with much respect. People, however, think differently of the matter now; and at all events, it is curious and interesting, at the present time, to observe Metcalfe's prognostications of the coming storm, and not uninstructive to mark in what manner he was wont to suggest that we should prepare ourselves to meet it. I have, therefore, given, in the second volume of this edition, several passages from Metcalfe's correspondence (not in the original edition) illustrative of his ever-prevailing sense of danger, and of his views with regard to the best means of strengthening and securing our position in the midst of a conquered people.

Besides these more important changes, which I trust will be considered improvements, there are some less important alterations, to which it is scarcely necessary to advert. Some documents public and private, which seemed to encumber the text and impede the flow of the narrative, have either been omitted altogether or removed to the Appendix, where they may be read, or not, according to the taste of the reader. I would not, however, recommend any one to abstain from the perusal of Dr. Goodall's letters to his old pupil, although I have removed them to the end of the book.

In conclusion, I will only say, as an utterance of pure gratitude, that I owe much to this work; for, if it has not increased the little literary reputation that may have before been earned by its author, it has added to his stock of private friendships, and that, in his estimation, is a far more valuable possession. It would be a solace to him to think that he had, in any way, repaid such service by extending or perpetuating the fame of the subject of this biography.

London, March, 1858.

PREFACE TO ORIGINAL EDITION.

The biography of a statesman to whose care "the three greatest dependencies of the British Crown were successively entrusted," calls for no introduction to explain or to justify the circumstance of its publication. But something may be said, in this place, respecting the materials upon which the present Memoir is based, and the considerations which have influenced the manner of its construction.

When, in the autumn of 1846, Lord Metcalfe was mercifully removed from what had long been to him a world of suffering, there was found in his will a special clause, giving and bequeathing to one of his trustees "all his papers, as well those in his own possession as in the hands of his agents, Messrs. Cockerell and Company, consisting principally of private correspondence," to be disposed of by the said trustee under instructions from the testator, and failing such instructions at his own discretion. Lord Metcalfe died, leaving no instructions regarding the papers. They, therefore, became absolutely the property of the trustee, who, after taking counsel with some of the nearest and dearest friends of the deceased, did me the honour to request that I would take charge of the papers, with the object of founding upon them a Memoir of the life of Lord Metcalfe.

The collection was one of considerable bulk. It comprised several large boxes, containing an immense mass of private letters addressed to Charles Metcalfe, from the time when he was a boy at Eton almost to the very day of his death. Here and there I found a few drafts or copies of letters written by Metcalfe himself, mixed up with those of which he had been the recipient. There were, also, one or two collections of Metcalfe's letters, written in a strain of unreserved confidence and familiarity to intimate private friends, who had died in India, and whose executors had seemingly returned the correspondence to the writer. In addition to these there were some early journals and common-place books —written at Eton, on the voyage to India, or during the first years of the writer's residence in that country; copies of all his letters written whilst on his mission to Lahore in 1808; of all, or nearly all, his minutes written when a member of the Supreme Government of India; and of his confidential letters and despatches written subsequently from Jamaica and Canada. Nor must I omit to state that there was one large box entirely filled with public addresses of congratulation or condolence—

of welcome or farewell—voted to him in the three great dependencies of which he was sometime the head.

After the first hasty examination of these papers, I had little doubt that they had been preserved for the purpose to which I was about to devote them. Nothing fortifies and encourages a biographer so much as such an assurance as this. Metcalfe had a very early prescience that he was destined to be great. When yet little more than sixteen he wrote, not lightly and jestingly either, of the "fervent biographer," who was to seize upon the traits of character indicated in the self-searching entries in his Common-place Book. But carefully as all these papers had been preserved, and multitudinous as were the records, they were hardly to be regarded as the best, or most legitimate materials of biography. Of the thousands of letters which passed into my hands, there was hardly one which was not of some use, as suggesting an idea, strengthening an impression, contributing something to the full comprehension of a trait of character, or supplying a clue to the elucidation of some incident in Metcalfe's life. Yet the entire collection did not supply complete materials for a biography. Whilst there was a superabundance of letters addressed *to* Lord Metcalfe, there was an obvious want of letters written *by* him. The want, however, was soon supplied. Although some of his most intimate friends and cherished correspondents had either not retained, or had destroyed upon leaving India all the letters they had received from him, or had been deprived of them by some of those moving accidents by flood and field which are the constituents of a stirring Indian career, others had carefully preserved the letters of their friend, and, in some instances, these memorials had survived the recipients of them.

In a little time, either my own inquiries, or those of influential friends who entered heartily into the undertaking and were eager to contribute all they could to its success, elicited from different quarters all that I desired. There was one collection of early letters preserved by the late Mr. John Walter Sherer, of the Civil Service, one of Metcalfe's earliest friends, which, as illustrating a most interesting epoch of his career, the records of which were by no means plentiful, I have found of the greatest service. Some family letters in the possession of Lord Monson—Metcalfe's first cousin—which were freely placed at my disposal, afforded additional materials, for which I am most grateful; whilst others, illustrative of what may be called the mid-career of the writer, were forwarded to me a very little time before his death, by Sir Richard Jenkins, one of the most distinguished of Metcalfe's diplomatic contemporaries. Of letters relating to a later period, after Metcalfe had become famous, it may be supposed that there was no lack. It is the want of authentic records of early life that is commonly the biographer's great stumbling-block.

It will be seen that I have had no such difficulty to surmount. The records of Metcalfe's early life, some may think, have, in these pages, been unduly amplified. But, rightly or wrongly, what I have done, I have done advisedly—systematically. What is for the most part a necessity often comes in time to be accepted as a rule. But I have not been able to persuade myself that because, in a large number of biographical works, three-fourths of the space is assigned to the few closing years of a distinguished career—to the record of circumstances illustrative of a great man's made reputation—that this is necessarily the way in which biography ought to be written. Doubtless, however, it is often the way in which it must be written, or not at all. I am inclined to think that the narrative of the steps by which a man has risen to greatness is neither less interesting, nor less instructive, than an account of his achievements, after the ladder of public life has been ascended, and he stands on an eminence of popularity before the world;—in a word, that the history of promise is not less valuable than the history of performance. The history of a great man's public performances are often part and parcel of the history of the country which he has served. They belong rather, indeed, to the historian than the biographer; and though ignorance may misunderstand, or party-spirit may misrepresent them, there is little chance of their being overlooked. Not always is that, which is historically the most important, biographically the most interesting. It is the function of the biographer to supply what is beyond the scope of the historian. When he reaches that stage of his inquiries at which the history of the individual becomes the history of the country, it would seem to be less his duty to expand than to contract the narrative. At all events, it is not his business to confine his efforts mainly to the illustration of those events which would be known to the public without his assistance.

If I have erred in devoting too much space to the earlier career of Charles Metcalfe, I have done so at least with design and intention. The first volume embraces the first thirty-five years of his life, including the first twenty years of his official career. In the second volume are contained the annals of the last quarter of a century of his life. It so happened that the last twelve years of his Indian career embraced a season of remarkable historical uneventfulness—a state of quiescence very much the result of those measures which he had advocated with so much energy and ability when in a more subordinate official position. It is well known that Sir Charles Metcalfe liberated the Indian Press. It is well known that he differed from his Council, in Canada, on the question of "Responsible Government." But it is not known how large a share he had in the authorship of those great measures for the consolidation of our Indian Empire, which shed so much lustre on the administration of Lord Hastings, which have preserved the whole continent in peace, and prepared the country for those internal improvements which could take root only in an undisturbed soil and under a quiet sky. During the first twenty years of Metcalfe's Indian career it was his fortune to live in stirring times; and, although in a comparatively subordinate position, the character of his mind and the impress of his opinions were stamped largely upon them. During the whole of the administration of Lord William Bentinck, and the earlier years of Lord Auckland's reign, when Sir Charles Metcalfe occupied a prominent station in the Indian Government, India was lapped in repose. With one or two remarkable exceptions, it may be said that the history of his public life during that period of his career is to be found in his Council minutes. A collection of these minutes would form one of the most valuable works on the subject of Indian administration that could be given to the public—but it is hardly within the scope of legitimate biography to insert them in these volumes.

At the same time I am not unconscious it may be said that, in some parts of this work, I have myself suffered the biographical to merge into the historical —and such a stricture would not be without justice, so far at least as regards the fact. But here, again, if I have erred, I have erred designedly, and after mature consideration. I am sorry to say that Indian and Colonial biography cannot be tried by the same test as that which is applied to memoirs of English soldiers and statesmen. In the latter case, the biographer may fairly assume the possession by the reader of a certain knowledge of the leading events of English history, to which reference is made in the course of his work. There is no necessity that he should halt to explain who was Napoleon Bonaparte or Daniel O'Connell; or what was the Catholic Emancipation or the Parliamentary Reform Bill. But I am afraid that it is necessary to explain who were Dowlut Rao Scindiah and Jeswunt Rao Holkar—what was the position of the King of Delhi after the first Mahratta war—and what the constitution of the Agra Government after the passing of the Charter Act of 1834. I have had all along an uneasy consciousness, that whilst there are many readers for whom such explanations are wholly unnecessary, there are others for whom I must explain these things, or leave the narrative of Metcalfe's connection with them in a state of total obscurity. It is better to err on the side of fulness and perspicuity. I have endeavoured to supply just the necessary amount of general information and no more; and as I have drawn the historical portion of the work mainly from original and exclusive sources,

I am not without a hope that even the instructed reader will find something in these passages not altogether unworthy of his attention. There are difficulties peculiar to Indian biography. No man will rejoice more than myself when they are removed.

Whenever I have had the opportunity, I have allowed Charles Metcalfe to tell his own story. When the choice has lain before me of using his words or my own, I have always employed the former. I might have made the narrative briefer, but it would have been less authentic. As it is, I feel that I have omitted much illustrative matter, to me of very great interest; and it is not impossible that some readers might wish that certain points of his career had been more minutely elaborated. This, however, more or less, will always be the case. In the present instance, the reproach of such insufficiency is hardly to be escaped, for nothing has been more apparent to me since I commenced this biography, than that there is a remarkable difference of opinion regarding what were the most important epochs of Charles Metcalfe's life. I have seldom found any two men to agree upon the subject. In like manner, some will think that I have devoted too much space to the Statesman, others, too much to the Man. I have endeavoured from first to last to bear in mind that Charles Metcalfe was both. I am not without a hope that those who knew him, as intimately in the one relation as the other, will be the most ready to acknowledge the fidelity of the entire portrait.

My obligations are numerous to those who have spontaneously aided me with valuable materials, or with counsel scarcely less valuable; nor less to others who, in eminent public or private stations, have responded promptly and courteously to applications made to them for permission to make use of correspondence in my possession, in which they have personally or officially had any original or acquired property. If I were to follow only my own inclination, I would make individual acknowledgments of all my obligations, but such expressions of thankfulness it is often more pleasant to utter than to receive; and, perhaps, the most acceptable manifestation of gratitude for the assistance of all kinds that has been rendered to me, will be found in the earnestness with which I have endeavoured to turn it to account in the pages of this Biography.

London, August, 1854.

CONTENTS OF VOL. I.

CHAPTER V.

CHAPTER VI.

CHAPTER VII.

CHAPTER VIII.

CHAPTER IX.

CHAPTER X.

CHAPTER XI.

CHAPTER XII.

CHAPTER XIII.

THE LIFE OF LORD METCALFE.

CHAPTER I.

[1785—1800.]

BOYHOOD.

Birth of Charles Theophilus Metcalfe—The Metcalfe Family—Major Thomas Metcalfe—Theophilus and Charles—Early Days—The School at Bromley—Eton—The Writership—The Voyage to India.

On the 30th of January, 1785, a few days before Warren Hastings ceased to be Governor-General of India, was born in the city of Calcutta to Major Thomas Theophilus Metcalfe, of the Bengal Army, and to Susannah his wife, a second son, who in course of time was christened Charles Theophilus. The house in which he was born, was then, and afterwards, known as the "Lecture House."* Whether it still exists, or to what uses it may have since been put, I have not been able to discover.

* My authority for this statement is a letter from Major Metcalfe to his son, written during the first year of Charles's residence in India, in which he says: "I give you some credit for having determined, and I think with some judgment, not to have a room in the Lecture House. Your objections were just, though it required some forbearance—*particularly being the house you were born in.*"

The Metcalfes appear to have been of a good old York-shire stock; and to have numbered many members of their family distinguished in their generation. One Thomas Metcalfe was Chancellor of the Duchy of Lancaster, in the reign of Richard the Third. The valour of James Metcalfe displayed in the battle of Agincourt, earned for him the honour of knighthood, and he was dubbed Sir James Metcalfe of Nappa. In the 15th century, another Thomas Metcalfe was High Sheriff of the County, and it is narrated of him, that he rode to the assizes, attended by fifteen Metcalfes, all mounted on white horses. In the reign of Charles the Second, another Metcalfe, Theophilus by name, distinguished himself in another way. He was the first to reduce short-hand writing to a system, and to publish an account of it. He went to London, was rewarded for his invention, and in remembrance of it was especially permitted to add a hand and pen to the heraldic adornments of his family scutcheon. He, or his son, afterwards settled in Ireland, and from him the subject of this Memoir was lineally descended.

I can nowhere find it recorded that Charles Metcalfe was learned in these genealogies, or held his ancestors of any account. But he was greatly and reasonably proud of his father. That father was the son of Thomas Metcalfe, an officer of the King's Army, who married the daughter of the Reverend Thomas Williams. At an early age he was despatched as a cadet to India, with a letter of introduction to Lord Clive; but any expectations he may have based upon it were disappointed, for the great man had left the country before young Metcalfe's arrival. So the friendless boy was thrown upon his own resources, and for a time so cheerless was his situation, and so sombre his prospects, that he determined to leave the service, and actually called upon the commanding-officer of his regiment to tender his resignation. An accident caused him to abandon the intention as hastily as he had formed it;* and from that time he determined to achieve success by a steadfast course of professional perseverance.

And in due time he did achieve it. Those were days in which rapid fortunes were sometimes made by lucrative Government contracts. It seems that Thomas Metcalfe soon contrived to detach himself from the go-cart of regimental routine, and to obtain employment on the staff. He was for several years "Agent for Military Stores;" and it was, doubtless, in this situation that in course of time he made a respectable fortune.†

Whilst thus Thomas Metcalfe, having risen through the different gradations of the service up to the rank of major, was supplying the army with stores and making a fortune, he took unto himself a wife. In the year 1782 he married the widow of a Major Smith, of the Bengal army. Five or six years before, this lady, then Susannah Debonnaire, daughter of a gentleman resident at the Cape of Good Hope, had gone out with a sister to join her father in that settlement; but it was deemed expedient that the young ladies should pursue their voyage to Madras, where Lord Pigot, a friend of Mr. Debonnaire, was then governor of the presidency. Between the Cape and the coast her sister died, under very melancholy circumstances, and she narrowly escaped a similar fate. Arriving, however, alive, though in shattered health, at Madras, she attracted the regards of Major Smith, to whom she was married in August, 1776, and soon afterwards proceeded with her

* Major Metcalfe's own version of this anecdote is given in a subsequent chapter, page 60. He was a cadet of 1767.

† The fact stated in the text is given on the authority of the Company's Records, whence it was extracted for me by Mr. Waud, under whose admirable arrangements all the historical wealth of the India House has been rendered peculiarly accessible to the student.

husband to Bengal. He died, leaving no issue; and in 1782 the widow became the attached and devoted wife of Thomas Theophilus Metcalfe.

The eldest son, born on the 19th of September, 1783, was called Theophilus John; the second, as I have said, Charles Theophilus. They were very young when their parents returned to England. Soon after his arrival, Major Metcalfe bought a house in Portland-place, and began to canvass for a seat in the Direction of the East India Company. He was a man of active business habits, good sterling common-sense, and an integrity beyond all impeachment. Altogether he was a reliable man. In process of time he became, as he intended, an East India Director.* Then he bethought himself of obtaining a seat in Parliament; and in due course he was returned for the borough of Abingdon, which he represented in several Parliaments. A loyal gentleman, a Tory, and a staunch supporter of William Pitt, on whose recommendation, in 1802, he was created a Baronet, he was an active and assiduous rather than a brilliant member of the House of Commons. But he often spoke, and with good effect, bringing his sound practical sense and his extensive experience to bear on many of the questions of the day; but more especially on those relating to the conduct of our Indian affairs. He was also an active Director of the Globe Insurance Company in days when insurance offices were few, and to be a director of such a company was esteemed an honour by men of high repute. He had brought with him no languor or lassitude from the East; and altogether was as robust a man of business as if he had never wiped the baked dust of Calcutta out of his blinded eyes.

He had several children born to him, of whom five survived their childhood. They were brought up, with a

* At the general election in April, 1789.

sensible kind of indulgence, under the eye of their mother, who was a woman of strong understanding, and of great sincerity of character. Her affection for her children seldom displayed itself in any maternal weaknesses, but was manifested in an eager desire to advance their worldly interests, whatever might be the immediate sacrifice of self. If she had any partialities, they were in favour of her eldest son, Theophilus—a fine manly boy, of whom frequent mention will be made in subsequent portions of this narrative.

Of the infant days of Charles Metcalfe little is known beyond what he afterwards recorded of himself. He seems to have encountered, like most other children at the threshold of life, the great stumbling-block of an unprincipled or an injudicious nurse. "The woman to whom my infant years were entrusted," he wrote in a commonplace book which he kept in his youth, "used to convey me, by way of punishment, to a dark room, and represented the coming of the *Old Man* (a famous bugbear in the mouths of nurses) as every minute to be expected. Here was I left, whilst probably the foolish woman would groan and make use of several other means to terrify me. The consequence was, that throughout my childish and boyish years, I was a prey to the most horrid fears; and such an effect has this treatment had on my imagination, that I am even now much weaker on this point than I could wish to be."

At an early age Charles Metcalfe was sent to school at Bromley, in Middlesex. The establishment was kept by a Mr. Tait. How it was obtained I do not know, but this gentleman had a considerable "Indian connection;" and among his pupils were divers Pattles, and Plowdens, and others bearing names with which East India Registers have long been familiar. It was partly on this account, and partly, perhaps, because some members of Mrs. Metcalfe's family resided in the neighbourhood of Bromley, that Mr. Tait's academy was fixed upon as the first training-house for the young Metcalfes. Its recommendations were, I believe, chiefly of an extrinsic character. Scholastically, perhaps, there was not very much to be said in its favour.

To this period of Charles Metcalfe's early career there are but few allusions in his letters and journals. In 1841, nearly half a century after he had been boarded and birched at good Mr. Tait's, being then Governor of an important Crown colony, he wrote to a near relative, in answer to some family inquiries:

"I remember, at Bromley, a fine-looking old gentleman, of the name of Debonnaire, who, with his family, occupied the pew in church next to that of our school, and whose broad shoulders and peculiar coat of remarkable pattern are impressed on my memory. I quitted Bromley in September, 1795. I also remember 'Aunt Winch,' as she was called, who used to board and lodge in Tait's house, and had my brother Theophilus and myself sometimes in her room. I paid her and the school at Bromley a farewell visit on my departure from England for India, on which occasion she gave me 2*l*., encumbered with a laudable injunction to purchase the 'Whole Duty of Man.' . . . . I have a faint impression that the Lefevres, whom I then understood to be relatives of the Debonnaires, had been the occupants of the house then in Tait's possession, which had some old ceilings of carved wood that we boys used to think very fine."

From Charles Metcalfe's own recorded reminiscences, little more can be gathered regarding his sojourn at the Bromley school. His surviving school-fellows are not many; but I am told that he was then a boy of a reserved and retiring nature, and that the more showy qualities of his elder brother entirely shone him down. It is remembered that Mrs. Metcalfe would pay occasional visits to the school; and it was well known even to the boys that Theophilus was the mother's favourite. Among the most memorable incidents of that period of Charles Metcalfe's life, was the preparation of a dramatic entertainment, which caused great excitement for many weeks in the school. The play was "Julius Cæsar;" and there was a great show of people to witness the performance. Theophilus Metcalfe played Mark Antony. To Charles were assigned the two humble parts of Flavius and Friend to Brutus.*

After the Christmas holidays of 1795-96, Charles Metcalfe, being then just eleven years old, was entered at Eton. He went to that famous seminary as an Oppidan, and boarded with his tutor, Mr. Goodall, afterwards head-master and provost of the college; Dr. Heath being then preceptor-in-chief. As at the private school, so at the public, he was known as a quiet retiring boy. He was not celebrated for his adroitness in any athletic exercises. He was neither a cricketer nor a boater. I am not sure that he ever played at fives. But it is on record, and on very sufficient authority, that he was once seen riding on a camel. "I heard the boys shouting," says Dr. Goodall, many years afterwards, "and went out and saw young Metcalfe riding on a camel; so you see he was always orientally inclined."

Many who knew Charles Metcalfe will, doubtless, accept the worthy Doctor's interpretation of this feat, for such gymnastic achievements were not at all in the young gentleman's way. It is not even on record that, in those early days, he ever trusted himself on the back of a pony. He was, at all times of his life, so miserable a horseman, that he seldom took equestrian exercise for any length of time without falling off and hurting himself. So that except upon the hypothesis that the boy was orientally inclined, it is not easy to account for the camel-riding exploit of the studious Etonian.

* A printed play-bill, containing a list of the *dramatis personæ* and the names of the performers, was preserved by Charles Metcalfe to the latest day of his life.

For very studious, indeed, he was at Eton. He went there when he was eleven years of age, and left when he was only fifteen. But Goodall was always of opinion that Metcalfe *minor* was a boy of very high promise; and, perhaps, there was not among his many pupils one to whom he was more sincerely attached. The affection was reciprocal. And it was lasting. Death only put a period to it.

When it is said that Charles Metcalfe was studious, it is not meant that he merely learnt his lessons—that he sapped at Latin and Greek, got up his derivations, wrote lyrics with great success, and was sometimes sent up for good. Doubtless, all this was done in the common course of things. But a boy may accomplish all this at Eton and still have much time for the playing-fields or the river. Neither had any charms for Metcalfe. His play-hours were spent for the most part in-doors. He read English, he read French, he read Italian. He wrote poetry. He was fond of drawing. Already was he becoming somewhat prone to disputation. A whole holiday was for him of value only as it gave him more time to puzzle over "Rowley's" poems, to read Gibbon, to translate Ariosto and Rousseau, and to tread the echoing cloisters, immersed in day-dreams of future renown. "Ah!" he said, a few years later, "those were days of real happiness! In those cloisters has my youthful and ardent imagination planned to itself a life of greatness, glory, and virtue—there have I been the orator, and discussed important topics in the senate-house—there have I been the statesman prescribing terms to the wondering nations of Europe—there have I concluded peaces, commanded armies, or headed a party struggling for liberty; or, descending from these lofty views—there have I found myself in private life, in the enjoyment of domestic happiness, the honoured patron of a neighbouring hamlet."

ETON JOURNAL.

Towards the close of his career at Eton Charles Metcalfe began to keep a journal.* His entries in it exhibit clearly the studious life that he led. They exhibit, too, something more than this. The annals of his last month at Eton afford some curious indications of the resolution of the boy—of his disposition to do what he afterwards called "holding out" against opposition. It appears that, in defiance of their tutor's orders, Metcalfe and some other boys were determined to drink tea in each other's rooms after the hour prescribed by authority. Some of the entries in the following passages relate to this act of sedition :

JOURNAL BEGUN IN MARCH, 1800.

"*Monday, 3rd.*—Whole school-day. Not well. Wrote an anecdote to the editor of the *Naval Chronicle.* Drank tea after six in Hervey's room, according to agreement. Afraid the plan of bringing in that custom won't succeed. Passed the evening in Hervey's room. Supped with Neville; went to bed full of turkey.

"*Tuesday, 4th.*—Whole holiday. Not well. Employed at verses; good theme. Read the 'Age of Louis XIV.' Mem. Write to the editor of the *Military Journal.* Heard of Parson Grey's being drunk. Drank tea solo. Finished verses ; gave to tutor ; he liked them. Passed the remainder of the evening in Neville's room, reading.

"*Wednesday, 5th.*—Whole school-day. Did translation. Drank tea in Neville's room, according to agreement, after six. My hopes gain on my fears, though the latter are still predominant. Re-translated four pages of my translation from Rousseau. Passed the rest of the evening in Neville's room, between reading and rowing.

"*Thursday, 6th.*—Half-holiday. Wrote a letter. Tonson sat in

---

* On the cover of his first diary the young journalist wrote: "First conceived the idea of this journal on the 1st of March; intend not only to make it a relation of facts, but also to intersperse it with observations, reflections, &c., &c.; so that it will be the general rendezvous not only of my actions, but of my thoughts."—C. T. M.

my room one hour and a half. Adjourned to Spires's. Tutor jawed about drinking tea after six. Drank tea with Tonson. Drew. Passed the remainder of the evening in Neville's room.

"*Friday, 7th.*—Whole school-day. Drank tea with Shaw, according to our convention, after six. Tutor jawed with great spirit. Destruction of our plan must in the end come on: we are at our last struggle; all our endeavours now are the exertions of despair, and we must only think how to resign nobly; in such cases as these, unanimity is required to obtain success, and that has not been obtained. Did Greek with my tutor. The remainder of the night in Neville's room.

"*Saturday, 8th.*—Common Saturday. Saw Rooke just going to Ireland, and thence expects a trip to France. Gave Nepean tea. Passed the evening in Neville's room, reading. Finished Voltaire's 'Life of Louis XIV.' Mem. Follow up the inquiry about the Iron Mask; ask my tutor to lend me Gibbon.

"*Sunday, 9th.*—Did theme. Read Ariosto with Melville and Shaw; make laws for the sake of due attention to the book.

"*Monday, 10th.*—Whole school-day; did some Homer. Mem. These epic poets are very free in their ideas; for instance, in the 290th line of the Book εψιλον, Æneas has got a stone in his hand in the act of throwing it at Achilles, who is rushing with his sword drawn on Æneas; but Neptune, who perceives destruction impending over Æneas, is determined to ward it off; accordingly addresses the other gods in a speech of sixteen lines, to which Juno makes answer in one of nine; in the mean time, we must suppose the stone pendent in the air, and Achilles in the act of rushing forward, but both very complaisantly waiting till their godships have finally decided. Perhaps it would have been better to have introduced Minerva with her ægis, turning these heroes into stone till the speeches were done with. To be sure, that would be comprehensible, whereas the other idea is so sublime as to be above the weak understanding of us mortals. Gave tea to Neville, Hervey, and Shaw, after six, according to agreement. Had a most tremendous jaw from my tutor, who said nothing but that it was a serious inconvenience, but could not bring one argument to prove that it was so. After supper did verses.

"*Tuesday 11th.*—Whole holiday. Gave Lamb breakfast. Finished verses. Gave Tonson tea. Began a French letter. Read riost o with Neville and Shaw. Began 'Life of Charles the Twelfth.'

"*Wednesday, 12th.*—General fast. Drank tea with Shaw. Read Ariosto with Neville and Shaw. . . . . . .

"*Thursday, 13th.*—Play at four. Read some of Lucan and Cicero. Drew. Read Ariosto with Neville and Shaw. Read Voltaire's 'Life of Charles XII.'

"*Friday, 14th.*—Read part of Horace's 'Art of Poetry.' Whole school-day. Read some Lucan. Drank tea with Hervey after six. We have conquered; and my tutor, not finding an argument against us, was obliged to consent; so that now we do it lawfully. Had it not been for our last despairing struggles we should have failed. Read the continuation of the 'Iron Mask' (which Voltaire mentions in his 'Siècle de Louis XIV.') in Gibbon. It is most probably, as he says, a son of Cardinal Mazarin and Anne of Austria, as indeed I think there are strong suspicions that Louis XIV. was. Read Gibbon's 'Antiquities of the House of Brunswick and Este.' Read Gibbon's 'Observations on Bishop Warburton's Explanation of his Sixth Book of the Æneid.' Read part of Gibbon's 'Journal;' and finished Voltaire's 'Life of Charles XII.'

"*Saturday, 15th.*—Common Saturday. Read Lucan. Greek Testament. Read Rowley's 'Poems.' Gave Shaw tea. Passed the evening in Hervey's room.

"*Sunday, 16th.*—Learnt 'Fourth Satire' of Juvenal for my tutor. Read Rowley's 'Poems.' Gave Grose tea. Did verses.

"*Monday, 17th.*—Whole holiday. Read Rowley's 'Poems.' Drank tea with Nepean. Did some lyrics.

"*Tuesday, 18th.*—Whole school-day. Read Homer. Cicero. Finished Rowley's 'Poems.' Drank tea with Shaw. Finished lyrics. Translated three pages of Rousseau.

"*Wednesday, 19th.*—Whole school-day. Read Homer. Virgil. Read a dissertation on Rowley's 'Poems,' tending to prove from the language that they were not written in the 15th century, but by Chatterton. Gave Neville, Hervey, and Shaw tea. Wrote a letter. Entered into a train of thoughts on public schools in general, and Eton in particular. . . .

"*Thursday, 20th.*—Half-holiday. Read Lucan. Drank tea alone. Read Ariosto with Shaw and Neville.

"*Friday, 21st.*—Whole school-day. Read Horace. Lucan. Read Bryant's 'Dissertation on Rowley's Poems,' tending to prove they were actually written by him. Drank tea with Hervey. Read Ariosto with Neville and Shaw. Read Xenophon with my tutor.

"*Saturday, 22nd.*—Common Saturday. Read Callimachus. Continued Bryant's Dissertation. Saw the College Library. Read Xenophon with my tutor. Read Ariosto with Neville and Shaw.

"*Sunday, 23rd.*—Learnt part of the Fifth Satire of Juvenal for my tutor. Dr. Norbury, the deceased Fellow, was buried in the church. Did theme. Read Ariosto with, &c. Read Bryant's Dissertation. Drank tea with Tonson.

"*Monday, 24th.*—Half-holiday. Read Homer. Did lyrics. Read Bryant's Dissertation.

"*Tuesday, 25th.*—Whole holiday. Wrote a French letter. Read Bryant's Dissertation.

"*Wednesday, 26th.*—Whole school-day. Read Homer. Virgil. Concluded Bryant's Dissertation. Began Tyrwhitt's, tending to prove that they were written by Chatterton. Took a solitary walk, and employed myself in making a few verses to Solitude. Drank tea with Neville. Re-translated part of my translation of Rousseau. Read Ariosto, &c.

"*Thursday, 27th.*—Play at four. Read Lucian. Cicero. Wrote a letter. Finished Tyrwhitt's Dissertation. Began Warton's on the same side of the question. Read Ariosto, &c. Took a walk with Tonson and Kelsale.

"*Friday, 28th.*—Whole school-day. Read Horace. Lucian. Finished Warton's Dissertation. After having finished all the Dissertations, I am now quite at a loss which to give it to: had I read the poems, and taken no trouble about convincing myself, I should have formed an opinion that they were Rowley's, and could have supported my opinion with arguments; but now I am quite in the dark. I think Bryant proves they were not written by Chatterton, and Tyrwhitt that they were not written by Rowley. The idea of a third person is still more chimerical than either of these. Who were they written by, then? I believe they must have written themselves. Drank tea with Shaw. Read Ariosto.

"*Saturday, 29th.*—Whole holiday. Read Goldsmith's 'Deserted Village.' Drank tea with Grose. Some more poems, said to be Rowley's. Turned first Eclogue of Rowley's poems into modern English verse.

"*Sunday, 30th.*—Took a solitary walk. Made a few stanzas, a Simile to Human Life. Gave Tonson tea. Took a walk with him. Read Ariosto.

"*Monday, 31st.*—Whole school-day. Read Homer. Cicero. Gave tea to Neville, Hervey, and Shaw. Packed up. Read Ariosto."

There is much in all this that is worthy of notice. In after days, Charles Metcalfe used to say that nearly all the literary knowledge which he had acquired in the course of his life, had been gained as a boy at Eton—he had never been able to read much at a later period of his career. How great was his application then, how varied his pursuits, may be gathered from these extracts. Great men are not to be tried by ordinary rules; they make rules for themselves. I would rather think of a fine open-spirited boy, boating, swimming, playing, even getting into mischief at school, and in the holidays spending half his time on the back of a pony; and I should, as a rule, believe that in such training there were more hopeful assurance of turning him, in due time, into a useful servant of the State, than in the discipline of such continued book-work as is recorded in Charles Metcalfe's journal. But it was fortunate, in this instance, that the bent of the boy's inclination was rather towards intellectual than muscular exercise—that he spent his leisure hours with Ariosto and Chatterton, with Gibbon and Voltaire, rather than with the boats' crews and the Eton elevens. If he had been captain of the boats, and beaten Harrow and Winchester off his own bat, he could not have grown into a manlier character. The finest physical training in the world could not have made him a robuster statesman. But if he had not acquired a love of literature, and some knowledge of books at school, he would never have acquired them at all; and though he might still have distinguished himself greatly on the theatre of the world, it is hard to say how much might have been wanting from the completeness of the character, which it is the business and the privilege of the biographer to illustrate.*

* It is probable that these studious habits were strengthened, if not generated, in the boy, by the exhortations of his mother, who was wont to stimulate him to new exertions in such a strain as the

That he read what he did at Eton, Charles Metcalfe in after years continually rejoiced; but he lamented that he had not enjoyed more extended opportunities of self-improvement. "Were I disposed," he wrote two years afterwards, "to lament that which is irretrievable, I should never cease to regret that I was removed from Eton at the time that I was. I left it at the age of fifteen, at a time when my ideas were ripening—when I was attached to the studies in the pursuit of which I was engaged, had objects towards which I was directing my exertions, and had formed plans which promised success. Five years more might well have been spared to Eton and a University, after which there would have been plenty of time for India." But now he was taken away from Eton, that he might be shipped off to India at once.

It was an awkward fact in the lives of the two young Metcalfes—Theophilus and Charles—that their father was an East India Director. So, doubtless, at least they regarded it. Already was the elder brother under sentence

following: "I am glad you persevere in your endeavours," she wrote to Charles, in 1799; "you must succeed; but to acquire knowledge requires resolution, without which nothing can be attained. Mrs. S. made a very deep impression on me the other day, by telling me that a very clever man said, if a person would read three hours a day seriously, and well-chosen books, for four years, he could not fail of being so clever and able, that he might fill any office or place in the kingdom—that the Ministers would be happy to have his abilities. . . . . I have read more regularly every day since her observation. I wish it had made as deep an impression on Theophilus—but books seem to give him no pleasure. What a pity! With his quickness and comprehension, he would, if he chose, be a very shining character. I think, if I were you, I would adopt the plan. It's astonishing what a number of volumes you will get through in that time." Her maternal penetration had not at this time discovered that it was not Theophilus, but Charles, who was destined to be the shining character.

of banishment to China. And now it was decreed that the younger should be despatched to Bengal. A China writership was, in those days, the best bit of preferment in the world. It was a certain fortune in a very few years. The appointments in that service were so few and so lucrative, that they were commonly reserved for the Directors' own sons. Major Metcalfe saw clearly the advantages of such a provision for his eldest boy. He had an easy fortune of his own; but he had a large family, and, divided among so many children, his 4000*l.* a year would not have secured a sufficiency to any. The baronetcy had not then been attained, nor a family estate purchased; and if they had been, it is doubtful whether Thomas Metcalfe would have "made an eldest son" and left Theophilus to amuse himself. As it was, he wisely determined that the boy should work for himself; and there being no easier and no more rapid road to fortune than the Company's Factory at Canton, the prudent father determined, in 1799, to despatch his first-born, in the following year, to "Cathay."

To Theophilus, who had left Eton some little time before, and had been dissipating, as he called it, in Scotland and Wales, this decision was a heavy blow. He was already tasting the sweets of independent life in England—making friends, falling in love, acting at masquerades, drinking his bottle of wine, and exhibiting other symptoms of premature manhood. The thought of being cut short in this career of glory was grievous to him in the extreme. So he cast about in his mind how he could escape the sentence recorded against him; and began to think whether Charles could not be persuaded to go to China in his room.

The two brothers had not always walked hand-in-hand with each other. The breaches between them were frequent—as frequent they will be between boys of different character, each with pretensions of his own, each after his own fashion egotistical and intolerant (and there is no egotism and intolerance equal to that of clever boys); but there was a fund of good brotherly love at the bottom of their hearts, even when they were most vehement in their denunciations of each other. All through the year 1799, this fraternal antagonism seems to have been at its height. Their good mother declared that she quite dreaded the approach of the holidays on this account, and strenuously exhorted them to peace. Her exhortations were not at first successful. Early in November, the two brothers fell to quarrelling over the politics of the day. Charles was at that time, like his father, a Tory and a Pittite; whilst Theophilus was in Opposition. Charles declared that the Ministers were the only men capable of governing the country, and called his brother a democrat. Upon this Theophilus fired up, and, adverting to the expedition to Holland, asked what was to be said of "Ministerial liberality, which now accuses the Russians, accuses the Austrians, accuses anything but those who would have taken all the credit if it had succeeded—so much for Ministers, for the only men who can govern the country, or in other words, can lose our credit by secret expeditions." Men got from politics into personalities more expeditiously in those days than they do now; and boys followed their example. So Theophilus, having disposed of Pitt and his colleagues, told Charles that as he treated all his opinions with insolence, he desired that the correspondence might drop. "You may," he added, "(by dint of application) have made yourself a better classical scholar than I (by idleness) have made myself; but still, I do not lower my abilities, in my own opinion, so as to need advice from a younger brother." Charles was, doubtless, inclined to be a little self-opinionated and dictatorial (and in this there were the germs of what afterwards came to be a noble self-reliance); but, although the rupture for a week or two was complete, it was not likely to be of long continuance between two such fine-hearted boys, and they were soon writing to each other in fitting terms of brotherly love.

Then it was that the great question of the China writership rose up for consideration. When Charles Metcalfe came home to Portland-place for the Christmas holidays of 1799-1800, Theophilus was in Wales, on a visit to Lord Newborough. Thence he wrote to his brother to sound him about China, bravely assuming at the outset that Charles could not possibly object to so excellent a provision for a younger brother:

> "When I consider," he wrote, in January, 1800, "of the difference between you and me, I am astonished. You, a studious, grave fellow, studying five hours a day; me, a wild idle dog, who does not look into a book from the rising to the setting of the sun. You, who would like to go to China to make a large fortune; me, who would like to stay in England and spend what I have. . . . . . Added to this difference between us, another great one is, you would not give a —— for a glass of wine, and I, with pleasure, will drink a bottle with any friend. Would, Charles, that you were to bend your way to China in my stead! and I know not why I should be refused remaining in England, when I seem so anxiously to wish it. . . . . . What, because the world styles it good, is a young man to be sent to a place which least of all suits his disposition, to be shut up for ten or twelve years from all relations and friends."

But Charles having no stronger taste for China than Theophilus, wrote his brother to that effect. The elder, however, would not still abandon all hope of the vicarious sacrifice to Mammon, on which he had set his heart. "If you are inclined to make money," he wrote, "which your disposition in some degree shows, China is the best place. . . . . I have written to my father on this subject; but I have one question to ask you. If it is offered to you, are you determined not to go? I request you to keep this letter, and you will see hereafter that I was your brother."

Charles was not to be persuaded, though he kept the letter. He still said, that if the decision depended upon himself, he would have nothing to do with the China factory. He hoped his brother would not be offended; but he had no wish to be offered up a sacrifice in his place. To this Theophilus frankly replied that he could not conceive why he should be offended; "as it is a maxim of mine," he said, "first to please myself, and then my friends, I cannot be angry at your doing the same."

But whilst these young gentlemen were arranging for themselves the business of their future disposal, the elder Metcalfes were settling everything for them, and leaving little choice to the boys. Both, after a few years, acknowledged that their parents were right. But when it was finally decided—and all escape from the decision was impossible—that Theophilus should be despatched to China, and that Charles should go as a writer to Bengal, the two boys were ready to die with vexation. Charles was very sorry to leave Eton. He loved the school. He loved his tutor. He loved many of his school-fellows; and he loved his books. He was sorry to think of leaving England; for he loved his parents, and he loved his sisters. Mrs. Metcalfe, though Theophilus was her favourite, sometimes acknowledged that Charles was the more dutiful and attentive of the two. By his sisters, into whose school-room he would make frequent disturbing incursions, he was held in the fondest affection. He was very loving and very loveable. He was not one who could be banished to a distant country without grievous laceration of the heart.

In the year 1800, and at the end of March, Charles Metcalfe quitted Eton. In those days boys were sent fresh from public or private schools, or from no school at all, to embark on board ship, and sail for the land where they were to become judges, or ambassadors, or ministers of finance. That under this system some great administrators rose into eminence is not to be denied. But in the character and qualifications of the general body of the Indian Civil Service, under an improved educational system—a system of special training still to be improved—a great and progressive advance during the last half century may be clearly discerned. When Major Metcalfe entered in his list the name of his son Charles Theophilus, the service of which he was about to become a member had emerged from the slough of corruption in which it had once been sunk; and though some who had belonged to it in the old bad times were still in its ranks, it had become a respectable profession. Lord Cornwallis and Sir John Shore had nursed the infancy and sustained the childhood of its respectability; and now Lord Wellesley was watching the progress of its adolescence. Instead of a race of men, who were more than three-fourths traders, growing rich upon irregular and unrecognised gains, there was fast growing up an army of administrators, receiving fixed pay for fixed service, and adding nothing to their stores that was not to be found in the audit-books of the Government. All that they wanted was more training to fit them for the public service, and this was soon about to be supplied. At no period were the prospects of the profession better; at no period were higher emoluments to be obtained with more honour; at no period was there finer scope for action, or a greater likelihood of a youth of energy and ability soon rising to fame and fortune.

Of Charles Metcalfe's abilities his father had a high opinion. He knew, too, that his son had great powers of application; and he predicted that the union of the two would enable him to command success. He was one of the few India Directors who neither at that nor a later period were alarmed by the vigour and determination of Lord Wellesley. He believed that under the government of that great man there were the fairest prospects of his son laying the foundation of his future eminence as a statesman; and though, if he had been swayed only by the impulses of parental affection, he would have retained both his elder sons in England, he now resolutely decreed that they should seek their fortunes in the East.

It was arranged, therefore, that Theophilus should sail for China in the spring, and that Charles should embark for Calcutta in the summer. In the meanwhile the boys were to enjoy themselves as best they could. Charles, though of a retiring disposition, did not dislike society; and there were a few families, in the neighbourhood of his father's house, to whom he was a frequent visitor. In one of these there was a young lady, a little older than himself, with whom he fell in love at first sight. He was first introduced to her, on the day after he left Eton, at a ball in his father's house.* After that event he frequently saw her, either at his own house or her mother's. The charms of the young lady, not merely those of external beauty and grace, made a deep and abiding impression on his mind; and he was long afterwards of opinion, that this boyish attachment, pure and disinterested as it was, had a beneficial influence on his character. He corresponded with her for some time afterwards, and her "sensible letters heightened his admiration." They are almost the only part of his correspondence which has not survived him. The exception tells its own story.

* He entered in his journal at the foot of a page, under date April 2, "Ball at home. I was first introduced to Miss D——; danced with her." What followed this simple statement can only be conjectured, for the next leaf in the journal is (very expressively) cut out of the book. Soon afterwards there was another ball in Portland-place—"a very pleasant one," wrote Charles; "danced four dances with Miss D——." Two or three nights afterwards he "passed the evening at Lady D——'s. Supped there; a most delightful party." On the next day he "called on Miss D——, sat an hour with her;" and so on.

All through the months of April and May, and the first half of June, Charles Metcalfe's head-quarters were in Portland-place. There he spent his time, improving himself in French and drawing, under masters; reading the Naval and Military Magazines, and sometimes writing for them; walking in the Park or in Bond-street with old schoolfellows; turning Rowley's Eclogues into modern English; writing letters to his "friend and tutor Goodall;" going to the opera; getting up masquerade costumes;* paying visits; painting a chess-board; sitting for his picture; and reading whenever he had time.†

In the beginning of May he went to Eton, spent a day or two there, and took leave of Dr. Heath, his schoolfellows, and his friend Goodall. It was, as he said afterwards, "a sad, sad day." It moved him deeply to say farewell to his old tutor; and the tutor, too, was greatly affected. He had recognised the many good and great qualities of his pupil; and whilst he was fondly attached to him on account of the former, there was a strong assurance in his mind that the latter would secure for the studious boy a not undistinguished career. Two or three years afterwards, he asked a gentleman from Bengal if he knew Charles Metcalfe, and being answered in the affirmative, he said, "Then you know a very good young man—a very superior young man. I have done for him what I never did for any one else—I wrote a letter in his favour to Lord Wellesley!"

In the middle of May, Theophilus Metcalfe embarked for China, on board the *Exeter;* but the fleet being delayed in the Channel, he came up to town and very

* He went to one masquerade as a Quaker, and to another as a Petit Maitre. He was wonderfully unlike both.

† The reading, however, was but scanty. It did not embrace much beyond Symes' "Embassy to Ava," and Turner's "Embassy to Thibet."

nearly lost his passage. He re-embarked at the end of the month, but was detained by stress of weather in Torbay, whence he wrote to Charles to "give him a bit of advice" about his love affair, as one who had "experience in such matters."* But it may be doubted whether the younger brother needed to be told that it was necessary to act with caution and diffidence. He was always very diffident about himself, and used sometimes to speak almost painfully of his want of personal attractions. For as he grew up, the beauties which developed themselves in the person of Charles Metcalfe were, for the most part, those of the mind. He was short and somewhat homely in appearance. But in the intelligence of his countenance, and the habitual sweetness of his smile, there was something that atoned for all such defects.

The vessel (the *Skelton Castle*) in which a cabin had been secured for Charles Metcalfe, was to sail with the June fleet. In the early part of the month, therefore, he took leave of his friends, and among others, of his first preceptor, Mr. Tait, of Bromley,† and his wife. The former died a quarter of a century afterwards, and Mrs. Tait survived Charles Metcalfe. Whether he ever saw

* The following amusing passage in this letter is extremely characteristic of Theophilus Metcalfe:—"Here we are lying in company with Lord St. Vincent and the Channel Fleet—wind S.S.W. My Lord is determined to put to sea the first opportunity, and we are to go with him. It will be a fine sight, the two fleets together. He has given orders that not one of us shall go ashore. He is a proud, overbearing fellow, and I should like to show him there is one in the fleet who does not see he has any right to fear him. If there were any of my friends ashore here, I would go in spite of the old fellow. One of the ships, the *Phœnix* by name, ran foul of him on entering the bay. I rejoiced to see it. The old fellow swore at him, I'll be bound."

† Reference to this visit has already been made. It is duly entered in his journal under date June 12: "Went to old Aunt Winch at Bromley."

her again I do not know; but when he died, he had for many years been paying a pension which he had settled on her; and after his death, a passage was found in his will, directing that, in the event of her surviving him, it should be continued during her life.

The 14th of June, as he wrote in his journal, was "the last he was destined to spend with his family." On the following day, he "took leave of all his friends and left London, not to enter it again for twenty years." After a few days spent at Portsmouth, off which place the fleet was lying, in making ready his cabin, visiting the Dock-yard, and writing letters to his friends, including Goodall and Miss D——, he "took leave of his dear father," who had accompanied him, and resigned himself to his fate.

After some detention in the Channel, the fleet got fairly out to sea; and then Charles Metcalfe began again to practise that system of "holding out," which had enabled him to defeat his friend Goodall, at Eton, and which afterwards secured him great moral triumphs over Eastern princes and Western partisans. But neither before nor after, neither in the east nor the west, did he encounter so troublesome and contumacious an opponent as his enemy of the *Skelton Castle*. Resolute in all things, Charles Metcalfe was resolute not to be sea-sick; and though his sufferings were considerable, he still entered in his journal from day to day that he "held out" against the enemy; and in spite of the frequent entries of "very squeamish," he almost accomplished success.

He had a friend on board, Mr. Bazett, with whom he "read Moors;" and in his own cabin he studied the Abbé Raynal's East Indies, Howell's Tracts, the Memoirs of Abdul Kurreem, and other books; and wrote poetry to Miss D——.

On the 22nd of September, the fleet came-to off the Island of St. Helena. Under the auspices of Mr. Bazett,

Charles Metcalfe landed, and was most hospitably entertained. He seems to have spent a week very pleasantly there, and to have come away with some lively impressions. I have heard it doubted whether Metcalfe was much alive to the beauties of external nature. I do not find many allusions to such things in his writings, nor can I gather that, at a later period of his life, the associations of the picturesque had much effect on his mind. But he was charmed and awe-struck by the beauty and sublimity of the scenery of St. Helena. The enthusiasm which they engendered within him may be gathered from some passages in a descriptive account which he wrote of the island. He thus speaks of his first ride: *

"In the first ride I took I was struck with astonishment and admiration. Every step I took afforded a new scene of delight; every winding of the valley, every twining of the mountain, offered a magnificent view to our eyes; the contrast was wonderful. If I looked behind, I saw a bleak, barren rock, without a stalk of cultivation; if I looked before me, I was struck with the pleasing view of the sides of the hills covered with verdure; a fine breed of cattle browsing on the declivity, and every here and there waterfalls, pouring their contents into the bosom of the most fertile valleys, where they formed a meandering stream, the banks of which were covered with water-cresses and other herbs in the greatest abundance. Everywhere something grand or something beautiful opened upon us, and everywhere there was fresh substance for admiration. But I need not attempt to describe what cannot be described; I shall overrun my imagination, and be lost in the maze of wonders."

---

* Having spoken lightly of Metcalfe's equestrian skill, it may appear strange and contradictory that I have so soon set him on horseback, and that too in a rocky, precipitous, and dangerous country. He himself affords the explanation. "The roads," he wrote, "throughout the island are situated on the edge of precipices—nor would I trust myself on them on any English horse—but the animals here are so quiet, and sure-footed, and careful, that I should not be afraid to trust myself asleep on the back of any of them."

In another passage he thus describes one of his mountain walks:

"From Rosemary we walked to a ridge of rocks, piled loose one on another by the hand of nature; some of them are so heaped up as to form the figure of a man, which goes by the name of the Friar, and taken in one point of view, it has that appearance. From this ridge you look down on an immense abyss, which from its depth and steepness is called Eternity; and, indeed, any despairing lover might in one instant, without any trouble or noise, put an end to his existence in one step; the appearance cannot be better described than by making use of the allegorical term, 'Beauty in the lap of Horror.' There are many other situations similar to this in the island which I had not an opportunity of seeing; their names will give a better idea of them than anything I can say; such as Purgatory, Break-neck Valley, Hold-fast Tom, and others, which have escaped my recollection. I clambered up High Peak, one of the highest points (as its name indicates) in St. Helena; from this I looked down upon Ladder Hill (which, as I observed, stands half a mile perpendicular from the sea), as upon a deep valley. I found myself, for the first time in my life, when on High Peak, above the clouds. The prospect is noble, and the eye grasps at one view nearly the whole island; but we were prevented from enjoying it by the clouds, which seemed to shut us out from the world and oppose a barrier to our communication with humble mortals; but the barrier was but vapour, through which we descended from the regions of air to grovel once more amongst the herd of terrestrials. I was inclined to loiter, when a cry of *descende cœlo* from Mr. Bazett, drove away my fanciful ideas; and I found in descending, that there was more difficulty in scrambling down than in clambering up rocks."

The remainder of the voyage furnished little worthy of record. An eclipse of the sun, a storm off the Cape, an enemy in sight, and a fall down the hatchway,* were the

* "*October* 30.—Had a terrible fall from the gun-deck to the orlop, by which I cut open my chin, and at the time imagined I had received an internal injury; but the next day, being bled, the pains went off, and in a few days I felt no more of it."

principal incidents recorded in young Metcalfe's journal.* At the end of December they were in soundings, and sighted land.

* His studies at this time were principally in a poetical direction. He read Dryden and Pope—*Othello*, *Jane Shore*, *Venice Preserved*, and the *Pursuits of Literature*. On the 21st of October he "began a poem, intended to be entitled 'Eton,' in imitation of Pope's 'Windsor Forest.'"

CHAPTER II.

1801.

THE FIRST YEAR IN INDIA.

The First Year in India—Arrival at Calcutta—The Young Writer's Reception—Hospitalities of the Cold Season—Oriental Studies—The College of Fort William—Depressing Influences of the Climate—Yearnings after Home—The Prescience of Young Ambition—Appointment to the Public Service.

On the first day of the present century, the vessel which conveyed Charles Metcalfe to India entered the Hooghly river, and at night-fall anchored off Kedgeree. On the following evening, as there was a likelihood of the ship's detention, the young writer put himself into a rowing-boat, and made his way towards Calcutta. After a "tedious, disagreeable expedition," owing, as the eager boy declared, to the "stupidity of the fellows," he arrived on the night of the 3rd of January, off one of the ghauts, or landing-places, of the great city; and in outer darkness, seeing nobody, and knowing not where he was, first planted his foot on Indian soil.*

* *MS. Journal.* "*January*, 1801. *Thursday*, 1*st.*—Having got our pilot on the preceding evening, we proceeded up the river, and anchored at Kedgeree.

"*Friday*, 2*nd.*—A number of boats came to us with fruits, and the appearance of the boats, as well as men, is very curious and entertaining to a stranger. As there was a likelihood of the ship's being detained, I got into the chokey boat at six in the evening, which, after a most tedious, disagreeable expedition,

After half an hour's delay, young Metcalfe contrived to obtain the assistance of a man, who showed him the way to Mr. Colvin's house—the house of one of those great Calcutta merchants, who were fast rising into the "princely" dignity which at a little later period they attained. Thither his baggage was conveyed, and there he spent the first night of his sojourn in India. On the following morning, Mr. Colvin lent his young visitor a carriage; and Metcalfe, with a bundle of letters of introduction, set out to pay a round of visits. Among others, to whom he presented himself, was Mr. Bristow, a member of the Civil Service, who invited the boy "to remain with him."* On the next day, he officially reported himself, ordered a palanquin, and hired a retinue of servants.†

And now commenced Charles Metcalfe's Indian career. He was fairly launched as a "young writer." He belonged to the great privileged class; he was the son of an East India Director; he had many friends in the settlement, for his father had preceded him there; he had a passport to the best society in Calcutta. It was the season of social activity, the height of the cold weather, when dinner-parties and balls are abundant, and young civilians are in

owing to the stupidity of the fellows, brought us up to Calcutta on Saturday night. When I landed, I know not where, I saw nobody, till, after half an hour's delay, I got a man to show me Colvin's house, where I got my baggage, and slept."

* *MS. Journal.* "*Sunday, 4th.*—Got into Colvin's carriage and went to Graham's—thence to Cotton's, and after that to Bristow's, who invited me to remain with him. Despatched my letters—wrote to my uncles." [Mr. Richardson and Colonel Monson.]

† *MS. Journal.* "*Monday, 5th.*—Reported myself to Crommelin, Secretary in the Public Department; saw Plowden and Higginson. Went to Mr. Brown, the provost. [The Rev. David Brown, minister of the Old Church, and provost of the College of Fort William.] Ordered a palanquin (160 rupees). Got a Khitmudgar, Hircarrah, Masaulchee, and Tailor."

constant requisition. So for some weeks after his arrival, the entries in his journal consist of little more than records of the places at which he dined and at which he danced. At the end of the first fortnight, he bethought himself of the duty of studying the languages; and he secured the services of a moonshee. But after two days' trial, he dismissed him, "finding him of no use;" and "determined to teach himself." The laudable determination, however, went the way of young civilians' resolutions in general; and for many weeks there is no record of anything beyond the hospitalities of Calcutta. A page or two from the boy's journal will indicate what they were:

"*Tuesday, January 6th.*—Went with Plowden to see Miss Baillie at Barlow's.* Received an answer from Crommelin. Dined at home.

"*Wednesday, 7th.*—Went with Plowden to Brooke's. Saw Golding. Dined at Thornhill's. Got a Dhobee.

"*Thursday, 8th.*—Changed my residence from Bristow's to Chapman's. Dined at home. Went to Lady Russell's.†

"*Friday, 9th.*—With Plowden in the morning. Was introduced to Sir Alured Clarke‡ and General Baynard. Dined with the Governor-General, who talked much about Eton. Went to Lady Anstruther's ball.§

"*Saturday, 10th.*—Shopping in the morning. Got a cocked-hat (20 rupees). Dined and passed the evening at Dr. Dick's.

"*Sunday, 11th.*—Called on Mr. Bazett. Dined with them.

"*Monday, 12th.*—Strolling about in the morning. Went to the levee. Dined at home, and passed the evening at Colvin's.

"*Tuesday, 13th.*—Dined at college. Went to the Governor's ball.

"*Wednesday, 14th.*—Dined at Sir Alured Clarke's. At Dick's in the evening.

---

* Mr. G. H. Barlow, then one of the chief officers of the Secretariat Department; afterwards Sir George Barlow, Governor-General of India.

† Wife of Sir Henry Russell, one of the puisne judges.

‡ Commander-in-Chief.

§ Wife of Sir J. Anstruther, Chief Justice.

"*Thursday, 15th.*—Dined at Mr. Graham's. Went to Brooke's ball. Sat up till sunrise at a second supper.

"*Friday, 16th.*—Dined at Tucker's.* Went to bed very much fatigued, not having slept the preceding night.

"*Saturday, 17th.*—Dined at college. Sat at Higgonson's. Had a moonshee.

"*Sunday, 18th.*—Dined at home. Had a moonshee.

"*Monday, 19th.*—Dismissed my moonshee, finding him of no use. Determined to teach myself. Went on board the *Shelton Castle*, the *Malartigue*, and *London*, taken from the French; and the *Countess of Sutherland*, a very large ship, in company with Plowden, Impey, Hamilton, and Chester. Dined at home. Went to Lady Anstruther's.

"*Tuesday, 20th.*—Dined at Dick's.

"*Wednesday, 21st.*—Breakfasted at Bristow's. Wrote journal. Dined at Bristow's.

"*Thursday, 22nd.*—Tiffed at Hamilton's. Dined with Plowden.

"*Friday, 23rd.*—Answered my uncle Monson's letter. Ditto Richardson. Dined at home. Went to the Governor's ball.

"*Monday, 26th.*—Dined at Barlow's. Great A.'s rout.

"*Tuesday, 27th.*—Dined at Bazett's.

"*Wednesday, 28th.*—Dined at college. Spent the evening at Hamilton's.

"*Thursday, 29th.*—Dined at Brooke's.

"*Friday, 30th.*—Dined at Buller's.† Ball at Brooke's.

"*Saturday, 31st.*—Tiffed at Law's."

After this, appears a long hiatus in the journal, and towards the end of February there is a brief admission that the writer had nothing but idleness to record:—"This long vacuum," he wrote, "would be filled by nothing but accounts of my idleness. It is, therefore, as well to drop it. I got into my own house on Sunday, 22nd (February)."

Having established himself in a house of his own, and being now in all respects the master of his own time and

* Mr. Henry St. George Tucker, then Financial Secretary.

† Probably Mr. C. Buller, of the Civil Service, father of the late Mr. Charles Buller and of Sir A. Buller, now one of the puisne judges of the Supreme Court of Calcutta.

his own actions, Charles Metcalfe began seriously to think about qualifying himself for the active business of his profession. The native languages were to be mastered at the threshold. It was to be a toilsome, systematic operation. No longer were Persian and Hindostanee to be acquired by chance. No longer were young men, fresh from Eton or Harrow, to be flung loose upon the surface of Indian life to acquire, as best they could, without any formal training or scholastic discipline, the knowledge that was to fit them to become judges and ambassadors and ministers of finance. Earnestly and assiduously had Lord Wellesley addressed himself to the great work of improving the administrative machinery of the Anglo-Indian Government. And foremost among his projects was the establishment of a nursery for young Indian administrators, under efficient direction and control. Clinging with peculiar fondness to those academic reminiscences, which no Etonian will willingly let die, he had conceived the idea of planting an *Alma Mater* on the banks of the Hooghly; and now the college of Fort William was fast springing into life. The history of this great project—of its rise and its fall—has been written, and may be written again. But it has not yet been recorded that Charles Metcalfe was the first student ever admitted into the college of Fort William.

It was on the 27th of April that he signed the declaration preparatory to his formal admission. He had been diligently "sapping"* all through the two preceding months. In spite of his determination to teach himself, he had secured the services of another moonshee; and day after day had been deep in Persian and Hindostanee, occasionally varying his Oriental studies with snatches of

* No Etonian need to be told that "sapping" means *studying*—literally, *growing wise*—but to other readers the interpretation may be necessary.

French and classics. The entries in his diary at this time relate almost exclusively to the continuance of his studies:—

"*Wednesday, February* 25*th.*—Attended Hindostanee lectures, second and first class. Breakfasted with Tucker, and dined.

"*Thursday*, 26*th.*—Dined at college.

"*Friday* 27*th.*—Attended first, second, and third classes of Hindostanee, and studied with my moonshee. Read Gibbon.

"*Saturday* 28*th.*—Studied with my moonshee. Read first vol. of Gibbon's Roman Empire. Breakfasted at Cotton's.

"*Sunday*, 1*st of March.*—Went to church. Hindostanee.

"*Monday*, 2*nd.*—Hindostanee.

"*Tuesday*, 3*rd.*—Ditto.

"*Wednesday*, 4*th.*—Ditto. Went to Bazett's in the evening.

"*Thursday*, 5*th.*—Dined at Tucker's. Hindostanee, &c.

"*Friday*, 6*th.*—Hindostanee lectures. Dined at Dashwood's.

"*Saturday*, 7*th.*—Classical.

"*Monday*, 9*th.*—French. Sapping.

"*Tuesday*, 10*th.*—Persian. Ditto.

"*Wednesday*, 11*th.*—Hindostanee. Ditto." [And so, all through the remainder of the month, continued "sapping to April the 1st, when the term closed;" and again "sapped to Sunday the 5th."]

A few more extracts from this journal will carry on the history of the young writer's life better than anything I can substitute for them. It will be seen how he continued to devote himself diligently to his studies; how he endeavoured to accustom himself to his new way of life, and to absorb himself in the occupations of the present; but how the cherished associations of the past would rise up to distract his mind and unhinge his resolutions. Do what he would, he still thought less of the Calcutta course than of the Eton playing-fields—less of Brown and Buchanan than of Heath and Goodall—less of Writers'-buildings than of Portland-place:

"*Thursday*, 23*rd.*—Wrote a long letter to my father. Got a new moonshee, the other having left with much insolence.

"*Friday*, 24*th.*—Wrote to Goodall.

"*Saturday, 25th.*—Ditto.

"*Sunday, 26th.*—To my mother.

"*Monday, 27th.*—Read and signed the declaration, and was admitted into college—being the first ever admitted into the College of Fort William.

"*Tuesday, 28th.*—Wrote to my mother.

"*Wednesday, 29th.*—Wrote to Lloyd, bookseller. Dined at Cruttenden's. Mure arrived from Cawnpore.

"N.B. During this month I daily did something in the way of studies, and found myself at the end of it improved. I have not written down an account of them, as my memory could not afford one. Of what nature they may have been, must be hereafter proved at the college examinations, and the degree of praise, or discredit, I may receive, will be the best criterion by which to judge whether my time has been thrown away or not. I cannot boast of having applied so much as I ought, for, of all disagreeable studies, the first steps of a language are most disagreeable.

"*Saturday, 2nd of May.*—At Bazett's in the evening.

"*Sunday 3rd.*—Church. Barton came and took up his quarters with me.

"*Monday 4th.*—Went to the Provost's chambers, read the declarations, &c., and was admitted the first on the list of the College of Fort William. Signed my name to the Hindostanee, Persian, Greek, Italian, French, and Latin languages. [Remark particularly. This is the anniversary of my going to Eton, and my taking leave of Dr. Heath.] There was a grand dinner at college, where the Governor-General, Lord Wellesley, was present. He was remarkably attentive to me. Went to Mrs. Palmer's.

"*Tuesday, 5th.*—Had a dinner at home. Sherer, Chester, Potts, and Plowden.

"*Wednesday, 6th,*—Anniversary of my leaving Eton. The last time I saw Goodall, Tonson, and Grose—a sad, sad day. Called on Mrs. Potts after college dinner.

"*Thursday, 7th.*—Dined at home. Bayley came. Received a letter from my mother and Grose.

"*Friday, 8th.*—Heard from Cawnpore. [From this to Monday, 18th, forgot.] Monday, examined in Persian by Edmonstone and Bayley.* Put in the sixth, or actually the second class.

---

* This should have been written Baillie. Captain Baillie was then one of the Professors of the College. He was subsequently a distinguished political officer, and an East India Director.

"*Tuesday.*—Hindostanee lectures. Got a new moonshee; Hilal-ood-deen.

"*Wednesday.*—Latin lectures.

"*Thursday, 22nd.*—This day twelvemonth, my brother left the fleet at St. Helen's; and came up to London, the last time I saw him. Not have I heard from him. God forbid he should have met with any accident.

"*Thursday, 4th of June.*—Was at the levee. The Lord behaved to me with marked attention, and gave me a general invitation to Barrackpore. Such civility from Lord Wellesley is no common thing.

"*Wednesday, 17th.*—Heard from my brother in China. This day week, moved into the Buildings.

"*Thursday, 18th.*—Wrote to my father requesting to return. On his answer depends my happiness in life."

This was written in the middle of June. The exhausting climate of Calcutta had now for some months been doing its sure work upon the young stranger; and he felt, as hundreds before and after him have felt—worn, weary, and dispirited; needing some great exertion to shake off the depressing influences which were surrounding him, and yet utterly incapable of making it. He had been applying himself somewhat too closely to his studies; the mind had been on the stretch, and the body had been inactive. He had neglected to take that regular exercise which, in moderation, contributes so much to the health of the resident in hot climates. He was not addicted to field sports; he did not excel in athletic exercises of any kind. He said that he was "out of his element" amid such scenes; and, now that the time for the more strenuous activities was past, he had not, like most of his cotemporaries, the unfailing resource of the saddle to fall back upon—seasonable in all months, from January to December. The brisk Arab and the open plain were nothing to him, for he did not delight in equestrian recreations. Foul vapours gathered about him; and there was nothing to disperse them. In these fiery months there is a general stagnation of the social atmosphere. A few languid dinner-parties feebly indicate that the spirit of hospitality is not dead, but sleepeth. Even the natives of the country shrink from the fierce glare, the scorching winds, and the intolerable dust of the summer solstice. How, then, when the sun is up, can English gentlemen pass about from house to house? In dreary isolation, in feverish imprisonment, they exist, through the long days, if they can; every one has enough to do in looking after his own individual life; he has little of any kind to bestow upon his neighbours. Doubtless, therefore, Charles Metcalfe, at this time, found himself lonely and dispirited—languid and exhausted—with all sorts of sickly fancies preying upon his mind. He was dissatisfied with the Present; he was hopeless of the future; and, worse than all, he was regretful of the Past. "Sorrow's crown of sorrow" was pressing heavily upon him; for he clung to the memory of "happier things."

Life seemed to him to be without an object. It is a great thing, doubtless, to "study the native languages." It is very right that this should be the unvarying formula of advice to all embryo Indian statesmen; but, however advantageous the results may be, this study of the native languages is a dreary occupation in itself. A young man in his teens may be forgiven if his spirit is not stirred by it to any very lofty pitch of enthusiasm—if he does not appreciate the privilege of gathering under the guidance of a moonshee the unlovely knowledge of the Eastern world, with a thermometer standing at 90° in the shade. I do not, therefore, seek to disguise the fact, that before Charles Metcalfe had been a year in India, he was eager to go home again. Let us read his own account of the matter.

"At the latter end of June," he wrote in his journal some months afterwards, "there was an examination, which placed me fifth on the list of Hindostanee scholars, and last of the first class. This brought praise upon me, as I had arrived in the country after all those who were examined with me, to the number of thirty. Lord Wellesley told me he considered my progress greater than that of any other. His attentions to me have been, on every occasion, marked and flattering. I spent a week of the July vacation at Umooar, or Oorcapara, on a hog-hunting party. I was out of my element. I afterwards wrote my essay on the College; it was one of the ten best sent in to the Lord. The next term passed over my head without any attention to my studies—my mind being too much occupied with the thought of my melancholy situation. I wrote repeated and urgent letters to my father on the subject of return, and know not how my fate is to be decided. I cannot exist here; the idea that my father may refuse, renders me thoroughly miserable. I had projected a trip up the river, for the vacation, with Hamilton, and we were on the point of setting off when a disorder broke out upon me, which stopped us, and now confines me to Calcutta, and almost to the house. I find from it how much inferior the most excruciating bodily torment is to mental agony—the result of reflection and too much sensibility. I cannot exist in absence from my family. I have been exceedingly unwell throughout the rains. Ill-health is a very inferior consideration with me. I am, however, willing to believe that the sufferings I at present labour under will be shortly removed, and that it hath pleased Almighty Providence to ordain me this time of penance that I may learn Humility, Patience, and Obedience to his Divine will. How awful is the thunder of the Lord, which, growling o'er our heads, proclaims his power—how mighty is his vengeance—how dreadful his wrath! Who shall oppose it? Man, remember the fall of our Great Ancestor. He sinned, and mark his punishment."—[*October 5th*, 1801.]

There would be enough in the mere fact of the physical ailments, to which reference is here made, to account for all this depression of spirit. The hot weather had exhausted young Metcalfe's strength, and the rainy season had utterly prostrated him. But the sufferings which he endured are not wholly to be attributed, directly or indirectly, to these causes. He was a youth of very quick affections. The pulsations of that warm human heart were ever keeping him in a state of unrest. From the solitude of his chamber in the City of Palaces, his thoughts went back with reverential love to his old home in Portland-place. And there was one fair form, which, filling all his boyish imagination with visions of delight, was ever flitting between him and his books, making dim to his dazzled sight the Oriental characters which lay before him. His whole heart untravelled turned towards England; and he was twelve thousand miles away.

Nor was it only his boyish love that made India distasteful to him. His boyish ambition had already been fired. A mysterious power within him had suggested that he was destined to be great. The day-dreams of the Eton cloisters were dreamt over again. He thought that he saw the end clearly before him; but so little did he understand the adaptation of means to that end, that he believed his success in life depended upon his immediate return to England. Under the influence of a strange intermixture of prescience and blindness, he implored his father to obtain for him, through the influence of Lord Grenville, an appointment in a public office at home,* for he believed that such an appointment, however insignificant, would be a stepping-stone to ultimate greatness.

* It is said that the Duke of Wellington, in early life, petitioned his friends to procure for him some small civil appointment, that he might retire from the military service, in which he saw little chance of rising.

He was a mere boy at this time—he had not completed his seventeenth year. But he had begun to think of the day when his biographer would trace, with deepest interest, his puerile aspirations through the records of his commonplace book. "No man," wrote young Charles Metcalfe, in the autumn of 1801, "can be forced into greatness without ambition. But will every man who has ambition be great? No one possesses more ambition than I do; and am I destined to be great? If I quit this country, I may be; and it is one of the reasons for my desiring it so ardently. I cannot help thinking, should I hereafter be great, of the fervour with which my biographer will seize upon these slight memorandums, and record them to an eager public as a proof of my indulging in youth, and in distant climes, the idea of becoming a great character on the theatre of the world. Ambition takes its rise from vanity, and in proportion as a man is ambitious, he is vain. I am, therefore, one of the vainest creatures upon earth—and I believe I am. There is, however, a vast distinction between vanity and presumption. The latter will show itself when the other cannot be perceived. I am free from the latter, for I have always the appearance of modesty. This modesty is not assumed; it proceeds from bashfulness, and however superior I may internally fancy myself, I have never the boldness to communicate my thoughts before any number of persons. Even if a third person is present, I have a padlock on my mouth. But whence arises vanity? A vain person would answer himself, 'From knowledge, abilities,' &c. I, indeed, am inclined to believe that all men of ability so possess vanity (distinct from presumption), viz., they have a consciousness of their own powers, which is an innate vanity. It does not, however, follow, that all men who have vanity should possess ability. Ambition arises from a consciousness of our own powers, or vanity; and this again from ability. The most ambitious are the most vain; but the most vain are not always the most able. I believe egotism arises from vanity; otherwise I should not have devoted two pages to an examination of my own character. If we were to search our hearts, we should find them very faulty."*

Thus reasoned the clever boy, not unmindful of the possibility of all this finding its way into print half a century afterwards, from the hands of a "fervent biographer."† It seems to have been his ambition at this time to take part in the strife of English politics, and to make his way to eminence through the House of Commons. He could not believe that Hindostanee and Persian would help him on the road to fame. "Language," he wrote, "is the most disgusting; history the most delightful of studies; law is the most perplexing; politics the most noble of professions. To be an independent member of the British House of Commons is the highest honour next to being Prime Minister of Great Britain. Pitt is the first man in Europe; still greater by his resignation." And still thinking of the career of English statesmanship which might lie before him, the young civilian pushed aside his Persian dictionaries and grammars, to write eager letters to his father, dwelling upon the misery of his condition and the hopelessness of his prospects, and praying for emancipation from the thraldom which was destroying all the happiness of his life.

How these letters were received at home will presently be told. In the meanwhile, what he called a slight

* MS. "Common-place Book," 1801.

† It is not unworthy of remark, that young Metcalfe had been studying Rochefoucault and Rousseau. The entries in his common-place book are either Maxims or Confessions, or a mixture of both. At this early period of life cleverness is always imitative. The impress of some favourite author may generally be discerned upon the writings of the young. The imitation is not the less striking for its unconsciousness.

reprieve came from another quarter. All through the months of October and November, he had been a prey to anxiety and dejection, but the remedy was close at hand. What young Metcalfe needed at this time to disperse the vapours which were clouding his happiness, was simply a life of action. He was weary of the stagnation of student-life, and, perhaps, he was beginning to understand that the "misery" which, as he said, was pressing so heavily upon him, was in part at least the result of physical causes, and that movement might alleviate, if it could not wholly cure the disease. So it happened, that when it became known that the Government purposed to despatch an embassy to the Arab States, he solicited Lord Wellesley, who was not unwilling to sanction the young writer's premature escape from college, to appoint him an attaché to the mission. The request was readily granted, and Mr. Charles Metcalfe was gazetted as Assistant to the Embassy to the Arab States.

But he never joined the appointment. "I was appointed," he wrote in his journal, a short time afterwards, "Assistant to the Embassy to the Arab States, on the 3rd of December. I afterwards (having the option, for which I feel sincere gratitude to Lord Wellesley) had my appointment changed; and on the 29th of December I was appointed Assistant to the Resident with Dowlut Rao Scindiah." Colonel Collins, an old friend of young Metcalfe's father, was then Resident at Scindiah's court. The appointment was, therefore, full of favourable promise; and not the least of its advantages was that, in order to join it, the young civilian was compelled to undertake an extensive land journey, at a season of the year when travelling in India is a long delight. So Charles Metcalfe, emancipated from the trammels of college, packed up his goods and chattels, and set out for the upper provinces.

And so ended Charles Metcalfe's first year in India.

The experienced Anglo-Indian reader will see in it, peradventure, the reflection of his own trial-year. When throughout the hot months and the rainy season of this year 1801, the young exile felt an irresistible desire to return to his old home, with all its charming associations of love and liberty, his longings were only those of a large proportion of the young exiles who, in loneliness of heart and captivity of person, struggle feebly through this first dreary season of probation. By the old, forgetful of their own experiences, this despondency, attributable as it is in part to physical and in part to moral causes, may be regarded as boyish weakness. But it is weakness better than any strength. Charles Metcalfe had a very warm human heart; and I do not think the reader will admire him less for being forced to love him more.

CHAPTER III.

[1802.]

FIRST OFFICIAL EXPERIENCES.

Departure from Calcutta—Meeting with Lord Wellesley's Camp—Pageantry at Lucknow—Progress of the March—Arrival at Agra—Letters to Mr. Sherer—Life at the Residency—Colonel Collins—Home Correspondence—Return to Calcutta.

CHARLES METCALFE had now made his election. In the civil service of the East India Company, there were several departments. The purely commercial line of business was fast becoming extinct. Though retaining the name of merchants and factors, the civilians had ceased to be traders on their own account, and now traded but little for their honourable masters. A large majority of them were employed in the collection of the revenue and in the administration of justice. The "political," or diplomatic, department of the public service, was not then closed against them, although its highest offices were held by military men—by the Kirkpatricks, the Closes, the Collinses, and the Scotts. It was to this branch of the service that young Metcalfe now directed his regards. It was the only one that could fire the ambition of the boy who had dreamt in the Eton cloisters of prescribing terms and concluding treaties. So he made his choice, and, having made it, he resolutely determined to cling to it. It was only, he judged, by adhering to one line, that there was any prospect of attaining distinction.*

* It was, I believe, at the suggestion of his godfather, Mr. Jacob Rider, that Colonel Collins recommended young Metcalfe to the situation of an *attaché* to the Residency at the Scindiah's

In the middle of the month of January, 1802, Charles Metcalfe quitted Calcutta, travelling in a palanquin, to join his appointment. He had a long journey before him; for

Court. In the course of the preceding August he had written an affectionate letter to his godson, in which he said:—"In spite of your present dislike to the country, I have been planning stations for you, in one of which I hope in due time to see your appointment. Amongst others, it has occurred to me that Colonel Collins, who is under great obligations to your father, should endeavour to get you appointed his assistant. It would be fixing you in one of the most respectable lines in the service, and your father, I am sure, would be very much pleased with it. It does not at all follow that military men are always to hold diplomatic appointments, and I should hope, old as I am, to see you Governor-General's agent to Scindiah. If you are for a rapid fortune, for a scramble, and to run off with what you can get, you should get appointed assistant to a collector. These principles, I trust, you are not come out with, and I should be sorry to hear of your getting into that line, or as assistant to either of the judges of Adawlut. Much better will it be for you to get into either of the offices below, under the Secretary-General, the Secretary in the Public Department, the Persian translator's office, or in the Secret Political and Foreign Departments. From any of these offices you will be qualified to hold any appointment in the Mofussil; but I say to you as I would to my own son—keep as long out of the judicial line, and the line of collections, as you can—altogether, I hope, or till that some great reform takes place in those lines. Recollect, my good fellow, that I write to you in perfect confidence, and not for general communication. There's scarcely a man in either of the lines I allude to that will agree with me in opinion. The diplomatic line is what I would recommend your turning your mind to.

"Your dislike to the country can't be greater than mine was for the first twelvemonth; it will wear off I am convinced, but perhaps not so soon in a college. However, when you reflect what satisfaction it will give your father and mother to hear of your getting a medal, I am sure you will study hard to deserve one, and then I will attack Collins, for I hope to see you fixed either with him at Lucknow, or at Poonah. I should be most happy to see you, but I would not on any account have you think of leaving College under any pretence whatever."

his destination was beyond the limits of the Company's dominions, in the heart of those provinces lying between the Jumna and the Nerbudda, which had been at this time little explored by British residents in the East. The Mahrattas were then dominant in that fine country. The hereditary enmity of Scindiah and Holkar was rending and distracting it. It was what the natives called *gurdee-ka-wukht*—a time of trouble.

At Oujein Scindiah held his court. British interests were represented there by Colonel Collins—an officer of the Company's army, who in more than one political situation had done good service to the State; but whose private amiability was not equal to his diplomatic address. He had been the friend and associate of the elder Metcalfe, to whom he was much beholden; but still it was not without some misgivings that the young writer now found himself on his way to join the family of a man who was not reputedly of a temper calculated to win the confidence and affection of youth. These doubts, however, did not much or long disturb him. He started under happy auspices, which became still happier as he proceeded northwards. Lord Wellesley was then on his way to the Ceded Provinces of Oude, progressing with the true pomp of the Sultan; and at Cawnpore young Metcalfe came up with the viceregal *cortège*, and was invited by the Governor-General to join it.

"I left Calcutta," thus journalized the young writer, "on the 14th of January, and arrived at Benares on the 19th, where I was very kindly entertained by Mr. Neave, and saw my godfather, Jacob Rider. I quitted Benares on the 21st, stopped some hours with Colonel Kyd at Allahabad, and arrived at Cawnpore on the 24th. Here I found all my friends and relations, and was very happy. But, alas! happiness cannot last long. I quitted Cawnpore on the 30th (my birthday) with Lord Wellesley, whose permission to accompany him was very graciously given; and after very agreeable marches (considered the whole time as one of his family) arrived at Lucknow on the 5th of February, 1802. Our time was most agreeably passed in a variety of magnificent shows. The fireworks exceeded any I ever saw. The elephant fights did not equal my expectation. I returned on the 14th of February to Cawnpore."

From this station, where he resided at the house of Mr. Richardson,* a member of the civil service, he wrote to one of his college friends—John Walter Sherer, then a young man of good promise, which his after-career of usefulness fulfilled—the following enthusiastic account of the pageantry at Lucknow. In the suite of Lord Wellesley he had begun to think that the bright Oriental tinting of the "Arabian Nights" had nothing fabulous about it.

CHARLES METCALFE TO J. W. SHERER.

"*Cawnpore, Feb.* 17, 1802.

"MY DEAR SHERER,—I have lately returned from Lucknow, whither I accompanied the Marquis. I consider myself fortunate in having had such an opportunity; for such a one will never most probably occur again. We left Cawnpore on the 30th of January, and, after four days' very pleasant march, encamped within three miles of Lucknow. The Nabob's tents were pitched between us and the town, which he had not entered since his return from Cawnpore. His Lordship's escort consisted of his Majesty's 76th, and 18th Regiment of Native Infantry, with the 3rd Regiment of Native Cavalry, and two troops of the 27th Light Dragoons, exclusive of his own body-guard. With camp followers, &c., we must have formed an encampment of above 20,000 men. Two of the Nabob's sons came to Lord Wellesley's tent to conduct him, and shortly after he commenced his march he was met by the Nabob, the Resident, and all the English and native respectable inhabitants of Lucknow. His Lordship and the Nabob mounted the same elephant (the whole party were provided with this conveyance), and commenced the procession

* Mr. Richardson was the husband of one of Metcalfe's aunts.

with every possible parade of magnificence. I do not think a finer spectacle could have ever before been seen. Every display of Asiatic and European magnificence was to be seen in our procession. We had a large body of European soldiery (the finest sight we know of in England), at the same time everything of Asiatic splendour which the mind can fancy. The innumerable concourse of elephants (the grandeur of which animal seems to have appointed it particularly for a procession of this nature), decorated with costly trappings, was no small part of my admiration. The very dresses formed a spectacle of magnificence, and the two nations seemed to vie with each other in their splendour. The Calcutta cavalry, I can assure you, was not the least elegant. His Lordship, in the true style of Eastern pomp, distributed his rupees with a liberal hand. The streets had been fresh painted, and those of the merchants were lined with the most beautiful silks of various patterns. The tops of the houses (with which we were brought to a level by our elephants) were covered with musicians and dancing-girls; the streets under our feet crowded with millions anxious to see so grand a procession. Everything recalled to my memory the 'Arabian Nights,' for every description of any such procession which I ever met with in history, even the celebrated Triumph of Aurelian (I think it was the Emperor), when he led Zenobia and Tiridates * captives, of which Gibbon gives an account, was completely beggared by it. I am aware that any attempt of mine to give an idea of what I saw will be very vain. We were received at the Nabob's at breakfast under a salute. There were some inconveniences, as there always will be in a thing of this kind,—such as the noise of the music, the cries of the scramblers, the crush of elephants, which was sometimes truly alarming.

"The Nabob and the Lord grew so attached to each other, that the Nabob declared that he could not exist unless he always dined and breakfasted in company with the Lord. We were, therefore, constantly annoyed with ceremony. The fireworks and illuminations which he exhibited to us were the most splendid I could ever have conceived an idea of. I was rather disappointed in the elephant fight: this animal does not seem to possess valour equivalent to his size or strength; yet to have seen it is certainly a matter of curiosity. The Nabob's horses are remarkably fine. His pleasures are all in the English way; he is fond of horses,

* This should have been written *Tetricus*.

dogs, hunting, &c. &c. His breakfasts, dinners, houses, are completely English. It struck me very forcibly as worthy of remark, that a Mussulman prince should sit after dinner merely for the purpose of handing about the bottle, though of course *he* did not drink. He has a French cook and a military band of English instruments. I at length grew quite tired of the variety of ceremonies, and, after gratifying my curiosity in seeing whatever was to be seen, I paid my last respects to his Lordship on Sunday. He has not quitted Lucknow. He was very attentive to me and kind. Remember me to all friends. Direct for the present to 'T. Richardson, Esq., Cawnpore.'

"Yours very sincerely,

"C. T. METCALFE."

"After enjoying the society of my friends for another fortnight," continued the young journalist, writing at Mynpooree on the 7th of March, "I left it on the 26th. Arrived on the 27th at Futtehghur, which I quitted on the 5th of this month, after having experienced a great deal of kindness from Mrs. Collins, and of attention and politeness from General Stuart. The change of scene which I have for the last two months experienced has, in some measure, diverted my mind from that constant brooding over my misery to which I have for too long a period given way. But no variety, no pleasures, can prevent me from frequently recurring to the probability of my happiness being sacrificed to worldly ideas of prudence. Alas! how little is happiness consulted in general. But I must not indulge in these reflections."*

* *MS. Journal, March 7th*, 1802. On the previous day he had written:—"*March 6th.*—I made a forced march from Mahomedabad to Bever, and thence to Bhogong, where I ordered the tents to be pitched. . . . Towards the evening I walked towards some distant ruins, which I found to be the burying-place for the followers of Mahomed. As I passed over their interred remains, I could not check my reflections upon the fallen state of this race of beings, who but half a century back were everywhere supreme." He had abandoned the palanquin, and was now riding on an elephant.

At this time young Metcalfe kept two journals; one a diary of his travels, the other what he called a "common-place book," or record of his thoughts; the objective and the subjective being scrupulously separated from each other. In the latter he wrote as follows, on that same 7th of September, in his tent at Mynpooree:

"SUNDAY.—I have just been reading divine service. What a strong impression does it always leave upon the mind, and how well calculated are the prayers to inspire one with a true spirit of religion. The Sabbath is (to the shame of mankind be it said) but very seldom attended to; in India, it is particularly neglected; so that even the day when it returns is not known, nor marked by any single act of devotion. It appears to me necessary to religion to bring it to one's serious attention at fixed periods. For the want of this, the English in India have less virtue in them than elsewhere, and cannot impress the natives with a good idea of our religion."

On the following day the young traveller left Mynpooree, and on the 10th he crossed the confines of the Company's territories. The narrative of his travels cannot be carried on better than in his own words:

"*March 9th.*—From Ghurriwal to Shekoabad. A battalion of sepoys was encamped at the latter place. I saw nothing, however, of any of the officers. It is a strange circumstance that, so far from all white faces, and not having seen one since quitting Futtehghur, I should not have greedily seized upon this opportunity of obtaining society. I did not, however, for reasons peculiar, I believe, to my own disposition. It seems equally strange that no one here should have thought me worthy of notice.

"*March 10th.*—From Shekoabad to Ferozabad. I this morning quitted the Company's territories. Ferozabad belongs to Scindiah, and is part of General Perron's Jaghire. The aumil, or governor of the place, came to pay his respects. He is a civil, shrewd, sensible man. He had heard the news of the peace, and inquired if a monarchy had been restored in France. Our conversation was chiefly political; and he observed, turning to my moonshee, who was in the tent, that the English were the only nation who could defeat the French, and that this was owing to their navy. He made many other clever observations; among others, he said that the design of the French in invading Egypt was clearly to forward their plans upon India; and concluded by observing that he did not think it would be a lasting peace. I never met with a native of India who appeared to have such rational ideas of European politics. He was a native of Lahore, and his ancestors were Uosbeck Tartars.

"*March 11th.*—From Ferozabad to Eatimadpoor. On the road I frequently passed ruins of palaces and mausoleums."

The next stage brought the young traveller to Agra, then a city garrisoned by Mahratta troops, under a Dutch commander. To the English in India it was little known except by report, and Charles Metcalfe, when he explored the wonders of the Taj-Mahal, trod where few of his countrymen had trodden, and sat down to describe in letters and journals what had seldom at that time been described by an English pen. Half a century has passed away, and the Taj has become the standing lion of the English traveller and the stock-subject of the English journalist. But custom cannot stale its infinite variety; and every new writer has something new to say about it. To young Metcalfe it appeared as the realization of the legendary and traditional, with all the charm of freshness about it. He said that it was very beautiful, and "beyond description;" but that it wanted grandeur, and suggested no solemn thoughts. The entries in his journal are brief:

"*March 12th.*—From Eatimadpoor to Agra. The eye was everywhere struck with the view of heaps of ruins, lamenting in forcible language the oppressive ravages of time. A considerable time elapsed before I could get my baggage over the river—the elephants swam. Whilst my tents were preparing, I took up my quarters in the Taj-Mahal. This is said by many—amongst others by the artist Zoffany—to be the finest building in the world. To attempt to describe it would be presumption, for it is far above description. Shah Jehan is buried here with his wife; this building was originally intended for her, and it was his design to have built a fellow to it on the opposite side of the river for himself. The ground for the purpose was enclosed with a wall, which still remains, though in a very ruinous condition. The centre building of this wonderful edifice is composed entirely of white marble, inlaid with different coloured marbles, cornelians, agates, and other curious stones in the form of flowers, ribbons, &c., &c., which are executed with wonderful nicety and real taste. I went to the summit of the minaret. They are more elevated than those of Lucknow, and present a very fine view of the fort and town.

"13th.—I breakfasted by invitation with the Dutch commander, Colonel J. Hessing. I found with him his son, who commanded in the engagement at Oujein, where his battalions were defeated; a Mr. Marshall, an Englishman; and two others, whose names I have not learnt. The breakfast consisted of kedgeree (rice and eggs), fish, game, fowls, curry and rice, stews, oranges, pears, pomegranates, eggs, bread and butter, cakes of all kinds, pancakes, and a number of other dishes, which have escaped my recollection—among others I had forgotten to enumerate cheese. The Dutchman was as polite as a Dutchman could be, and very well-meaning I am certain. I walked over some of the buildings. They are in general of marble, beautifully inlaid, and admirably executed. The roofs of many have been silver. These, however, have fallen a prey to the destroying hands of the Mahrattas, who have even stripped the rooms of the leaves of gold which covered the flowers in many places. Some of the rooms are lined with small mirrors. I was conducted by Mr. Marshall and another gentleman, who showed me the place where Shah Jehan was confined while his sons were contending for his empire. It is a small octagon room where the ruler of all India spent this wretched portion of his life, not in the command of a single slave. The walls were white, but in many places the plaster had dropped, and disclosed a coloured wall, with gold and silver ornaments. It is said that the Emperor had it whitewashed that he might not be troubled with the sight of such pernicious metals."

On the following day he "breakfasted and dined with the Dutchman, and examined the Taj-Mahal with more attention." It was a happy day, for his affectionate heart was gladdened by the receipt of a letter from his friend Sherer, which he sat down at once to answer. "I cannot better," he wrote, "express the joy I feel at receiving yours of the 1st, than by answering it immediately. It has not been in my hands ten minutes. It finds me an inmate of the far-famed Taj-Mahal at Agra." "It is above description," he added; "but I may endeavour to give you an idea of its materials." And then he went on to speak of the wonderful mosaic, of the precious stones inlaid, of the elegant devices—but confessed that there was something unsatisfactory in it all. "If," he wrote—and the passage is worth more than whole pages of such description—"if you are not already tired of the subject, I will tell you the impression that all this beauty and elegance left upon my mind. Although I have by no means done it justice, yet you will be surprised when I tell you it left *no* impression upon my mind; I was not inspired with any of those sentiments of awe, delight, or reverence with which I have viewed much less magnificent buildings, particularly the colleges of the universities, or with which I have heard the echo of my own footsteps even in the cloisters of my much-loved Eton." Then he fondly reverted to the day-dreams of his boyhood;* and contrasted them with his actual state. "How crushed," he exclaimed, "are all my hopes, my honours, and my fancied glories! But you will say I am wandering, and in looking over the last page I find that I am."

On the 15th of March, Charles Metcalfe turned his back upon Agra, and proceeded upon his journey to Scindiah's Court. On the evening of that day, halting at Mundakor, he wrote again to his friend Sherer. After having dismissed one moonshee because he was stupid, and another because he was insolent, the young student had found a third, who was neither; and, as he was as ready to appreciate good qualities as he was to resent bad ones in his native instructors, he had come to the resolution, after leaving college, to reward the services of the man to whom he believed himself so much indebted for the proficiency which, during his year's residence in Calcutta, he had acquired in the knowledge of the native languages. What

* The passage omitted is given by anticipation at page 8.

shape the young writer's gratitude assumed may be gathered from the following letter, which deserves record as a characteristic manifestation of the kindliness and generosity of the writer:*

CHARLES METCALFE TO J. W. SHERER.

"*Camp of the Anglo-Mahratta Allied Forces, Head-quarters, Mindakor, March* 15, 1802.

"MY DEAR SHERER,—My letter of yesterday should have sufficed you for the present had I not forgotten in it to mention a subject which I particularly wished to write to you upon. It relates to our common friend Hilal-ood-deen. He is the only native of India for whom I entertain any particular esteem, which his merits loudly demand. It is no fault of his that I am not at this moment a tolerable proficient in some one or other of the Oriental languages. I am ashamed to say he was thrown away upon me. He has now to deal with a better subject, Jenkins,† who will do him the justice he deserves. The good old man must have thought it very extraordinary that I should have left Calcutta without giving him any memorial of my regard: the reasons why I did so have been explained in a letter to Hamilton. I have been considering of the means by which I can do him some *permanent* service; and I think that a monthly allowance will be the most so. Tell him, therefore, that he is to consider himself entitled to twenty rupees per month from January last inclusive. If I return to England, I must make amends for the loss of this allowance by a sum of some small value, but if I remain in India, it will continue to Hilal's death, unless I am carried off before him. It is a slight recompense, and by no means comes up to my wishes; but as I have not the slightest idea of my own salary, and as, exclusive of camp equipage and travelling

---

* On the following day he wrote in his common-place book:—"*Hilal-ood-deen.*—I have determined to settle twenty rupees per month upon this man, who so well deserves all that I can do for him. This added to his other salaries will render him extremely comfortable.—[*Futtehpore Camp, March* 16*th*, 1802.]"

Nearly a year afterwards he wrote opposite to this passage:—"I was dissuaded from this as being beyond my means. I gave 200 rupees."—[*Feb.* 19*th*, 1803.]

† The late Sir Richard Jenkins, G.C.B.

expenses, I am obliged, for the sake of appearance, to maintain a much larger establishment than I ever should have done in Calcutta, the sum which I have set apart for Hilal-ood-deen is as considerable as my ability, consistent with convenience, will admit of; this, however, I shall not feel in the least burdensome, and only regret that it cannot be larger. As it is, it may serve to add to his comforts. I will shortly contrive some means for his being regularly supplied; yet you must be aware that I must have some trifling increase before I can effect this. Give him, however, to understand that this allowance is to commence from the 1st of January, 1802, and to continue until some circumstances as above mentioned shall interfere to prevent it. I, however, by no means consider this trifling recompense as acquitting me from further obligation; on the contrary, Hilal-ood-deen will ever have a strong claim to any services I may be able to render him or his family, and in thus disposing of any benefits, in addition to gratifying my own sentiments of gratitude, I shall have the satisfaction of serving a man of solid merit and intrinsic worth. . .

"I have never experienced any comfort in India until of late, since I have been travelling quite alone. I do nothing but read English, Latin, and French, and I have procured another small but good selection of books. I rise early, read constantly, eat heartily, and sleep soundly—four blessings I never before enjoyed in India. I never allow myself to think of England, and I feel the good effects of my resolution, though my views with respect to it are the same as ever. I have no room to tell you all my plans. Persuade Hamilton to write; I have not had a word from him in answer to either of my letters. Remember me to him and Wood. Lord W. did not see the second and third essays. Depend upon it I feel more gratified by his approbation than I should by the prize itself. Buchanan* appears to have been officiating priest on the occasion, and I cannot admit that his judgment was by any means good; remember, I speak of the first lot—I know nothing of the others, not having seen them.

"Yours very sincerely,

"C. T. METCALFE.

"N.B. I have entirely deserted Oriental literature for the present, and shall see the arrivals of yesterday in a short time

---

* The Rev. Claudius Buchanan, Vice-Provost of the College. I find a letter from him to Metcalfe, written at this time, in which

turning up their noses—*en passant* [blood must have blood; I'll give you Gil for Gil*] who are the hopes of the rising generation?"

On the 17th of March, Metcalfe left Futtehpore, and on his way to Radowul his "baggage was attacked by the banditti of the country, who were repulsed." Many of his marches, at this time, were performed by moonlight. The increasing richness and beauty of the country through which he passed excited pleasurable emotions in the mind of the young traveller; and day after day, as he encamped "under the elegantly-spreading banyan-tree," or "in a most elegant grove of banyan-trees, every one of which is in itself a grove," he recorded his favourable impressions of the abundant fertility and the romantic picturesqueness of the country of the Mahrattas. Here and there he came up with battalions of Perron's troops, and received complimentary presents, and visits, not merely of compliment, from their officers.† At other places he was warned of the contiguity of Holkar's marauding bands; and "obliged to keep a

he says: "Some gentlemen were praising your essay lately, when an old civilian observed, he did not see it was anything remarkable. 'Pray can you do as well, John?' On which John said that he thought he could, if he had time."

* The reference is to some colloquialisms of Dr. Gilchrist.

† Under date March 22nd, he writes:—"*Pilowdil to Koshulghur.*—At the latter I found encamped four more battalions of Perron's roops. One of the officers came to visit me—anxious to hear of his father, Colonel ——. . . . I obtained some information from him relative to the Mahratta service. It appears that promotion depends on General Perron, who is naturally disposed to favour his own countrymen. So far, however, as the rank of captain, every officer obtains a step annually—*i. e.* in four years a man must be a captain. The rule extends no higher. The uniform of the sepoys is the same as the Company's; so are the accoutrements, with the exception that they carry a sword as well as a bayonet and musket. The band, which was in full tune, as they marched by my little camp, played nothing but marches—perfectly the European style."

sharp look out." But these things did not much disturb his tranquillity, or break in upon his meditations. Even in the near neighbourhood of the banditti his habit of moralising was not to be repressed, and we find him, with Holkar's troops within a few miles of him, opening his common-place book, and recording his opinion on the formation of character and the disposition of children.*

At Kotah, it became apparent to him, for the first time, that he was a person of some consequence, and he was compelled to act a dignified official part. The Dewan, or minister of Zalim Singh, came to pay him a visit of ceremony, which it was his duty on the following day to return. Through streets lined with wondering inabitants, "as if to view some strange spectacle," the young diplomatist went forth, more full of wonder than all the rest. He could not help reflecting on the little notice that would have been taken of him on entering any country town in England; and perhaps in his young ambition he may have begun to think that Indian official life has its compensations after all. The incident is thus detailed in his journal:

"*April 2nd, Kotah.*—In the afternoon [the Dewan] came to pay the complimentary visit. I had spread a white cloth over the satringee in the tent. I received him and his relations and friends before the tent, and after having embraced them led them in. I seated myself with them according to the Hindostanee custom, and after the ceremony of distributing Pan and Attr, ordered the presents to be brought, consisting of a gold watch, a brace of pistols, penknife, scissors, and Hindavi manuscript curiously minute. To my great annoyance, he accepted the whole, which I had never intended, and which is not a very general practice.

"*April 3rd.*—The necessity of returning the visit detained me here this day. The streets were lined with inhabitants as if to view some strange spectacle. I could not help reflecting with what indifference I should be suffered to pass into a town in

* A portion of the essay is given in Chapter I.

England, and yet how much happier I should be. I was received with the same ceremony which I had practised. The presents consisted of four shawls, three pieces of muslin, one of silk, and one of orange-coloured cloth."

After a slight detention, caused by the accidental death of one of his followers, and the kindly desire of the young diplomatist to allow time for the friends of the deceased to "perform their last duties" to him, and a subsequent halt in expectation of receiving letters from Colonel Collins, Charles Metcalfe pushed on, through a bleak, barren country, differing greatly from the fertile regions between Agra and Kotah, to Oujein.* And on the 16th of April

* The following descriptive passages from the young writer's journal, are worth giving :—

"*April 6th.*—Waited till after breakfast for letters from Colonel Collins. Receiving none, marched with thirty-eight men from the Rajah, and my havildar's guard, to Humihuttea, distant eight coss through the most savage, bleak, dreary desert I ever had any idea of—one vast rocky plain or plain rock, for there was scarcely an inch of earth, and wherever flowers grew, they were without a single leaf; every tree that appeared had its branches entirely bare. In the midst of this wild stands Juypoora, like Palmyra or Tadmor in the Desert—a spot which appears to great advantage, for between Rota and it, a distance of ten miles, there was not an inhabitant nor a hut, nor a single drop of water. The wind blowing, as if through a furnace, was too high to admit of my using any chatteh (umbrella), so that I was exposed on my elephant to the burning rays of the sun, the reflection from the rock, and the scorching influence of the wind; all these circumstances rendered me unwell during the day and night.

"*March 9th.*—Jalsepatam—five coss. The road was tolerably good, the land as wild as before. This country differs very much from the beautifully fertile and well-cultivated lands between Agra and Kotah. Here, whenever a tree has sprung up, the soil appears to confess its inability to support it, and has left it, seemingly, to wither. Whether this be owing to the seasons, or the barren soil, I know not; but the branches of every tree are completely bare. This country may very properly be called 'India Petræa,' for it is one continual rock."

he wrote the words "*Labor Ultimus*" in his journal. "After a long march," he recorded elsewhere, "rendered pleasanter by my resolution and recreation than I expected to find it, I arrived at Oujein." There he became a member of Colonel Collins's family, and entered upon the duties of his appointment. . . . . . .

But he had leisure still to discourse of love and friendship, and there was no growth of new attachment at Oujein to displace the old. The truth being told, it must appear that Charles Metcalfe, at this time, was driven to seek solace in reminiscences of the past. Disappointed, vexed, sometimes perhaps irritated, he peopled his lonely tent with the images of his absent friends, and as he pored over the letters of some beloved correspondents, or looked eagerly for the coming of the post, thought that he was again in London or Calcutta. The entries in his common-place book show what was the warmth of his young affections:

"Attachments.—Attachment to a female is generally inseparable from desire; yet when this is not the case, how much more tender and pure it is! The effect Miss D——'s virtue, sense, and beauty had, and still have, upon my mind, can never, I think, be effaced. Yet was my attachment pure and warm, but unaccompanied with any desire. I longed for her heart. . . . . The love of a boy of fifteen is a laughable subject; and is considered too childish to be lasting. Two years of absence have only served to strengthen the most disinterested attachment to her, and her sensible letters have heightened my admiration. She is far removed from any thoughts of obtaining her hand, and good sense and reason prohibit my aspiring to it. Her happiness is my first wish in preference to my own; and whoever the happy man to whose arms she is consigned, may he prove worthy of the inestimable blessing."—[*Camp near Oujein, April 25th*, 1802.]

"Neglect of Friends.—How painful is the neglect of friends, or the appearance of it! Although it is more than probable that my correspondence has not been slighted, and that the friend of my heart has actually written to me,* yet the doubt and anxiety occasioned in my mind by the non-arrival of his letters are really tormenting. With what eagerness do I wait for the coming of the post, and when my hopes are daily disappointed, with what impatience do I look forward to the next morning, and the possibility of their being realized. I may say with Rousseau, I was born for friendship; but, alas! how few are—how few feel it in its sincerity—how often is it abused—how very few look upon it as more than a temporary intimacy, which after separation is no longer to be maintained."—[*Camp near Oujein, April 25th.*]

The official connection of Charles Metcalfe at this time with Scindiah's Court was brief and unsatisfactory. "My situation was very disagreeable," he wrote in his journal, before he had been more than a few weeks attached to the Residency; and he very soon formed the resolution of seeking more congenial employment elsewhere. But, painful and embarrassing as was his position, he was becoming more reconciled to Indian life. The great panacea of action had been applied, with unfailing efficacy, to the mental ailments of the eager youth; and though his home-sickness had not been wholly subdued, it had considerably abated. He no longer felt that he was stagnating. The great world was opening out before him.

So it may be believed that when, in the summer of 1802, Charles Metcalfe received, from his parents, answers to the letters which he had written from Calcutta in the preceding year, imploring permission to return to England, and found that those answers gave no encouragement to the project of abandoning the profession which he had entered, the denial inflicted upon him less pain than he

* I believe that the friend here alluded to was Mr. Terrick Hamilton, then a student in the college, and afterwards a not undistinguished member of the Madras Civil service—one of the few of Charles Metcalfe's old friends and associates now living. The missing letters were afterwards received. The friend had not been neglectful.

had anticipated. He had begun to take new views of life, and of life's duties. Perhaps it had become apparent to him that distinction might be achieved in the East as rapidly as in the West. All his friends in India, old and young, had dissuaded him from the project of returning to England, and now the letters of his parents brought conviction to his mind that he could not take the rash step without plunging them in deepest grief. Most kindly, but still most firmly, did Major Metcalfe reply to the solicitations of his son. How wise his counsel was need not be told:

FROM MAJOR METCALFE TO CHARLES METCALFE.

"*Feb.* 24, 1802.

"MY DEAR CHARLES,—Your letter of the 30th of June reached me this day, and has, of course, caused much uneasiness to your mother and me. The two letters you allude to have not yet been received. On a retrospect of my own feelings with regard to my children, I can with great truth declare, that their care, comfort, and establishment in life has been the great object of my endeavours. If I had considered my own inclination, I should never have suffered your brother or you to leave this country. In the vale of life, the company of two sons, of whose abilities and acquirements any father might be proud, would have been a solace that a selfish mind would readily embrace; but, looking forward to the period when I must pay the debt of Nature, it became an indisputable duty to give up personal enjoyment for their future welfare, and to consider how to place them in the most advantageous situations. Judge then, my dear Charles, what I experienced at finding you so dissatisfied with your station in the Civil Service, after so short a trial. Let me ask you in what line of life I could have placed you that could hold out any prospect of a direct support, much less of a future independence? The army and navy you always objected to; and with respect to your present idea of a clerkship in the Secretary of State's office, if I could have obtained such an appointment, the situation is neither so pleasant nor so profitable as a clerk in a merchant's counting-house—a place which you would soon discover to be too degrading for any son of your father's. That the prospect in

Bengal always appears unpromising on first entering into the service, is a fact I have innumerable instances to prove; and many men now in England with large fortunes, and several in Bengal in good circumstances, held the same language as you now do. I remember well my own feelings when I was an ensign, and had been in the country about three months. I one morning (in a fit of the bile) waited on the commanding officer with an intention to resign the service, and return to England. Fortunately for me, the conversation at breakfast took a pleasant turn, in which I bore an active part, and a hearty fit of laughter got the better of my *blue devils*. I returned to my quarters with a determination to persevere; and by that prudent resolution have reached the situation which I now hold. Let my example not be thought unworthy of being followed by my sons; and I shall look with anxiety for your next letter being written in better spirits than the one now before me.

"God bless you, my dear Charles; let me hear from you by every opportunity.

"Your most affectionate father,

"THOMAS T. METCALFE."

From his mother the young writer received letters couched in more emphatic language than this. Mrs. Metcalfe was a woman of strong sense and of plain discourse. She did not deal in half-truths, and was not given to reservations. She knew that the prosperity of her son's career depended upon his continuance in India, and she was resolute not to encourage a humour which, in her conviction, was fraught with ruin. So she went straight to the point, and told her son that he ought to be ashamed of his instability; that he did not know his own mind; that he talked about distinguishing himself in England, but that he really thought more of indulging a boyish fancy; that he had been reading too much and had got the vapours; and that it would be good for him to "dissipate" a little. A little more tenderness would not have spoilt the letters, but there was wonderful sagacity in them. They touched the whole matter as with a needle's point—and Charles Metcalfe must have felt their prickings.*

Fearful as they were lest, under the influence of the despondency which beset him during his first year of probation, their son might be tempted to abandon all his fair prospects of success, and precipitately to return to England, it was with no common satisfaction that the elder Metcalfe learnt that Charles had been appointed an assistant to their "old friend Jack Collins," and was on his way to Scindiah's Court. And how much this satisfaction was enhanced by the assurances they received from all

* A few extracts from these letters may be given in a note:—

"If you have a grain of ambition, you are in the field for it, and the ball is at your foot. . . . . What is it you want? With friends, money, attention, credit, good sense, abilities, and a prospect before you which hundreds, I may say thousands, in that country have not, you want, I fear, my dear Charles, a contented mind. . . . . You study too much. You should dissipate a little. On account of your health, you should relax. Ride on horseback. When intense thinking is joined with the want of exercise, the consequences must be bad."—[*March 14th*, 1802.]

"Your letters by the *Georgiana* have given your father and myself little satisfaction. We did not expect this, and are, therefore, the more chagrined. Instead of your parents being the objects of your wish to relinquish so important a situation, if you examine your heart, you will find it is Miss D—— . . . . Your father has not the means of interest to get even the paltry appointment of a clerk in Lord Grenville's office; and if he had, there you might stay, whatever were your abilities. . . . . If you are ambitious, the field is open before you where you are; and in no place will you stand so good a chance. . . . . You will laugh at my sending you out a box of pills by Miss S——; but I think you are bilious, and they will be of great service."—[*April 8th*, 1802.]

"I do not know what to say to alleviate your seemingly discontented mind. . . . . I feel most severely your letters, and think it a great misfortune that you should have taken so great a dislike to a situation which seems best calculated to bring forth your abilities. It shows a want of energy, a want of manliness, to be so cast down."—[*November 24th*, 1802.]

quarters that their son was treading worthily the appointed path, and was already considered a youth of uncommon promise, may be gathered from Major Metcalfe's subsequent letters:

FROM MAJOR METCALFE TO CHARLES METCALFE.

"*India House, July* 28, 1802.

"MY DEAR CHARLES,—I received your short epistle informing me of your appointment to the Arabian embassy; and while I was writing to you by the way of Constantinople received an account from Mr. Balfour of your destination being changed to the assistantship to my old friend Jack Collins—the situation of all others which accords most with my wishes, and I hope this letter will find you happily situated with the man who of all others in India is most interested in the welfare of my son. You are now in the high road to diplomatic fame, and as the country languages are to be acquired in greater perfection where you are stationed than in Calcutta, and your attention will be called officially to the general politics of India, my expectations are sanguine you will soon be considered well qualified for the situation Government has placed you in, and which must of course lead to something better in time. . . . . .

"Tell Collins I saw his boys lately; they are going on extremely well, and as I intend giving the eldest my best nomination when he is of the proper age, you will have to take as much care of him as I am convinced his father will take of you.

"THOMAS T. METCALFE."

FROM THE SAME TO THE SAME.

"*August* 30, 1802.

"MY DEAR CHARLES,—In a few days after I sent off my last letter, Colonel Monson, to our great surprise, made his appearance, and gave us the most satisfactory account of your progress to Agra, with several particulars respecting health, &c., that made your mother and me completely happy, feeling as we naturally do more interested in the welfare of you and your brother, who are removed to so great a distance, than for the children immediately under our eye. Our whole mind is constantly employed in thinking of your prospects in life; and as nothing can be more flattering than the commencement of your public line, I am sanguine in my expectations that you will continue to reflect honour upon your father. Indeed, my dear boy, I feel the most heartfelt pleasure at the accounts I receive from all quarters about you, and only regret that you have not been a little more communicative about yourself, but look forward in expectation that when you are settled in your diplomatic employment you will make amends by frequent accounts of yourself and my friend the Resident. The Marquis (Wellesley) has desired to have a successor appointed, and in his letter of the 1st of April, mentions an intention of embarking for England in December, 1802, or January, 1803. I am of opinion that we shall not appoint a new Governor-General till he arrives, and think Lord Castlereagh is likely to be the man—in which case, I think I shall be enabled to make a favourable impression both for Collins and you, as I am upon good terms with Lord C.

"Tell Collins his charming boys are returned to school. With love to him, and every blessing a father can bestow,

"I remain, my dear fellow,

"Your most affectionate parent,

"THOMAS T. METCALFE."

FROM THE SAME TO THE SAME.

[*Without date.*]

"MY DEAR CHARLES,—The accounts I have received from various quarters of your character and general conduct is so flattering, that I assure your mother with confidence you will turn out a distinguished man when an opportunity offers of bringing your talents forward; and your parents want nothing to complete their happiness but information from yourself, that you are satisfied with your present situation. The share of good sense you are evidently master of, will, I trust, reconcile you to the line of life you are placed in, and convince you of the impossibility of a compliance with your former request. I think you did right in selling your books, as your library was by far too large to travel about with; and when you get a settled situation, I will supply you with as many as you may write for.

"Tell my friend Collins I saw his boys yesterday. They are all we can wish.

"The Marquis's conduct to you has made a deep impression on my mind. I shall feel more devoted to him than to any other man who was ever in high station. His last letter, dated in April, intimates an intention of leaving India in December or January, and desires the Directors to appoint a successor. But when he receives a *request* from the Court, as well as from Mr. Addington to remain another year, I think there is no doubt of his continuing. The change in the office of President of the Board of Commissioners is an advantage to the Public and Company. Lord Castlereagh is the most promising young man in England. He comes nearer to Mr. Pitt than any other person in public life. I stand well with him and the Minister—an object of no other consequence than as it may furnish the opportunity of promoting the interests of my two sons. Give my unfeigned love to Collins. Let us hear from you frequently, to give happiness to

"THOMAS T. METCALFE."

But long before these last letters had reached Charles Metcalfe, he had turned his back upon Scindiah's Court, and bidden adieu to his father's "old friend Jack Collins." A trial of a few weeks satisfied him that he could not serve under the Resident; so he made up his mind to resign his appointment. What the immediate cause of the rupture may have been I know not. In all probability it resulted from general incompatibility and an aggregation of minute circumstances not easily to be described. Something, however, may be gathered from the following characteristic passage of a letter to his friend Sherer, dated "Camp near Abzunpoor, June 20, 1802."

"I have suffered one precious year of my life to pass away without any adequate improvement. In the year 1801 I really acquired nothing, unless a smattering of an Oriental jargon be termed an acquisition. I suffered a very large library to be useless whence I might have extracted that which would have been of much more service to me than running about to tiffins and noisy parties, where instruction, and even amusement could never be procured."*

---

* In this letter the young writer alludes to his want of personal comeliness, saying,—"Let mankind say what they will, a pretty face is an excellent introduction, and before now I have had to regret the bad effects of an ugly phiz—particularly with the ladies. Never for a moment hesitate, under the idea of my being foolishly offended, to tell me what you think. Believe me, I am the last man who would at all take ill even your censure."

"I am always happy to be of your opinion, which in the present case carries conviction along with it, and I have much satisfaction in telling you that I have acted according to it, for although I regret the want of public employment, which is to me the most agreeable of all employment, yet I have endeavoured to gain what knowledge I could, and improve my ideas. My short stay at Scindiah's Court has prevented my knowledge being very complete, but in a short time one may observe something. There is great justice in your reproach, which, whether meant or not, I have applied to myself, respecting my injunctions of caution to you. I could, I know very well, have trusted to your judgment, which, for the future, I shall do. As to Collins, I scarcely know what to say. . . . I say that from my soul what I believe to be true, yet I am aware that it is possible that I may see things with a jaundiced eye, for his conduct towards me has been such that I have not words to express my contempt of it. . . . . Any general description of Collins will convey no idea of it; it is only from hearing particular anecdotes that you would be able to judge of his extraordinary character. To say the best of him, he is a man whom one ought immediately to quit."

That Jack Collins and Charles Metcalfe had their differences, and could not agree to differ amicably and philosophically, is clear. The story is a very old one; within every man's experience; intelligible; without mystery. Colonel Collins was cold, imperious, and overbearing. He was known by the name of "King Collins;" and he had little toleration for those who did not recognise his sovereignty. He looked upon Charles Metcalfe as a vassal and as a boy. He stood upon his position, and he stood upon his age. He exacted a deference which the youth was slow to concede; he claimed a superiority which was not willingly acknowledged. The boy thought the man arrogant and domineering. The man thought the boy forward and presumptuous. It is probable that both were right. It is almost a condition of early talent to be vain and self-sufficient. It does not much matter. The vanity and self-sufficiency are soon rubbed off. But in the meanwhile it is hardly to be expected that age and experience should benignantly regard the manifestation of these qualities only as a sign of what is called in the above letter a "consciousness of power." Still, a little more toleration in such cases is to be desired; and it would have been well if the elder man had smiled at the self-sufficiency of his young friend, and borne with it for the sake of his finer qualities. Charles Metcalfe was, doubtless, fond of arguing, and King Collins did not like being argued with by a boy of seventeen.* This in a few plain words seems to have been the cause of their rupture. They parted with at least outward civility; and became sufficiently good friends—at a distance.†

* It was, doubtless, after some similar collision with an elder, that, a few months afterwards, Charles Metcalfe wrote in his common-place book,—"ARGUE. We are often reproached for what we are taught to do. To differ in opinion from men of greater age and experience is looked upon, in a young man, as a great presumption. Yet are boys at school and college taught and compelled to criticise the best and most celebrated authors that the world has known, and to argue on all subjects even in favour of an untenable proposition."—[*February* 18*th*, 1803.]

† Several letters from Col. Collins, written shortly after Charles Metcalfe's departure, are preserved by the latter. They are written probably with as much warmth as the man was capable of feeling. They sometimes acknowledge the receipt of a "friendly letter" from Metcalfe, and generally express a hope—often an assurance, that the young man will succeed in the line of his profession. In one letter he says: "I had little doubt but that Mr. Barlow would recommend your fixing in Calcutta, and on more mature reflection, I believe that his judgment is perfectly correct. Since he seems so well disposed towards you, I am certain you will not fail to cultivate his esteem and regard—not merely because his friendship may be useful in forwarding your interest, but principally on account of the high character he bears, as well for integrity as ability. Do you know, I by no means despair of drinking a bumper with your father, at some distant period, however, to the health of Charles Metcalfe, member of the Supreme Government

in Bengal. Jesting apart, you have talents to justify the most sanguine hopes of your friends; and as you have come to the resolution of continuing in the service, I have no doubt of your application. Indeed, the former would be of no use without the latter. . . . . Pray let me hear from you sometimes. Be assured that I shall ever feel warmly interested in your success in life, and, consequently, must be desirous of knowing how you get on. Remember, also, I am your banker, as well as your sincere friend.—J. COLLINS."—[*September 24th*, 1802.]

CHAPTER IV.

[1802—1804.]

TRAINING AT THE PRESIDENCY.

Return to Calcutta—Appointment to the Chief Secretary's Office—His Studies—Extracts from his Common-place Book—Visit of Theophilus Metcalfe—Appointment to the Governor-General's Office—Early Official Papers—Rupture with Scindiah—Appointment to the Staff of the Commander-in-Chief.

On the 10th of September, 1802, Charles Metcalfe, having dropped down the river in a boat lent to him by Captain Collins, arrived, a second time, at Calcutta; and on the 4th of October he was appointed an assistant in the office of the Chief Secretary to Government.

It seems to have been his desire, at this time, to obtain employment at the Presidency, under the eye of the Governor-General, and to fit himself in the Secretary's office for advancement in the diplomatic line, to which he had determined to adhere. Lord Wellesley had looked favourably upon the young writer, and was obviously well inclined to serve him. Mr. Barlow, who was then second in influence and importance only to the Governor-General, recommended him to remain at the Presidency. He had friends, too, whom he dearly loved at Calcutta; so that all his inclinations were gratified by the arrangement that had been made. His trip to the camp of the Mahratta had not been without its uses. He had returned with enlarged experiences to the viceregal city. He had traversed a large extent of country. He had acquired a more extended knowledge of the people of India than he could have gained in many years of Calcutta life, And though he had rendered no great service to the state, as assistant to the Resident at Scindiah's Court, he brought back some local information which subsequently was turned to profitable account, and he had begun to interest himself in the tangled politics of northern and western India.

Little by little he had learnt to reconcile himself to Indian life, and, still not without some fond regrets, he now looked his profession steadfastly in the face, and applied himself sedulously to the duties of his office. Much of his leisure time he devoted to his books. And he was no careless reader. He sat with a note-book before him, and as he pored over the pages of Gibbon, of Russell, or of the Abbé Raynal, he jotted down such landmarks of history as would be most useful for after reference, and kept his memory fresh as he proceeded. His old habit of philosophising, at which some of his friends laughed irreverently, was as strong as ever, and his common-place book was often opened. To many of the entries a peculiar value belongs, for they are snatches of self-portraiture or incidental reflections of the character of the youthful statesman. They contain, indeed, his inner history, and are a little autobiography in themselves.

EXTRACTS FROM THE COMMON-PLACE BOOK OF CHARLES METCALFE.

[*Ætate* 17—18.]

"Human Intellect.—It has often occurred to my mind, as a doubt which I have never been able to solve, how far active talents and a sedentary disposition are compatible. By active talents I do not mean that activity of the body which delights in the sports of the field and corporeal exercise, but that activity of the mind, that superior ability, which is formed for the rule of empires, is at all times ready for action, perceives instantly, and decides without hesitation. Were I to decide hypothetically, I should say that active talents were never accompanied by close application. There is a degree of drudgery, quiet, and, I had almost said, inertness required in close application to a particular study which I think incompatible with a mind such as I have in view. Instead of sedentary disposition, I ought to have said confined attention, to a science or a pursuit, for it is certain that there is no activity so great as that of the mind engaged in the pursuit of knowledge. But I am of opinion that active talents cannot be bent to a particular branch of study, and that they will universally fly off from particular to universal knowledge. Many men of quick but quiescent parts have rendered themselves famous in some one art or science, whilst others of more active talents, having made universal knowledge the object of their pursuits, have not been driven beyond the circle of their acquaintance, for human intellect is confined within such narrow bonds that it can never possess more than a very moderate knowledge of general subjects. And it is one of the innumerable proofs of the vast extent of Divine Wisdom that the human mind should take such various turns, and proceed by such different ways, to the acquisition of knowledge, improvement of science, refinement of the world, and to the accomplishment of the views of the Omnipotent Deity. For I take it to be an indisputable fact, that there are no two minds, and never were two minds, which are not essentially different."—[*Calcutta, October* 29*th*, 1802.]

"CHRISTIANITY.—I cannot help thinking that too strict an inquiry into the truth of the Christian religion ought to be discouraged in very young persons. It is an inquiry which requires vast fortitude of mind, and which we ought to commence with perfect faith. Youth is very easily led astray by plausible arguments, and the system of natural religion is too pleasing not to engage a young imagination. It is thus that M——, who has brought these reflections to my mind, at first set off as an enthusiastic admirer of Christianity, and carried his attention to its principles and duties to a great excess, but has now (most probably from the sophistical argument of some persuasive genius) entirely given up his faith in our blessed religion, and devotes himself to natural religion and universal philanthropy. A mind, however, so easily and suddenly converted may, without much difficulty, be brought back to a just belief of the doctrines of our Heavenly Saviour."—[*November* 19*th*, 1802.]

"FRIEND.—It is less difficult to conciliate an enemy than to preserve a friend. There are no enmities so strong that the parties are not desirous of a reconciliation. I have seen no friendship which has not been interrupted by many petty jealousies, which always produce temporary contentions, too frequently lasting separations, and which are the more acute as the attachment is more ardent. I must eradicate from my mind that propensity to form romantic attachments which my youth and inexperience have encouraged. Never again will I nourish the seeds of a rising friendship; never will I love the man who has not obtained by long intercourse my respect and esteem; and so aid me ye powers of prudence and good sense in my resolves! I am too well convinced that there are very few hearts capable of the friendship which I feel, and would wish others to feel; and, young as I am, I am taught by painful experience that the sacred name of friendship is too often violated; that equal and mutual attachments are seldom, and I doubt if ever, to be found; and that an ardent attachment unreturned shackles the independence of the mind, and cannot fail to be attended with vexation and unhappiness. I am determined to resign the man whose apparent indifference has cost me so many sighs, and hope that in a short period I may be able to turn back to this page and smile at the reluctance with which I evidently part from him, and which is still more painful than it is evident."—[*December* 18*th*, 1802.]

"SELF-LOVE is a most consoling companion. Let every man search his own heart. I have a very good opinion of myself, and, as far as I remember, always had the same. Self-love is the guide of all men's actions. One man feels a pleasure in feeding his own desires, another in feeding his neighbour's; but the principle is the same. Self-love is always at the bottom. The one is bent on present happiness, the other on future. I can tell which is the wiser, but I cannot which is the better man. We appear all to be instruments in the hands of an Almighty, All-seeing Being, and is one more blameable than another? Can we go in the right way without the assistance of Providence? And shall he, who for want of that assistance goes wrong, be punished? Do we suffer for the sins of others? For what were we created? When, and how, shall we be destroyed? The inquiry is endless. Guide me, O Lord, in the right way."

"TO MYSELF.—Mind—little Mind—thou art envious—not so as to give me much trouble, but sufficient to convince me that thou art in want of reform; so set about it instantly, and learn to feel as much happiness at the good fortune of others as thou wouldst for thine own."—[*February* 19*th*, 1803.]

— "Nothing is more irksome than in submission to the rules of society, or to the natural inclination which the mind has not to offend, to feign a liking to one whose qualifications do not render him an object of our esteem, or to appear gratified with the society of him who could not be too far from us. Such a man is R——."—[*April* 22*nd*, 1803.]

"MIND AND COUNTENANCE.—The features of the countenance are formed after those of the mind." *—[*April* 25*th*, 1803.]

But whilst Charles Metcalfe was thus from time to time recording in his common-place book the history of his inner world of thought and feeling, in the outer world of incident and action there were circumstances developing themselves which tended in no small measure to shape the after-career of the man. These were partly of a domestic, and partly of an official character. In the month of January, his elder brother, Theophilus, came round from China to Calcutta, and on the 4th of April, Charles Metcalfe was appointed an assistant in the office of the Governor-General.

His brother's visit was quite unexpected. The dawk of the 8th of January brought him a letter from Theophilus, not dated from the Factory at Canton, but from the "Ship *Betsy*, below Ingerlee," on the Hooghly river. "You certainly will be astonished, my dearest Charles," wrote the elder brother, "to receive a letter from me dated from this place; but the cause is, ill-health having compelled me to take a trip to sea, I took the opportunity of spending a few months with you, my dear fellow, and, thank God, have arrived safe, and perfectly recovered." The announcement filled Charles Metcalfe with delight. "My God," he exclaimed to his friend Sherer, on the evening before Theophilus' arrival, "he is the finest fellow in the

* Opposite to this he had subsequently written, under date *August* 9*th*, 1803—"Why, then, are mine so ugly?"

world!"* Not many hours afterwards the two brothers were shaking hands, after three years' separation—yet little more than boys in age, but in experience and position men. They were still as unlike as ever; but years and absence had taught each brother to appreciate the qualities of the other, and they met as the most affectionate of friends.

It is not to be doubted that this fraternal visit was very beneficial to Charles Metcalfe. His brother was a fine, manly youth—by no means inclined to meet the troubles of life half-way, but in the cheerfulness of his disposition and the strength of his endurance, sufficiently case-hardened against them. He had gone out to China much against his will, but had soon reconciled himself to his position, and had earnestly persuaded his more desponding brother to do the same.† But when he found that Charles con-

* *Sherer to Metcalfe, January* 17, 1806.

† On the 5th of November, 1801, dating from Canton, Theophilus Metcalfe wrote:—"The receiving a letter from you afforded me much pleasure, but I am sorry to find that India has not turned out so pleasant as you expected. But, my dear brother, it does not seem to be the profession you dislike, or the mode of making the money (which is my dislike to the country), but a regret at leaving England. Consider, Charles, it is not in the nature of things for us to be always with our family. Therefore, as you like your profession, and say 20,000*l.* would not suffice for you, what place can you sooner realise that sum in than India? You will perhaps say, that I am much altered. It is not so. My remaining here is only from the same motive which induced me to come out—that of satisfying a parent. . . . . . No more of this; I have two requests to make: that you will not go home unless you are ill; but if you find the climate will not agree with you, return home immediately, and I promise you that, when it is in my power, your situation in England shall be made pleasant. If you cannot stay in this country, go home and make my dear friend Anne my sister. I have another request to make, that you will place confidence in me, let me know your debts, your movements, everything—

'Take courage, man, and me your sorrows tell,
And safely think nane kens 'em but yoursel.'"

tinued firm in his eagerness to return to England, with a generosity and self-devotion which did him the highest honour, he seconded his brother's solicitations, and promised his father, that if he would permit Charles to settle at home, he himself would engage not to swerve from the line of his profession, but make a fortune for himself in China.* Such conduct had greatly endeared him to his brother, and had raised him in the estimation of his parents. But the elder Metcalfe had made up his mind on the subject; and whilst Theophilus was crossing the Bay of Bengal, he was writing to Charles that the generous conduct of his eldest son had not induced him to swerve from his old resolutions. "The last letter from your brother," he wrote, "was of the most pleasing nature. He feels perfectly satisfied with his situation, and with a degree of affectionate liberality, which does him great honour, desires me to let you come to England, and allow him to shift for himself. You, my dear boy, know my sentiments on this head. I should feel wanting in the duty as a father to the true interests of his son, were I to indulge my own desires to have my family with me by complying with the request of either of my sons to abandon the line of service I have had the good fortune to place them in; and my confidence in your good sense is such that I flatter myself you will, ere this arrives, be convinced my determination is founded in your prosperity—the only object I could possibly have in view."

Before this letter was received, Charles Metcalfe and his

* He, however, discouraged the idea of "Lord Grenville's office," and suggested to Charles to turn banker. . . . . "Believe me," he said, "you will not find yourself happy in Lord Grenville's office; the situation I would recommend, if you are determined to leave India, and which in my letter to my father I shall point out to him, as I believe, if he could succeed in placing you in it, he would consent, is the banking line."

brother had many a time talked over the subject-matter of it together; and it is not to be doubted that the former profited largely by the sensible advice, and perhaps still more by the cheerful demeanour of the young Chinaman, and the affectionate intercourse which was maintained between them. Theophilus Metcalfe was determined to enjoy himself. He had scented a party at Government House even from the Sand-Heads, and had written up to his brother that he should "require a *friseur*" immediately upon his arrival. He now stimulated the social activity of his more studious and quiescent brother, and even brought him somewhat reluctantly into a cricket-match, which the Etonians of Calcutta had adventured against the whole Presidency.* These things did the young statesman no harm. And, apart from all these secondary influences, there was an abiding consolation in the presence of his brother, which seemed to bring home nearer to him, and greatly diminished the sense of isolation which had before pressed so heavily on his heart.

Even when Theophilus Metcalfe turned his back on Calcutta, and set out to visit his aunt Richardson, at Cawnpore, whither he vainly endeavoured to persuade Charles to accompany him, there still remained with the latter a feeling that he was not alone. Seldom did a day pass on which the young civilian did not receive a letter from his brother reporting the progress he had made upon

* In a little manuscript volume, which he kept at this time, and which he called an "Account of Reading," Charles Metcalfe wrote under date of January, 1803.—"Continued Arabic. My studies and reading much interrupted this month by the arrival of my brother from China, which rendered me, on his account, more inclined to pleasures of every sort."—The month's reading only included "Browne's Travels in Africa," "Lucani Pharsalia," "Carmen in Pisonem," and "Volney's Travels in Egypt and Syria."

his travels. All this had an unfailing tendency to encourage and to strengthen him at a time when other influences were at work in the same favourable direction—when his official position was such as increasingly to flatter his boyish vanity and stimulate his boyish ambition. He was, I have said, appointed in April, 1803, an assistant in the office of the Governor-General. Lord Wellesley had, some time before, conceived the idea of planting in Government House an office under his own immediate superintendence. He was not guilty of the folly of attempting to mystify the secretaries to Government—of embarrassing his own movements by keeping them in ignorance of his designs. The Government secretaries, indeed, were a part of the machinery of his own office. But he believed that in matters of great political importance, involving the necessity of secresy, the subordinate agency of supreme direction could best be carried on by educated gentlemen, the covenanted servants of the Company, immediately responsible to himself. In prosecution of this design, it was his wont to select from among the young civilians at the Presidency those who had given the fairest promise of intelligence and zeal, and to make them his confidential assistants. And it is an eminent proof of the sagacity of this great statesman that he seldom made a selection that was not more than justified by the after-career of the man on whom he had fixed his regards. Nor was it the least pleasing of his retrospects forty years afterwards to recall the persons of the young men whom during the first years of the century, he had assembled in Government House—the persons of John Adam, of Bayley, of Jenkins, and of Metcalfe, and to think of the distinction that in the interval had been attained by his pupils.

In that grand viceregal school the clever boys of the civil service ripened rapidly into statesmen. They saw there how empires were governed. The imposing spectacle fired their young ambition, and each in turn grew eager and resolute to make for himself a place in history. Of all men living, perhaps Lord Wellesley was the one around whose character and conduct the largest amount of youthful admiration was likely to gather. There was a vastness in all his conceptions which irresistibly appealed to the imaginations of his disciples. Their faith in him was unbounded. The promptitude and decision with which he acted dispelled all doubt and disarmed all scepticism. Embodied in the person of Lord Wellesley, statesmanship was in the eyes of his pupils a splendid reality. They saw in him a great man with great things to accomplish. As he walked up and down the spacious central hall of the newly-erected Government House, now dictating the terms of a letter to be despatched to one political functionary, now to another, keeping many pens employed at once, but never confusing the argument or language proper to each, there was a moral grandeur about him seen through which the scant proportions of the little viceroy grew into something almost sublime. There could not be a finer forcing-house for young ambition. Charles Metcalfe grew apace in it.

He soon began to feel that he was acquiring something that would cling to him all his life—that the training to which he was subjected was well calculated to fit him to tread the path that leads direct to fame. What had once appeared to him petty and objectless, was now expanding into bulk and significance. The day-dreams of the Eton cloisters might be realized after all on the scenes where he once believed hard fate had condemned him to waste his existence. The future seemed very different to him now that Government House had become his college, and he had for a moonshee the Governor-General himself. The example of his father, too, was at this time conspicuously before him. Major Metcalfe, who had gone out to India with none of those advantages which had environed his son, had been sent to Parliament by the people, and created a baronet by the King.* The glad tidings of this latter event reached Charles Metcalfe early in May; and some days afterwards he wrote in his common-place book these memorable words:

"MY FATHER.—Early in the month I learnt that his Majesty had conferred the dignity of baronet upon my father. I rejoiced at it, because I was certain that this honour was not sought for by any of those mean arts which generally soil modern titles. I rejoiced at it because I was certain that it was not purchased by the loss of independence. My good father is a strong instance of what may be done by ability and integrity. He is an example which I shall ever have before my eyes, and if I steadily pursue his footsteps I have little doubt that I shall raise the second branch of the family to the same honours."—[*May* 16*th*, 1803.]

From this time Charles Metcalfe looked steadily forward. There were no more vain retrospects; no more idle regrets. The *vestigia retrorsum* were not to be taken. He had formed the resolution of not leaving the country until the governor-generalship of India was in his hands. And that such would be the end of his career was not a mere passing thought—an impulsive hope—but an abiding and sustaining conviction.†

* Writing of the dignity that had been conferred upon him to his son, the elder Metcalfe said:—"The dignity of Baronet which his Majesty has lately conferred upon me, was done in the most handsome way, and our reception at St. James's, when your mother was presented on coming to the title, was flattering in the highest degree. At my time of life the adding *Sir* to my name is of little importance, but to your mother, your sisters, and the whole family, I think the object desirable."

† He did not scruple to say in early youth, that he would be Governor-General of India. And this not lightly and jestingly; but with all sincerity of meaning and gravity of manner. Among others to whom he mentioned this conviction, was that excellent man, the late Dr. Marshman, who often spoke of the prophecy in after years, when Charles Metcalfe had reached the gaol towards which he had long been steadily advancing.

All through the year 1803 and the earlier part of 1804, Charles Metcalfe continued to graduate in Indian politics, under the directorship of Lord Wellesley. It was a season of unusual excitement. At no period, perhaps, of our connection with the East, has the aspect of affairs beyond the frontier presented such a knot of difficulties for the disentanglement of British statesmanship. I shall come presently to speak more in detail of our own relations with the Mahratta States. At present it is enough to say, that the complication of affairs, threatening, as it did, to involve the British power in the greatest war in which it had ever been engaged in India, threw a large amount of work into the Governor-General's office, and taxed all the energies of his assistants. Lake and Wellesley were in the field, waiting the opportunity to strike. It was certain that no statesmanship, that no diplomacy, could avert the inevitable collision. Whatever may have been the wishes of the Governor-General, I am afraid that it cannot be said that the boys in his office were very desirous to arrest the war. They were deeply interested in the progress of events, and their sympathies were not with the peace-makers. So it happened that, when intelligence reached Calcutta that the anticipated rupture had actually taken place, and that Colonel Collins had quitted Scindiah's court, Metcalfe and his associates were thrown into a state of excitement in which there was no great intermixture of pain. It was, indeed, a memorable day. There are men still living who, after the lapse of half a century, remember all the circumstances of that evening as vividly as though they had occurred in the present reign. For some days, the "glorious little man," as his disciples affectionately called Lord Wellesley, had been pacing one of the halls of Government House, girding himself up for the approaching crisis; and now he was prepared to meet it. Aided by Edmonstone, the Political Secretary, whose knowledge was as ready as it was extensive, he now dictated instructions to Colonel Collins, now to General Lake, now to Arthur Wellesley, now to John Malcolm, and now to Close and Kirkpatrick, the Residents at the courts of the Peishwah and the Nizam. All day long these weighty despatches grew beneath the hands of the young scribes. The brief twilight of the Indian evening passed and left the work only half done. But still, by the bright lamp-light, the young writers resolutely plied their pens, as hour after hour the Governor-General continued to dictate the despatches, upon which the fate of principalities depended. Words of encouragement, little needed, came freely from him, as he directed this great work. And still, as Adam, Bayley, Jenkins, Metcalfe, Cole, Monckton, and others, wrote and wrote these weighty despatches, upon which the events of the great war were to turn, he told them ever and anon that their work would soon be done, and that there was a table spread for them in the banquet-room, at which they might presently drink success to the campaign. Though it was now the exhausting month of August, and rest and food were denied to them throughout many long hours, there was not one of them who flagged at his desk. Sustained by their youthful enthusiasm, they continued at their work till past midnight; then weary, hungry, and athirst, they were conducted to the table which had been spread sumptuously for their entertainment. It was a festival not soon to be forgotten. A special message from Lord Wellesley instructed them to give full vent to their hilarity—to use his cellar as though it were their own, and not to think that they were bound to be quiet because they were in Government House. So they drank success to the campaign in good earnest; toasted the glorious Wellesley and his glorious brother; toasted General Lake and Colonel Stevenson; toasted the British soldier and Jack Sepoy; and finally toasted one another. And the Governor-General did not complain that next day his office was not very efficient.

Incidents of this nature were surely calculated to bind such warm-hearted, earnest youths as Charles Metcalfe by the strongest feelings of personal attachment and fidelity to Lord Wellesley. They not only worked for him, they worked with him. And the endearment thus engendered was reciprocal. No statesman ever took a livelier interest in the intellectual development of the disciples who sat at his feet. He watched their progress with affectionate concern: he encouraged and stimulated them by judicious praise. He was at once their master and their friend; and there was not one of them who did not identify himself with his policy, and was not eager to contribute to its success.

And that even these clever boys could contribute something to the successful issue of Lord Wellesley's magnificent designs, abundant proof was frequently given. Eager for an opportunity of rendering some service to the State, in a higher capacity than that of a mere scribe, Charles Metcalfe was not long in finding one. His visit to Colonel Collins, I have said, was not barren of profitable results. He had traversed a great part of the Mahratta country, and he had been no inattentive observer of its local peculiarities. The information which he had acquired on the spot was most useful in the conjuncture which had now arisen; and the young statesman knew well how to turn it to profitable account. When, at the close of 1803, by a succession of victories unparalleled in the annals of Indian conquest, Lake and Wellesley had broken the power of the Mahrattas and brought Scindiah to their feet, a second treaty was dictated to the prostrate chief, by which he undertook to receive a subsidiary force into his dominions. The disposition of this force, dependent necessarily on local circumstances, was likely to become an important subject of consideration; and as Charles Metcalfe had something to say upon it, he resolved to draw up a memorandum, to be submitted to Lord Wellesley, recommending Kotah as the fittest place for the location of the subsidiary force, if it were to be planted in one central cantonment, or for a part of it, if it were to be broken up into several detachments. This may not have been his first state-paper, but it is the earliest that I have been able to find.*

This memorandum greatly pleased Lord Wellesley; he saw its importance, and was glad to acknowledge it. Taking up a pencil, as was his wont, he wrote on the margin of the document: "*This paper is highly creditable to Mr. Metcalfe's character and talents. It may become very useful. A copy of it should be sent to the Commander-in-Chief, and another to Major Malcolm.*—W." This was Charles Metcalfe's first great success. It fixed him in his resolution to persevere, and dwarfed the proportions of Lord Grenville's office. The boy of nineteen was drawing a salary of a thousand a year,† and writing state-papers for the information of the highest military and diplomatic authorities in the country.

But, although he was now turning his attention towards the strenuous realities of life, studying the Government records, and dwelling rather upon the circumstantial than upon the abstract, he still found time to moralize in his common-place book, and to read a large number of printed volumes, English, French, Latin, and Italian. Nor were the Oriental languages wholly neglected.‡ He applied

* The original, in Charles Metcalfe's handwriting, was preserved by the late Mr. Edmonstone, to whose representative, Mr. Neil Edmonstone, I am indebted for a mass of valuable historical materials.

† Eight hundred rupees a month—from the 3rd January, 1804. —[*Letter of Mr. Edmonstone to Mr. Metcalfe, March* 17, 1804.]

‡ In February, after enumerating the books he had read, he wrote:—"These, with a slight occasional attention to French

himself to the study of Persian and Arabic, and seems to have mastered them sufficiently for all practical official purposes. From the entries in his common-place book at this time, I make the following selections: they are contained in the last private journal that he ever kept:

EXTRACTS FROM THE COMMON-PLACE BOOK OF CHARLES METCALFE.

"SELF-SUFFICIENCY.—I often, in moments of reflection, take myself to task for my self-sufficiency in fancying a superiority of knowledge and sense over the generality of mankind, and examine upon what claim this fancied superiority is founded. I have read and observed more, and have devoted more of my time to reflection, than, I may almost say, any man of my own age. Does not this give a claim to superiority? One would think so; and yet I am much staggered when I see men acquiring fame and consequence whom I do not conceive entitled to either. I know no right that I possess to fancy any superiority, and yet my mind will fancy it. It is, however, an opinion which, I believe, can only inspire good

---

and Arabic, form the sum total of my February reading."—In March he wrote:—"In the latter part of this month I paid some attention to Persian."—In April, "Continued studies in Persian, and a general perusal of records. The improvement of this month, if not so various, is equally solid with that of the last, or perhaps, more so." In May, he "read a great variety of interesting records." Studied Persian, and reported that his improvement had been "progressive and satisfactory."—In June, he "continued studies in Persian, and had a great deal of office business. On the whole, improvement inadequate." In July, he recorded "A considerable degree of office duty—improvement very decent, but might have been better."—August, "Commenced with a very hard press of public business."—[In this month he read a vast number of plays, chiefly comedies and farces—many of them Fielding's.] And in September there was "an increase of official business." With the cold weather came a diminution of his literary industry, and the entries in his "Account of Reading" were few.

and honourable actions. I believe that every man has some vanity, derived from a fancied superiority in person, manners, accomplishments, talents, or mind; and I do not know that mine is the most unworthy. That vanity only is disgusting which is proclaimed; and here I hope that I shall never be so weak as to fall. One circumstance which may render this advisable is, that I am constantly reminded of this fancied superiority by the avowed opinions of others, and we are so willing to believe what others say in our favour, that I would without scruple resign my case to a just judge, and ask with confidence—'Have I sinned beyond the hope of grace?'—[*July*, 1803.]

"GOOD FELLOW.—A character I have taken much pains to gain, which is that of a good fellow, is a very contemptible one in the enjoyment of it. The term itself is not at all appropriate to the character, and the character is the most insignificant possible. It is bestowed without distinction upon the sensible, the generous, and the really good, as well as upon fools and ignorant and unprincipled men. What are the qualifications which are requisite to obtain this name it would not be easy to define, since it is so indiscriminately bestowed. Generally speaking, they seem to consist in a resignation of one's words and actions to the whims and follies of the society in which we move; in a total departure from the dictates of good sense and right reason, and too frequently from those of religion and morality. The greatest merit which some men possess, the highest ambition which some men cherish, is to be a good fellow—a character too prostituted to be valuable. If I am never entitled to greater praise, or excited by a nobler ambition, may my ambition be eternally smothered, and the tongue of praise be hushed for ever."—[*August 5th*, 1803.]

"BEAUTY.—Men may talk as they will about the little necessity for beauty in a man; but beauty is a real advantage. A handsome, interesting countenance is a man's best recommendation at first acquaintance; and although I by no means mean to say that internal worth will not be admired, when known, even under an ugly external, yet we are much more ready to receive to our arms the man whose pleasing countenance we are willing to believe to be the index of his mind. Are there not countenances which at first sight seize, as it were, upon our hearts, and establish an interest in the welfare of their possessors? The influence does not end with the first introduction; if tolerably good qualities are visible in a handsome man, his beauty will never fail to heighten and adorn them, and as it is his best friend in obtaining the countenance of society, it will be his steady supporter in securing its admiration. Instances without number occur to me of the truth of these observations, and in no place can they be more strongly marked than in the society of Calcutta. An ill-looking man, whatever may be his good qualities, is never so much the object of our praise as a handsome one. Beauty, however, has its disadvantages. It secures so good a reception everywhere, that a man possessed of it is persuaded that he has nothing left to acquire. The ugly man, finding his face against him, is obliged to lay his claim to being agreeable on the solid foundations of good sense, knowledge, and virtue. But if this emulation is not excited, the consequences are dreadful. A pretty fool may pass through the world pretty well, but an ugly fool is a most unfortunate wretch. Who would not discover that the writer of this is an ugly fellow?

"With the female sex the beauty of a man is everything. . . . . I believe there are very few indeed who consider worth as essential in a lover, and as few would regard it in the choice of a husband did not selfishness lead them to do so.

"A man may mar the effects of his beauty by affectation, but particularly by effeminacy; for the men will despise him, and the nearer he approaches to the female sex the women will too."—[*Calcutta, August 9th*, 1803.]

"FORTUNE.—Men who rise in the world are much more indebted to their good fortune than to their merit or ability; and he is the most clever who is best able to profit by good fortune when it comes to him.

"Among the favours of fortune may be considered a good face or figure, which, if a man knows how to take advantage of them, are not the least of her favours."

From this date there is no further entry until the spring of the following year, when he thus recorded the fact of his brother's marriage, and closed his journal-books for ever. "My eldest brother, Theophilus John, was yesterday married to a charming young woman, Miss Hannah Russell.* His age is twenty. He will be twenty-one on

* Niece of Sir Henry Russell, one of the Judges of the Supreme Court of Calcutta.

the 19th of September next. May they enjoy every happiness which good hearts ought to enjoy".—[*March 2nd, 1804.*]

Soon after this, the two brothers parted, with full hearts. Their meeting in Bengal had endeared them greatly to each other, and the affection thus engendered was never subsequently diminished. They differed greatly in character, but both were of a loving nature and a generous disposition; and although in childhood opposite qualities breed conflicts and divisions, in manhood they blend with and adapt themselves to each other, and there is more love where there is more diversity.*

Not long after the departure of his brother, Charles Metcalfe also quitted Calcutta. A life of active excitement was before him. The grand army of General Lake was in the field. The campaign against Holkar had commenced. Metcalfe was well versed in Mahratta politics; he was acquainted with the views of the Governor-General; and he was conversant with the native languages. Lord

* "As schoolfellows," wrote the elder brother two years afterwards to Sherer, "we were continually squabbling, and I believe from the different turn of mind, which you must have observed, our parents thought it would be the case through life. Thank God, those who saw us in Bengal must convince themselves of the contrary, and I may safely say, that there never were two brothers more sincerely attached; and, indeed, had I been totally devoid of brotherly love, his kindness and attention to my dear girl would have gained him my warmest affection." This Sherer communicated, in one of his letters, to Charles Metcalfe, who wrote in reply:—"The passage which you transcribed is, as you rightly judge, peculiarly gratifying to me. The difference in our habits, which was acquired in our childhood, will probably stick to us, and it is possible that we may have different opinions on controversial points, as you may remember we used to have, but in fraternal affection and friendship Theophilus and I will ever have, I am sure, the same mind and spirit." The letter in which this passage occurs is given entire in Chapter VI.

Wellesley believed that in the camp of the Commander-in-Chief the young civilian would render good service to the State. So he placed him at the disposal of General Lake as a political assistant, and despatched him to join the head-quarters of the army.

CHAPTER V.

[1804—1805.]

LIFE IN LAKE'S CAMP.

Conclusion of the war with Scindiah and the Rajah of Berar—Jeswunt Rao Holkar—Recommencement of hostilities—Charles Metcalfe joins the army—The Battle of Deeg—Letters to Sherer and others—Prospects and intentions—Adherence to the Political Line.

UNDER the conduct of Lake and Wellesley, the war with Scindiah and the Rajah of Berar had been brought to a glorious close, and followed by an honourable peace. But the rest which ensued was but of brief duration. There was another chief still willing to try the temper of those formidable battalions which, on the bloody plains of Assaye and Laswarrie, had routed the Mahratta horsemen, and captured the French cannon, and who had fought their way, through the breaches they had made, into the strongest fortresses in Central India. Holkar now appeared on the field. "After the conclusion of the late glorious war with Scindiah and Boonsla," wrote Charles Metcalfe, in an unfinished memorandum, "by a peace which secured great advantages to the British interests, and afforded a fair prospect of future tranquillity and security, Jeswunt Rao Holkar began to operate against us. The power of this chief, who had taken no active part in the contest against us, although undoubtedly a principal member of the hostile confederary, was increased by the events of the war. In its commencement Scindiah, in order to secure his co-operation, ceded to Holkar all the territories which had been conquered from him in their former disputes. Holkar, whilst Sciadia and Boonsla were carrying on hostilities, took advantage of the favourable opportunity to take possession of his ceded countries, and the British Government did not consider him as an enemy. At the conclusion of the war, the chiefs and troops who had served the confederates, having no hopes of pay from either the Rajah of Berar or Dowlut Rao Scindiah, joined the army of Holkar. Jeswunt Rao had nothing to fear from his former opponent, Scindiah, nor from any power in India but the British Government, and that Government did not wish to attack him. Perhaps, therefore, Holkar was never so powerful as at that time.* Just at the conclusion of the war, he had advanced with his cavalry and menaced the territory of the Rajah of Jypore, who had previously entered into a defensive alliance with the British Government. The Commander-in-Chief was obliged to keep the field, to watch the movements of Holkar, and ascertain his intentions. After some vain attempts to negotiate, war became inevitable."† The language of Holkar was insolent and defiant. He threatened to overrun the country, and to destroy his enemies by lakhs. So our British chiefs again prepared themselves for action, and, without a fear of the result, launched boldly into a second campaign.

* "It could not be expected, after the glorious events of the former war, that Holkar would singly engage in a contest with the British power. The thing was considered almost impossible. Holkar was despised, and his power underrated."—C. M.

† The memorandum from which this is taken is unfinished; but I am glad to use Metcalfe's words when I can.

Some partial successes at the outset raised the hopes and increased the presumption of Jeswunt Rao Holkar. Nor was this elation confined to himself. The Mahratta chiefs, who had been so crushed and mutilated during the last war, now began to think that there was a prospect of recovering what they had lost. Their restless ambition would not suffer them to subside into inaction. History, properly written, is but a bundle of biographies. It is in the characters of individual men that we see the sources of great events which affect the destinies of nations. That Dowlut Rao, left to his own unaided councils, would have sought to try the issue of another conflict with the British Government, or would have desired to league himself with Holkar, would seem to be at least uncertain. But he was wrought upon by one who, after the old fashion of Oriental courts, had gained an infamous ascendancy over him by administering to his pleasures—a man of vile character, of degraded personal habits, and of unscrupulous malignity, who hated the English, and was continually inciting his master to compass their overthrow. This man, Sergiy Rao Gautka by name, had energy and ability sufficient to enable him to carry out his designs. Obtaining an influence over Scindiah sufficient to enable him to thwart the more moderate and judicious counsels of the Maharajah's other advisers, he persuaded him that, by entering into an alliance with the Nizam, the Rajah of Berar, and his old enemy Holkar, he could effect the entire overthrow of the British power in Central India. In pursuance of this design, agents were employed at the courts of Hyderabad and Nagpore, and were despatched to all the principal chiefs of Malwa, inviting them to enter into the great combination which was to achieve such mighty results.

But in the meanwhile, eager to repair the disasters

which had beset the commencement of the campaign, Lake had taken the field against Holkar, and was soon again asserting the supremacy of British arms. It was on the 3rd of September, 1804, that the head-quarters of the army left Cawnpore to unite with other detachments at Agra, which had been fixed as the place of general rendezvous. Charles Metcalfe, who had left Calcutta on the 23rd of August, was then on his way to join the camp of the Commander-in-Chief.

He started in good spirits, and under happy auspices. Such a deputation was as honourable to his character and his talents as it was indicative of the discernment of Lord Wellesley, who may have been mistaken sometimes in his measures, but who seldom mistook his men. The young writer was to retain his situation in the office of the Governor-General. But it had already lost much of its attractiveness in his eyes: for some of the best and most cherished of his associates had already been selected for detached employment, and he was beginning to think that the office was being rendered a little too "open." It could not always be stocked with Bayleys, Jenkinses, and Metcalfes; and the very mutations of which the young writer complained were a necessity inherent in the constitution of such a training-school for public servants. Personally attached as he was to Charles Metcalfe, Lord Wellesley parted from him with regret; but the Governor-General rejoiced to see him fairly launched upon a journey towards the theatre of those great events which were changing the destinies of Hindostan, for he knew that the talents of the young diplomatist would there find free scope for action, and that the national interests would profit by their exercise. So Charles Metcalfe started for the camp of the Commander-in-Chief, and the strongest possible recommendations preceded him. How greatly Lord Wellesley appreciated him, at this time, may be gathered from the following letter written by his Military Secretary:

"CAPTAIN ARMSTRONG TO CHARLES METCALFE.

"*Barrackpore, August 24th, 1804.*

"DEAR METCALFE,—Lord Wellesley having heard this morning of your departure by dawk, directed me to write a letter to Lieutenant-Colonel Lake, and to send it by express, lest you should arrive without an introduction.

"I have great satisfaction in informing you that, in following his Excellency's instructions, I never saw so strong and handsome a letter in my life, both as to your public and private character, and his Lordship's personal regards for you. I can only say, I would not wish a better letter for Arthur Cole.

"I have wrote to Colonel Lake from myself, requesting his attention to you as my particular friend; and I have no doubt you will find every attention and kindness.

"I intended to have sent you my letter to deliver, but Arthur Cole wrote me that you wished me to write to Colonel Lake direct.

"I wish you a pleasant campaign, and every success you can wish for.

"Believe me,

"Yours very sincerely,

"J. ARMSTRONG."

Resorting to the most expeditious mode of travelling which the country afforded, Charles Metcalfe left Calcutta, journeying in a palanquin, and proceeded for some distance without any interruption. But before he reached Cawnpore, at some point of the road which I cannot precisely indicate, he was set upon by robbers. He was asleep in his palanquin when he fell among these thieves, and, according to custom, was abandoned by his bearers. One of his assailants had a club in his hand, which young Metcalfe seized; another then struck at him with a tulwar, or sword, cut off the ends of two of his fingers, and wounded him on the head and on the breast. Single-handed, it was impossible to save his property, but his life he might save; so, finding resistance useless, he staggered away from his assailants, and following a path through the jungle, he soon found himself on the bank of a broad river, or stream. There, faint from loss of blood, he sank down; and, as he lay on the ground, thoughts of home came thick upon him. It flashed upon his mind that his parents were not improbably at that very time at Abingdon Races, talking with some friends about their absent son, and little thinking of the danger and the suffering to which he was at that moment exposed. These thoughts made a deep impression on his mind; but he presently roused himself to action, and tottered back as best he could to the spot where his palanquin was lying; but found that the robbers had not yet made off with their spoil. After a little while, however, they went, having despoiled the traveller of all the baggage which he carried with him*—never any great amount on a dawk-journey—and effected their escape. Metcalfe was then carried on to Cawnpore, where, under the care of his aunt, Mrs. Richardson, he soon recovered from his wounds, and proceeded onwards to the camp of the Commander-in-Chief.'†

* There were two small articles, of inestimable value to him—one, a seal given to him by his father; and another, a toothpick case, containing locks of all his family's hair. It is said that he was wounded battling for these treasures.

† This event occurred about the first week of September. I have been able to discover no account of it from the pen of Metcalfe himself. The details which I have given are derived principally from family tradition. His godfather, Jacob Rider—ever affectionate and generous—wrote to him on the 18th from Nerozapore: "Badly as you are wounded, yet after the first report we had of you, I congratulate you on the narrow and great escape you have had, and that you have fortunately fallen so early after the disaster into the friendly care of your good aunt. As you will have everything to furnish yourself with before you can proceed on your mission, draw upon me at sight for four or

Lake was then on the banks of the Jumna. Holkar was hanging on his rear; and, in the full indulgence of the predatory habits of his tribe, was carrying off our baggage, cutting off stragglers, and always avoiding a general action, inflicting upon our troops that desultory annoyance, in their capacity for which they were almost without a rival. In the course of October, Charles Metcalfe arrived at head-quarters, and was met with all outward marks of courtesy and kindness. But the welcome which he received was mere cold formality. The truth is, that he was not wanted. In spite of the excellent credentials which he carried—credentials which bore witness no less to his personal than to his official qualities—he was regarded with some mistrust. His position, indeed, was not a promising one. He was a civilian in the midst of a community of soldiers. He came fresh from the office of the Governor-General, and it is not improbable that men who knew little of the real character either of the one or of the other, were inclined to look upon him as a spy. There always has been a certain jealousy of political officers in a military camp, even when those "politicals" have been soldiers. Their presence is regarded as a tacit reflection on the short-comings of the general

five thousand rupees, if it will be any immediate accommodation to you." Vague reports of this disaster reached England, and greatly disquieted Charles Metcalfe's parents. The intelligence first reached Mrs. Metcalfe, in the middle of the following March, at a ball; and was repeated to her next day at the Royal Institution. Afterwards Mrs. Plowden, her first informant, sent her an extract from a letter from Mrs. Dashwood, saying: "I was sorry to hear Mr. C. Metcalfe was attacked by robbers travelling up the country, and had lost a joint of one of his fingers, and received a cut on the head; but is now (Sept. 21) quite well, and going on his journey. He was obliged to spend some days with his aunt Richardson. He is a very fine, sensible young man." This was all the information that the family received for some weeks—Charles Metcalfe's own letters not having arrived.

and his staff. But, superadded to these impediments to the *entente cordiale*, there were in the present instance to be contended with those class prejudices, which, more or less, exist at all times between the civil and the military professions. It was young Metcalfe's business to assist the Commander-in-Chief in his negotiations with the native chiefs, to carry on the necessary correspondence with the civil officers in our own newly-acquired districts, to collect information relative to the movements of the enemy, and to conduct other miscellaneous business comprised under the general head of "political affairs." Such a functionary at the head-quarters of Lake's army was not unlikely to be called a clerk, and sneered at as a non-combatant. But Charles Metcalfe, though he wore neither the King's nor the Company's uniform, had as much of the true spirit of the soldier in him as any officer in camp.

And this he waited only for an opportunity to prove. I believe it had reached his ears that something had been said about civilians participating in the pleasant excitement of the march and the socialities of head-quarters, but not sharing the active dangers of the campaign. Whether this was said or not, he was determined to show that, civilian as he was, he shrunk from none of those perils to which his military comrades were exposed. And an opportunity was not long wanting to him. The fortress of Deeg, distant some forty-five miles from Agra, was garrisoned by the allied troops of our enemies Holkar and the Rajah of Bhurtpore. In the month of December, General Lake, who had determined upon the reduction of the place, encamped within sight of it, and awaited the arrival of his battering-train from Agra. On the 13th, having been joined by his guns, he took up his position before the fortress, and commenced an attack upon the outworks. On the 17th, the breaching battery was ready for action; but such was the strength of the walls, that it was not until the 23rd, that the breach was reported practicable, and dispositions made for the assault on the following day.

The storming party was told off, and Metcalfe volunteered to accompany it. He was one of the first who entered the breach. There are soldiers now living who remember that memorable Christmas-eve, and delight to speak of the gallantry of the young civilian. The "clerk" fairly won his spurs, and shared with the most distinguished of his comrades the honour no less than the dangers of one of the most brilliant achievements of the war. In the Commander-in-Chief's despatch, the name of Metcalfe was honourably mentioned. "Before I conclude this despatch," wrote Lord Lake, "I cannot help mentioning the spirited conduct of Mr. Metcalfe, a civil servant, who volunteered his services with the storming party, and, as I am informed, was one of the first in the breach."* Afterwards, the fine old soldier called him his "little stormer."

The chivalrous impulses of a youth of nineteen are not to be inquired into with too much nicety, or reasoned about with too much wisdom. Doubtless, it may be said that Charles Metcalfe was not despatched to Lord Lake's camp to help the Commander-in-Chief to carry fortified towns by assault.† This is an objection one scarcely need

* It is worthy of remark, however, that the historian of the Mahratta war, Captain Thorn, is significantly silent regarding both the fact of Metcalfe's presence with the storming party, and the Commander-in-Chief's mention of it in his despatch; although throughout the entire narrative he has scrupulously recorded the names of all the military officers who were officially noticed by their chief.

† And this was said both in India and in England. Very different opinions were expressed on the subject. Writing to her son, in a letter expressive of mingled pride and anxiety, now commending his gallantry, now reproaching him for his temerity,

care to answer. And yet it may be answered with all gravity, and with due regard for the strictest rules of official propriety. It was of no small moment that the young civilian, representing as he did the Governor-General in the camp of the Commander-in-Chief, should be held in high estimation by the men with whom he was thus officially associated. It became him, by all honourable means, to increase his influence at head-quarters. And there were no surer means of doing this, than by showing his comrades that he was willing to share their dangers—even the dangers of the forlorn hope—and to emulate their worth on their own field of professional enterprise. Nothing is so intelligible—nothing is so generally appreciated—as personal gallantry. There is no position in life in which a man does not increase the prestige of his authority by demonstrating his possession of such a quality. There could be no more sneers at the clerk

Mrs. Metcalfe said: "Every one views it in a different light. Some give you a great deal of credit. Others think that you were wrong, not being of the profession; and one military man, in particular, met me the other day, and said: 'I hope you will scold your boy—scold him from me.' It was a man who has been at the head of the army in India." (Probably Sir Alured Clark, who had met Charles Metcalfe in Calcutta.) "There is one thing strikes me," adds Mrs. Metcalfe, with her wonted penetration—"you must have had some good and strong reasons to have gone out of your line. I hope it will not happen again; and that, should you have the military ardour upon you, Lord Lake will not permit you to throw yourself in the way of danger. One would think you imagined that your prospect in life was desperate, instead of its being one of the finest. Your outset has been beyond the most ardent expectations. Your abilities, being of a very uncommon kind, and your conduct regulated by a fine judgment (except in the storming business—forgive me, but a mother can never reconcile that to herself), must ensure you, if please God you live, further success, and that of the most distinguished nature."

and the non-combatant, after young Metcalfe's appearance in his shooting-jacket on the crest of the breach at Deeg.

Whatever may have been thought of this exploit by others, by Charles Metcalfe's young friends and associates in the Governor-General's office it was contemplated with enthusiasm and delight. There was a little group of young civilians at the Presidency, including some of the most promising members of the service, who a short time before Metcalfe's departure had erected themselves into a sort of club or association, which, in honour of Admiral Lord Howe, was called a society of "Howe Boys." These Howe Boys were in the right frame to appreciate gallantry of any kind, and most of all in one of their own associates. So, when the news of Metcalfe's conduct at Deeg, followed speedily by Lord Lake's despatch, reached Calcutta, the Howe Boys held a meeting, the result of which is set forth in the following amusing letter:

"TO CHARLES THEOPHILUS METCALFE, ESQ., HOWE BOY.

"*Howe Boys Office, January, 18, 1805.*

[Official—No. I.]

"SIR,—By the despatches of his Excellency the Commander-in-Chief we have been made acquainted with the glorious success of the British arms in the assault of the outworks of Deeg, and in the subsequent capture of that important fortress.

"2. His Excellency the Commander-in-Chief having been pleased to testify his high approbation of your conduct on this occasion, we consider it to be an act of indispensable justice to record our decided and deliberate judgment that the ardent spirit of zeal, energy, valour, and resolution manifested by you in the unsolicited offer of your personal services, and in the actual assault of the outworks of the fortress of Deeg, have been seldom equalled, and never excelled, by any of the youths in Lord Howe's Establishment.

"3. Your fortitude in refusing to submit to the imperious

dictates of a haughty ambassador,* your invincible resolution and consummate ability in opposing the establishment of a vicious and immoral institution,† and your ardent patriotism and honourable ambition in voluntarily exposing yourself to the dangers, hardships, and privations of an active campaign, had commanded our approbation, and had enabled us to anticipate with a considerable degree of confidence the continued advancement of your character and the unrestrained augmentation of your renown.

"4. We have no hesitation in declaring that your conduct has fully answered the high expectations which we had formed of it, that you have acted in strict conformity to those sentiments and principles of public virtue which ought to regulate the conduct of all the individuals in our society, and that you have deserved well of your country and of the members of Lord Howe's Establishment.

"5. Under these circumstances we have unanimously determined to testify our sense of your conduct by presenting you with a silver pen as a mark of our applause, esteem, and approbation.

"We are your affectionate friends,

(Signed) "J. ADAM.
"A. H. COLE.
"C. D'OYLY.
"CHARLES PATTENSON.
"C. LUSHINGTON.
"JOHN WAUCHOPE.
"WM. HENRY TRANT.
"JOHN FORBES.
"W. BUTTERWORTH BAYLEY."‡

---

* "King Collins." Alluding to Metcalfe's breach with Colonel Collins, narrated in the previous chapter.

† The reference here is to a controversy which a little time before had agitated the Civil Service, relative to the basis upon which the proposed Pension Fund for the relief of the widows and orphans of its members was to be established. Of one section of the service John Adam and Charles Metcalfe were the leaders, and conjointly the mouthpiece; the principal manifestoes were issued in their name.

‡ With the exception of Mr. Adam, who had by this time become Deputy Secretary in the Political Department, the gentle-

From Deeg the Grand Army marched upon Bhurtpore—the most formidable stronghold of Central India. It was a maiden fortress, and had always been deemed impregnable. The Bhurtpore Rajah was a Jaut chief, who had at one time professed friendship for the English, but whom the first successes of Holkar had induced to throw off the mask and to unite himself with the Mahratta chieftain. Deeg was one of his strongholds. The decided part which he had taken had compelled Lake to reduce that fortress, the garrison of which was partly composed of Bhurtpore troops, and partly of Holkar's fugitives; and now the British commander determined to attack the Rajah in his capital. Indeed, since the battles which had been fought at Deeg* and Furruckabad, and in which both the infantry

men signing this letter were all assistants in the Governor-General's office. Mr. Adam rose to the highest offices of the State. After a long and distinguished career in the Secretariat he became a member of the Supreme Council, and was Governor-General during the interregnum between the Hastings and Amherst Governments, and died on his way home. Mr. (the Honourable A. H.) Cole was a Madras civilian, and for many years resident at Mysore. Mr. (afterwards Sir Charles) D'Oyly and Mr. Pattenson served chiefly in the revenue and commercial lines. Mr. Lushington was for twenty years in the Secretariat, and was Chief Secretary in 1825. Mr. Wauchope was a distinguished magisterial and judicial officer; and for some time Governor-General's agent in Bundlekund. Mr. Trant served chiefly in the financial department. On his return to England he was sent to Parliament by the electors of Dover. Mr. Forbes quitted the Civil Service very early, and went home in the same vessel with Lord Wellesley. And Mr. Bayley, after holding the the highest offices under Government, and sitting as Governor-General of India on the departure of Lord Amherst, returned to England to enter the Court of Directors, was twice elected Chairman of that body, and is still one of its most distinguished members.

* On the 13th of November. This battle was fought before Deeg by General Fraser and Colonel Monson. The siege did not take place till some weeks afterwards.

and cavalry of Holkar had been signally defeated, the Bhurtpore Rajah had become our most formidable antagonist. On the first day of the new year, the army moved from Deeg, and, on the following, took up their position before the walls of the formidable Jaut fortress. Lake, who had under-estimated its strength, flung himself upon it with a precipitancy that could only result in failure. Four times the British troops were led to the attack, and four times they were repulsed. The enemy defended their works with remarkable vigour, and neglected no possible means of harassing their assailants and increasing the difficulties of the siege.

Nor were the enemies within the walls the only ones with whom we had then to contend. Holkar was reassembling the scattered remnants of his broken force, and Ameer Khan, a soldier of fortune, originally attached to the service of that chief, was at the head of a large body of marauding troops. This man, a Rohilla by birth, of a bold and enterprising character, and of abilities beyond the level of his countrymen, finding that little was to be gained by the alliance with Holkar and the Rajah of Bhurtpore, and having little sympathy with men of an opposite creed, determined to operate on his own account, and to invite the followers of the Prophet to flock to his standard in the Doab and Rohilkund. He had been in the near neighbourhood of Bhurtpore, looking after our convoys, intent upon plunder; but now that he had formed more ambitious designs, he determined at once to cross the Jumna, to attack the Company's newly-acquired territories, and to excite the people to aid in our expulsion. Occupied as was Lake's army with the exhausting siege of Bhurtpore, and unable to detach any large bodies of troops for service on the other side of the river, the danger of this threatened incursion was not to be lightly regarded. But what the British commander could do, he did—and he did it promptly. He despatched a brigade, consisting principally of light dragoons, under General Smith, in pursuit of Ameer Khan; and out rode the British horsemen, on a February morning, from Lake's camp, determined, in camp-language, to "give a good account" of the Rohilla.

With this force rode Charles Metcalfe, as Smith's political *aide*. It was his duty to conduct all the diplomatic business of the campaign. Of this, the collection and the diffusion of accurate information relative to the movements of the enemy, and of our detachments in different parts of the country, was no insignificant part. He was at once the secretary and Persian translator of General Smith, and the representative of the Governor-General in the districts which Smith's force was sent to defend. He said afterwards, that his position at this time was a pleasant one. It was a pleasant, because it was a responsible one. In his own department, at least, he was supreme; and his young ambition delighted in the thought of being thrown upon his own resources.

All the correspondence of the expedition not strictly relating to matters of military detail passed through his hands. Veteran officers, who had seen good service in the field before the young civilian was born, addressed him respectfully, and sent him reports of their movements. Members of his own profession who had served under Cornwallis, recognised the importance of his position, and, clearly discerning the merits of the man, were eager to maintain a frequent correspondence with him. Nor were the communications of which he was the organ confined to his own people, or to his own language. He wrote Persian letters to the chiefs, and issued proclamations to the inhabitants of the country through which he passed—not in his own name, but what was of more importance—in his own ideas and his own words. There was much in all this to satisfy the ambition—or, as he, in his self-searching candour, would have said—to gratify the vanity of the young diplomatist. He was fast becoming a personage of some political importance—taking, indeed, a place in history—and that, too, before he was of age. India, he began to think, was, after all, the place for eager aspirants of his talents and his temper. There was nothing like this in Lord Grenville's office.

It was believed by the most experienced civil officers in Rohilkund that Ameer Khan was so strongly planted, that General Smith's cavalry would not be able to dislodge him without strong reinforcements of infantry from Lord Lake's camp. The civilians, however, were mistaken. Smith crossed the Jumna, pushed across the Doab with uncommon rapidity, and soon appeared in Rohilkund. It was a harassing, but an exciting service. Men took little account of distance or fatigue, and their horses seemed to be sustained by the spirit and impelled by the enthusiasm of their riders. The fine bracing climate of Upper India, and the noble scenery which opened out before them, as they neared the great mountain-range of the Himalayah, invigorated and refreshed our English officers, as they pursued the Rohilla freebooter across his own fair province, and tried to tempt him to a general action. Many long night-marches across difficult tracts of country deprived the trooper of his accustomed rest; but he went on without a murmur. He was on the track of the enemy, who were plundering and devastating along their whole line of march; and as he passed the smoking remains of villages, and crossed the fields laid waste by Ameer Khan's reckless Pindarrees, he pricked on with renewed impulses of zeal, eager to stop their desolating career. At last the long-wished-for opportunity arrived. Smith found himself near Afzulghur, face to face with Ameer Khan's army. There was a short but sturdy conflict, with the anticipated result. The British cavalry did terrible execution among the Patan levies of the Rohilla chief, whilst our horse-artillery guns played with terrible effect upon his cavalry. Beaten at all points, there was nothing left for him but a precipitate flight. Making a forced march, he re-crossed the Ganges, and as he went, the wreck of his army melted away. He had nothing to look upon, as the result of his temerity, but a disastrous and ignominious failure.

Having effected the expulsion of Ameer Khan from Rohilkund and the Doab, General Smith returned with his detachment to head-quarters, and joined Lord Lake's army before Bhurtpore on the 23rd of March. Two days before this, the Rohilla chief, abandoned by all his troops, save a small body of predatory horsemen, had re-crossed the Jumna, and arrived at Futtehpore Sikree. His power of independent action was entirely gone, and he was willing to take service under some more fortunate and influential leader.

In the meanwhile, Holkar, with the characteristic elasticity of his tribe, had sufficiently recovered from his late reverses to muster a strong body of horse, and to threaten Lake's camp at Bhurtpore. Upon this, the English general, placing himself at the head of his cavalry, and taking with him a detachment of infantry, moved from his position to beat up the Mahratta quarters. But Holkar, prepared for flight, evaded the meditated attack, and retired to some distance from Bhurtpore, where Lake, thinking that the enemy would be less on the alert the further he was removed from our camp, again endeavoured to surprise him. The attempt was not wholly unsuccessful. Holkar, having gained information of our approach, had sent off his baggage, and was prepared to march on the following morning; when Lake, on the night of the 2nd of April, determined not to wait for the dawn, but, guided by the enemy's watch-fires, moved at once on the Mahratta camp.

Aware of the advance of the British troops, and little desiring to meet them in fair fight, Holkar again attempted to escape; but our cavalry were close upon him, and the pursuit was a most effective one. Some brilliant charges made by the pursuers told with terrible effect on the flying Mahrattas, who, utterly broken, and unable to rally, dispersed themselves in disordered masses about the country. After a rapid march of some fifty miles, Lake reappeared on his old ground, and prepared to commence anew operations against Bhurtpore, if the enemy were not inclined to make overtures of peace.

On these occasions Charles Metcalfe accompanied the Commander-in-Chief, and it was of them that he wrote in the following letter to his friend Sherer. The stirring life in camp, and the active business of the public service, had left him little time for private correspondence, and when at last he took up his pen to address some of his old associates at the Presidency, he could only write by snatches in the midst of the incessant interruption of the camp:

CHARLES METCALFE TO J. W. SHERER.

"*Camp near Bhurtpore, April* 6, 1805.

"MY DEAR SHERER,—Welcome back to Bengal; and accept the congratulations of your old friend Metcalfe upon your safe return. . . . You will not, I think, have been surprised to find me absent from Calcutta. You know me to possess a love of change, and a silly desire to deviate from the beaten track. I am much pleased with the determination which sent me again abroad, and have derived much satisfaction from the new scenes which have opened upon me. . . . .

"Within the last few days we have twice surprised Holkar's camp. Yesterday was the last time. [*Written on the 3rd.*] They thought themselves perhaps secure, as they were twelve or fourteen miles distant. We got upon them at daylight, and gave a close and galloping chase for many miles. We were mounted twelve hours, and went above forty miles. These *dours* must have a fine effect, and will sicken our enemy very much. I go on all these expeditions. Without their occasional occurrence, camp would be dull. I do not know how soon I may return to Calcutta. I am anxious to see you again, and talk over our respective adventures.

"The arrival of your letter within the last few minutes gives me great joy [*April 6th*], but with that joy a great deal of shame and contrition is mixed. You expected—and you had a right to expect, and I should have been hurt if you had not expected—that I should have been one of the first to congratulate you on your return, and that 'long ere I read yours you would receive a letter from me, greeting you on the occasion.' The guilty wretch trembles before your judgment-seat; but I cannot suffer you to condemn me without an explanation. The fact then really is that office-work has left no leisure to write. When I say no leisure to write, I mean to write *to you* as I would wish to write with my mind abstracted from all other things, and occupied solely with friendship. A hasty note I might have snatched a moment to pen; but I wished to converse with you at length. This letter was commenced on the 26th of last month, and has, as you will perceive, been several times interrupted. Even this page was commenced four hours back; and although I had determined to-day to set business at defiance, I could not prevent the invasion of visitors. When I consider the long period which must pass before this reaches you, I dread that I may suffer in your opinion in that time, and regret that I did not send all documents to the devil, and finish my letter to you before.

"I expect much from you when we meet; when that may be I am not sufficiently long-sighted to decide. If you recollect any particulars of my brother's house, situation, habits, &c., you will give me great pleasure in communicating them to one to whom the most trivial anecdotes will be interesting. I am rejoiced to find that Theophilus still continues to be satisfied with his situation; but rather surprised that his ambition is satisfied within the limits of the Factory of Canton.

"My situation with General Smith was a very pleasant one; here I am more subordinate. I confess to you that I should not be sorry (many of my objects being fulfilled) to return to Calcutta; and your arrival has added another inducement. From a former part of this letter you will perceive that I anticipated some remarks from you upon the *new Cabinet*. Those which you have made are such as I expected, and I perceive that the same ideas have passed through your mind which have been in mine upo that subject. You will readily imagine that the association of the new party did not diminish the weight of the motives which induced me to quit the cabinet for the field. The situation was deprived of its credit when it became so open. . . . . . My only views are, to return to office when I am satisfied that it will be right in me to quit the army. I am not at all tired of it, but I think that I may be losing some advantages attending upon the Governor-General's office, which at a future period I may not regain. I should grieve if anything occurred which should fix me in this part of the world; I see no prospect of such an event, but should lament it exceedingly. A short time ought to decide what will be done with us. I do not admire a doubtful state of things. It is my intention, I hope that I may fulfil it, that you should frequently hear from

"Your sincere and affectionate friend,

"C. T. METCALFE."

A few days after this letter was written, a treaty of peace was concluded with the Rajah of Bhurtpore, and, on the 21st of April, Lord Lake broke up his camp, and marched down to the Chumbul, where, having crossed the river, he formed a junction with the Bundlekund force under Colonel Martindale, and, with the object mainly of holding Scindiah in check, halted there during the greater part of the month of May. A subsidiary treaty having been concluded with the Rana of Gohud, Lord Lake, warned by the painful obtrusiveness of the hot winds, made preparations for the march of his army to cantonments at Agra, Futtehpore, and Muttra; and re-crossed the Chumbul at the end of the month. On the 30th they were at Dholpore, and from this place Metcalfe wrote again to his friend Sherer:

CHARLES METCALFE TO J. W. SHERER.

"*Camp, Dholpore, May* 30, 1805.

"MY DEAR SHERER.— . . . . . . I have lately had some most delightful letters from my father, which will, I am sure, heighten your opinion of him when I have an opportunity of showing them to you. I shall not fail to *storm* your *quarters*, and make a lodgment within your walls, or, to speak in a more *civil* way, I shall avail myself of your kind invitation, and pay my respects in Post-office-street immediately on my arrival in Calcutta. In short, my friend, I heartily thank you, and hope speedily to be with you. Your advice, which will always be most acceptable, agrees, I rejoice to find, with my own resolves. You will have seen from my letter to Bayley, that on other grounds than those mentioned by you I had determined to go to Calcutta. I am still ignorant when I shall quit the army; I hope soon. I had intended to have loitered on the road, and, as I have always hitherto travelled up and down in haste, to have taken a leisurely view of all the stations on the river. What you say will hasten my voyage, for I would wish to see Lord Wellesley as much as can before he goes.

"As far as my present thoughts go, I can sincerely tell you that I have not the wish to obtain any situation; for, to tell you the truth, India does not contain a situation, which would come within the bounds of my just claims, that would give me any pleasure. I understand the presidency secretaryships are reduced to a despicable degree by our very noble and approved good masters. I will postpone a dish of politics until we meet. I shrink from them as from a serpent, for I have seen things in them which sicken me. I am amazed at the state of your finances, which are almost as bad as mine. Cole is not yet with us. The expectation of his arrival has been the only cause which has prevented an endeavour to get away from the army before this. This is short, but shall be followed soon.

"Your very sincere friend,

"C. T. METCALFE."

It will be gathered from this letter that Charles Metcalfe had determined at this time to leave the army, and to return to Calcutta. It had been made known to him, by his correspondents at the Presidency, that Lord Wellesley was about to return to England, and he was eager, on many accounts, to see the statesman, to whom he owed so much, before his final departure. But soon after the despatch of this letter an incident occurred, which caused him, after much consideration, to forego the intention he had formed. He had gone on to Muttra, with one division of the army, for the purpose of spending a few days with his friend Arthur Cole; and there he met Colonel John Malcolm.

"I recognise in all your letters," wrote Malcolm to Metcalfe, fifteen years afterwards, when both were in high place, "the same unaltered Charles Metcalfe with whom I used to pace the tent at Muttra and build castles; our expenditure on which was subject neither to the laws of estimate nor the rules of audit." Malcolm came with a high reputation—a reputation made in that very line of the service to which Metcalfe had determined to adhere, and the attentions of the experienced diplomatist flattered his vanity and stimulated his ambition. They had a common bond of fellowship in their attachment to Lord Wellesley; and Malcolm, as they talked over their future plans, and discussed the affairs of the empire with eager interest, was charmed with the enthusiasm and frankness of his young friend, and clearly recognised in him, one who some day would do good service to the state. What impression these meetings made on the mind of the young civilian may best be told in Metcalfe's own words, as contained in the following most interesting letters:

CHARLES METCALFE TO J. W. SHERER.

"*Camp, Muttra, June* 10, 1805.

"MY DEAR SHERER,—A thousand thank for yours of the 24th. I shall, in the first instance, waive any discussion of the important contents of that letter, and shall make you acquainted with the inconsistency of my own conduct. You have, doubtless, expected that my departure from the army has taken place before this time, and you will be surprised to learn that it is now most probable that I shall make another campaign, if a campaign is necessary, or assist in any political arrangements which may happen in this part of India. I shall proceed regularly to state the causes which have produced this change in my intentions.

"From my last letter you will have believed me to be decided in my plan of returning to Calcutta, and I never was more decided in my life. Colonel Malcom and Cole joined us on the day when the army separated for their different destinations—to Agra, Futtehpore, and Muttra. I should have, undoubtedly, accompanied the Agra division as the nearest road to Calcutta, but the desire of having Cole's society for a few days brought me on to Muttra. On the day after his arrival in camp, Colonel Malcolm, to my surprise (for I could scarcely call myself acquainted with him), entered, in a full, friendly, and flattering manner, into the question of my intention, which Cole had mentioned to him. With full confidence he laid open to me the various plans which were in contemplation, gave me admission to all his papers, and, by appearing to interest himself in my welfare, prepared me to listen to him with great attention. He expatiated on the great field of political employment now open in Hindostan, the necessity of many appointments and missions, the superiority, as he seems to think, of my claims, and the great risk, if not certain injury, of my quitting the scene of action. By holding out the offer of distinction, he gained the important outwork of Desire, and the citadel of Resolve was in danger of falling. It did not immediately yield, however; and, notwithstanding all he said, I clung fondly to my rooted and long-indulged intention of returning to Calcutta, and of paying my last respects to Lord Wellesley. There was, however, sufficient in what Malcolm said to induce me to reflect seriously on the step I should take.

"I did not converse again with Malcolm for five days, and in that period the subject was ever in my mind, and I never experienced such irresolution on any occasion in which I had the power of self-decision. Exclusive of the reasons suggested by Malcolm for my remaining, others occurred to me which he could not mention. I have long, as you know, looked upon the political as my line of service; and although I have seen what people call native courts, and have passed over many countries, I have had the misfortune of being under men whose talents, knowledge, and character, or rather want of these, I could not admire; who gave no encouragement to my desire to learn, who, on the contrary, rather made me sick of my pursuit of knowledge. I have felt myself degraded by my situation, and, instead of studying acquaintance with the natives, I have shrunk from notice as much as possible. My knowledge, therefore, is only that which I acquired in the Governor-General's office, and which, though highly useful, does not in itself qualify a man to be a political agent. The opportunity of acting under a man with Malcolm's talents and reputation, established knowledge, inquisitive genius, and communicative disposition, promises advantages of the most solid and certain nature, and of real importance. I could not, however, give up my desire to visit Calcutta, and my second conversation with Malcolm ended in our agreeing that I should run down to Calcutta and return quickly. On the same evening, however, he strongly advised me not to go, and the next day we had a long conversation, which ended in my being very uncertain what to do. I think, however, clearly that I shall stay, but I never did anything with more reluctance. I long to see our glorious Wellesley before he quits us. Malcolm tells me that I cannot better show my gratitude to Lord Wellesley than by assisting in scenes in which he will always have great interest.

"Farewell! I shall write to you to-morrow again, for I have much to say. Cole desires to be particularly remembered; I believe that few respect you more than he does. Show this to Bayley, with my love, to account for my conduct. Remember me to Fagan, and Adam, and Trant.

"Your sincere friend,

"C. T. METCALFE."

THE SAME TO THE SAME.

"*Camp Muttra, June* 11*th*, 1805.

"MY DEAR SHERER,—I wrote to you yesterday and said that I would write again to-day—I forgot to tell you that one reason conspiring with the rest to induce me to remain is this—Mercer will go to Calcutta, and Malcolm, who will manage all political concerns at head-quarters, has expressed a wish that I should remain on his account, expecting to derive more assistance from me than I fear he will. This subject fills my mind, and it is with very great difficulty that I can reconcile myself to the overthrow of my plans—plans which I have so long ruminated over with anticipated delight. I rest my chief consolation on Malcolm's character, and the useful knowledge that I shall obtain whilst with him. It is my intention to cultivate his intimacy zealously—his advances to me have been very flattering—I foresee one thing; he is a likely man to give my mind a turn towards literary pursuits, which have scarcely ever entered my imagination—nay, he already has; he himself is an enthusiast.

"I do not know what opinion to give upon Lord Cornwallis's appointment; I cannot help thinking that he will not come out. If the supercession of Lord Wellesley is occasioned by an alarm existing in consequence of Monson's retreat before Holkar, the conduct of the directors and ministers has been equally unjust and contemptible. It is unjust that confidence should be removed from a Governor-General whose whole conduct has been accompanied by the applause and confidence of his country, because a check is experienced for a time in one part of the immense empire under his charge. It is unjust to imagine that he is not equal to meet the approaching difficulty. It is contemptible to have been alarmed seriously at the retreat of a detachment of five battalions before all Holkar's force. I do not foresee any change of measures or system under Cornwallis. I am convinced that any change will be unwise. To recede I think is ruin.

"This is not a new observation. Conciliatory measures are, I think, impossible; they have already been pursued too long. It is with regret that I have perceived the last six months of Lord Wellesley's administration marked by an indecision and weakness (caused, I imagine, by his dread of people at home) unworthy of the rest of his wise and dignified government. He has, however, been kept ignorant of the real state of things, and his *agents* have not done their duty. I do not believe it possible to persuade the Mahrattas *yet* that we have moderation. They know no such thing themselves, and why should they attribute that quality to us, if we hold the language of submission when they hold that of insolence? Shall we, Sherer, sue for peace, when a Mahratta, in violation of all treaty, insults our Government, and in every act and word hurls at us a thundering menace of war? Peace is, I think, impossible, unless we prepare most vigorously for war. We should breathe the spirit of an insulted and mighty power; I should not be surprised if the dread of our determined attack were sufficient to scatter all our enemies. When they are reduced and humble, when we have crushed their insolent pride, then I would display moderation. But I do not see the prospect of permanent tranquillity whilst our controlling influence is spread over every part of India. We had this in our power once, I think twice, but lost it for want of information in one quarter, and want of foresight in another.

"It would require a long discussion to explain my meaning. We may command all India in a few months more. We need never interfere in the internal government of any state, but we ought to regulate the external relations of all. I have made many bold assertions without much troubling you with arguments. You know my way. I shall respect the opinions of the men the opposite to my own; what I have put down are, at present, decidedly *my* real ones. You know me too well to be surprised at the self-satisfied impudence with which I have settled this *trifling* subject.

"I want Hufeezoodeen here very much. I wish that you would send him up. He will require some handsome inducement to quit his situation in the College. I empower you to grant him anything between his college salary (60 rupees) and 100 rupees *per mensem*, and to grant him some allowance for his journey up to me, either in the way of a monthly travelling allowance, or present; I wish him to set off immediately. You know my prospects as well as I do, and can make known to him what will be his.

"There are appointments for natives in *our* line of 100 and 200 rupees *per mensem*. Of course if he follows my fortune it will be incumbent on me to provide for him, and it is not improbable that he may, at some time not far distant, obtain a situation under Government, which will secure to him a handsome provision in the event of my death, &c.* Let him come to Agra, and there wait upon Wemyss or Mr. Munro, where he will have introductions ready for him.

"I am, dear Sherer,

"Your affectionate and sincere friend,

"C. T. Metcalfe."

THE SAME TO THE SAME.

"*Muttra, August* 6, 1805.

"My dear Sherer,—It is long since I received your friendly letter of the 28th of June. I shall be very glad of Hufeezooden, for I think that he is a respectable man. I am not certain that he is a man of business, and I am not anxious that he should be, for I should like to form him for my own habits. I thank you truly for the trouble you have taken about his voyage to me. I shall, I think, increase his allowances when he arrives. Your letters are the only encouragements that I receive to pursue the life which I have laid down for myself. Your sentiments and expres-

* Hufeezoodeen joined Metcalfe, and was for many years attached to him as head moonshee. He followed his master to Delhi and Hyderabad, and made a considerable fortune. Some allusions to him will be found in subsequent chapters of this Memoir.

sions would make me proud of it; Bayley, Hamilton, and Cole think it unhappy.

"I am at a loss to know what is hereafter to become of me; I sometimes long for quiet and a select few of my friends; but if I were in the enjoyment of those things, I think it not improbable that I should long again for bustle and motion. I see that all secretaries are swept from the face of the earth; this, in all probability, will affect my prospects. One part of your letter particularly strikes me, and I am not prepared to give a serious opinion on the subject. You speak of our inability to maintain our supremacy when we have acquired it. It is a prodigious question. I do not know that I could acquiesce in your way of thinking. At present I have no idea that deserves the name of a thought. Inconsiderately speaking, I should say that we are better able to maintain our supremacy over the whole than we should have been, in a few years, to preserve a portion of our dominions. And I look upon the events which have accelerated the establishment of our government over almost all India as necessary and unavoidable consequences of the events which preceded them. I should be happy to see your sentiments on the whole subject. In 1803, there certainly were powers in India which were very formidable; now I think undoubtedly there are none.

"I cannot reflect without indignation upon the conduct which has been adopted to Lord Wellesley. It appears a surprising instance of determined malice or desperate ignorance when a patriot, who has rendered the services that Lord Wellesley has done to his country, is superseded in his government, and is exposed to the most active measures to disgrace him. Disgraced he cannot be, I think, and the darts which his enemies fling at him will return upon their own heads. Now, if a proper spirit exists in the settlement, now is the moment for an address. Lord Wellesley's departure from this country should surely be accompanied with every possible mark of respect, gratitude, and attachment. I see no harm that is likely to arise from Lord Cornwallis's government. On the contrary, I look at it with confidence. His internal government will be excellent I have no doubt. I am anxious about his politics. The tame conduct which when he was here before would have been wise, might now be very otherwise. With regard to his appointment personally I am quite indifferent. No man could have come to India upon whom I have fewer claims, and from whom I expect less.

"I continue to like Malcolm much. As a person who is to be my immediate superior, I do not fancy a better. . . . . . I am more worked, and more incessantly and more variously worked, than I ever was. I literally have no time to myself. My private correspondence is entirely suspended, and my answer to you has been thus long delayed. I find it more than is pleasant, for I have no relief. A day of labour makes society in the evening delightful. There is no such thing here. The Commander-in-Chief's table is full of restraint, and never has society. So, to confess the truth, I am much bored. Some snug dinners with you, Bayley, Fagan, and one or two others, would be delightful. I wish you financiers would find some money for *us* soldiers. How we apples swim!

"Your affectionate friend,

"C. T. METCALFE.

"Kindest remembrances to Bayley, Fagan, Adam, Trant. Tell Plowden I will write to him soon to explain that I am toughly worked."

So the intended visit to Calcutta was abandoned, and Charles Metcalfe, now resolute not to sacrifice his fair prospects of advancement in the political line of the public service, despatched a letter to the Presidency in his place. Doubtless, this was the wiser course. The letter addressed to Lord Wellesley's private secretary, fully expressed the gratitude and admiration of the young civilian, who owed so much to the departing Governor-General:—

CHARLES METCALFE TO MAJOR MERRICK SHAWE.

"*Muttra, June* 20, 1805.

"DEAR SHAWE,—The intelligence of Lord Wellesley's intention to quit India has caused universal regret, and it would be very surprising if I were not afflicted by it.

"I should be very sorry that his lordship should quit this country without receiving the humble assurance of my eternal thankfulness and gratitude; but the various acts of his goodness towards me have long filled my heart with sentiments which it would be vain for me to attempt to express.

"In common with every man who loves his country, and particularly with those who have watched the course of affairs, I must lament Lord Wellesley's resignation of the government at this moment, as a most grievous public misfortune, and however improbable it may be that his lordship would be induced to remain under the confederacy of ignorance, ingratitude, and malice which has been formed against him by the majority of the Court of Directors, yet whilst there is a possibility of such a change in his lordship's resolution, I cannot, and will not relinquish the hope of it.

"In speaking of the directors as I have done, I of course separate my father from those men with whom he happens in station to be associated. His opinions are widely different from theirs, and there is not in the United Kingdom, nor in India, nor in the world, a man who has a greater admiration of Lord Wellesley's talents and virtues, or a higher sense of the vast advantages which our nation has derived from his administration.

"You well know that I must lament Lord Wellesley's departure, from private and personal considerations. I have been so long used to look up to his lordship's approbation as the highest reward which I could receive, that in his departure I shall lose one great incitement to exertion; I trust that I shall always do my duty to my country, and prefer the public interests to any other. If I do not, I must lose sight of everything that I have learned in the Governor-General's office. Yet, if ever I perform any services which may deserve to be approved, I shall regret that Lord Wellesley is not here to approve them, for his approbation would be more precious to me than that of any other Governor-General ever can be. His lordship's favour first distinguished me, brought me out of the beaten track of the service, and placed me in situations from which prospects of future eminence and success opened upon me. If ever these prospects are realised, I shall owe their fulfilment to Lord Wellesley, and I shall carry with me through life the firm conviction of an endless obligation.

"You may remember when I quitted Calcutta that I particularly requested Lord Wellesley's permission to return to his family and office at the end of the campaign; the hope of doing so has ever been uppermost in my mind. When I received the melancholy news that his lordship was preparing to quit India, I was more than ever anxious to proceed to Calcutta, in order that I might have the honour of paying my respects to him before his departure.

"When I was on the point of requesting Lord Lake's permission to quit head-quarters, my intentions were checked by Colonel

Malcolm's expressing a wish that I should remain here, as he has the goodness to suppose that I might be useful.

"He tells me that I cannot better show my gratitude to Lord Wellesley than by assisting in scenes in which he will ever feel an interest. If I could, indeed, flatter myself that I could be useful, or that the motives of my stay should meet with his lordship's approbation, I should less feel the disappointment of not being able to pay my best respects in person. The expression, however, of a wish for me to remain, on the part of an officer in Colonel Malcolm's situation, I consider to be a public call. Under an officer with Colonel Malcolm's great knowledge and abilities, I expect to acquire information and experience which may hereafter enable me to perform useful public services.

"I have no favour to ask from his lordship; the cup of his kindness has been already filled beyond my deserts.

"My last request is, that his lordship will believe me to be bound to him by the most sincere gratitude and attachments. It would be presumptuous in me to pretend to offer my humble services to his lordship, yet I should be favoured if he would consider me as his devoted servant, ever anxious to receive, and eager to obey his commands.

"All India will anxiously watch the future course of his lordship's public life, and I hope that he will continue to guard the fate of India. I hope that his lordship will long enjoy every happiness that he can wish, that he will soon overthrow all his enemies, and see the accomplishment of all his designs.

"I trust that I shall be excused if I have taken any improper liberty in writing this letter. I am, and can never cease to be, actuated by the greatest reverence for Lord W.'s character, and the most respectful attachment to his person.

"Wishing you, dear Shawe, a pleasant voyage, and a happy life,

"I remain yours sincerely,

"T. C. METCALFE."

This letter, which was very gratifying to Lord Wellesley, produced the following reply, under the hand of his private secretary :—

MAJOR MERRICK SHAWE TO CHARLES METCALFE.

"*Calcutta, July* 10, 1805.

"DEAR METCALFE,—In this season of hurry and packing up you will not expect from me so long a letter in reply to yours of the 20th of June as the subject of your letter merits. It will be sufficient to inform you that Lord Wellesley was extremely gratified by its contents. His lordship has received it as a warm and unequivocal testimony of your attachment to him. The sentiments which the present state of affairs has excited in your mind do credit to your judgment and to your feelings, and as Lord Wellesley entertains a most favourable opinion of both, your expressions were highly satisfactory to him. Lord Wellesley is disposed to form the most favourable expectations of your future success from his opinion of your public zeal and talents, and I hope he is too good a judge to be disappointed. I beg leave to add my sincere good wishes, and the expressions of my hopes that his expectations may be fulfilled.

"Lord Wellesley would have been very glad to see you previous to his departure, but he entirely approves your resolution to remain at your present post at this crisis.

"I trust that the state of affairs at Hindostan is rapidly advancing towards an advantageous and permanent settlement, and if your father could bite his brethren in Leadenhall-street, all would be well with respect to the future safety of this country.

"Believe me to be, ever yours sincerely,

"MERRICK SHAWE.

"Pray remember me to Cole, who will always do credit to Lord Howe's Boys."

On the 20th of August, 1805, Lord Wellesley took his final departure from Calcutta, and in the beginning of January, 1806, he set foot again on English soil. Soon after his arrival he expressed a wish to see Sir Theophilus Metcalfe, who called upon him, and received from the lips of the retired Governor-General an account of the talents and disposition of his son, which might have gladdened any father's heart. It was the fortune of Lord Wellesley, as it was the fortune of another great Indian statesman, to be assailed and reviled, under the shelter of parliamentary privilege, by men who could not understand his measures or appreciate his character. Among the foremost of his defenders in the House of Common's was Sir Theophilus Metcalfe, who had done battle for him, too, in the Court of

Directors, and being in the minority at the India House, had thereby sacrificed his chances of succeeding to the Chair. It was an honest and a manly defence, based upon sincere convictions, the result of much knowledge and experience, and it was not persevered in with less heartiness for the reflection that, whilst defending the character of an able statesman, he was serving the friend of his favourite son.

CHAPTER VI.

[1805—1806.]

THE "GREAT GAME" ENDED.

Arrival of Lord Cornwallis—His Policy—Necessities of an Exhausted Treasury—Charles Metcalfe's Views of the New System—Letters to Mr. Sherer—State of our Relations with Scindiah and Holkar—Advance to the Banks of the Hyphasis—Treaty with Holkar—Return of the Army—Metcalfe appointed to the Delhi Residency.

On the 30th of July, 1805, Lord Cornwallis took upon himself a second time the office of Governor-General of India. He went out to extricate the country from political entanglements and financial embarrassments which had disquieted and alarmed the Home Government, and not without solid reason for their anxiety. The British power in the East had been for some time subjected to all the exhausting influences of a state of chronic warfare. No sooner had one campaign been brought to a close than we were continually finding ourselves at the outset of another. And whilst we were putting down our new enemies, our old ones, in spite of the most solemn engagements, were bracing themselves up to renew the contest. It seemed, indeed, without any hyperbole, to be a great national illustration of the old story of Hercules and the Hydra.

The East India Company were at this time essentially a merchant-company. They were restrained by act of Parliament from wars and conquests, and from treaties with native princes likely to entangle us in wars and conquests. They desired, both upon principle and upon policy, to abstain from the extension of their empire; for they believed that there was only weakness in such extension, and that by seeking new fields of political enterprise we should neglect the good government of the old, and utterly sacrifice the trade. It was not strange, therefore, that they should have viewed with the liveliest apprehension the recent great conquests in Upper India; the treaties and the acquisions that had attended them. We were rapidly becoming masters of the whole continent of India, in spite of the principles, and in spite of the policy, of the Company; and the Court of Directors, viewing the progress of these great events from a distance, could only see in this universal dominion the forerunner of universal prostration and decay. The gigantic military enterprises which we had undertaken had not only exhausted the treasury, they were also forestalling the revenues of the country. The Government of British India, indeed, was fast approaching a state of bankruptcy; and in the eyes of a commercial company this was the most alarming contingency of all.

It is not to be doubted that our position in India at this time was beset with difficulties and dangers of no ordinary kind. It is not to be doubted that those difficulties and dangers were only to be removed by the establishment of peace. But they who attributed to Lord Wellesley a disinclination to peace, were ignorant and unjust. His steadiest friends and warmest admirers were shaking their heads and saying amongst themselves that the "glorious little man" was losing heart—that he had become far too prone to compromises and concessions—that he was overlooking insults and offences which ought to be resented, and rewarding as friends or welcoming as associates men who deserved only the chastisement due to the most unscrupulous of our enemies. And, doubtless, they rightly estimated the deserts of the Mahratta chieftains. But wisdom wears one garb on the banks of the Jumna; another on the banks of the Hooghly; and another, it may be added, on the banks of the Thames. Neither the players of the "great game" in Lord Lake's camp, nor the merchant-statesmen in Leadenhall-street, whilst they set up theories of their own, both wise after their kind, took account of those practical impediments to war or peace with which the Governor-General had to contend. They did not reflect that peace at one time might be as difficult as war at another. They did not reflect—to use an expression the emphasis of which atones for its want of elegance—that it might happen that, in making war or in making peace, Lord Wellesley "could not help himself." He was forced into war by circumstances not to be controlled or resisted; and by circumstances equally uncontrollable and irresistible, he was compelled to make every effort, compromises and concessions included, to restore the country to peace.

In 1803 the conduct of Scindiah and the Rajah of Berar rendered war inevitable; in 1804 the excesses of Holkar again compelled us to take the field; but in 1805, though we had still wrongs to redress, and insults to chastise, the exhausted state of the Company's treasury, and the host of evils which these wars had entailed upon the country, rendered it necessary that, even at some loss of national dignity, peace should be speedily restored. And when Lord Cornwallis arrived in India, the paramount object of Lord Wellesley's desires, the chief subject of his thoughts, and the main occasion of his labours, was the speedy re-establishment of peace, and the restoration of the financial prosperity of the empire.

That Cornwallis, armed with specific instructions from home, having no parental interest in the condition of affairs that had arisen in Central India, and regarding the men to whom the conduct of our military and political affairs had been entrusted as mere abstractions, may have set about the work before him in a more resolute and uncompromising manner than if he had himself been concerned in the measures, and associated with the personal agency to which this state of things was in no small degree to be attributed, is hardly to be doubted. But the policy which he intended to pursue differed but little in its essential features from that which Wellesley himself would, at this time, have adopted. The two statesmen were for some days both resident in Calcutta. During that interval, Sir George Barlow, who was the link between them, drew up an elaborate paper on our relations with the States of the North-West, in which past events were recited, and prospective measures were mapped out, for the guidance of Lord Cornwallis. It was intended to embody the views of Lord Wellesley, as modified by the circumstances in which Government were then placed, and it was submitted to him for approval. A single sentence, not affecting the general tenor of the document, was inserted by the retiring Governor-General, who then declared that it fairly represented his opinions. There was, indeed, but little antagonism between the sentiments of the two statesmen. Both recognised a necessity against which it was impossible to contend; but it fell to Cornwallis to commence the execution of those measures which, under other circumstances, neither might have willingly initiated, but which in the conjuncture that had then arisen, seemed equally inevitable to both.

It need hardly be said, that in Lord Lake's camp these measures were grievously unpopular. Every military and political officer on the banks of the Jumna cried out loudly against them. And Charles Metcalfe, earnest among the earnest in his disapprobation of the new system, or no-system which was now to be enforced, could hardly bring himself to believe that the Governor-General was not somewhat of a bigot, wedded indissolubly to his own theories, and utterly regardless of the opinions of all the experienced practical men in the country. Before Lord Cornwallis had been more than a month in India, the young diplomatist entered into a critical examination of the venerable nobleman's conduct. The letters which he wrote at this time forcibly express not only his own views of North-Western politics, but those of the party to which he belonged; I may give at least one specimen of them;—

CHARLES METCALFE TO J. W. SHERER.

"*Camp, Muttra, August* 31*st*, 1805.

"MY DEAR SHERER,—Your silence has lasted very long. I have been particularly anxious to know your sentiments upon the change which the arrival of Lord Cornwallis has produced. It is very probable that I look upon things in a wrong light, but I confess my opinion is, that as far as I am able to see, all the acts of Lord Cornwallis since his arrival have been deficient in wisdom; and I believe that it may prove to be a great misfortune that his Majesty's ministers or the Imperial Directors should have selected for the government of this country a man of experience and knowledge. . . . Had the genius of our country led the choice to a man of judgment, who had not before been in India, he would certainly have applied for information to those persons who might be supposed the most capable of giving it, and, whatever might have been his decision, after he had collected his knowledge, it would, we may suppose, have been the result of unprejudiced deliberation.

"Lord Cornwallis's manner and substance of speech are precisely the same now as they were on the first day of his arrival. There is some immovable notion in his head. Has Lord Cornwallis sought information from any man who was likely to give it? If he has not you will, I think, agree with me that he has been wanting in his duty, and that such self-sufficient importance may be injurious to the public interests. I should suppose that the persons whose opinions upon the political state of India would be useful for the consideration of a governor-general would be Lord Wellesley, Lord Lake, Sir G. Barlow, Lumsden, Edmonstone, Colonel Close, Colonel Malcolm, Mr. Webbe (if he had lived) Colonel Gerard, and Mercer (these two have had opportunities of acquiring great local knowledge, and have in person seen what the nature of our situation in Hindostan is, and what is the extent of difficulty and danger in pursuing one course, and may form a judgment of the probable effects of another). If these are not the persons whose opinions are to be estimated, the political management of India must have been wretchedly conducted for the last seven years. But Lord Cornwallis knows better than all these. Surely Lord C. might suppose that a great change having taken place since he was in the Government before, his knowledge of the present state of affairs might be improved by communications with others. 'No,' he says, 'I know best, and what I say must be right.'

"All our communications are, of course, most confidential, and I will mention one of Lord C.'s remarks, which shows his own character. He says, 'There is a general frenzy for conquest and victory even in those heads which I had believed to be the soundest.' Setting aside that this sweeping observation is false and unfounded, as the records of the Government will prove, let us observe the nature of it. He agrees that the wisdom or necessity of a particular course of policy, which he is pleased deliberately to term a frenzy, is strongly impressed upon those heads which he had believed to be the soundest. Respect for the judgment of those men would have led common characters to examine into the causes of such a prevailing conviction, and would have induced them to suspect that such an universal effect might have some good cause which it would be right to search for. But this man has a head so very sound, that the only thought that arises in his mind is that there is not a sound head in India. He proves either that he is no judge of heads, or that he disagrees with the soundest heads. I believe there is no soul who does not heartily wish for peace, but it would surely be unwise to purchase a temporary peace by concessions.

"I believe that affairs would be immediately settled with Scindiah if the armies were advanced; and I believe that Holkar could not survive long. They have had frequent disputes lately. A settlement with Holkar does not appear practicable until he is quite reduced; unless it is intended to grant him such concessions as shall establish him into a mighty power; and if this is done it will not be long before we repent of it. At one period he was very nearly extinguished. His junction with Scindiah has revived his power in a small degree; but he is very much reduced. It will be melancholy to see the work of our brave armies undone, and left to be done over again. I hope for the best from Lord C.'s administration; but I am, I confess, without confidence. It is surely unwise to fetter the hands of the Commander-in-Chief, and to stop all operations until his own arrival. We shall have Holkar near us in a few days. I wish you would send us money.

"Yours affectionately,

"C. T. METCALFE."

In the last words of this letter there was mighty significance—"I wish you would send us money." Unhappily, there was no money to send. This was the only circumstance that weakened the force of Charles Metcalfe's arguments. But it was a practical answer of such cogency and comprehensiveness, that it rendered all else superfluous. Sherer, who was then in the Finance department of the Administration, must have smiled sorrowfully at the utterance of such a wish in such a crisis.

Three weeks after the despatch of the above letter, the young diplomatist wrote in somewhat better spirits of the prospects before him. "The army," he said, "is ordered to assemble. *We want money only*. Holkar talks of visiting Delhi again. His motions have neither been active nor menacing as yet. There is, I think, no prospect of Scindiah presuming actually to contend with us, if we are disposed to forgive him all his past sins; but I make no doubt that he will regulate his conduct in the way that will be suited best in his opinion to induce us to purchase his good-will by concessions; and I am sorry to say that the political conduct of our Government for the last year is likely to encourage a hope in him that an appearance of an intention to aid Holkar may succeed." And, doubtless, there was much truth in this. The recent bearing of Lord Wellesley towards Scindiah had been conciliatory in the extreme. Eager to avoid an open rupture, he had overlooked some grievous insults and offences, had accepted unsatisfactory explanations of indefensible acts, and by such concessions had plainly indicated to the restless chief that we were eager, almost at any cost, to restrain him from flinging himself into the arms of Holkar. When Lord Cornwallis arrived in India, he wrote to the Home Government, that he had found the Company at war with Holkar, and scarcely at peace with Scindiah. This, indeed, was the true condition of affairs. The latter chief was oscillating between the state of a treacherous, presumptuous ally, and an open, defiant enemy. And, in the meanwhile, Holkar, who had lost none of his old energy or his old elasticity, was recovering from the effects of his late discomfiture. He had, indeed, nothing more to lose. He was reduced to the state of a mere soldier of fortune; and carried, as he said, all his possessions on the saddle of his horse. But that dominion of the saddle was still formidable. It was in the very nature of things that Upper India should be swarming with desperate adventurers—the scattered fragments of all the armies we had beaten in the field—eager to reunite again under some common standard. So it was not long before Holkar, attended by Ameer Khan as his lieutenant, had raised a considerable army, and collected a large number of guns. With these he marched towards the Sutlej. He had opened a correspondence with the Sikh chiefs; and he believed that they would unite themselves with him. It was a combination which promised great results; and already the turbulent Mahratta saw himself at the head of an immense body of predatory horse, streaming from the country of the five rivers, plundering the fairest regions of Northern India, and carrying everything before him in his desolating career.

But these visions were destined soon to yield to the pressure of waking realities of a far more sombre complexion. Holkar had men with arms and horses; and he had an imposing train of artillery;* but he had no money to subsist them. He was even poorer than we were ourselves; and we were in a melancholy state of pecuniary destitution. Wherever he went, his poverty compelled him to make enemies for himself, by demanding money or plundering the country. In the Cis-Sutlej Sikh states he exerted himself especially to obtain the assistance of the Rajah of Putteealah, from whom he demanded two lakhs of rupees; but by this time Lake had set his divisions in motion. General Dowdeswell, with a force of all arms, was ordered forward to Saharunpore, from which advanced position he could defend the Doab, and open communications with the Sikh chiefs. With Dowdeswell's division went Charles Metcalfe, as Political Agent. The service was the same as that which he had rendered in the spring of the year with the division of General Smith, that had gone in pursuit of Ameer Khan into Rohilcund; and the position, which was one of independence and responsibility, was peculiarly pleasing to him.†

There was fine weather, a fine country, an exciting adventure, and plenty of work. Young Metcalfe was in good health and good spirits. It was his business now to conduct, in the General's name, an important correspondence with the Sikh chiefs; to detach them from an alliance with

* It was that, indeed, and nothing more. I believe that it was a mere imposition, for most of the guns were unserviceable.

† Sir Theophilus Metcalfe called this "nursing King's officers;" and in his letters to his son rather made light of the employment. But it was, and has been ever since, the most important duty that can be entrusted to a young man of ability acquainted with the languages, the habits, and the political condition of the people in whose country our armies are moving. These "nurses" have since come to be called "politicals." Half a century ago, when Charles Metcalfe "nursed" Generals Smith and Dowdeswell, the employment was a new one. He was, indeed, almost the first of the race.

Holkar, if they had formed one; and to deter them if they had not. Of these the Rajah of Puteealah was the most important. The letter which Metcalfe addressed to him, with the Rajah's answer, may be given in translation, as an illustration of the work in which the young diplomatist was engaged, and a not unamusing specimen of the diplomatic correspondence of the East:—

TO RAJAH SAHIB SINGH OF PUTEEALAH.

"I have heard of your many good qualities, and have become anxious for your acquaintance. The reports of your enemies state that you have joined the cause of Holkar, and have consequently placed yourself in the situation of an enemy to the British Government. I cannot believe that you would act in a manner so adverse to your true interests.

"The power of the British Government is known to the whole world. It is terrible to its enemies, and a sure protection to its friends. Holkar is a fugitive, and has fled from Hindostan to the country of the Sikhs, from dread of the British troops. Wherever he goes he brings destruction on those who assist him. Whilst he remains in your country, he destroys your crops and plunders the inhabitants. It is not consistent with your famed wisdom to associate yourself with such a man. Convinced that the reports which I have heard are false, I write to you, in a friendly manner, to inform you that I am advancing with a large army of infantry, cavalry, and artillery, and that I shall in three or four days arrive at the banks of the Jumna. If you act openly against the enemy, you may depend upon assistance from the British Government. The Government regards the Sikh chiefs as friends, and has no intention of interfering in their concerns. Its sole object is to defeat the hostile designs of Holkar. Whoever joins the desperate fortunes of that freebooter must expect to draw upon himself the vengeance of the British Government; and whoever acts against him will be rewarded with great kindness. Attack the enemy, and your interests will undoubtedly be promoted. If you have any communications to make, I shall be happy to receive a confidential person from you. Make me happy by the transmission of friendly letters, with accounts of your welfare."

FROM RAJAH SAHIB SINGH TO MAJOR-GENERAL DOWDESWELL.

[*" Despatched at night, immediately on the receipt of your letter.*]

[After compliments]—"I have had the honour of receiving your friendly letter. . . . I have derived great happiness, confidence, and satisfaction from the perusal of it. The case is, that since the bright sun of British rule has enlightened the countries of Hindostan, I have sincerely and faithfully fulfilled the duties of submission and attachment to the Government, and have preserved the relations of friendship and good-will with its officers, with whom I have always held, and now hold, a friendly correspondence.

"In no instance has our friendship been interrupted. God is my witness! From the time when my heart first received the impression of attachments to the Government, the impression has always increased, and is not to be erased.

"When Holkar, suddenly flying with fear from the victorious armies of the British Government, brought his ill-boding train into the country, and sought my assistance and alliance, preserving in its purity my faith and friendship to the British Government, I paid no attention to him whatever. When the plundering oppressor fixed his camp of wretchedness between Puttealah and Syfabad, it was suggested to me that my enemies would perhaps join him and procure success to their designs, and I was persuaded that the necessity of the time made it advisable to keep up an outward intercourse with him. From necessity I submitted to one or two conferences. Still, however, notwithstanding my apparent good-will, the rascal did not refrain from plundering and destroying my country, which he has made a desert. I at one time hoped by his means to punish my enemies; but this, also, was not brought about. The wretch, whose profession and livelihood is plunder, has marched to plunder towards the Sutlej. I have no asylum but in the British Government, to which I shall ever look up. From it I shall always, I know, derive protection and prosperity. I feel great confidence from your near approach. May it be propitious. I have answered your kind letter in haste. I shall immediately despatch a person in my confidence."

The sincerity of all this may be doubted. Had Holkar's prospect of success appeared, in the eyes of the Sikh chiefs, to have sufficient encouragement in it, it is not improbable that they would have united themselves with that desperate freebooter, and taken part in the proposed incursion. But the Mahratta appeared before them as a fugitive and a mendicant. The British troops were pressing forward in pursuit of him. On both banks of the Sutlej the Sikhs regarded our advance with lively apprehensions, and were eager to see the battalions, both of Holkar and the Feringhees, on their way back to Central India. Both armies, before the close of the year, were encamped in the Punjaub. On the 9th of December, the British army was posted on the banks of the Hyphasis, opposite to the Rajpoor Ghaut, and were gladdened by the sight of the noble scenery which opened out bewitchingly before them.* Holkar had marched to Umritsur, and taken up his position there, in the heart of the Sikh country, relying upon assistance that was never afforded to him. The promptitude of Lake's advance had cut off from the fugitive Mahratta all hopes of such coadjutancy. Thus, feeble and alone, he saw that resistance was useless. There was nothing, indeed, left for him but to obtain the friendly offices of the Sikhs to bring about an amicable arrangement with the dominant state which he had so injured and insulted. It was whilst affairs

* See Thorn's "History of the Mahratta War." "In the extreme distance from north to east arose the snowy ridge of old Imaus. . . . . The fleecy softness of its faint and irregular outline appeared to great advantage, in resting upon immense masses of nearer elevations, whose rocky eminences in chaotic confusion were most beautifully contrasted with pine-clad hills, still closer to the view, and these again relieved to the eye by the prospect of a fine undulating country of hill and dale, covered with luxurious vegetation, and enlivened by numerous villages, temples, and ruins, to the extent of thirty miles, bounded by the noble river which, flowing in majestic grandeur immediately before us, brought to our recollection that we were standing as it were on classic ground."

were in this condition, the army still halting upon the banks of the classic river, that Charles Metcalfe wrote to his friend Sherer a letter in which he thus spoke of his position with the army:—

"I sent off yesterday a letter to our friend Bayley, to which, in order to avoid repetition, I refer you for an account of myself and my movements since I last wrote. From it you will perceive that I am exceedingly happy in my present situation, and wish nothing more than to remain in it. I see much novelty and variety, and my spirits are kept alive by the change. I was with General Dowdeswell's division of the army when I received yours of the 22nd October. I have taken my leave of the subject of Lord Cornwallis. Whatever may be my opinion of his designs, let it rest. I do not wish to assail his respected and respectable memory. . . . . Mention to me any new works of note that have appeared lately. I rejoice at Tucker's appointment on public grounds.* I hope that it does not interfere with your private prospects. I go on here as well as I wish. I have not been much troubled with business lately. What I do is under Malcolm, with whom I have always been on very good terms. I have not, however, any particular intimacy with him; and prefer to consider myself as distinct from his establishment. Cole has been ill, and is not yet strong. Few have withstood the late sickly season; I have, and I thank God for, the enjoyment of uninterrupted health and increasing strength."

On the day after this was written (December 19, 1805), an agent from the Lahore Government appeared in our camp charged with the office of mediator between Holkar and the British Government. On the following day arrived an emissary from Holkar himself to negotiate the terms of a treaty of Peace. There was no difficulty now in arranging a settlement of affairs. The Indian Government, under-

* The appointment to the Accountant-Generalship of Henry St. George Tucker, whom, as the ablest financier in India, Sir G. Barlow had induced to leave the house of business with which he had connected himself, in order that, in the great crisis that had arisen, he might assume the direction of our pecuniary affairs.

peremptory instructions from home, and utterly unable in the embarrassed state of their finances to prosecute another great war, were compelled to pacificate upon terms which, under other circumstances, they might have regarded as derogatory to the character of a great nation. Concessions were made to Holkar which the Commander-in-Chief, and all his staff on the banks of the Hyphasis, declared to be disgraceful; but which the Governor-General* at Allahabad and the Accountant-General at Calcutta believed to be necessitated by the pressing exigencies of the times. At the same time, Scindiah, whose agent had been for some while in our camp, reaped his share of the benefits arising from the conciliatory spirit of the British Government. A treaty of peace was concluded with that Prince, by which most of the advantages conceded by the old treaty of Surjee Angenjaum, made by Arthur Wellesley, were secured to him, in addition to a pension of four lakhs of rupees; and he on his part undertook to grant an indemnification for the losses sustained by the British Resident, and engaged thenceforth to exclude the unprincipled Minister, Ghautka, who had been the real mover of all the outrages against the British Government, for ever from his councils. This treaty, the terms of which were subsequently rendered still more favourable to Scindiah, was ratified under a royal salute on Christmas-day. What Charles Metcalfe thought upon the subject will presently be seen.

In the mean while, Holkar's agent had returned to his master to take counsel with him relative to the terms offered by the British, and not until the beginning of the new year did he present himself again in our camp. Then it appeared that Holkar was inclined to presume upon the pacific spirit of his adversaries, and to obtain better terms,

* Sir George Barlow, who, on the death of Lord Cornwallis early in October, had succeeded as provisional Governor-General to the chief seat in the Administration.

if he could. But Lord Lake was not to be frightened or to be cajoled into further concessions. He declared that if the treaty were not signed within three days, he would at once cross the river, and move upon Holkar's camp. This threat had the desired effect. And on the 7th of January a treaty which restored large possessions to the man who, a little time before, had declared that he could carry his all on his saddle, was ratified with all due ceremony in the presence of several of the Sikh chiefs.

On the following day, attended by an escort of two battalions of sepoys, Charles Metcalfe, under instructions from Lord Lake, set out for the Mahratta camp. The visit of friendship was intended to give assurance to Holkar's people, who, weary of a war from which they derived but little, either in the shape of plunder or the shape of pay, could hardly bring themselves to believe that the peace they desired was at hand. He was received in full Durbar, with every mark of satisfaction and respect. There was but one gloomy face—one moody spirit in the conclave. Ameer Khan had reluctantly attended the meeting, and was now little inclined to do honour to the representative of the British Government. The scene in Holkar's Durbar-tent was an interesting one; but I need not describe it, for on his way back with the army, which broke ground immediately afterwards on its return to the provinces, Charles Metcalfe related the circumstances of the interview in a letter to his friend Sherer:*

"*Camp, Sirhind, January* 26, 1806.

"MY DEAR SHERER,— . . . The peace with Holkar and our march from the Punjaub are already known to you. Bayley or Jenkins will have told you that I have been in Holkar's camp. My visit to him was occasioned by his request that some gentleman might be sent to him, as a mark of friendship and confidence from the British Government. It was, indeed, necessary to give

* See also Appendix A, for Metcalfe's official report.

satisfaction to his people, who would not give credit to his proclamation of a peace. They considered it as a trick such as he had often before practised to raise their fallen hopes; and, consequently, the arrival of the mission which confirmed the fact was hailed with every demonstration of unbounded joy and rapture.

"The conduct of Holkar and his chiefs was equally expressive of the highest delight; and made my mission a very pleasing and happy business. My task was easy, being in its nature only to convey assurances of friendship. One subject only of discussion occurred, and that was attended with no difficulty. It was my duty to urge his immediate departure from the Punjaub on his return to Malwa. I got from him a promise to move on the 13th, which he maintained, to my surprise. *Ek-chushm-oo-doula's* † appearance is very grave, his countenance expressive, his manners and conversation easy. He had not at all the appearance of the savage that we knew him to be. The same countenance, however, which was strongly expressive of joy when I saw him, would look very black under the influence of rage, or any dark passions. A little lap-dog was on his musnud—a strange playfellow for Holkar. The jewels on his neck were invaluably rich. With these exceptions, there was nothing extraordinary in his Durbar, which was just as might have been expected under the circumstances of his situation. All his chiefs were present. Ameer Khan is blackguard in his looks, and affected on the occasion of my reception to be particularly fierce, by rubbing his coat over with gunpowder, and assuming in every way the air of a common soldier. But for his proximity to Holkar, he would have passed for one; indeed, I did not know that he was Ameer Khan. I consider his behaviour to have been affectation. He had the impudence to ask from me my name, which must have been known to him; and his conduct was so evidently designed to bring himself into notice, that I felt a gratification in disappointing the unknown impudent; and answering plainly to his question, I turned from him and continued a good-humoured conversation with Holkar and Bhao Bhaskur. I was better pleased that I did so when I learned his name, for he had on a late occasion behaved with egregious impertinence.

"I have been very much gratified with this accidental mission because, though of no importance, it is a little distinction. Lord Lake has made use of it to say more in my favour than I have ever deserved in a despatch to the Governor-General.

* A nickname for Holkar, signifying One-Eyed.

"I hope that I shall be with you in a very few months. What say you to my proposed trip to England, as mentioned to Butterworth? Let me have the benefit of your advice on that subject. I shall be better pleased when you write more; but am now, and ever,

"Your very affectionate friend,

"C. T. METCALFE."

The army was now on its way back to the British Provinces. It was a season of comparative leisure, which Charles Metcalfe turned to advantage by devoting more time to his private correspondence. The following letters have a double interest; for while they treat of public affairs, they afford also some glimpses of the personal character of the young writer :—

FROM CHARLES METCALFE TO J. W. SHERER.

"*Paneeput, February* 12, 1806.

"MY DEAR SHERER,—I had the pleasure, a few days ago, of receiving your kind letter of the 17th ult. I am greatly indebted to you for its contents. It brought the latest intelligence of my brother that I have yet received; my last letters are dated in the early part of November. He continues, I am rejoiced to see, in every way happy and content. . . . I have been a very bad correspondent to my brother, and he complains against me in his last. He knows, however, that my idleness is not caused by want of affection. The passage which you transcribed* is, as you rightly judged, peculiarly gratifying to me. The difference in our habits which was acquired in our childhood, will probably stick to us, and it is possible that we may have different opinions on controversial points, as you may remember we used to have, but in fraternal affection and friendship Theophilus and I will ever have, I am sure, the same mind and spirit.

"We are moving on to Dihlee.† Four battalions, with a body of 1200 horse (Skinners' Corps), will be left here (Paneeput) under Colonel Burn. Another battalion is at Kurnal. We shall reach Dihlee in five days. That rascal, *our friend* Holkar, has been playing tricks; and by way of a specimen of what may be

---

* See *ante*, page , *note*.

† Metcalfe always spelt Delhi in this manner.

expected, has already violated the treaty in a *few* articles. From our pacific, mild, moderate, amiable character, Holkar may play as many tricks as he pleases, and we shall have the generous magnanimity of overlooking them. I am getting tired of Politics, and am not disposed to trouble you much more with them, or Sir George Barlow. We can discuss subjects fully *tête-à-tête*. You will, I dare say, be able to show me his merits in revenual, judicial, and financial administration since he has ascended the throne. I have been so situated as to see him *only* in one point of view, and he has not, in the light in which I have seen him, appeared to advantage. It may be the fault of my optics. But I cannot with temper see his incorrigible wantonness in wasting and throwing away our strength and influence. He has not actually yet done the mischief; and I wish that our guardian genius would convert his hard heart.

"Lord Lake has acted in a dignified and noble manner. He declares his sentiments in opposition to those of the Governor-General, and he urges every argument and fact which he hopes will induce him to alter his plans. Having done this, he is determined not to embarrass or counteract the views of the Government; and feeling that he cannot be a fit instrument for the execution of measures which he entirely disapproves, finding also that Sir G. B. does not know how to exercise his supreme authority without deviating from the respect due to Lord Lake's rank, situation, character, and services, his lordship is resolved to resign all political powers, and to confine his attention to military arrangements. His despatches are marked equally by proper respect and manly firmness. They show that he is attentive to what is due to Sir G. B., and to what is due to himself.

"Of myself I know nothing more than that I am well and happy.

"Your affectionate friend,

"C. T. Metcalfe."

FROM THE SAME TO THE SAME.

"*Camp, Dihlee, March* 14, 1806.

"My dear Sherer,—I received yours of the 16th ult. a few days ago. I am extremely concerned that any expression in my letter should have conveyed the insinuation which you very justly reprobate. Such never existed in my mind; if it had, it would have caused to me very severe unhappiness. Believe me, Sherer, the confidence that I have in your friendship, and in the firmness and continuance of it, as long as I may be not quite unworthy, is a consoling pleasure to me in our separation. I look forward to finding you at our meeting the same kind, unaltered friend that you used to be. Without this reliance I should be very wretched, for I consider the regard of respected friends as an inestimable blessing, and any diminution of it would be an insufferable affliction. Do not, therefore, think that I could ever mean to insinuate that distance of time or place could affect your sentiments. We are anxious about what we prize, and my anxiety to hear from you perhaps made me complain more than I had any right to do. Indeed, when I consider the incessant business which you go through, I ought to be grateful for every line that you bestow on me, but have no right to complain. It would be unconscionable, indeed, to expect that you should not in your leisure hours seek refreshment from harassing fatigues in those pursuits to which your mind is bent. Forgive my impatience.

"You speak of the variety and opportunity of improvement which occur in my situation. I feel the value of them, and look back over the whole time that I have spent in this manner with very great satisfaction. I have, however, I am sorry to confess, thrown away my opportunities of improvement. I have acquired habits of idleness and indifference. I am almost afraid I love wandering for its own sake, rather than for the knowledge which it might enable one to acquire. Works and ruins which would have made me mad with solitude formerly, operate with much diminished effect now. I know not whether it is that the repetition of novelty blunts the edge of curiosity, or that human art cannot produce much variety, but from some cause my curiosity is not so sharp and lively as it was. There is, however, something in this place to which the mind cannot be indifferent. The ruins of grandeur that extend for miles on every side, fill it with serious reflections. The palaces crumbling into dust, every one of which could tell many tales of royal virtue or tyrannical crime, of desperate ambition or depraved indolence, that have caused the accomplishment of the most important events, and yet have never reached the ear of history; the myriads of vast mausoleums, every one of which was intended to convey to futurity the deathless fame of its cold inhabitant, and all of which are passed by unknown and unnoticed, eclipsed by the grandeur of one or two which attract the traveller. These things cannot be looked at with indifference. The view at present before me from my tent contains the history of ages. We are about a mile from what we now call Dihlee. I have before me the magnificent tomb of Humaioon; the ruined fort where Shah Alum was deprived of sight; a ruined palace where another poor king was thrown out of a window (the very window is staring at me), and many other buildings of which my ignorance knows nothing, but which, doubtless, have had their share of blood and murder. I should like much to go over the history of India whilst here, but there is not a book in this army. The Commander-in-Chief does not patronise literature in his troops. 'D—— your writing, mind your fighting,' is his maxim—a maxim, too, the latter part of which he has taught by example as well as precept. If I were a poet . . . I could write something at this place, in an elegiac strain about—

'The pomp of heraldry, the pride of power,' &c., &c.

The ground on which we are encamped was occupied by Holkar's army, when it besieged Dihlee. The defence was one of the greatest and most important actions that has been performed, but the man whose exertions caused the success of it, has met his reward from this encouraging Government in an unrecompensed dismissal from his office.* Speaking of Holkar, he has in true character made a point of breaking all the articles of the treaty that he has not had it in his power to fulfil. He is at present engaged in plundering the Sikhs. Be it said to his credit, that he plunders most those who befriended him. We are detained here until he chooses to march towards his own country. This is a happy state of Peace.

"Cole and the sporting ones of this quarter are on a hog-hunting party. All the riding that I have had has not given me a grain more of enterprize on horseback than I used to have, so I enter no more into those dashing amusements than formerly. What proceeds perhaps from timidity is put down to the score of gravity, and as there is not a soul here whose pursuits are like mine, my want of vivacity is generally pitied."

The war was now at an end. The Grand Army was to be broken up. Charles Metcalfe's occupation as the nurse of Queen's officers was gone; and he soon ceased to disquiet himself about the inglorious peace on which he had so earnestly descanted. In the years 1805-1806,

* Colonel Ochterlony, who had been removed from the office of Resident at Delhi to make room for Mr. Seton.

political controversy rose to a higher pitch of excitement than it had ever risen before, or than it has ever risen since in Indian official circles. Men spoke and wrote in those days eagerly and emphatically, according to the light that was in them; and it is not for us, after the lapse of half a century, to condemn them for that one-sidedness which is apparent in all their arguments. The Lake party were right at Muttra and Delhi. The Barlow party were right at Calcutta. The views of both parties were tinged by local and incidental circumstances. If Barlow had commanded the army, he would, probably, have been as eager for the prosecution of the war as Lake, if he had been at the head of the Administration, and immediately responsible to the Home Government, would have been for its cessation. And I do not doubt that Charles Metcalfe, if he had been Accountant-General, would have written just such letters as flowed from the pen of Henry St. George Tucker.*

* The correspondence between Mr. Tucker and Sir G. Barlow in the years 1805 and 1806, recently published in the Memoirs of the former, very fairly reflects the views of the Peace party. From that correspondence, and from the letters of Metcalfe and Malcolm, a just conception may be derived of the antagonistic arguments of the soldiers and the financiers.

CHAPTER VII.

[1806–1808.]

THE DELHI ASSISTANTSHIP.

Charles Metcalfe's Prospects—His Visit to Calcutta—Appointed Assistant to the Resident at Delhi—Administration of the Delhi Territory—The People and the Court—Character of Mr. Seton—Charles Metcalfe's Duties—Letters to Mr. Sherer —Pecuniary Circumstances—Better Prospects.

It has been stated that Charles Metcalfe, when he joined the camp of the Commander-in-Chief, still retained his situation as an assistant in the office of the Governor-General. But among other retrenchments which were effected by the new administration was the abolition of the "Office." This, although it entailed upon him a considerable loss of salary, Metcalfe scarcely regretted. Without Lord Wellesley and his old associates, who were now scattered over the country, the "office" would have been nothing to him. What his prospects were at this time it was hard to say. The orders of Government were, that he should remain with Lord Lake until his services were no longer required, and that then he should "return to the Presidency, in order that when opportunity should offer he might be employed in some other branch of the public service." *

There was nothing very hopeful in this. He had resolutely determined, as long as it was possible, to adhere to the political line; but in that department of the public

* *Mr. Edmonstone to Mr. Metcalfe, May* 29, 1806.

service great retrenchments were being made, and Metcalfe believed that Sir George Barlow was not likely to extend towards him any very great amount of favour.* He was in no hurry, therefore, to return to the Presidency to wait for a new appointment. Indeed, he seriously contemplated at this time a visit to England, and wrote both to his friends at Calcutta and his family in England, to consult with them on the expediency of the step. He received, however, little encouragement from either quarter. Before, indeed, the answers from his home-letters had arrived, he had made up his mind to continue at his post.

From the following letter, written from Cawnpore at the end of May, may be gathered more distinctly what were his feelings and intentions at this time:

CHARLES METCALFE TO J. W. SHERER.

"*Cawnpore, May* 29, 1806.

"MY DEAR SHERER,— . . . . I shall quit this place for Calcutta about the middle of June, and suppose that I shall reach it about the first week of August. I have settled to join Mal-

* Barlow, however, it must be said, had recognised the great ability and the fine character of young Metcalfe from the very commencement of his career, and predicted for him a rapid rise in the service. "I have great pleasure in acquainting you," he wrote to Colonel Collins, "that young Metcalfe possesses very pleasing manners, and that he appears to unite quick parts with a very solid understanding. If I am not mistaken he will eminently distinguish himself among his cotemporaries." When it was ascertained that the King's Government had refused to appoint Sir George Barlow permanently to the Governer-Generalship, in spite of the earnest support of the Court of Directors, a report obtained in Calcutta that the whole Court had voted for Sir George, with the exception of three members, and that Sir Theophilus Metcalfe was one of the three. But the statement was entirely erroneous—Sir Theophilus was one of Barlow's most strenuous supporters.

colm's party on the voyage down. Without waiting for an invitation, I shall inform you that I intend to make your house my home, but I shall hope to hear from you on that point, as it may be possible you are so situated with regard to room or something else, as to make my invasion an inconvenience to you. As I have nothing now to do here, I wish as soon as posible to be at the Presidency, in order that my destination may be decided, and that I may again be employed.

"I am determined, if the Governor-General will allow me, to adhere to the line in which I have made my outset, even if I should be obliged to submit to a temporary loss or degradation, and the scene on which I wish to be employed is that which I have just quitted. I think that it will be the busiest; I therefore give it a preference. On the whole, prospects are not so flattering as they once were to me, but every dog has his day, and *le bon temps viendra*, I trust. I do not mean to make immoderate haste, nor to put myself to any inconvenience in my journey to Calcutta. I shall proceed leisurely. Under more encouraging circumstances, I think that I should have been there before this time, for I feel every wish to be again engaged on public service. By-the-by, I was long ago ordered down, and am perhaps guilty of disobedience by staying so long.

"My letters from England are very pleasing. My father says that he is proud of my conduct. You know, my dear Sherer, what pride a son must feel at such praise from an honoured father. One sentence of his approbation is an ample reward for any exertion, and more than consolation under every disappointment. God bless you, dear Sherer.

"Your sincere friend,

"C. T. METCALFE."

In fulfilment of the intention here expressed, Charles Metcalfe started on his river-voyage to Calcutta in the course of June, and about the third week of the following month he found himself again at the Presidency. He was now only in his twenty-second year; but he had passed nearly six of these in the public service, and was already a ripe diplomatist. By all who knew him—by his private friends and official associates, he was held in such estimation that not one of them hesitated to predict his speedy attainment of the highest honours of his profession. There was much in all this to solace him under what he believed to be a lull in the prosperity of his career; but nothing cheered him so much as his father's letters, which breathed the warmest affection, and expressed the exultant pride with which Sir Theophilus contemplated the honourable progress of his favourite son.

But there was little occasion for despondency of any kind. Charles Metcalfe had not long to sojourn at the Presidency, waiting for the dawn of official re-employment. On the 15th of August, he received a letter from the Secretary of Government, announcing that the Governor-General in Council had been pleased to appoint him "First Assistant to the Resident at Delhi."

This was not a very brilliant appointment. Time was when he would have regarded it with some contempt—but the political service was not then what it once had been in the palmy days of the "glorious little man" who had set Charles Metcalfe on the high road which leads to fame and fortune. He had come now to look more soberly at these things, and so long as he was not removed to the revenue or judicial departments, he was content with his situation. Indeed, Delhi was of all others the place in which, under these altered circumstances, he had recently desired to be posted.

Mr. Seton was then resident at Delhi. A little time before he had been the Governor-General's agent in Rohilcund; but Sir George Barlow entertained so high an opinion of his zeal and ability, that he removed Colonel Ochterlony from the Delhi Residency to place the civilian there in his stead. To Seton, who was a man of peculiar delicacy and generosity of feeling, the circumstances under which he had been ordered to proceed to Delhi would have been extremely painful, if such an explanation of these circumstances had not been offered to Ochterlony as to convince him that he had not forfeited the high opinion of Government.* But Seton was a man whose whole soul was in the public service, and who, once appointed, was eager to join his appointment, and to devote himself day and night to its duties. Of Metcalfe he knew little, but that little had kindled within him a fervour of admiration for the young *attaché*, and one of his first wishes on being nominated to the Delhi Residency was to associate with himself, in the performance of his new duties, one whom he emphatically described as "a young man of most uncommon abilities and acquirements." "Although my personal knowledge of Mr. Metcalfe," he wrote to Colonel Malcolm, "is but slight, it is sufficient to convince me of the truth of what you say respecting him. We met but *once*. But it was SUCH AN ONCE!' So interesting a meeting! I already knew a great deal of his character

* See letter of Mr. Seton to Colonel Malcolm, Bareilly, March 12, 1806.—"It must give the sincerest gratification to every honest heart to learn that the explanation of the grounds of the present arrangements have been such as to convince Colonel Ochterlony that he stands as high as ever in the estimation of Government. But surely Government will not content itself with merely soothing the wounded feelings of a public officer of his great and acknowledged merits; nor can I bring myself to think that it is not in contemplation to make a handsome provision for him, although it was not, perhaps, announced or recorded at the same time with the arrangements, inasmuch as it was a public measure."—[*MS. Correspondence.*] The supercession of Colonel Ochterlony had not been decreed without manifest reluctance. "The ground of hesitation I have with regard to this arrangement," wrote the Governor-General, "is the service rendered by Colonel Ochterlony in the defence of Delhi. Is this consideration such as should prevent me removing him? and will it justify my making the sacrifice of the public interests, which I know I should make, if I were to relinquish the arrangement? I consider Mr. Seton's appointment to Delhi to be of the most essential importance in a variety of points of view."—[*MS. Notes of Sir G. Barlow.*]

from having seen many of his private letters, and from having been in the habit of familiar intercourse with many of his friends. As a young man of most uncommon abilities and requirements, not to have known him would have 'argued myself unknown.' When, therefore, we met, I could not meet him as a stranger. Ever since, I have been one of his many enthusiastic admirers. In the arrangments to be formed for conducting the public business at Delhi, the claims of such a candidate cannot be overlooked. I recollect, however, hearing one of his friends and correspondents observe, that he would not like to be stationed at Delhi, and that Calcutta was the station he preferred."* Such (every allowance being made for

* *MS. Correspondence.*—The observation in the last sentence must be supposed to have reference to the days when Lord Wellesley was Governor-General. Metcalfe himself subsequently applied for the appointment. Some passages of another letter from Mr. Seton may be introduced here in illustration of this and other points. The communication quoted in the text had been sent to Metcalfe, who wrote to thank Seton for the kindness it expressed. On this the latter wrote :—"Think not, my dear sir, that I mean frivolously to compliment or poorly to flatter, when I assure you that our meeting at Kangur made an impression upon my mind—upon my heart, which no time can weaken. The unspeakable interest, which the circumstance of my being then introduced to your personal acquaintance gave to my visit to camp, makes me consider it as one of the leading epochs of my life ; and ever since that memorable period, I have longed for the means of being brought into nearer connection with you, and of being indulged with an opportunity of cultivating your friendship. In this avowal, which is dictated by the heart, you have, my dear sir, a vertical reply to one part of your letter. I shall only add, that if Government comply with your application, and render you my associate in the political branch of the business attached to the Residency at Delhi, I shall feel as if eased at once of one-half of my care. That it will be complied with I cannot for a moment doubt." The meeting alluded to in these letters was in General Smith's camp, when his force was in pursuit of Ameer Khan, in Rohilcund.

Seton's habitually over-courteous style of language) being the opinion of the young assistant entertained by his official superior, there was little chance of Metcalfe's connection with the Court of the Mogul terminating as did his first diplomatic experience at the Court of the Mahratta. Perhaps no two men were ever more unlike each other than Archibald Seton and Jack Collins. Each, as the young Assistant soon discovered, lacked what the other had in excess.

Starting to join his appointment without much loss of time, Metcalfe proceeded by dawk to Delhi, and reached the imperial city on the 23rd of October. The journey was not a pleasant one; but his reception was of the kindest and most flattering description; and he soon began to find, that if in his new official position he had anything to contend against, it was the excessive delicacy and humility of the Resident, who shrank from employing the services of his Assistant in the manner contemplated by Government in such an appointment. What Charles Metcalfe thought of this, may best be described in his own words:

CHARLES METCALFE TO J. W. SHERER.

"*Dihlee, October 25th*, 1806.

"MY DEAR SHERER,—I arrived here on the 23rd, after a very troublesome and uncomfortable journey. From Mynpooree to this place I encountered several difficulties. I scarcely anywhere found a sufficient number of bearers, and what there were were old and tottering wretches. I met with a remarkable instance of respect in an officer of the Udalut, a Darogah, or, as the people in this part of the world call him, Udalut-walla. I passed the whole night in the street of the town of Koorja, because this gentleman had chosen to seize the bearers that had been stationed for me, and had carried them on his own pleasure to a village some miles distant. For the last thirty or forty miles, by mistake no bearers had been stationed, because by an erroneous calculation I was not expected so soon. I therefore abandoned my palkee, &c., and after a long walk, and when I could walk no longer, a long ride upon a sowar's horse, which I had the good luck to obtain, I at last reached the object of my labours.

"All is well that ends well, and now I am as comfortable as I could wish. Seton is most kind. I foresee that I shall have some difficulty in persuading him to break through a bad habit which he has acquired of doing every part of business, even the minutest, with his own hands. I commenced my attack yesterday, and mentioned to him several duties which he daily performs, and which in my conception ought to devolve upon the Assistant. But he says that he is shocked at the idea of degrading my &c., &c., &c., to such mean occupations, and that the assistance which he expects to derive from me is in the aid of my &c., &c., &c., on the great questions of politics. This is very fine and complimentary, and of course not displeasing, but, as I observed to him, how can that be degrading to an Assistant which is daily performed by the Resident? and what is the use of an assistant, if he does not relieve the superior from some part of the drudgery and detail of official duties? He was at last brought to say that we would relieve each other. Such is his delicacy, or the inveteracy of his habit, that I foresee some difficulty; but I shall persist, and do not despair of accomplishing the object. And if once he can be brought to throw off the unnecessary trouble that he takes upon himself, he will, I am sure, be much happier, for at present he worries himself with detail, and the clearest head in the world must be confused by the mixed and multifarious nature of the minute duties to which he gives his attention. He seldom comes either to breakfast or dinner. He rises before the day, and labours until the middle of the night. He does not move out, he takes no exercise, and apparently no food. The real duties of his situation do not require such toil, and I must persuade him to relinquish a part to me.

"The collections are ridiculously trifling, and the districts in a sad and irremediable state of confusion. Orders have been issued for a settlement. Spedding has not commenced on it. It is a funny duty for me to perform, who am entirely ignorant of such matters; but I must undertake it, and as I am completely under Seton's orders, I am not so terrified as I should otherwise be. I shall probably, but not positively, go into the Mofussil to make the settlement, and it is possible that I may take the field against my refractory subjects, of which there are more than there are tractable? God forbid that this business should end in leading me into the revenue line. I must endeavour to prevent that.

"I am, ever yours affectionately,

"C. T. METCALFE."

Charles Metcalfe was now fairly settled at Delhi—the imperial city of the Great Mogul. The Emperor, Shah Allum, old, blind, and infirm, still held there the mockery of a court. The victories of the British army on the banks of the Jumna had rescued him from the thraldom of the Mahrattas to impose upon him another yoke. In our hands he was as helpless, but less miserable. He was at the mercy of men who respected his fallen fortunes, and desired that he should enjoy as much of the luxury and the pomp of royalty as could be purchased for a certain sum of money, to be appropriated to him out of the revenues of our new possessions. How this was best to be done—which, indeed, was best un-done—was a question which for some time perplexed the Calcutta council. Upon the first establishment of our supremacy in the Delhi territories, it was determined that a maintenance for the royal family should be provided by means of certain assignments of land, and an annual stipend payable to the Shah. These territories were not to be brought under the operation of the rules and regulations of the Company which were to be introduced into other parts of the ceded and conquered provinces; and it was, therefore, arranged that the fiscal administration of the districts which had been set aside for the maintenance of the royal household should be entirely in the hands of officers appointed by the Shah himself, with the sanction of the British Government. The principal officers for the collection of the customs and duties of the city of Delhi and the management of the police, were also to be appointed by the Shah, in concurrence with the British Resident. But this functionary was "not to interfere with the executive duties of any of those officers; nor with the municipal or revenue arrangements of the city or territory, except by his advice and recommendation."* There was, indeed, to be a sort of *imperium in imperio*. A remnant of regal power was to be delegated to the Mogul, that his money might pass into his hands rather in the shape of revenue than in the shape of pension, and that he might still flatter himself with the thought of possessing some officers and some subjects of his own.

In sanctioning this arrangement, the British Government thought more of the feelings of the Shah than of the prosperity of the people of Delhi. The evils of the system were apparent; and Ochterlony soon pointed them out. "I lose no time," he emphatically wrote to Government, on the 30th of November, 1804, "in earnestly requesting, from a knowledge of the disposition and temper of his Majesty and his probable successor, that the provision intended for his Majesty should be a fixed stipend, payable in ready money from his treasury. Any lands assigned for this purpose would, I am fully persuaded, be unproductive of the real value, nor could the controlling power intended to be vested in the Resident prevent much oppression in the Pergunnahs, and exorbitant taxation in the city."† This was one side—the people's side—of the question; but looking only at the King's side, it appeared that the new arrangement, though it might flatter the vanity of the Shah, was calculated to inflict upon him a solid injury, by placing it in his power to waste his substance upon favourites and parasites. "Any assignment of lands," wrote Ochterlony, in the same letter, "though it might, and, I have no doubt, would, flatter his pride, would only open a path to grants which

* Memorandum by Mr. Edmonstone (April 27, 1805)—"On the Subject of an Arrangement for the Maintenance of his Majesty Shah Allum and the Royal Household."—[*MS. Records.*]

† *MS. Records.*

would in a short time deprive him of nearly the whole of his country; nor would any influence of the Resident be able to control his bounty, which has been, during his life, weak, ill-placed, and indiscriminate."* And in a subsequent letter, pointing out more in detail the evil consequences of placing the collection of the town-customs in his hands, especially in time of scarcity, the Resident wrote: "To give the Shah all that is realised, exclusive of the pay of establishments, would be an easy and a sacred duty in the Customs as in the Pergunnahs; but to invest him with a control, is to give him a power to injure himself, to which the avarice and self-interest of numberless dependents would undoubtedly lead."†

Nor were these the only evils inherent in such a system. It was only too probable, as, indeed, experience had already shown, that in the assigned districts the revenue-payers might sometimes contumaciously withhold the sums claimed by the officers of the Shah. In this case coercion would become necessary. The taxes could only be collected under the constraint of a military force. A choice of difficulties then presented itself. Either this constraint must have been exercised by the miserable rabble which the King or his officers would be compelled to retain; or the Company's troops must have been employed for the purpose. In the one case, there was no reliance to be placed on the support of men who might at any time have sided with the recusants or been defeated by them; and in the other, the British Government would have been placed in an anomalous and embarrassing position, for they would have exercised military control where they had no civil power; would have

* *MS. Records.* "His (the King's) probable successor," added Ochterlony, "is imbecility personified, and under the guidance of a woman of low extraction, originally a servant of the household, weak, proud, and in the highest degree avaricious and rapacious."

† *MS. Records*

been compelled to enforce measures for which they were not responsible; and to counteract evils which they were not suffered to prevent.

On a review of these important suggestions, the Supreme Government, after much consideration, moved by the recommendations of the Resident, resolved on a notable compromise. They were desirous to spare the feelings of the Shah; but, at the same time, not to invest him with powers which might be exercised to the injury both of the people and of himself. So they gave him a nominal authority over the assigned districts; but arranged that, at the request of his Majesty, the Company's servants should undertake their administration in his name.* The authority of the Shah was to be a harmless fiction. The actual administration was to be vested in the Resident; but there was to be a great parade of the name of Shah Allum; and the British officers, whilst dandling the miserable puppet, were to appear to be the humblest of his slaves.

But all this was to be merely an experiment. "All circumstances considered," wrote Sir George Barlow, then senior member of the Supreme Council, "and particularly the attention necessary to be paid to the feelings of his Majesty, would appear to render the system of management here proposed the most advisable, at least for the present. But it might be intimated to his Majesty, that if the system should not prove to be well calculated for the

* "The lands might be considered as Khalsa lands, placed by his Majesty under the charge of a British authority, and the collections might be made and all other acts done in his Majesty's name; and as the Resident further suggests, inferior officers might be appointed by his Majesty to attend the Collector's office, for the purpose of satisfying his Majesty's mind that no part of the collections is embezzled by the executive officers of the British Government."—[*Mr. Edmonstone's Memorandum. MS. Records.*]

improvement of the country, for the realisation of the revenue, and the maintenance of tranquillity, such alterations in the system will be hereafter suggested for his Majesty's approbation as shall appear advisable. It will ultimately, I imagine, be found to be necessary for the attainment of the several objects above stated, to extend the British Laws (Regulations) to the assigned territories."* And, under the orders of Lord Wellesley, instructions were sent to the Resident in conformity with Barlow's suggestions, based as they were on Edmonstone's abstract of Ochterlony's recommendations. And this was the system of management in force when Charles Metcalfe joined his appointment.

But that the system did not work well was soon apparent. Even upon the vestige of authority that remained to him the Shah was inclined to presume; and the excess of delicacy and generosity with which a man of Mr. Seton's temper was sure to treat the poor puppet, tended to increase this natural presumption. That this, however kindly the intention, was in effect but cruel kindness, Metcalfe believed; but he did not come hastily to the conclusion that his official superior was at fault. He had been nearly a year at Delhi, during which he had seen many proofs of the evil working of the system, when he wrote the following letter to his friend Sherer:

CHARLES METCALFE TO J. W. SHERER.

"*June* 16, 1807.

"MY DEAR SHERER,—I have had so little of any satisfactory matter to communicate, that it has not been incumbent on me to transmit to you an account of my affairs; nay, more, that I am

* MS. Notes of Sir George Barlow, on the margin of Edmonstone's Memorandum. The paper is endorsed by Lord Wellesley with the words, "Draft of Instructions to the Resident at Delhi, to be sent in conformity to this Memorandum, including Sir George Barlow's remarks, in which I concur.—W."

on the whole doing so badly, that it is almost a duty to be silent. Now, having laid a heavy charge on your back, and prevented, as I conclude, by invincible arguments, any retort on your part, I proceed to tell you that I am, with respect to health, as well as usual, and that, I thank God, is very well; in spirits, too, pretty well; and though the place is very dull, and I myself am no great enlivener of society, never fail to be merry on a favourable opportunity. I am tired of business, and long to have less to do, the nearest to nothing the better; for I see that I could spend my time much more satisfactorily and advantageously to myself in my own way, than by attending to the politics, police, revenue, and justice of this quarter; and now comes the dreadful tale. My finances are quite ruined, exhausted beyond hope of any reasonable repair. You know that I am very prudent; prudence is a prominent feature in my character; yet, ever since I came to this imperial station, I have gradually been losing the ground which I had gained in the world, and at length I find myself considerably lower than the neutral situation of having nothing; and without some unlooked-for and surprising declaration of the Fates in my power, I see nothing but debt, debt, debt, debt after debt, before me.

"The last stroke that has involved me in utter despair, has been the necessity of building. I have been up to my neck for some time in bricks and mortar, mud and dirt, and I am threatened, in consequence, with being over head and ears in debt. After all, I am only building a small bungalow fit for a bachelor. Notwithstanding, all things conjoining, the expense is considerable. Seton would have had me, very kindly, to live with him; but I declined it for a thousand reasons. The one that I used to him, which was a principal one, was, that I could never enjoy a moment's privacy at the Residency; which is as true as that you could not enjoy privacy seated in a chair in the middle of the Cossitollah. Every part of one is no less thronged with natives than the other. . . . .

"I do not exactly conform to the policy of Seton's mode of managing the Royal Family. It is by a submission of manner and conduct, carried on in my opinion far beyond the respect and attention which can be either prescribed by forms, or dictated by a humane consideration for the fallen fortunes of a once illustrious family. It destroys entirely the dignity which ought to be attached to him who represents the British Government, and who, in reality, is to govern at Dihlee; and it raises (I have perceived the effect disclosing itself with gradual rapidity; ideas of imperial power and sway which ought to be put to sleep for ever. As it is evident that we do not mean to restore imperial power to the King, we ought not to pursue a conduct calculated to make him aspire to it. Let us treat him with the respect due to his rank and situation; let us make him comfortable in respect to circumstances, and give him all the means, as far as possible, of being happy; but unless we mean to establish his power, let us not encourage him to dream of it. Let us meet his first attempts to display imperial authority with immediate check; and let him see the mark beyond which our respect and obedience to the shadow of a King will not proceed.

"Seton, however, seems to think (which if it is, as I think, an error, is a kindly one), that we cannot study too much to soothe the feelings of a family so situated; that the most obsequious attentions do not at all hurt the Resident's dignity; and that by yielding to the King the exercise of power in small points, we shall be able to oppose him with a better grace on great and important occasions. To what length the idea of small points may be carried is uncertain. One man will think one thing, and another another. A great deal is left to discretion; and it has often happened, that what Seton has assented to as a mere trifle, has struck me of such importance as to require opposition. Two authorities exist in the town, which circumstance gives rise to much trouble and confusion. A riot lately took place in the town, threatening to be very serious, which arose, I am convinced, entirely from that circumstance, which would never have taken place if the people had not expected that the King would (as he did) protect them; which had, in fact, its origin in the palace, and which, if traced to its primary cause, proceeded, I believe, from the effect of Seton's too delicate and submissive conduct. Ideas of the exercise of sovereignty ought, I think, to be checked in the bud; it may be attended with difficulty to destroy them when they have been suffered to grow for some time; at least, greater difficulty than there is in suppressing them altogether.

"Enough.—This letter begins to smell of the shop. Of mighty importance to be sure are the politics of Delhi! What progress that infernal villain Buonaparte has made; I long to hear more of affairs in Europe. We have had a long interval of darkness since the last accounts. No letters either from home. I have just heard of the sudden death of Colonel Collins. There is always something more shocking in a sudden death than in a forewarned demise. I felt a stronger spirit of resentment against him than I have ever felt towards any other man. He has reached that goal at which all enmities subside; mine are at an end. I sincerely forgive him for the wrong he did to me; and I trust that God will forgive me if I ever wronged him.

"Remember me to all friends, and believe me,

"Ever your sincerely attached,

"C. T. METCALFE."

The "riot" of which Metcalfe speaks in the above letter was this. The Mussulmans of Delhi had risen up in rebellion because a Hindoo banker of influence had carried an idol through the city, and had been suspected of an intention to impart undue pomp to the proceeding. A cry was raised that the interests of Islam were in danger. The banker's house was attacked. There were tumultuous gatherings in the streets. Seton was absent, in attendance on the princes, who were performing certain ceremonies in honour of the late King's memory;* so the responsibility of quelling the disturbance devolved upon Metcalfe. He did it promptly and well—with energy and with judgment. He went first to the officer in command of the troops, and desired him to get his men under arms, and prepare to march into the city. Then he went to the palace, and called upon the King to exert his authority to suppress the tumult. The answer of the King was unsatisfactory; so Metcalfe proceeded at once to the lines, called for the immediate aid of the military authority, and returned with the battalion to the scene of disorder. The presence of the troops damped the energies of the rioters; the crowds dispersed, and there was almost a bloodless victory. Had the King done his duty in the emergency, not a shot need have been fired.†

* Shah Allum had died in December, 1806.

† Metcalfe's conduct in this matter elicited the praises of the Supreme Government. The Chief Secretary wrote:—"You will be pleased to communicate to your First Assistant, Mr. Metcalfe,

Leaving for a while this poor shadow of a "Great Mogul," with his pension of 200,000*l.* a year, let us dwell for a moment on the former part of this letter, and bestow a thought upon the "pecuniary circumstances" of the Assistant to the Resident at Shah Allum's Court. If biography were to take note of things, and to expatiate upon them in proportion to the amount of thought devoted to them by the subject of the "Life" or "Memoir," a very large space in all these lives and memoirs would be devoted to the "pecuniary circumstances" of the man whose character and career are in course of illustration. The greatest among us will think about money and be disquieted by the want of it. To be in debt is with young civilians almost a condition of existence. Some never get out again. Now Charles Metcalfe never had been extravagant; but he had been in debt before this, had extricated himself from it, and now he was "in difficulties" again. The fact is, that, pecuniarily speaking, his fortunes had not lately been on the ascendant. When attached to the Governor-General's Office, in 1804, he had drawn a salary of 800 rupees a month. An additional (deputation) allowance of 12 rupees a day had been subsequently granted to him, when he was serving in Lord Lake's camp; and as the order for this grant was not passed till many months after he had joined the army, and then took retrospective effect, the accumulations enabled Metcalfe to pay off all his old debts. But on the 15th of December, 1805, the Governor-General's Office having been abandoned, the salary which he had drawn as an assistant in it ceased, and in its place he was allowed a salary of 400 rupees a month, with the

the Governor-General in Council's high approbation of the firmness, judgment, and promptitude of action manifested by Mr. Metcalfe on that critical occasion. To the exertion of those qualities the Governor-General in Council primarily ascribes the speedy suppression of the disturbance."

same deputation allowance as before. He was now, in 1807, drawing 750 rupees a month as Assistant to the Delhi Resident—being nearly 500*l.* a year less than he had received three years before.* This might have sufficed him—but the necessity of building a house at Delhi caused an increase of immediate expenditure, which he could not meet; so the curse of debt sat again upon him. He had a liberal and a wealthy father, who at this time was so proud of his son's success in life, and of the repeated eulogies that were passed upon him, that he would have done anything for him, and often said so; but on this very account Charles Metcalfe was slow to ask—he would rather have suffered all the miseries of debt for years than have presumed on the kindly emotions which he had raised in his parent's breast. He determined therefore to extricate himself; and before long the means were placed at his disposal. Some new arrangements for the civil administration of the Delhi territory caused an increase of his official duties, and with it came an increase of his salary, the accumulations of which he left to form themselves into a sinking fund for the reduction of his debts.† And never after this reduction did he feel the burden again.

But there was much in Metcalfe's estimation to detract from the advantages of this increased salary. The new duties imposed upon him were connected with the fiscal administration of the Delhi territory; and he had a great and increasing dislike of revenue business. Even when the Commission, appointed in 1807 to report upon the civil administration of the ceded and conquered provinces, was in course of construction, and Mr. Tucker, the working member of the itinerant Board was anxious to see Charles

* These facts and figures are taken from the original official letters preserved by Lord Metcalfe. It is needless to make separate references to each.

† Letter to Sherer, *post*, page 236.

Metcalfe attached to it as secretary, he was unwilling to accept such a situation lest it should lead him away permanently from the political line to which he was resolute to adhere. On other accounts, the appointment had many attractions—and when he found that his friends Sherer and Bayley were attached to the Commission—the former as secretary, the latter as interpreter, he often longed to be one of the party. In the following letter to the former his opinions and feelings are clearly expressed :—

CHARLES METCALFE TO J. W. SHERER.

"*July* 10, 1807.

"MY DEAR SHERER,—I am rejoiced to see your appointment and Butterworth's to the Commission, as I indulge the hope of seeing you here, though not immediately. It of course has taken place with your entire consent, and both you and Bayley, I imagine, retain your respective situations in Calcutta. It will be a delightful trip for you; you will see a great deal which you must greatly wish to see. You will obtain a most extensive knowledge of a most important branch of our affairs, and your situation being only temporary, it will not interfere with your plan of always keeping your head-quarters in Calcutta, nor with your views of promotion in that most successful field of action. Considering these circumstances, I look upon your appointment as a most pleasant and fortunate event, and congratulate you upon it accordingly. The same to Bayley, to whom I shall shortly address my sentiments on his conduct, although he has behaved so shockingly lately as almost to be unworthy of my notice. My love to him notwithstanding. I already anticipate some delightful days with you two in my bungalow at Delhi. You have a most respectable deputy and agreeable companion in Fortescue, to whom I beg you to remember me kindly. My remembrance also to the Commissioners in proper terms and degrees. By-the-by, Tucker will, doubtless, have mentioned to you what I read in a letter from him to Richardson, that at first, with the assent of Cox, he had proposed to Sir G. Barlow, through Lumsden, my appointment as Secretary to the Commission. Of course at that time he could not have expected that the Secretary's office would be put on so respectable a footing. He could have had no idea that the

Government would spare you, Bayley, and Fortescue, otherwise he would never, it is clear, have thought of me. I will tell you the effect that this had on my mind when Richardson sent me Tucker's letter. I must observe that Tucker wrote just after Lumsden left him to carry the proposition to the Governor, and therefore could give no hint of the result. I was, of course, flattered by the circumstance, and obliged to Tucker, but I wished that he had not made the proposal, and I did not like the thought of getting so deep into the revenue line, and so far from the political. I did not know what I should do if any reference were made to me, as on the one hand to give up my hold on a favourite line, and on the other to reject so respectable a situation likely to be attended with considerable advantages would be either way difficult. My hope was that Government, without any reference to me, would make its own arrangement excluding me, and so relieve me from the responsibility of guiding my own destiny. The sight of your appointment was the first and is the only intelligence which I have yet received, and besides the pleasure of seeing your appointment to a post which I thought would be pleasing to you, I felt on my own account great relief. Although I am much obliged to Tucker for thinking of me, I am glad on many accounts that the present capital arrangement has taken place. If I could take the tour which you are about to make in company with you and Bayley, what happiness I should feel! But alas, alas! I must rest contented with the hope of seeing you here. With respect to the object of your commission, it is my private opinion—but I am not, you know, a mighty wise man in these matters (nor indeed in any other)—that the ceded and conquered provinces are not ready for a permanent settlement. But you come, I suppose, with discretionary powers, and I trust with full and efficient control.

"If the Commission wishes to try its hand at unsettled countries, it will have a glorious opportunity in those which have lately been under my management (perhaps it would be more properly called mismanagement). All my efforts to call the attention of Government, or even the proper and active attention of the Resident, to the subject have been vain. I thank God, Spedding will be here in two or three days, and I shall be relieved from the charge. Then there will remain the confounded Udalut in which, from circumstances peculiar to Delhi, there is work for ten judges without there being one. If these duties continue, it will be a farce to call myself in the political line, whilst I am continually fagging from morning to night in the judicial and revenue. I shall, on Fraser's arrival, astonish Seton, by requesting permission to confine myself to *my own* line; and perhaps shock him by this proof of my insensibility to the prayers of a numerous people petitioning for justice; for Seton, in theory, is an enthusiast for the administration of justice. . . . We have been and are, and I believe, ever shall be, on the best of terms. We have had our different opinions on public matters, and argued them, and finally adhered each to his own, without any interruption of harmony or diminution of confidence, and considering our relative situations the merit of this rests entirely with him. More of him another time. For myself, I never, I assure you, can lose sight of the object to which you guide my thoughts; I mean Adam's office. I despair, indeed, of ever gaining it, but I do not the less desire it. It is the only situation in India that I think of. I would make any exertions to obtain it if I expected success. But I fear, I fear, I fear that I have no chance. I wish that you could make out an *obvious connection* between it and the trifling affair which lately happened here. I sincerely thank you for your kind expressions relative to the business here. It was a trifle, and you have heard all relating to it that is worth mentioning. I have much left unsaid, but will resume at another time; it is now very late. Believe me ever, my dear Sherer, not forgetting the glorious defeat of the Corsican wretch,

"Yours most affectionately,

"C. T. Metcalfe."

In this letter we see with sufficient distinctness that Charles Metcalfe could not easily reconcile himself to the performance of the uncongenial duties of the revenue and judicial departments; but in the following, his dislike of these services breaks out with more manifest impatience; for he had been disquieted by an unexpected call to act as Collector of Saharunpore. There was a scarcity of civilians at that time in the ceded and conquered provinces; and there were geographical reasons, if none other, why Metcalfe should be taken from Delhi to officiate for Mr. Guthrie, during his leave of absence from the station; so he received a missive from one of the Government secretaries, ordering him to act as Collector of Saharunpore "for one month"—an "insignificant duty," of which he could not refrain from expressing his disgust:—

CHARLES METCALFE TO J. W. SHERER.

"*Meerut, August* 27, 1807.

"MY DEAR SHERER,—I have just now received your letter from the Ganges, between Mirzapore and Allahabad. I rejoice to find that you are so much pleased with your trip. It appears to me to be a great relief to the sameness of your official duties, and altogether an event which must be attended with incalculable advantages. I am not surprised that your mind wanders occasionally from regulations, reports, and plans, to seek refreshment in the elysium of interesting literature. I should be very much astonished to hear the contrary of *you*, though it might do very well for M——. In saying what you did to Tucker concerning my views, you acted like a true friend. If the offer of such an honourable post had ever reached me, I might have hesitated before I declined it. An ambition to be so distinguished would, doubless, have tingled in my breast; but my reason tells me, that in order to secure any success in the political line, or any other, the only wise way is to adhere to that line most tenaciously; and as my choice is fixed, I mean to pursue what appears to be the best way to attain my object. With these sentiments, you will be able to conceive that my disgust and annoyance is not small in being sent on the insignificant duty of acting as Collector in the absence of Guthrie from his station.*

---

* Metcalfe wrote to his friend John Adam, who was then in the Secretariat, emphatically setting forth the inconvenience of detaching him from his regular duties to act temporarily out of the line of his profession; and it may be gathered from the following extract from Adam's reply that he obtained something of an assurance that he would not be sent on deputation again:—"I am sorry," wrote Mr. Adam, on September 17, 1807, "that I am not able to give you a positive promise that you will never at any future time be employed on deputation; but I think it extremely improbable that you will, after what I have said to Edmonstone on the subject, and the manner in which he has spoken to Dowdeswell. D. excused himself on the subject of your being sent to Saharunpore on the ground of there being no other fit person whom they could employ on that duty within a

"This is a dreadful blow to all my plans, because it may be repeated whenever the convenience of sending me from Delhi to act for any collector in the vicinity may suggest itself to the wise head of an unaccommodating secretary. What would I not give, if I must act out of my line, to change my present situation to be made your deputy! I should like very much to know what answer *my friend* Sir George gave, when I was proposed as secretary. If you should ever hear from Tucker, let me know. I dare say it was, that I was too young and inexperienced.

"I hope that I shall be able to spend some time with you and Bayley, but I shall not be so much my own master as you expect. I shall, most likely, have a troublesome year of it. I expect to be out the greater part of the season with a considerable military force, to *reduce* a barren unproductive country to subordination. It will be a most unpleasant duty; but Seton's heart is set upon it, and I do not know how I can get rid of it. Unfortunately, our districts are not put under your commission—if they were, I should expect some good in them. Our Customs at Delhi particularly require your interference; which, from the absurdity of keeping up all the old Sayers, and refraining from introducing a a new system, are in a most abominable state. A representation that I made on the subject, in order to get rid of the worst part of them, went no further than Seton's desk.

"I am much of your way of thinking with regard to his Majesty of Delhi. If I do not go all lengths with you in destroying every part of the shadow of his royalty, I am, at all events, for letting him see very clearly that he is a mere shadow; and if

---

very great distance, and he assured him that it should not occur again. Edmonstone himself is fully impressed with the impropriety as well as the unfairness of sending you to perform duties so foreign to your own profession and to your inclination. . . . . It so happened, too, that one day at Barrackpore Lord Minto was asking me about your situation (which he introduced by saying that Seton had been writing of you in terms of high praise), and I took the opportunity of telling him your objections to the temporary employment you were upon, and your wish to devote yourself altogether to the political line. He made some observation about the superiority of the political line, and that your deputation would not last long; but whether the impression will remain, I cannot tell. I should hope, however, there is no danger of your being again made a collector."

this could not be done completely without destroying even the empty name which I would wish for the present to leave to him, I would destroy even that. Thinking as you do, you will be vexed, as I am, to find that the tone, language, and behaviour of the *Court*, together with all the outward marks, and, in some respects, the real operative influence of royalty, have become in an increasing ratio much more ridiculous and preposterous since the accession of the illustrious Ukbar than they were before. It has often made me wonder, and at the same time almost made me mad, to see a most worthy, excellent man blind to such gross absurdity, and a dupe to wild and romantic feelings.

"As we near, I hope that our correspondence may become more frequent. This hint is not necessary to Bayley; he at all times writes so frequently! My love to him. Remember me to Fortescue.

"Believe me ever, your sincere friend,

"C. T. METCALFE."

All through the cold weather of 1807-1808, Charles Metcalfe, actively employed in the performance of his official duties, had little time for private correspondence. Nor would there have been much to gather from it that would advance the progress of the narrative, if he had found leisure to keep up a constant interchange of sentiment with his friends. But the summer of the latter year came to him pregnant with great events. His ambition was now about to be signally gratified. Lord Minto was at this time Governor-General of India. From all quarters he had heard the praises of Charles Metcalfe, and though personally unacquainted with him, he had such confidence in his zeal and ability, that he rejoiced when the progress of events enabled him to give the Delhi Assistant an opportunity of distinguishing himself on an independent field of action. Metcalfe was now about to be employed on an important political mission, demanding for the due execution of its duties the highest diplomatic powers. In what state the summons found him may be gathered from a letter which he wrote in July to his friend Sherer. He had then either not received the official notification of his appointment, or it was a state secret—but soon afterwards, he was on his way to the Punjaub:

CHARLES METCALFE TO J. W. SHERER.

"*Delhi, July 3rd*, 1808.

"MY DEAR SHERER,—As it is long since I have written to you, I will give you some account of myself. As by the blessing of God I have a good constitution, and have never experienced any of those misfortunes which wound the heart or warrant any tendency to melancholy, I enjoy as usual good health and good spirits. My accounts from my family are in all essential points of a most pleasing nature. My father and mother continue perfectly healthy. My sisters are growing up all that their parents wish them to be; and Master Tom is said to be a quick, merry boy, with a *slight inclination* to idleness.

"From China I have no late intelligence. The only bad piece of news that I have received from England is, that my father has lost his seat in Parliament. I am sure that he must feel the want of it, and I confess that I felt much annoyed by the intelligence. There is some consolation, however, in thinking that, at my father's time of life, rest and retirement, if not required, ought at least to be beneficial.

"You are of course acquainted with the arrangement which has lately taken place here, attaching permanently to the situation of First Assistant the duties of the *ci-devant* Superintendent of Revenues. I am far from being pleased either with the arrangement or the mode in which it has been ordered; but there is no use in grumbling about it. To the charge of the business now settled upon me they have affixed the commission which the Superintendent used to draw, in order, I suppose, to soften the bitterness of the trial. I mean to make this a sinking fund for the reduction of my debts, which, owing to the expenses of my bungalow, has risen to a considerable amount. My political character will henceforth be little more than nominal, for I must necessarily give up my time and attention to revenue matters. In two or three days I shall take the field, and I do not expect to take up my residence again at Delhi before the next hot winds. . .

"Your faithful friend,

"C. T. METCALFE."

CHAPTER VIII.

[1808—1809.]

THE MISSION TO LAHORE.

Apprehension of an Invasion—Measures of Defence—Metcalfe appointed Envoy to Lahore—Meeting with Runjeet Singh—Conduct of the Rajah—Delays and Excuses—Metcalfe's Diplomatic Address—His Firmness and Decision—Advance of the British Troops—Progress of Negotiation—The Proposed Treaty—Collision with the Akalis—The Treaty concluded.

When, in the Spring of 1808, from the Council Chamber of Calcutta, Lord Minto and his colleagues looked out upon those vast tracts of country which lie beyond the Sutlej and the Indus, and saw already the shadow of a gigantic enemy advancing from the West, it was no idle terror that haunted the imaginations of our British statesmen. The pacification of Tilsit had leagued against us the unscrupulous ambition of the great French usurper and the territorial cupidity of the Russian autocrat. That among the mighty schemes which they then discussed for the partition of the world between them, the invasion of India was not one of the least cherished, or the least substantial, now stands recorded as an historical fact. We know now that it was nothing more than a design; but it was not less the duty of our Indian rulers in 1808, to provide against a contingency which then seemed neither improbable nor remote. The occasion was one which, if it did not warrant a demonstration of military power, at all events invited a display of diplomatic address.

It was sound policy, in such a conjecture, to secure the good offices of the princes and chiefs who were dominant in the countries which were supposed to lie on the great high-road of the invader. If the rulers of Afghanistan and the Punjaub could be induced to enter into friendly alliances with the British Government for the resistance of invasion from the North, it seemed to Lord Minto and his colleagues that more than half of the danger which threatened our position would be at once removed.

Already was French intrigue making its way at the Persian Court. That was the sure commencement of the great game that was about to be played—the safest and the wisest commencement. It was a great thing, therefore, to re-establish our ascendency at Teheran; and a great thing to achieve the diplomatic occupation of the countries between Persia and India before our enemies could appear upon the scene. To accomplish the former object John Malcolm was despatched to the Court of the Shah-i-shah; and to secure the latter, Mountstuart Elphinstone and Charles Metcalfe were ordered to proceed—the former to Cabul, and the latter to Lahore.

The prince to whose court Metcalfe was ordered to proceed was Runjeet Sing. Since, in pursuit of Holkar, Lake's battalions had encamped in the country of the five rivers, the rise of that chieftain had been rapid. He had gone on without halting, on his career of conquest. A man of unbounded energy and unfailing courage—with great natural sagacity and no inconvenient amount of conscientiousness either to control his energies or to direct his abilities—he had been recently absorbing all the small principalities beyond the Sutlej, and consolidating them into a great empire. Even the petty Sikh states on our side of the Sutlej were not beyond the scope of his ambition. He was eager to bring them also under the common yoke; and as he approached the confines of British dominion, was already beginning to excite the jealousy and mistrust of his Christian neighbours. In 1805 he was known to us merely as one of the chiefs of the Punjaub; in 1808 he was the Maha-rajah (or great king) Runjeet Singh.

Of the Sikhs we were long content to know little. In the first years of the century our British functionaries spoke of them as "miscreants," as a lawless and degraded people, either indulging their predatory habits abroad, or sunk in deep sensuality at home. Neither their territorial arrangements nor their military resources were matters of vital concern to us at this time; and if we took any account of the national character of the followers of Govind, it was in pursuit rather of ethnographical knowledge than in furtherance of any political ends. But the great war with the Mahrattas, and the conquests which it had forced upon us, brought us into proximity with these strange new people; and it then became apparent to us that we could no longer regard the Sikh states as a group of petty principalities, exercising no influence whether for good or for evil upon the security of our position, or the pacific character of our rule. It seemed, indeed, necessary to do something; but what that something was to be it was difficult to decide. In the disunion of the Sikhs there were elements both of safety and of danger to the British —of safety, because a power so utterly wanting in union and organization could never be formidable in itself; of danger, because the very causes which prevented the Sikhs from becoming formidable enemies rendered it impossible that they should become serviceable friends. There was, indeed, in these states, on both sides of the Sutlej, nothing of unity or stability out of which a barrier against external invasion could be erected. It was apparent that we could enter with them into no engagements that could bind them to oppose the advance of an European army. To protect themselves against spoliation it was but too likely that they would league themselves with the invaders, and swell the tide of devastation and destruction. It was difficult to deal with such a combination of circumstances as now presented itself, and yet to adhere strictly to those principles of non-interference which the British Legislature had established, and to which the Indian Government of the day declared its fixed determination to adhere.*

The advantages of giving something like a tangible form and substance to the scattered elements of the Sikh power on the banks of the Sutlej had been urged upon the supreme Government by Colonel Ochterlony whilst still Resident at Delhi. It was proposed by him, that the British Government should distribute the country between the Sutlej and the Jumna among four principal Sikh chiefs, the precise limits of the territory of each being assigned by *us*, and that we should enter into specific engagements with these chiefs. Or, if it were considered that such engagements were not likely to be observed, it was suggested that resort might be had to a more decided exercise of our paramount power—that the whole body of Sikh chiefs might be reduced to the condition of tributaries, and

* See, for the views of the Supreme Government in 1805-1806, minute drawn up by Mr. Lumsden for the Governor-General:

"The Sikh chieftains in the actual condition of their respective tenures could not by any arrangement be rendered efficient allies and auxiliaries against an invading enemy. It would be impracticable to unite them in a common interest and a common cause. In the event of invasion they would probably add by their junction to the number of the invaders, and increase their means of devastation. . . . We could not safely or prudently depend in any degree upon the sentiments of gratitude or the obligations of public faith and honour to govern the proceedings of such a tribe. The ruling chieftains would probably provide for their security from immediate plunder or destruction by conciliating and assisting, and perhaps by joining the enemy."—[*MS. Records.*]

compelled to pay for the maintenance of a British force to "watch their conduct," or, in other words, to hold them in absolute subjection. But this was not a course of policy likely to find favour in the eyes of Lord Cornwallis, Sir George Barlow, or Lord Minto. "The Resident was informed that the arguments which would justify such an exercise of our power would equally justify the annexation of the whole of the Sikh territory to the British dominions, and that the extension of our territorial possessions, or of our political control for purposes of expediency, or even of comparative security, unsupported by motives of indisputable justice and indispensable necessity, had never constituted an object of the policy of this Government."* A strictly defensive system was to be maintained —not that defensiveness which is nine parts aggression, but rigid non-interference, which turns its back upon its neighbours until it receives a blow from behind. The Sikh chiefs were to be left to themselves. But they were to be chastised if they offended us. Predatory incursions across our borders were to be visited in the first place by the expulsion of the offenders at the point of the bayonet, and in the second place by the partition of their lands among those chiefs who aided us in the suppression of the lawless excesses of their neighbours. And it was believed that we should best maintain the integrity of our frontier by showing that we were as unwilling to practise as we were able to resist aggression.

In this state, affairs remained until the year 1808, when the two circumstances to which I have referred at the commencement of the chapter induced Lord Minto to depart from the policy to which his predecessors had so religiously adhered—the increased apprehension of European invasion and the progressive consolidation of the empire of Runjeet Singh. A Sikh alliance had now

* Minute of Mr. Lumsden, *ut supra*.—[*MS. Records.*]

become more expedient and more practicable. We wanted an ally, and we had found one. Left to themselves, the Sikh chiefs on the further side of the Sutlej had, one by one, been compelled to own the supremacy of Runjeet, whilst those on our side of the river, awed by the threats of the Lahore chief, were trembling for the safety of their possessions. Of the influence and the ability of this chieftain the British Government had no doubt. His integrity and good faith they may have questioned, for he was a Sikh. But they believed that they might work upon his hopes and upon his fears, and by demonstrating to him that his own interests would be largely promoted by an alliance with the British, induce him to enter into an engagement for the protection of the frontier of Hindostan.

In the winter season of 1807-8 a favourable opportunity of establishing amicable relations with the Lahore chief seemed to have presented itself. Runjeet Singh, who had written a friendly letter to Lord Minto, contemplated a visit to Hurdwar; and it was resolved that a British officer should be despatched to meet him there. The functionary selected for this duty was Charles Metcalfe.*

* Metcalfe had applied for the Deputy-Secretaryship in the Political Department, on the translation of John Adam. Lord Minto had previously made other arrangements with respect to this office, but he directed his Private Secretary, in reply to Metcalfe's application, to express his lordship's high sense of his character and abilities, and the desired intention of the Governor-General to take an early opportunity of promoting so excellent a public servant.

"The esteem," wrote Mr. Elliot, "which his lordship has conceived for your character and talents, is founded as well on what has already fallen under his own observation as on the report of those whose judgment has been formed on a longer acquaintance. It will, therefore, give him great satisfaction to evince these sentiments by such marks of confidence and favour as he may find suitable opportunities of showing you."—[*Mr. Elliot to Mr. Metcalfe, October* 25, 1807.]

But the vacillating chief never fulfilled his intention; and when subsequently he declared that he contemplated a visit to Thanesur, it was felt that so little reliance was to be placed on his movements that it would be expedient to shape our own measures without reference to the uncertain procedure of the impulsive Sikh. So it was determined that a mission should be sent across the Sutlej, under the conduct of Charles Metcalfe; and on the 20th of June, 1808, the Supreme Government, under the hand of Mr. Edmonstone, formally announced his appointment, and the instructions by which the young ambassador was to be guided.

The duties of the mission were to be entrusted entirely to Metcalfe himself. He was to move without secretaries, assistants, or attachés. A military escort was to be provided; and a proper establishment of moonshees, writers and servants, was to be furnished. But the work of diplomacy was to be left entirely to his unaided counsels. He was to carry with him, however, the Oriental diplomatist's best auxiliary, a costly supply of presents; and, in order that his communications with the Government might be frequent and uninterrupted, he was instructed to establish a letter-post between Delhi and Umritsur. His personal salary was to be 2,000 rupees a month, and all the expenses of the mission were to be charged to the state.*

Such were the outer circumstances of the mission to Lahore. The letter which determined them carried also the instructions of the Supreme Government relative to the course of policy to be pursued by the British representative at the Sikh Court. It was such a letter as Metcalfe had never received before—such a letter as a young man of three-and-twenty has seldom, if ever, received from the government of a great empire. The object of the mission

* *Mr. Edmonstone to Mr. Metcalfe, June* 20, 1808.—[*MS. Records.*]

was of the most momentous character. It was simply to counteract the towering ambition of the gigantic despots of France and Russia. Of the great scheme of diplomacy by which Persia, Afghanistan, and the Punjaub were to be erected into friendly barriers against Russo-Gallic invasion, Metcalfe was to be the pioneer. He was to prepare the way for Elphinstone, and make things ready for the reception of Malcolm. He was to conduct a series of the most delicate operations alone and unaided in a strange country, and to negotiate a treaty of friendship with a prince of an uncertain and capricious temper, of selfish and unscrupulous ambition, unrestrained by any principles of Christian rectitude, or any courtesies of civilized life. But the very difficulties which beset such a position, and the responsibilities with which it was surrounded, only, in the eyes of Charles Metcalfe, enhanced its attractiveness. He had been panting for a great opportunity and now the great opportunity was come. They who have caught glimpses of the early character of the man in the recorded pages of his common-place book, and seen what were his aspirations, will readily conceive what were the pulsings of his warm heart, and the tinglings of his young blood, when he sat down to read the instructions of the Supreme Government, and to draw up for his future guidance the following memoranda, containing an abstract of the Chief Secretary's letter and his own interpretation of its contents:

"MEMORANDA FROM INSTRUCTIONS.

"General and conciliatory answers to be returned to any questions from the Cis-Sutlejean chiefs respecting the object of my mission. Arguments to be used to satisfy them that the improvement of the relations of amity between the British Government and the Rajah of Lahore involves no arrangement prejudicial to other chiefs. Applications for protection against Runjeet Singh to be referred to the Resident of Dihlee, but endeavours to be made to convince the chiefs that Government takes an interest in their welfare, and that the objects of my mission are entirely consistent with those friendly sentiments.

"Main object of the mission:—Counteraction of the designs of the French. The time of stating my ultimate purpose to be regulated by circumstances. Expedient first to make myself acquainted with the character and disposition of Runjeet Singh and his ministers, and to endeavour to create an interest with them by conciliating their confidence and good-will. Proper to ascertain the Rajah's disposition respecting my residence at his court. If he should be desirous of my continuance, to select my own time for opening the negotiation. In the meantime, to represent the object to be the improvement of the amicable relations so long subsisting between the states, and confirmed by the intercourse between Lord Lake and the Rajah, and by the treaty then concluded. Reference to be made to Runjeet Singh's friendly letter to the Governor-General, and the Governor-General's reply. To observe that the demonstration of attachment contained in that letter had augmented the solicitude of Government to cultivate the connection between the two states, and that I had been sent accordingly for the express purpose of cementing the bonds of friendship. That I had been despatched to Hurdwar with the same view; and that the failure of that opportunity of showing our friendship had suggested the still more distinguished mark of regard by a direct mission to his court.

"Cases in which it would be advisable to enter immediately on the proper object of my mission.—1st. If any French agent should have arrived at, or might be expected in, Lahore, or the adjacent countries. 2nd. If the designs of the French, and the state of affairs in Persia should have attracted the Rajah's notice. 3rd. Receipt of authentic intelligence of the actual advance of a French army towards Persia.

"General principle upon which to conduct the negotiation:—Opposition to the French to be urged as the only way of securing the Rajah's territories and independence from the insatiable ambition and unlimited encroachment and violence of the ruler of France. To persuade him that he will not be able to resist the enemy without a British force. To secure the Rajah's consent to the march of a British army through the Punjaub, and the exertion of his authority in furnishing supplies, with permission to establish depôts of provisions and military stores. To express the full confidence of the British Government in its power. To explain the facility of cutting off the supplies of the enemy, and withholding from them the produce of the country.

"To avoid a declaration of non-interference in case of the renewal of his attacks upon the Cis-Sutlejeah states, and to manage that delicate question as well as I can. To show a disposition to accede to engagements of a strictly defensive nature if proposed; but to refer the question for the decision of Government, except in an evident emergency.

"To facilitate the Mission to Cabul and establish a preliminary intercourse with the Court, and to establish a channel of intelligence and communication to the westward. Not to announce the intended mission to Cabul until after its departure from Dihlee, but to be prepared to remove from Runjeet Singh's mind any jealousy or apprehension. No objection to disclosing the object of the Cabul mission after having disclosed my own, otherwise to attribute it to motives which cannot injure him.

"To collect and communicate every information regarding the political state of the country, also respecting those points which it is expedient to ascertain with reference to the march and supply of troops. To ascertain the routes through which it is practicable for an army to march from Persia to the Indus. To communicate information respecting the geography of the countries to the westward of that river.

"To discover the real disposition of Runjeet Singh towards the British Government, and to regulate my negotiations accordingly. To inquire respecting his resources, troops, government, dominion, relations with other states, &c., &c. To discourage Mehtab Kour and her mother *quoad* their plot. To do away the effect of Captain Matthews's proceedings. To inquire into the reported intrigue with Holkar and Amnut Rao."

To one of Metcalfe's aspiring temper, not the least of the attractions of this new employment was derived from the considerations of the great extent of country over which he was to be permitted, under certain contingencies, to spread the network of his diplomacy. He already saw himself despatching emissaries to the Courts of Cabul and Teheran, and baffling the gigantic intrigues of Napoleon and Alexander throughout the whole expanse of Central Asia. But his enthusiasm was always tempered with sound good sense, and when, in the following paragraphs, he committed to writing, more for his own guidance than for any other purpose, his views of the course which it was expedient to pursue with reference to a correspondence with those distant Courts, there was nothing discernible in the paper but the workings of a plain, practical mind:

"It appears from the minute of the Governor-General and the instructions which I have received, that the mission to Lahore will considerably precede that to Cabul, and his lordship has expressed an expectation that I may have the means of facilitating the latter mission, and of establishing a preliminary intercourse with the Court of Cabul. It is proper, therefore, for me to consider how I can best carry these instructions into execution.

"The uncertainty existing respecting the time at which Mr. Elphinstone will proceed on his mission, gives rise to some doubt regarding the proper plan for me to pursue. If any great delay were in contemplation, I should think it right for me in the first instance to endeavour to open a correspondence with the Minister of the King of Cabul of a general friendly nature, and to refrain from any communication of the intentions of Government to send an Envoy to Cabul until I had ascertained the disposition of the Court, and found a proper opportunity. In this case, I should think it right to despatch a native agent to Cabul, with a letter to the Wuzeer, requesting permission for him to attend the Court on my part, for the purpose of sending me account of the welfare of his Majesty, and of establishing a medium of friendly communication. This is all that I should think it advisable to do at first; and I should expect that opportunities would occur of proceeding further in the course of the correspondence which would probably follow this introduction. I should not, if I were to act according to my own judgment, charge the native with any directions to sound the Ministers respecting the disposition of the King; nor should I make him acquainted with the views of Government, because I would not on any account put it into his power to commit the dignity of Government.

"In the case stated, it is supposed that there may be that interval between my arrival at Lahore and Mr. Elphinstone's departure from Dihlee, which would admit of a general friendly correspondence with the Court of Cabul previous to announcing the intention of Government to send an Envoy. But if Mr. Elphinstone is to proceed on his mission at an earlier period than has been supposed, the line of conduct above mentioned would not answer; and in that case it would, I think, be advisable, and most suitable to the character of the British Government, to announce its intentions in a dignified and open manner, by sending a native as the bearer of a letter directly to the Court. It is scarcely possible that the King of Cabul would wantonly insult the British Government by any improper reply to this notice; and the expediency of making this direct advance is considerably strengthened by the probability that a report of the intended mission may reach Cabul before the desired intercourse can be opened by the Court. It is, however, probable, that the measures already adopted by Mr. Seton will lead to a correspondence, which may afford opportunities of announcing the mission in a manner different from that above suggested.

"It may be a question whether it would be most advisable to conduct the preliminary intercourse with Cabul through the Resident at Dihlee, or through Mr. Elphinstone, or through the Envoy at Lahore; at present I am instructed to turn my attention to the object as well as to the necessity of opening a communication with Teheran immediately after my arrival at Lahore; and it is, consequently, necessary that I should be accompanied by natives qualified to be employed in these important matters, either according to such particular instructions as I may hereafter receive, or according to the best of my judgment, formed upon the general orders which I have already received. This consideration induced me to request from Mr. Seton the assistance of Fyzut-oolla at Lahore; and with the same view, I propose to carry along with me Syud Jafier Khan, who was formerly employed by Colonel Scott on a mission to Nadaun. One or the other of these, whichever may appear to be best qualified, I propose to send without delay, if all things remain as they are, to Cabul, charged with a letter from myself to the Minister; and the other I intend to employ in opening the communication with Persia. It is not my intention to confine my endeavours to obtain intelligence of the state of the Court and country of Cabul to the mission of a native to Cabul with a letter. We ought, besides, to have secret news-writers, not only with the Court, but in Cabul, Cashmeer, Peshawur, Candahar, Moultan, Herat, and as far as possible in the interior of Persia."

Little time was lost in making the necessary preparations for the departure of the mission. In the first week of August, Charles Metcalfe turned his back upon Delhi.

The weather was unpropitious. It was the height of the monsoon. The heavy rains and the bad roads for a while impeded the progress of the mission. After passing Kurnaul, the weather began to improve; but the travellers invariably found themselves either in a quagmire or a pool. "The country," he wrote, "is so full of water, and the roads are so deep with mud, and the soil so soft, that it is difficult for cattle of every description to move. We have been under the necessity of taking a circuitous route, the direct road not being passable; and we have not been able to make marches of a greater distance than about ten miles daily." On the 22nd of August the mission reached Puttealah, one of the chief places in the cis-Sutlej states, and here the serious business of diplomacy commenced.

The Rajah of Puttealah received the British Envoy with profuse demonstrations of compliment and congratulation; and at a public interview, unexpectedly produced the keys of the fort, and requested Metcalfe to restore them to him as a gift from the British Government. He threw himself, he said, entirely on our protection—all that he had was at the mercy of the British—his government and his existence would cease without our support. But Metcalfe read at once the true meaning of this proposal, and answered that he was not authorized by his Government to perform any such ceremony, but that the British were the friends of the Rajah, and ever desired his prosperity: and that the keys could not be in better hands.*

On the 1st of September the mission crossed the Sutlej.†

* Soon afterwards, the chief told him that he had heard it was the intention of Runjeet Singh to cross the Sutlej and to seize Fureed-kote, which was in the Puttealah dominions—an intention which was subsequently fulfilled. It was suggested, too, to Metcalfe, that it would be expedient for him to write to Runjeet to say that the British Government desired him to remain at Lahore to receive the mission.

† Before the mission had reached the banks of the river,

At Puttealah they had been met by an agent despatched by Runjeet Singh with a letter of welcome and congratulation; but as they advanced into the Punjaub, it became at every stage more and more obvious that that erratic prince had little intention of remaining at home, either at Lahore or Umritsur, to receive the British embassy in a becoming manner. It was reported, indeed, that he had crossed the river with the intention of making a descent upon the Puttealah territory; but this Metcalfe was slow to believe, and the Sikh agent who remained in his camp either was, or pretended to be, ignorant of the movements of his master. All doubts, however, were soon set at rest by the receipt of a letter from Runjeet himself, announcing his intention to receive the British mission at Kussoor. Troops, it appeared, were assembling there from all quarters; but Metcalfe believed that the chief cause of the assemblage was a desire on the part of the Sikh chief to make a formidable display of his military resources in the presence of the British envoy.

Metcalfe pushed on to Kussoor, which lay upon his road to Umritsur;* and upon the 10th of September he halted within a few miles of the Sikh camp, that the ceremonials of the reception might be arranged. On the following day Runjeet's prime minister † and his chief military officer,‡ with a retinue of two thousand men, came out to conduct

Metcalfe had despatched a confidential agent to Cabul with instructions to communicate all that was passing in Afghanistan, and to keep open the communications with Persia, to which country Malcolm was about to proceed at the head of a great embassy.

* He seems to have had some misgivings at this time regarding the external appearance of the mission at the Sikh Court—the clothing of his escort being in a most discreditable condition. He reported the circumstance to Government.

† The Dewan Mokun Chund.

‡ His adopted brother, Futteh Singh.

the mission to the ground that had been marked out for their encampment, at a distance of less than a mile from the Rajah's tents.

"On the 12th," wrote Metcalfe to the Chief Secretary, "I paid my first visit to Runjeet Singh, accompanied by the officers attached to the escort. The Rajah met us on the outside of a large enclosure, and having embraced all the gentlemen of the mission, conducted us within, where tents had been prepared for our reception.* As a compliment to us, the Rajah, from his own choice, used chairs at this meeting, partly collected from our camp and partly from his own, upon which he and the principal Sirdars present and the gentlemen of the British mission were seated. This interview was prolonged by the Rajah beyond the usual time of visits of ceremony; but nothing of consequence passed at it. The Rajah did not enter much into conversation, and made only two observations worthy of remark. One was an expression of regret for the lamented death of Lord Viscount Lake, of whom he observed that it would be difficult to find his equal, for that he was as much distinguished by his gentleness, mildness, humanity, and affability, as by his greatness as a military character. The other observation was in reply to one of his courtiers, who was remarking that the British Government was celebrated

* Metcalfe was of opinion that Runjeet ought to have come out to meet the mission, but this Runjeet declined. His representations, however, were not without some effect.

"It appeared to me," he wrote, "that the rank and dignity of the Government, which I have the honour to represent, required that the Rajah should come out from his camp to meet the mission, and I had it intimated to him that such was my expectations. He did not come into my wishes in that respect; but the references which I had occasion to make respecting the ceremonials, had a good effect, inasmuch as they produced a great change in them, for at the first the reception was proposed to be in a style far inferior to that which has been observed."—[*Metcalfe to Edmonstone, September* 13, 1808.]

for good faith; upon which Runjeet Singh said that he knew well that the word of the British Government included everything." Presents were interchanged, and in the evening a salute was fired in Runjeet's camp in honour of the day, which he intimated to Metcalfe was regarded by him as a day of rejoicing.

In spite, however, of these declarations of friendship, the reception given to the British mission had nothing of cordiality in it. Runjeet was plainly jealous and suspicious of the British Government. His better reason clouded by the false insinuations and the mischievous advice of councils of chiefs, who, from motives of self-interest, desired to embroil Runjeet with the Company's Government, he forbade all communication between the two camps, and for some time was unwilling to return the visit of the British Envoy. It was obviously his wish to enhance his own importance in the eyes of the assembled chiefs and the large body of troops encamped at Kussoor, by appearing to hold the British mission of little account. "In brief," wrote Metcalfe, "it would appear that I am regarded as a dangerous enemy to be guarded against, rather than as an envoy from a friendly state charged with the most amicable duties."

But the decided conduct of the young envoy soon induced Runjeet at least to pay the British Mission the compliment of a visit. On the 16th, Metcalfe received the Sikh with all honours. A suite of tents had been erected for the occasion, and a musnud in the oriental fashion prepared for the Rajah's occupancy. But Runjeet, preferring the European style, seated himself on a chair, and still eschewing business, entered into familiar conversation with the British officer, principally on military subjects.* After

* "He spoke with great respect of the British troops, and observed of the Mahratta army which he had seen in this country that it contained great numbers, but that it wanted union and command. He related the following anecdote, which happened when Jeswunt Rao Holkar was in the neighbourhood of Umritsur.

the interview, he expressed a wish to see the manœuvres of the detachment of Company's troops composing the escort, and mounted on an elephant, watched the exercise of the sepoys with interest and seeming pleasure. He took his final leave, to all appearance, much gratified; and such had been the cordiality of his manner, that Metcalfe believed a favourable change had taken place in the feelings of the Sikh, and that the business of the mission would soon proceed without interruption. Great, therefore, were Metcalfe's astonishment and disappointment when, on the following day, he received a letter from Runjeet Singh, which he characterised in his official communications to Government as "an extraordinary instance of suspicion, hastiness, and disrespect." The letter, in its Eastern phraseology, contained the meaning here embodied in an English dress:—

Translation of a Note from Rajah Runjeet Singh to Mr. Metcalfe, delivered by Misr Prebdial, Hukeem Uzeezoodeen, and Meean Imaum-oo-deen, on the evening of the 17th of September, 1808.

"I never before, at any time, under any emergency, or in any place, have made so long a halt as I have now, solely in consequence of the friendship between this Government and the Honourable Company, which by the blessing of God has been increasing and improving from the time in which his Excellency Lord Lake came into this country to the present happy hour. My camp has remained in this place so long, in the expectation of

---

A report was brought to Holkar that Lord Lake had crossed the Beeas in pursuit of him. Holkar immediately mounted his horse. The alarm spread through his army, and the whole fled to a considerable distance, leaving all their tents standing. It was pleasing to observe that this had made an impression on Runjeet Singh, and that he had no objection to mention it. He put questions concerning our favourite mode of fighting, the distance at which we erected our batteries in besieging, the distance at which our artillerymen could hit a target in practice, with others of a similar nature and tendency. He complained of the difficulty of introducing discipline among the people of the Punjaub."—[*Metcalfe to Edmonstone, September* 17, 1808.]

your arrival. Thanksgivings to the Throne of the Almighty, this wish of my heart, that is, your arrival, and the pleasure of seeing you, has been obtained in a proper manner.

"Although it is difficult to feel satiety from the interviews of friends whose hearts are united, and although the times of meeting, however many, seem too few, yet affairs of state must be attended to. Consequently, I am about to march immediately for the settlement of certain districts. In my nation it is considered very auspicious to march on the first day of the moon; and my march is appointed for that day. Therefore be pleased to make the friendly communications on the part of the Right Honourable the Governor-General, with which, from his lordship's letter I understand you to be charged, in order that I may act accordingly. My anxiety cannot admit of longer expectation."

Outwardly courteous and complimentary as was this effusion, its uncourteous and uncomplimentary meaning peeped out from every sentence of it. "This extraordinary document," wrote Metcalfe, "gave me notice in a plain manner that I was expected to take my leave in three or four days. It was calculated to repel, whilst it professed to call for communications, and in, I suppose, an unprecedented manner, evinced a design to shut the door against all intercourse, and to put an end to the proceedings of the mission, without even ascertaining in the slightest degree the object to which they might be directed." But Metcalfe believed that the obnoxious letter was hardly to be considered as the act and deed of Runjeet himself. It was, he knew, the result of suspicions instilled into him by others; and he did not yet despair of bringing the chief, by good diplomacy—by conduct at once firm and conciliatory, into a more reasonable frame of mind. So he sent back the following letter in reply:—

Translation of a Note from Mr. Metcalfe to Rajah Runjeet Singh, transmitted on the night of the 17th of September, in reply to that received from the Rajah on the evening of same day.

"By the blessing of God the relations of friendship have been firmly established between you and the British Government, from the time when his Excellency General Lord Lake was in this country, and have been daily improved, particularly since the period when you wrote a very friendly letter to the Right Honourable Lord Minto, the Governor-General, congratulating his lordship on his arrival in India. In consequence, when you formed the intention of visiting Hurdwar, in order to bathe in the Holy Ganges, his lordship deputed me for the purpose of receiving you with every respect, and attending you during your stay in that quarter. It happened that your intentions were postponed. The Right Honourable the Governor-General, wishing to display a signal mark of his friendship and regard, has now commanded me to repair to your Court, to express the satisfaction with which his lordship views the existing harmony and concord between the two states, and with a view to establish and improve the ties of intimacy and union. To-morrow I hope to have the honour of waiting upon you whenever you are at leisure, when I will make the communications with which I am entrusted by the Right Honourable the Governor-General, and present a letter which I have from his lordship to your address."

This letter was not without its anticipated effect. Metcalfe was right when he believed that Runjeet had been led astray by the instillation of some falsehood with which the men by whom he was surrounded had poisoned his understanding. He had been told that Metcalfe was on his way to Caubul; and that the British mission had not been despatched primarily and exclusively to his court, but merely instructed to pay him a passing visit. But this lie was soon exploded; and Runjeet again began to regard the mission with complacency. An answer was promptly returned to Metcalfe's letter; and it contained an eager invitation to the meeting proposed by the British envoy :—

Translation of a Note from Rajah Runjeet Singh to Mr. Metcalfe, received from Meean Imaum-ood-deen, on the 18th of September.

[After compliments.] "In an auspicious and happy moment your friendly letter, most agreeable to my inclinations, every letter of which refreshed my eye, reached me, and gave splendour to the unity and concord (subsisting between us). That which is written by your friendly pen respecting what has happened from the illustrious arrival of Lord Lake in this country up to your arrival, in order to confirm and improve the relations of intimate sincere friendship, which by the blessing of God have been so firmly established, and so manifestly displayed as to be known to all, collectively and individually; and the intimation which you give of your intention to visit me, and make me happy by the communications entrusted to you by the Right Honourable the Governor-General have given me thousand-fold pleasure and joy.

"My desire to see you cannot be postponed from this day till to-morrow, and my inclination is impatient of delay, but in consequence of the season, and state of my constitution, I have this day taken medicine. To-morrow, therefore, at three o'clock in the afternoon, bring pleasure to your friend's house. Hukeem Uzeezoodeen will arrive with you at that hour and conduct you."

Mollified by this outwardly friendly invitation, Metcalfe, on the 19th of September, visited Runjeet Singh, and, in the presence of the principal Sikh councillors, opened the discussion by accusing the Rajah of encouraging unjust and unworthy suspicions. This was denied. Evasive explanations of the offensive letter were given; and after a conversation conducted on both sides with the utmost good humour, it was determined that the propositions of the British Government should be received, as soon as the Sikhs had held a council of state to determine upon their plan of operations. But this was manifestly reversing the order of things. So, when subsequently a deputation waited on Metcalfe, to explain that the Sikhs could not determine upon the course they were to pursue until they were informed of the nature of the propositions to be made to them, the British envoy acknowledged the cogency of the assertion, and declared that he was willing on the following day to deliver the important message with which he was charged by his employers. It appeared to Metcalfe, indeed, that it was no longer desirable to keep Runjeet in ignorance of the real objects of his mission; for the mind of the restless Sikh might be diverted by thoughts of the anti-Gallican alliance from other objects on which it was not expedient that he should dwell.

So on the afternoon of the 22nd of September, Metcalfe went unattended to Runjeet's residence, and there found the Sikh ruler surrounded by his principal councillors of state. I give the history of the meeting in the young envoy's own words:—

"I opened the conference," he wrote, "by stating that the friendship which had happily existed between the Rajah and the British Government had induced the Right Honourable the Governor-General to depute me to communicate some important intelligence, in which the Maha-rajah's interests were materially concerned. I then mentioned that his lordship had received authentic advices that the French, who were endeavouring to establish themselves in Persia, had formed the design of invading these countries, and of seizing Cabul and the Punjaub—that his lordship's first care was to give warning to the states which this intelligence concerned—that feeling the interests of the British Government and those of the Rajah to be the same, his lordship had commissioned me to negotiate with the Rajah arrangements for the extirpation of the common enemy, and had appointed another gentleman to be envoy to Cabul for similar purposes with respect to that country, who would, in a short time, with the Rajah's permission, pass through this country on his way to the place of his destination. I added, that these measures had been adopted by the Government in the purest spirit of friendship, and that it was evident that the interests of all the states in this quarter required that they should unite their powers in defence of their dominions, and for the destruction of the enemy's armies.

"At the conclusion of this introduction the Rajah and all present following him, made an exclamation of admiration at the friendly conduct of the Right Honourable the Governor-General in making this communication, and expressed without hesitation a ready concurrence in his lordship's plans. The Rajah asked, how far the British army would advance to meet the French, and what force would be sent? I replied, that these questions would depend upon subsequent arrangements; but that it was our practice to seek our enemy, and that no doubt the Government would send an army beyond Cabul. With respect to the amount of the force, I observed, that would necessarily depend upon circumstances, but that such a force would of course be sent as would be amply sufficient to destroy the foe. He asked if troops were ready to advance, and when the French might be expected? I said that the moment at which the enemy might be expected could not at present be ascertained—that it might be sooner or later—but that there was no doubt of the design, and that it behoved wise governments to be prepared to counteract it; and that our troops always are, and always would be, ready to advance.

"After expressing in animated terms his desire to co-operate with the British arms, his sense of the friendly motives which had led to the communications from the Right Honourable the Governor-General, his approbation of the plan of attacking the enemy before they could reach Cabul, and his satisfaction at the prospect of a close alliance with the British Government, which had long, he said, been the wish of his heart, now spoke in a whisper to Misr Prebdial (one of his councillors), who, in consequence, carried aside all the persons present except the Rajah, Kurreem Singh, Imaum-ood-deen, and myself. Whilst the gentlemen apart were deliberating in a whisper, the Rajah continued to converse with me, sometimes on subjects connected with the objects of my previous communication, and sometimes on general topics. He started the idea that the King of Cabul might throw himself in the arms of the French, and asked what would be done in that case? I said, in that case we must attack the King of Cabul as well as the French; but that it was improbable that he would be so blind to his own interests; for that the French invariably subjected and oppressed those who joined them; plundered and laid waste their country, and overthrew the Government. In the course of this conversation I endeavoured, in conformity to the instructions of the supreme Government, to alarm the Rajah for the safety of his territories, and at the same time to give him confidence in our protection.

"The Rajah asked if all was right with Holkar? I said, "Yes?' and that since the peace with him made in this country, he had continued on the most friendly terms with the British Government. 'But,' replied the Rajah, 'he is a determined rascal (*pucka hurumzadah*), and no trust can be reposed in him.' I answered, that when we were at war with him, we used to call him a great rascal; but as we were now at peace, we always spoke of him with the respect due to a friendly chief. The Rajah mentioned, that when in this country, Holkar prohibited his troops from plundering as long as Lord Lake's army was near to him, but let them loose on the country as soon as his lordship had commenced his return to the British dominions.

"When the deliberations of the whispering council were concluded, the result was conveyed by Misr Prebdial to the Rajah's ears, and the Rajah delivered some order to him in the same manner; after which Misr Prebdial addressed me in a long speech, the substance of which was, that the Rajah concurred in everything that I had communicated, and particularly desired to have the closest connection with the British Government; but that the business not being of slight consideration, but of the highest importance, it was necessary to proceed with deliberation—accordingly, that the question would be fully discussed by the Rajah with those present, and that the result of their deliberations on that and other subjects should be communicated to me on the following morning. The Rajah said the same; and having enjoined profound secresy to all present, put an end to the conference."

The morrow came, and with the morrow a new light dawned upon the subject.* To the Sikh councillors it did not appear, upon consideration of the whole matter, that they had much to apprehend from the rumoured incursion of the French. The danger was at most something remote and conjectural. They hardly could bring themselves to believe that the counteraction of foreign influence in the countries of Central Asia was the real object of the mission to Runjeet's court. And if it were, they argued among themselves, the alliance which the British Government sought was mainly for its own advantage. Why then should not the treaty at the same time embrace objects more nearly and palpably advantageous to the Sikhs themselves? It was Runjeet Singh's earnest desire, at this time, to obtain from the British Government a recognition of his sovereignty over all the Sikh states on both sides of the Sutlej; and it was now intimated to Metcalfe that the Rajah suggested the expediency of including this and other provisions in the contemplated treaty. To all of this

Metcalfe listened patiently; but he firmly replied, that he had no authority to give any such guarantee on the part of the Government which he represented—that the alliance against the French was the first point to be arranged, and that the rest would be left for future consideration. But this was not a view of the case in which the Sikh councillors were inclined to concur. The interview, therefore, was not a satisfactory one; and nothing was settled except—the last resource of inconclusiveness—that the views of Runjeet Singh should be reduced to writing, and considered by the British envoy.

I cannot follow in detail all the consultations—many of them mere profitless repetitions of inconclusive discussions—which day by day Metcalfe reported to the Supreme Government. The difficulties with which the young diplomatist contended were many and great. He soon perceived that in Runjeet Singh he had to deal with a man inordinately ambitious himself, and out of measure suspicious of the ambitious designs of others. Untainted by any objects of aggression as was this mission to Lahore, it must be admitted that Runjeet's suspicions were not wholly without foundation. He had seen, within the space of a few years, the fairest provinces of Hindostan subjected to the yoke of the conquering Feringhee. If he had extended his dominions, our extension of territory had been far greater; and there was sufficient, at least in the antecedents of British conquest, to make him fearful of his independence, when he saw our battalions already approaching the banks of the Sutlej, and our diplomatists, the sure forerunners of our armies, beginning to spread themselves over all the countries of Central Asia. It is not strange, therefore, that one, by nature suspicious in the extreme, and wrought upon by evil councillors and treacherous adherents, should have regarded the advance of the British mission with distrust. From the very first his suspicions had broken out into acts of open discourtesy. He had forbidden, as I have before said, all intercourse between the two camps. Supplies had been refused to the mission. The native bankers were afraid to cash Metcalfe's bills. Runjeet's spies were continually in the British camp. The camp had been pitched on ground selected by Runjeet in the bed of a dry river, on whose banks the Sikh sentries were incessantly posted. Our messengers had been intercepted; our letters had been opened; and Metcalfe had excused himself to Government for submitting to many indignities which he pretended not to observe. He had certain great ends to accomplish, and he would not be arrested or turned aside by any obstructions but those of the greatest national import and significance.

But that which most embarrassed Metcalfe, at this time, was the unscrupulous course of territorial aggrandizement, which Runjeet was determined on pursuing in the face of the British mission. It was obviously his intention to turn to account what he hoped would be considered the implied sanction of the British Government to his conquests on the southern bank of the Sutlej. The suddenness of his movements baffled all diplomacy, and prevented all remonstrance. Thus, on the 25th of September, just as the negotiations appeared to be in a favourable state, Runjeet suddenly, without intimation to the British Envoy, and without consulting his Ministers, broke up his camp at Kussoor, and prepared to cross the Sutlej.* The primary object of the

* Reporting this to Government, Metcalfe wrote: "I was disposed to augur well from the spirit of this conference; and great was my surprise on rising this morning to find that the Rajah's army was moving. Uzcezooden at the instant came to me and said that he had been sent by the Rajah to inform me that he was about to march to the river Beeas, and to request that I would march too. I answered that I could not march to-day; but that I would follow the Rajah as soon as I could. I expressed my surprise at the Rajah's moving so suddenly, and

movement was the capture of the fortress and surrounding territory of Fureed-kote—a tract of country in the domain of the Rajah of Putteealah, one of the chief of the group of his Cis-Sutlej States;* but it was openly boasted in camp that the expedition was designed to accomplish the subjugation of the whole of the country lying between the Sutlej and the Jumna. And there were those who said that, this accomplished, some hostile movements against the British would certainly ensue.†

Following the Sikh camp at a convenient interval of time, Metcalfe, on the 28th of September, again met Runjeet Singh. The interview was held on an island in the river. The confidential servants of the Rajah were present; and the manner of Runjeet himself was courteous and conciliatory. But there seemed to be a hopeless gulf between the two negotiating parties, which it was impossible to bridge over. Metcalfe still asserted that he came for nothing but a defensive alliance against the French. "If the French invade your territory," he said, "you will profit greatly by the alliance. If they do not, you will

without giving me any previous intimation, and I desired to know what were the Rajah's intentions, where he was going, and whether he would cross the river or not. Uzeezoodeen could give me no satisfactory information. I therefore desired him to bring me an answer on these points from his master, saying, that until I should obtain the information required, I could not say whether it would be proper for me to accompany the Rajah or not."—[*Mr. Metcalfe to Mr. Edmonstone, Camp Kussoor, September 25, 1808.*]

* Fureed-kote was, however, at this time in the possession of rebels, who paid no revenue to the Puttealah Rajah.

† Metcalfe reported, among other things, that there was "a story on foot to the effect that the Rajah of Bhurtpore had applied to Runjeet for aid against the hostile designs of the British, that his application had been backed by Holkar, and that Runjeet Singh had agreed to co-operate for the defence of Bhurtpore."

not suffer by it." Reduced to this simple formula, the case was a convincing one; and Runjeet at first seemed to be staggered by it. But he clamoured for the sanction of the British Government to the extension of his sovereignty over all the Sikh territories; and was eager also to introduce into the treaty a clause, pledging us not to interfere for the prevention of any hostilities that he might be pleased to carry on in the direction of Caubul. Such was the unvarying tenor of his discourse; and every new meeting only served to convince Metcalfe of the difficulty of persuading the Rajah to abandon a design which lay so very near to his heart.*

In the meanwhile, Metcalfe's letters, despatched with unfailing punctuality, and admirably lucid in all their details, were exciting much grave reflection in the Council Chamber of Calcutta. The seeming determination of Runjeet to extend his conquests on the southern bank of the Sutlej, excited in Lord Minto a very strong desire to arrest by force of arms the progress of the ambitious Sikh. The first minute which he wrote upon the subject, hinted

* Summing up the whole state of the case after the lapse of another month, Metcalfe wrote to the Supreme Government: "It appears to me that he wishes merely to have a treaty of perpetual friendship with the British Government to be maintained hereafter with his heirs and successors; that he is indifferent to the proposed alliance against the designs of the French, as the danger is not near nor perceptible to him—that to that alliance generally, however, he has no objection, although he wishes to make his agreement to it the means of obtaining concessions from the British Government; but at the same time he does not view without uneasiness the progress of the measures in contemplation, and the probability of the introduction of British agents in his territories, the disclosure of the actual state of his country, army, and resources, and other imagined consequences of opening the means of communication between the British Government and the disaffected chiefs whom he oppresses."—[*October* 20, 1808. *Mr. Metcalfe to Mr. Edmonstone. MS. Records.*]

at the expediency of instructing Metcalfe to intimate to Runjeet Singh, that if, pending negotiations, any advance were made towards our frontier, or if any interruption were at any time given to the Caubul mission, it would be considered as a declaration of war. But he was a statesman of a calm and dispassionate nature, and he recorded at the same time, that these were only his first hasty reflections, and that he would, "in the course of the day, collect more deliberately such thoughts on the general question as might appear worthy to be communicated" to his colleagues, and to the Envoy in Runjeet's camp. And the result of these subsequent deliberations, aided by a memorandum drawn up by Mr. Edmonstone, was, that Metcalfe was instructed not to follow any course that would precipitate his abrupt departure from Runjeet's camp, but to protract his negotiations, and to avoid, if possible, such a rupture as would incite Runjeet to assume an attitude of open hostility. These instructions Metcalfe had anticipated. The course laid down for him was that which his own judgment suggested, and already he had entered upon it.

Having thus resolved to gain time and to amuse Runjeet, whilst they were maturing their plan of ultimate operations, and waiting to see what might be written down in the ever-fertile chapter of accidents, our statesmen at Calcutta began to take larger views of the whole question, and to consider whether it would be expedient to yield to the solicitations of the Rajah, or to maintain the independence of the Sikh chiefs on our side of the Sutlej. Lord Minto at once determined that the question was one which he was justified in deciding upon grounds of immediate policy, rather than upon any abstract principles; and after weighing the consequences of the adoption of either course—each being beset with its own peculiar difficulties—he resolved that the interests of the British Government demanded that the aggressiveness of Runjeet Singh should be stemmed, and that the lesser chiefs between the Sutlej and the Jumna should be supported. But this object was not to be gained by mere passive resistance. "A consequence of our refusing our assent to Runjeet's proposal," wrote Lord Minto, "must be the necessity of our affording open and immediate protection to the Sikhs, and employing a military force for that purpose. For to declare that we do not consent to the proposed conquests, and at the same time to look on whilst they are achieved, is a contradiction calculated alike to alienate the Sikhs and to provoke the enmity of Runjeet Singh. That we should advance," he added, "a body of troops to the Sutlej, and take post on that river in concert and connection with the principal Sikh chiefs, I should not think in itself a disadvantage, but in our present circumstances the reverse."* The Governor-General did not conceal from himself that this measure might precipitate an open collision with Runjeet, but he was prepared to abide the result.

In the meanwhile, Runjeet Singh, having taken possession of Fureed-kote, was dragging the British mission hither and thither, still evidently desirous that its presence should seem to sanction his aggressive proceedings, until Metcalfe demanded that the Rajah should name some fitting place where the mission might remain encamped until Runjeet had completed his operations, and was in a position again to give himself uninterruptedly to the pending negotiations. After much further discussion leading to no result, and some wild propositions at which Metcalfe only laughed,† it was agreed that the British mission should

* *MS. Memoranda of Lord Minto.*

† Amongst others was a proposition to the effect that Metcalfe should return to Calcutta, taking with him one of the Sikh chiefs as Runjeet's wakeel (or agent), and finish the negotiations at the Presidency. This Metcalfe treated as a "humorous proposal." Another scheme put forth by the Sikhs was that two treaties

halt at Gongrona, a place between the Sutlej and the Jumna, about twenty miles south-east from Loodhianah, until Runjeet had done his work. The Sikh army was now moving upon Umballah, and thus bringing itself into dangerous proximity to our own frontier-station of Kurnal.*

A lull in the more strenuous activities of the mission enabled Charles Metcalfe not only to take a comprehensive survey of past transactions, to clear up in his letters to Government any uncertainties or obscurities which his previous communications might have presented, and to draw up elaborate reports on the character of Runjeet Singh and the resources of his country,† but also to devote

should be drawn up—one according to Runjeet's wishes, one according to our own—and that the latter should be held in pawn until redeemed by the ratification of the former! It was with reference to one of these conferences (on the 24th of October) that Metcalfe wrote that the confusion produced by the eagerness of eight Sikh councillors to declare their opinions was almost sublime. "I beg you," he said, "to conceive an assemblage of nine persons, in which eight are endeavouring by all manner of means to obtain a particular point from one—the ministers being all eager to display before their master their zeal in the cause, their skill and acuteness; and the picture will completely represent the conference, which was preceded by a present of a horse from the Rajah's stable. There was little argument on either side. The subject had been repeatedly discussed, and nothing new remained to be said."

* At one of the conferences between Metcalfe and the Sikh Ministers, the latter had been asked whether he considered that Kurnal belonged to the British Government.

† There is an amusing passage in one of these reports relative to Runjeet's appreciation of artillery, and the means by which he contrived to scrape his ordnance together. "The Rajah's attachment to guns," wrote Metcalfe to Government, "and his opinion of their weight, are both so great, that he will never miss an opportunity of obtaining a gun. If he learns that there is a gun in any fort, he cannot rest until he has taken the fort to get at the gun, or until the gun has been given up to him to save the fort. He immediately dismounts the gun from the wall and drags it

some time to his private correspondence. In the middle of November he had received the distressing intelligence of the death of his aunt Richardson, to whom he was deeply attached. Some letters written by him at this time to his afflicted uncle, and to his "dear and now, alas! only aunt," Mrs. Monson,* express the strength of his grief. He was eager at first to know, whether his "dear, dear aunt in her illness ever thought of him? With her mind," he added, "occupied by thoughts of her children and her beloved sisters, I cannot expect that she did." But all thoughts of his own sorrows passed away as he dwelt on the sufferings of the husband and sister, and prayed that they might be comforted and sustained by Him, who alone has power to wipe away all tears from our eyes. "May the Ruler of all things," he wrote to his uncle, "give you patience and fortitude to support you under the heavy pressure. 'And now, Lord, what is my hope, truly my hope is even in thee. In the midst of life we are in death. Of whom may we seek succour but of thee, O Lord? Blessed are the dead who die in the Lord, for they rest from their labours.'"†

Whilst Metcalfe, thus halting at Gongrona, was dividing his thoughts between his public business and his private sorrows, Runjeet was extending his dominion over the more helpless of the Cis-Sutlej chiefs. Many of them, unequal to resistance, acknowledged that they were his

after him, as an addition to his field train. He boasted to me once, that he had made the Rajah of Puttealah give him a fine gun, which the Rajah wished to rescue for 20,000 rupees."

* Mrs. Richardson and the Hon. Mrs. Monson, then widow of Colonel Monson, of whom Charles Metcalfe said, "he was always an affectionate uncle and kind friend to me," were sisters of Lady Metcalfe.

† *November* 1808, *Camp Gongrona.*—In this letter Metcalfe says: "If my mission should soon end, which is possible, I shall endeavour to join you at Banda to share your sadness."

subjects, that they held their possessions only by virtue of his grant, and contributed their guns to the Rajah's collection; whilst others obtained temporary immunity for themselves by aiding him in these acts of spoliation.* But he still had time to think of the British mission, wrote courteous letters to Metcalfe, "evinced a desire to be friendly and conciliatory;"† and was sincerely desirous to protect the mission against any inconvenience that might result from the turbulent character of the people surrounding their camp.‡ Before the end of November, the restless

* "Including," wrote Metcalfe to Government, "those chiefs who have attended him in this expedition, his sovereignty has been completely acknowledged by all the Sikh chiefs with two exceptions"—the Rajahs of Puttealah and Thanesur.

† "Being informed that Gongrona was not a pleasant situation, he wrote to me," said Metcalfe, "in the most civil manner, to request that I would move to another place, which was ascertained to be better; but finding Gongrona sufficiently agreeable, I did not think it necessary to move."

‡ "It happened," wrote Metcalfe, "that in taking the air one evening I was fired upon from a village by mistake. This trivial circumstance was reported to the Rajah and magnified. In consequence, he gave orders to the commanders of his infantry and guns, on detaching them from Shuhabad on their return to the Punjaub, to attend me, and wrote to me to desire that I would cause them to plunder and destroy any village that had behaved in a disrespectful manner. After thanking him for his kindness, I requested him to forgive a fault which had proceeded from inadvertency and the divided state of the country." This humane interference, however, had not at first the desired result. In a subsequent letter Metcalfe wrote: "The Rajah's infantry and guns have been at this place for some days. As they were sent by the Rajah for the avowed purpose of destroying certain villages which had been represented to him as having behaved in a disrespectful manner to me, I endeavoured to prevent their advance, but did not succeed, as Kureem Singh, the possessor of the tents of Gongrona, had a strong interest in persuading them to come on. On their arrival I had some difficulty in preventing their attacking the villages. The commanders informed me that

chief had sent back his infantry and his guns to Gongrona, and purposed, after a friendly interview with the Rajah of Putteealah, to make his way to Umritsur and Lahore, and there to rest himself in the lap of pleasure after the fatigues of war and the anxieties of public business.

It was at this time that Metcalfe learnt the results of the deliberations which had been held in Calcutta at the close of the preceding month. The Chief Secretary communicated to him that Lord Minto had determined to resist Runjeet's efforts to subjugate the Cis-Sutlej States, and that henceforth these petty principalities were to be under British protection. The letter which announced this important intelligence was followed by a communication to the same effect to Runjeet himself, sent through the Delhi Resident, couched in the ordinary language of diplomatic flattery, but sufficiently unmistakeable in its import and decided in its tone. The ambitious Sikh was now called upon to arrest his career of conquest in the country between the Sutlej and the Jumna, and to surrender the places which he had recently wrested from the petty chiefs. But Metcalfe, still anxious to achieve the objects of his mission without violence, and believing that Runjeet was already on his way back to the capital, determined to delay the communication of the Governor-General's resolution, in the hope that the Rajah's withdrawal from the scene of his recent conquests might appear rather a spontaneous act upon his part than one forced upon him by the implied

they had positive orders to plunder the villages, and put to death the inhabitants. I saw their instructions under the seal of Runjeet Singh, giving orders for their guidance, and even laying down the plan of attack, and giving intelligence of the force that they might expect to be opposed to them. Fortunately, the Rajah had written other instructions, desiring them to obey my orders, which have enabled me by positive commands and written injunctions to restrain them until the result of my reference to the Rajah may be known."

menaces of the British Government.* The uncertainty and the impulsiveness which marked Runjeet's conduct, rendered Metcalfe, however, sceptical of the real intentions of the Rajah; and doubting whether he would return immediately to his capital, he wrote to him that he desired an interview at Eesroo, which lay on the road to Umritsur. The request was readily granted, but before the appointed time Runjeet had once more changed his resolution. He was tired of business. He was eager again to enjoy the delights of the wine-cup and the zenana. He had exchanged turbans as a token of amity with the Rajah of Puttealah; and he had now little else to do. So he wrote to Metcalfe proposing a meeting on the Sutlej. But before the British Envoy had reached the banks of the river, Runjeet had again changed his mind, and was moving in hot haste on the wings of love to Umritsur. His confidential physician-minister, Uzeezoodeen, was left behind to invite Metcalfe to follow him; and on the 10th of December the British mission arrived at the holy city.

The delay had not been without its uses. The instructions despatched to Metcalfe by the Supreme Government

* *Mr. Metcalfe to Mr. Edmonstone, November* 27, 1808.—"When I received your instructions of the 31st of October, I had every reason to expect the instant return of Runjeet Singh to Lahore from his own communications to me, as well as from general opinion and actual appearances. His infantry and guns, which generally form his advanced guard, were encamped in this place, which is within a forced march from the Sutlej; and the Rajah himself was lightly equipped with the seeming and avowed intention of advancing. Under these circumstances, it appeared to me that if the Rajah should immediately re-cross the Sutlej with his army, and remove his troops from all positions menacing to the safety and independence of the chiefs whom it is the intention of Government to protect, one of the most important objects of my instructions would be obtained without any immediate interruption of amicable negotiation, and time would be gained for the execution of the arrangements destined for the defence of this country."

at the end of October, and the letter to Runjeet Singh sent through the Delhi Resident, had been of a more peremptory and decided character than Lord Minto upon further consideration considered it expedient to confirm. The letter to the Rajah had now been modified into a communication less menacing in tone, and containing a less undisguised exposition of the intentions of the British Government. And when Mr. Edmonstone forwarded a copy of it to Metcalfe, he wrote a private letter, briefly explaining to him, in the following sentences, Lord Minto's wishes regarding the future conduct of his negotiations :—

"You will see that it is wished you should remain; and I will state in very few words what is intended. Government is satisfied that Runjeet Singh will never be the cordial friend of the British Government; an engagement with him for co-operation would be mere waste paper. His character, conduct, and views are such as to render it for our interest that his government were subverted. But we shall do nothing to promote that object. It would hardly be justifiable to do so; at the same time, it is desirable not to be embarrassed with engagements which might compel us to assist him against internal rebellion. Our object must be at present to remain as free as possible without breaking with Runjeet. It is not, therefore, desirable to accelerate the negotiation. The longer it is kept in suspense the better; and on the plea of awaiting the result of your report to Government that he has withdrawn his army, disclaimed any interruption to the Cabul mission, and treated you as an accredited minister of a great state ought to be treated, you can properly and plausibly suspend the conclusion of engagements. Though I apprehend from your despatch No. 29, just received, that you may have gone too far under your former instructions to admit of this course. Troops will be sent to the frontier as was at first announced in the letter to Runjeet; but it is now thought best to suspend any notification to him of this arrangement, so you are to know nothing of these matters."

On the evening of his arrival at Umritsur, Metcalfe, taking with him the Governor-General's letter, visited

Runjeet Singh. But the Rajah was in no mood for business. He was in the midst of a riotous career of self-indulgence. Instead of attending to the affairs of state which had called the British Envoy to his presence, he sent for his dancing-girls; and soon afterwards, the wonted strong drinks were introduced. In vain did Metcalfe call the attention of the Rajah to the business on which he had come; in vain did he speak of the Governor-General's letter of which he was the bearer. Runjeet was willing to receive the letter, but he was not prepared to read it. "The evening was devoted to mirth and pleasure." The Rajah was in a genial humour—full of cordiality towards his English visitor; familiar in manner, friendly in speech. Metcalfe, with right diplomatic address, entered into the spirit of the scene, within the limits of becoming hilarity; and when he took his departure, it was obvious to him that the Rajah and his friends were "incapacitated for business."*

But Runjeet Singh, drinking and revelling with the unopened letter of the Governor-General beside him, was as a man singing and dancing upon a loaded mine. Whether he had any suspicion of its actual contents, and was disinclined to mar the pleasurable excitement of the life to which he had now temporarily abandoned himself, content to live in the rapture of the present moment, and to lull all corroding anxieties to rest, can be only matter of conjecture. But the morrow passed away, and still Metcalfe heard nothing of the effects of the letter. So he wrote the Rajah a note under his own hand—a note giving no uncertain sound, but clearly and decisively stating the stage to which the discussion had now been brought, the various offences which had been committed by the Rajah, and the dangers which stared him in the face; and con-

* *Mr. Metcalfe to Mr. Edmonstone, December* 11, 1808.

cluding with the following specific declaration of the views of the British Government;—

"I am directed by the Right Hon. the Governor-General to protest against the invasion of the country between the Sutlej and the Jumna, in the name of the British Government; and further, to declare that the British Government cannot acknowledge any right in the Maha-rajah to any territories that he may have taken possession of situated between the Sutlej and the Jumna since the first reference of this question to the British Government.

"Moreover, the Governor-General feels himself authorised to expect, and entertains no doubt, that the Maha-rajah will restore all the places that he has taken possession of since that period to the former possessors, and will confine his army to the right bank of the Sutlej, since he can have no object in maintaining it on the left bank, except to overawe and subjugate the chiefs situated between that river and the Jumna, who are now declared to be under the protection of the British Government.

"In expressing these sentiments, I am directed to inform the Maha-rajah that the British Government is desirous of maintaining the most amicable relations with his Government, and wishes that the friendship subsisting between the two states may daily improve and increase. The British Government desires no country for itself. It has enough, and its only ambition is to improve the territories which it possesses, and to promote the happiness of its subjects. It wishes to live in amity with all mankind. It cannot consent to the subjugation of chiefs who are closely connected with it, and have claims upon it for protection. At the same time, it entertains the most friendly designs towards the Maha-rajah, with whom, notwithstanding the just causes of complaint which the Maha-rajah's conduct has afforded, it is anxious to cultivate the relations of intimate and cordial friendship.

"I trust that the Maha-rajah will duly appreciate the friendly sentiments of the Right Hon. the Governor-General, and meet them with reciprocal cordiality and confidence, so as to give an assurance that for the future the rights and privileges of the representative of the British Government shall be respected according to the established usage between states, and that the intercourse between the two Governments shall be carried on in the spirit of mutual confidence and friendship."

Of this unmistakeable communication Metcalfe's confidential moonshee was the bearer. It was soon apparent that the contents of the Governor-General's letter were utterly unknown to the Rajah, who, on perusing the Envoy's note, seemed to stagger under it, as though under the influence of a "sudden shock." But it was a shock of a salutary nature. It seemed to sober him. He spoke of the communication more humbly and more reasonably than, judging by his foregone behaviour, there was any ground to expect. He appeared sensible of the impropriety of his conduct towards the mission, and believed, or pretended to believe, that the determination of the British Government had been forced upon it by his want of courtesy towards its representative, rather than by his bearing towards the petty states. And he indulged the hope that a more favourable reply to his demands would speedily be despatched to his court.

The following day was fixed upon for an interview with the British Envoy; but it brought, after the old fashion, only excuses for delay. The Rajah had determined to proceed at once to Lahore, and he invited Metcalfe to accompany him. It was evidently Runjeet's object to gain time. Other thoughts were distracting his mind. There were dangers and difficulties bristling at his own door. He had hoped for a little while in the arms of his favourite mistress to forget all of royalty except its sensual delights. But that which was to have been to him only a source of refreshment and repose, became the exciting cause of unexpected trouble and alarm. His favourite was a Mussulmanee dancing-girl. It may have been in the plenitude of her Mahomedan zeal—or it may have been in the mere wantonness of power—that either by force or persuasion, she had recently converted a Hindoo to the faith of Islam, or at least subjected him to its external ritualities. The act, from whatever feeling it may have resulted, threw Umritsur into a ferment of excitement. The shops of the holy city were closed. The priests of the great temple issued their manifestoes, and forbade the people, under a ban of excommunication, to open them and return to their wonted business. The houses of the Mussulmanee dancing-girls—in expiation of the offences of one of their tribe—were plundered by the outraged Hindoos. There was a great strife between the temporal and the spiritual power; and the former was worsted in the encounter. So Runjeet was fain to withdraw himself from the scene of turmoil, and to make his escape to Lahore.*

And thither Metcalfe speedily followed him. But the change of scene did not induce a change of conduct. Runjeet still maintained a cautious silence, and "found fresh excuses for delaying his answer to the demands that had been made upon him" by the British Government. At length, on the 17th of December, just as the Envoy was writing a letter, peremptorily calling upon the Rajah to declare his intentions without longer delay, a message of invitation came from the Sikh, and Metcalfe proceeded to his presence. But even then the old reserve was upon him. Runjeet appeared careworn and thoughtful, and little inclined to address himself to affairs of state. His troubles had followed him from Umritsur to Lahore. The Hindoos were thronging round the walls of his palace, and sitting *dhurna* at his gates.† He was ready, therefore, with more excuses, and eager for more delay. He told Metcalfe that "his attention had been much engaged by the disturbances at Umritsur and Lahore; that he had had to dismiss his chiefs and followers to their homes; that several of those with whom he was in the habit of consulting were absent, and that, to say the truth, after four

* *Mr. Metcalfe to Mr. Edmonstone, December* 14, 1808.

† To sit "*dhurna*" is to sit in fasting and prayer at a man's door—an expressive kind of practical curse.

months' campaigning he felt "an inclination for some rest."* And all that Metcalfe, pressing him sorely, could extract from him was the old promise that he would see him, and make "a full communication on the following day."

But with the new day, after the old fashion, came new excuses. Runjeet's ministers had tried to reconcile Metcalfe to the eccentricities of their chief; but the English gentleman had answered with becoming firmness that, although the eccentricities were sufficiently apparent, he could not admit that they furnished any justification for is conduct. In vain they pleaded that Runjeet had never been habituated to control—that flushed with continual success he had ever regarded himself, and himself alone, as the arbiter of his conduct—that he was a man of a headstrong and ungovernable nature, and that some allowances ought to be made for him. Metcalfe was not to be driven from the position he had taken up. The business in hand, he said, was an affair between two states, and no considerations of personal character should be admitted in justification of conduct which violated the rights and lowered the dignity of the Government which he represented.†

* *Mr. Metcalfe to Mr. Edmonstone, December* 18, 1808.

† The passage in Metcalfe's correspondence descriptive of this scene merits quotation. "I asked," he wrote to the Chief Secretary, "what explanation I should offer to my Government for the delay which had taken place on the part of the Rajah. Imaum-ood-deen begged me to bear in mind that the Rajah, from the earliest age, had been without control; that his disposition had, in consequence, become ungovernable; that he had throughout life acted according to his pleasure; that God had prospered all his undertakings; that he had acquired a habit of acting without reference to the inclination of others; and that allowances ought to be made for these considerations. I observed, that the Rajah's eccentricities were evident enough, and that I had been often amused by them; that they would, indeed, be very entertaining if they did not interfere so much with important business; but that I could not state them to my Government to account for the Rajah's conduct,

And he desired the Sikh Minister to inform his master that he was surprised at the repeated excuses he had received, and impatient of further delay. But in spite of this, on the following morning, Runjeet's confidential advisers again appeared before Metcalfe as the bearers of further excuses, and to request one more day's delay. Everything, they announced, was in train for the conclusion of the business, and now, at last, procrastination was at an end.* There was, indeed, no longer a pretext for evasion; and so, on the morning of the 20th of December, the long-delayed conference appeared to be on the point of accomplishment. But instead of meeting the Rajah himself, Metcalfe met only a large assembly of his councillors. There was a long and animated, but an unsatisfactory debate. The young English statesman had a host of antagonists, but he was more than a match for them all. He told the Sikh chiefs that the plan which the British Government purposed to pursue was conceived in a friendly spirit, and to be prosecuted in a friendly manner; but that the determination which had been announced was fixed and irrevocable, and that it were well that this should be understood by their master.†

as any consideration for them would be inadmissible. The British Government, I remarked, could only judge of the Rajah by his acts, and if these were improper, could not think of justifying them by any reference to his education. I pressed upon the attention of Imaum-ood-deen that it was necessary for the Maha-rajah to reflect that every matter pending was between Government and Government; and that it was indispensable that he should lay aside the notion that he might act according to his own pleasure without regard to the rights and dignity of the British Government.

* One of the excuses advanced by Runjeet was founded on the absence of a councillor—Mith Singh—in whom he professed great faith. This man had been summoned to Lahore, and was now in attendance on the Rajah.

† "I was pressed," wrote Metcalfe, "to say distinctly whether the demands of the British Government were meant to be made

The object of this preliminary conference was plainly to sound Metcalfe. But the councillors retired carrying with them nothing that was likely to soothe the apprehensions of their chief. And when, at last, on the following day, the British Envoy met Runjeet himself, all that the wily Sikh could do was to repeat oft-refuted arguments, and to put unprofitable questions. The Rajah asked why we called upon him to withdraw from the left bank of the Sutlej—why we demanded that he should restore the places he had already captured? And Metcalfe answered plainly and firmly, with undeniable logic, that the British Government intended to take those principalities under its protection—and how could they be protected when the Rajah threatened them with his armies, or had absolutely brought them under his rule? But still a decisive answer was not to be elicited. In general terms the Envoy was told that an arrangement would be made honourable to both nations; but Metcalfe saw plainly that no arrangement was likely to be made without an appeal to arms.

amicably or not. I replied that that question was answered by so many circumstances, that I wondered it could be put. Why, I asked, was I here? Why had the Governor-General addressed a friendly letter to the Rajah? Why had I given in a long explanatory note? Why had the Maha-rajah expressed his satisfaction at the contents of these communications, and observed that friendly remonstrances could not be produced without regard? Of course, I said, the demands that I had presented were made with friendly intentions. In order to prevent the construction that might be assumed that my consent would be obtained to a protracted discussion of the respective rights of the British Government and the Rajah of Lahore to political supremacy in the country between the Jumna and the Sutlej, and to convince all present that it would be in vain to agitate that question, I declared decidedly that with respect to the demands that I had made, I must persist in them, and could not relax in any degree: that the orders of my Government were final, and that I would not exercise any discretion."

A crisis, indeed, was now fast approaching. It has been seen that the British Government had announced to Metcalfe its intention of moving forward a body of troops to take post upon the Sutlej. This announcement had not yet been made to Runjeet; but the time for a full revelation of our intentions seemed now to have arrived. It was doubtful, indeed, whether rumours of the threatened movement had not already reached the Sikh ruler, for he was collecting troops, seemingly in anticipation of a coming struggle. It appeared expedient, therefore, to Metcalfe to warn the military authorities of the probability of resistance being offered to the demands of the British Government. So he wrote a letter to the Commander-in-Chief, setting forth, distinctly and emphatically, the grounds on which he based his belief in the likelihood of a speedy collision. Having despatched this letter, his next care was to intimate distinctly and decisively to Runjeet Singh that the British Government purposed, without further delay, to advance a military force to the banks of the Sutlej. The game was now nearly played out. On the 22nd of December the British Envoy and the Sikh Rajah were again face to face. The communication was made. Runjeet told his attendant chiefs to consider of the matter; and, under the influence of self-control such as he rarely exercised, fell into friendly conversation with the English gentleman. Several questions were asked concerning the British detachment—what would be its strength?—where it would be posted—whether at Loodhianah, or what other place? To all of this Metcalfe answered, that the details of the movement were matters of future consideration. A hint from the consulting chiefs here drew the Rajah aside. A brief conversation between them ensued. The Runjeet, having ordered Uzeezoodeen to state his opinions to the British Envoy, left the room, mounted his horse, and with what appeared to Metcalfe "surprising levity," began prancing about the court-yard of his residence.* There was good reason afterwards to think that this was less an indication of levity than of the strong feeling which was working within him.

Whilst Runjeet was caracolling about the court-yard, Uzeezoodeen delivered his master's message. It was not a conciliatory one; and it was not given in a conciliatory manner. The Rajah, he said, had flattered himself that the intercourse between the two states would be conducive to his welfare; but instead of this, in reply to a friendly application, he had received a message of so extraordinary a nature, that he did not know what to make of it. What was the use, it was asked, of a small post on the Sutlej?—surely such a demonstration would not deter the French from

* Metcalfe's words are: "On a hint from the party aside, the Rajah withdrew to join them; and after a consultation, sent them to me with a message, and proceeded himself with surprising levity to mount his horse and prance about the court-yard of his residence." I am the more particular in giving the exact words of the writer, inasmuch as that this story has been variously narrated, and has obtained, perhaps, a wider currency than any other incident in Metcalfe's life. The current version of the story is this, which I find in a leading article of the *Times* newspaper, written in December, 1839: "When these terms were propounded to him, Runjeet, after a short and futile attempt to overbear the British Ambassador, rushed out of an apartment, an elevated summer-room, in which the conference had taken place, and in an incredibly short space of time, Sir Charles Metcalfe saw him on horseback, at the head of his immediate suite, galloping in the most furious manner over the plain below. When he had thus digested his spleen, he returned, and after telling the Envoy that he always took this extraordinary anodyne under extreme vexation, expressed his determination to submit implicitly to the requirements of the British Government." This story is so much more striking and picturesque than that which I have given in the text, that I have been really sorry to substitute the homelier version which I have found in Metcalfe's own handwriting, written on the day after the incident occurred.—[See also Appendix.]

advancing. To this Metcalfe replied, that all idea of deterring the French was out of the question—that he had made certain distinct propositions to the Rajah, and that he called for an answer equally distinct. The decided tone in which he spoke was not without its effect on the Sikh councillors. Runjeet had by this time dismounted and seated himself in another chamber, where Uzeezoodeen and his associates waited upon him with Metcalfe's message. What passed there can only be conjectured. The consultation was a long one; and when the Ministers returned, their bearing was strangely altered. They spoke now with an affable manner, and in a softened tone. They said that the plan of advancing a British detachment to the banks of the Sutlej would not be opposed by the Rajah, if it were done in concert with him, and in a friendly manner. The answer was, that if the requisitions of the British Government, from which the Envoy would on no account recede, were complied with, everything would be done in a friendly manner. Again the councillors sought the Rajah; and again, after a protracted consultation, they returned to the room where Metcalfe was quietly awaiting them. The answer they brought back was more satisfactory than he could have anticipated even in his most sanguine moments. The Rajah, they said, was confident of our friendly intentions, and agreed to all our proposals. "And so," wrote Metcalfe, "the demands that I had presented, respecting which I had not been able for a fortnight to procure the least answer, were now treated as if they were mere trifles with which there was not the smallest difficulty in complying."

But these were mere idle words—vague generalities meaning nothing. On the same evening a deputation waited on Metcalfe to inform him that the proposal to advance troops to the Sutlej was so extraordinary, that the Rajah could not give any definite answer to the requisitions of the British Government until he had consulted with his chiefs; that he therefore purposed to proceed on the following day to Umritsur; and that he requested the British Envoy to follow him there. At this, Metcalfe, wontedly so calm in his outward demeanour, fired up with becoming indignation. He thought, with the prophet of old, that he "did well to be angry." He denounced the conduct of the Rajah as mere trickery to gain time—trickery often repeated and now well understood. He declared that such conduct was disrespectful in the extreme to the British Government; that if the Rajah determined to march, in the midst of the negotiation, he could not control him; but that against such a proceeding he earnestly and indignantly protested.

The remonstrance was not without its effect. The precipitate movement to Umritsur was abandoned; and the negotiations were resumed. But there was still the old system of chicanery at work—still the old excuses and the old delays. Foiled in his attempts either to overbear or over-reach Metcalfe in oral discussion, Runjeet now resorted to epistolary communication. First of all he attempted a compromise; but the young English statesman was resolute to submit to no half-measures. He called for the fulfilment of the requisitions of the British Government without stint or reservation; and his unshaken firmness ere long achieved the desired victory. Little by little, Runjeet, not without fresh displays of procrastination and evasion, yielded to the demands of the British Envoy. He saw that the announcement of the intended advance of a British detachment was not an empty menace. Metcalfe, it has been seen, was in communication with the Commander-in-Chief, whose head-quarters were in Saharunpore; and under instructions from his Excellency, a detachment had been ordered for service on the banks of the Sutlej. This detachment was placed under the command of the fittest man in the army that could have been nominated for the performance of such a duty. It was placed under the command of Colonel David Ochterlony. Early in January it was ordered to advance.

The first service to be performed by this force was the expulsion of the Sikh troops from Umballah, where a considerable body had been for some time posted. But the Rajah promised to withdraw his men to his own side of the river, and desired Metcalfe to consider it as done. But performance in this case, as in others, lagged far behind promise; and Metcalfe, weary of all this falsehood and fraud, came to the determination that the time had come for his departure from Runjeet's court, if the state of the military preparations on the frontier seemed to warrant so decided a step. But it was now the policy of both parties to temporise. Runjeet was collecting troops, and eager to gain time. General Hewitt was making his dispositions, and eager also to gain time. Metcalfe was recommended to temporise; and by delay the war was averted. Awed by the resolute bearing of his antagonists, the Sikh began slowly and reluctantly to fulfil the conditions demanded by the British Government. On the 6th of January, one of Runjeet's chiefs was despatched to Umballah, to recall the troops posted there, and to make restitution of the place to its rightful owner.

In consequence of this, negotiations were resumed at Umritsur, to which place the court and the mission quietly proceeded in the middle of January. Presuming on what he had done in the way of concession, Runjeet demanded that now a treaty of general amity should be concluded. But Metcalfe pointed out that other conditions were yet to be fulfilled; that if Umballah were restored, Kheir and Fureed-kote were not; and he demanded the concession of all the territory acquired since the arrival of the mission. It would take long to tell how Runjeet promised and broke his promises; and how from day to day the restitution of these places was delayed; how the Sikh continued to demand a treaty, and how the British envoy called for the fulfilment of the conditions necessary to the attainment of what he sought. The month of January passed away; and the month of February passed away. Military preparations on both sides were advancing; but still Metcalfe remained at Runjeet's court—still the negotiations appeared every morning to be approaching a favourable issue, and still every evening it was clear that these appearances had been most delusive.*

It was whilst affairs were in this state that an incident occurred which awakened Runjeet to a sense of the danger which he would incur by a collision with the British troops. At the end of February the annual festival of the *Mohurrum* was celebrated by the Mahomedan sepoys of Metcalfe's escort. It is the custom of the followers of the Prophet to spend upon this great occasion considerable sums of money on the construction and decoration of gigantic cars, called tazeeahs, which are paraded about for several days in a noisy, obtrusive manner, to the great delight of all true Mahomedans, who pride themselves upon

* Among other complaints that Runjeet made, was one to the effect that Metcalfe treated him like a jageerdar (or pensioner). "He (Runjeet) observed (to Hafoozoodeen) on my note, that when he made any proposal, I replied that I had no authority; but when I brought forward my own proposals, I issued my commands to him as authoritatively as if he were only a jageerdar."—"Considering," wrote Metcalfe, "the efforts which I have always made to conciliate the Rajah—considering the patience and forbearance which I have exercised from first to last in my communications with him—considering that I have been barely acquitted by my own government of the fault of carrying moderation to a disgraceful length—and considering, moreover, that the late proceedings at this Court have put my patience to a severer trial than it had ever before undergone, I did not expect this charge from the Rajah."—[*Mr. Metcalfe to Mr. Edmonstone, January* 4, 1809.]

the grandeur of the ceremony, and are little disposed to be stinted in their demonstrations. Now the Mussulman sepoys of Metcalfe's escort, according to the custom of their sect, made a tazeeah at the appointed time, and paraded it about, with the usual ceremonies, in the neighbourhood of the mission camp. For three or four days this went on without interruption; and then Metcalfe was informed that the display of the tazeeah gave dire offence to the priests of the great temple of Umritsur. Had he known this before, he would have prohibited the celebration of the festival, however unpopular the prohibition might have been to all the Mahomedans in his camp. As it was—as the ceremonies were now nearly over—he contented himself with giving orders that they should be performed for the future in the most noiseless and unobtrusive manner, and that the tazeeah should not be any more paraded about in public. All this was done in concert with Runjeet Singh, who condemned the bigotry of the priests; and it was hoped that no evil consequences would arise from this periodical display of Mahomedan zeal. "I did everything that could be done," said Metcalfe, reporting the circumstances to Government, "to prevent any offence being taken, except destroying the tazeeah itself. That could not be done without exciting great indignation among the Mahomedans; and I had a right to expect that within the precincts of the British camp my attendants would be protected by the Government in the free exercise of their religion."

Still further to prevent the possibility of a collision, it was agreed between Metcalfe and Runjeet that the former should restrain the sepoys from going into the town, and that the latter should prevent the people from entering the mission camp. The English gentleman performed his part of the compact; the Sikh ruler did not. On the morning of the 25th of February a party of religious fanatics—

half-soldiers, half-devotees—known as Akalis, marched out of the town, with drums beating and colours flying, followed by a surging rabble, intent upon the plunder of the British mission. As they neared our camp, the escort, headed by Captain Popham, was drawn up in front of it, whilst Metcalfe sent out some persons to parley with the excited Sikhs. Still, however, they continued to advance in the same menacing attitude, and presently opened a brisk fire on the British camp. It took immediate effect. Our men were dropping in the ranks. There was now no time to be lost. Popham proposed that he should advance upon his assailants; and with Metcalfe's sanction he attacked them. The movement was a spirited and a successful one. The Sikhs were seen flying in confusion, and seeking shelter under the walls of the town.

The disturbance was immediately known to Runjeet, who rode out to the British camp, and exerted himself to quell the tumult. But all his endeavours could not quiet the fanatics. A party of Akalis again assembled and marched out of the town, threatening another attack on the mission. During the rest of the day, and all through the night, they continued in force upon the plain; so Runjeet sent out a body of his own troops to protect the British camp from further outrage. On the following day it was removed to a greater distance from the town, where it remained unplundered and unmolested, whilst the ceremonies of the Mohurrum were prosecuted to the end in the quiet manner originally intended.

The blood that was shed upon this occasion was not shed in vain. Runjeet, who had before seen our sepoys in the exercise of mimic war, now saw them in the stern realities of action. He learnt, for the first time, what was their temper—what was their steadiness, what their discipline in actual warfare. This little handful of British soldiers had routed a vastly superior body of Sikhs; and Runjeet began to ask himself how, if the people of Hindostan, drilled in the English fashion, could do such things, the English themselves must fight; and how it would fare with him if he were to meet many thousands of them on the banks of the Sutlej, supported by their far-reaching guns.

So, although this disturbance of course afforded a pretext for some further evasions and delays, Runjeet, beset by obstinate doubts and painful self-questionings, soon came to the conclusion that a war with the Feringhees was an event not much to be desired. But still it was not in the nature of the man to proceed to the performance of his past promises in a plain, straightforward manner. The old shifts, however, could not serve him much longer. Our military preparations were advancing; and already our attitude was an imposing one. Ochterlony had taken post on the Sutlej, and had issued a proclamation, declaring all the Sikh states upon the left bank of the river to be under British protection* A strong body of troops, under General St. Leger, was ready to move forward to his support. Nor was it only his confidence in these military preparations which, at this time, impelled Metcalfe to assume a bolder tone in all his negotiations. The great object for which he had been despatched to Lahore had now ceased to exist. The whirligig of Time had rendered an anti-Gallican alliance with the rulers of the Punjaub a matter of small concern to the British-Indian Government.† It little mattered now whether Runjeet

* The proclamation bears date February 9, 1809.

† These altered circumstances were duly announced to Runjeet. Writing, subsequently, a letter of recapitulation, Metcalfe said: "Immediately after I had the honour of receiving your despatch of the 23rd of January, I informed Runjeet Singh, at a conference which I had with him, that I had been instructed to intimate to him that authentic intelligence had been received of the French having suffered repeated defeats in Europe from his Majesty's armies and those of his allies; and of their being in embarrassments,

were our enemy or our friend. From the path of the British Envoy this change in the state of our European politics cleared away a jungle of difficulties and perplexities. He had now only to support the dignity of the great nation which he represented; and he was not slow to recommend the most decided measures, even to the extreme one of the invasion of the Punjaub. It was with no small delight that he flung behind him the thought of all further compromises and concessions, and prepared to give the signal for the immediate commencement of war.

But awed by the proximity of an event which must have overwhelmed him in disaster and disgrace, and for ever checked his career of ambition, Runjeet was now fulfilling slowly and reluctantly the behests of the British Government. In the early part of March, Kheir was restored to its legitimate owners; and now the restitution of Fureed-kote alone remained. A series of incidents of the most trivial character delayed the accomplishment of this; but it was plain to Metcalfe that the Rajah really designed to fulfil his promise, though he was thwarted by the trickery or the contumacy of those who, perhaps, desired to embroil him in a war with the British. In January he had talked vauntingly of discussing the restitution of Fureed-kote with his chiefs, at the head of his army on the banks of the Sutlej. But he was now, in March, again abandoning himself to pleasure, and rather suffering by his remissness, than really designing or desiring, the delays which obstructed the fulfilment of his promise.

which would render impracticable the prosecution of those hostile projects against this country, against which it was the object of my mission to provide—that, consequently, there was no necessity for the conclusion of the treaty which I had formerly proposed, or for any specific engagements between the two states, who were already bound by the relations of amity and friendship." The announcement had not much effect upon Runjeet. Metcalfe was obliged to acknowledge that "the Rajah did not express the disappointment which he had expected."

From this pleasant forgetfulnesss Metcalfe roused him by a missive, which flashed the sunlight into his sleeping face. "The Maha-rajah," he wrote to him on the 26th of March, "is revelling in delight in the Shalimar gardens, unmindful of the duties of friendship. What friendship requires is not done; nor is it doing. I entertained a great desire and hope that the relations of friendship might be firmly established through my mediation. I have nothing now remaining in my power but to require leave to depart. I, therefore, in the name of the British Government, require my dismissal, and trust that the Maha-rajah will furnish me with a proper escort to conduct me to the British armies, and prevent any aggression on the part of the Maha-rajah's army on the way."

To this Runjeet replied that the delights of the garden of friendship far exceeded the delights of a garden of roses—that the demand of the British Envoy for an escort would certainly excite great surprise—and that what he desired should immediately be done. And steps were certainly taken to do it. But just at that point of consummation, new difficulties supervened. A dispute arose about the grain in the fort; and the party sent to hand over the place to its old legitimate owners, retired without accomplishing their object. But Runjeet saw that any further obstructions would work grievously to his detriment. Metcalfe had written to General St. Leger desiring him to expel the occupants of Fureed-kote, and hinted to the Rajah that there was yet time to prevent this display of force. Throughout the whole of these protracted negotiations, no such potential argument had been used, though Runjeet now protested against it. "I must observe," he wrote with a hypocritical *naïveté* which is very diverting, "that when matters are settled in an amicable and friendly way, to talk of armies and such things is neither necessary nor pleasing to my friendly disposition." But the "talk of armies" effected at once what might, by dallying in the "garden of friendship," have been long delayed; and on the 5th of April, Metcalfe wrote to the Chief Secretary, "I have the honour to inform you, that Fureed-kote was finally surrendered to the right owners on the 2nd instant."

So now, after long delays and repeated evasions—after a systematic display of the most pitiful tortuosity, which now excited the anger and now the contempt of Metcalfe, and rendered necessary the exercise not only of consummate ability and address, but of the highest patience and forbearance—all that the British Government demanded was done by the Sikh ruler. And then came the question of the treaty. Whilst on the banks of the Sutlej time was being wasted in the manufacture of difficulties about the surrender of Fureed-kote, on the banks of the Hooghly Lord Minto and his councillors were discussing the expediency of concluding engagements of general amity with Runjeet Singh. At first it seemed advisable to them, now that the danger of European invasion had passed away, not to encumber the Government with any treaties which might embarrass their future proceedings. But they subsequently considered, that in the event of all our requisitions being complied with by the Sikh chief, it might be in some sort an act of justice to him to grant the treaty which Metcalfe had led him to expect, and which he urged the Supreme Government to allow;* whilst at the same

* This intention was first announced to Metcalfe in a private letter from Mr. Edmonstone, dated March 14, 1809: "Your letter of the 15th of February was received on the 11th, and it was yesterday resolved to grant a treaty to Runjeet Singh, of general amity, containing, however, some conditions respecting his troops on this side the Sutlej. I had occasion to draw up a memorandum on the subject, and to state in substance the same arguments which I found so ably stated in your letter, No. 69, which did not arrive till to-day.

time no great harm could result from it if it were unencumbered with inconvenient details. In accordance with these more mature considerations, instructions were sent on the 13th of March to the British Envoy, giving him authority to conclude a treaty with the Rajah, and forwarding to him the following draft:—

Draft of a Treaty between the British Government and the Rajah of Lahore.

"Whereas certain differences which had arisen between the British Government and the Rajah of Lahore have been happily and amicably adjusted, and both parties being anxious to maintain the relations of perfect amity and concord, the following articles of treaty, which shall be binding on the heirs and successors of the two parties, have been concluded, by the agency of C. T. Metcalfe, Esq., on the part of the British Government, and of [ ], on the part of Rajah Runjeet Singh.*

"Art. 1. Perpetual friendship shall subsist between the British Government and the State of Lahore; the latter shall be considered, with respect to the former, to be on the footing of the most favoured powers, and the British Government will have no concern with the territories and subjects of the Rajah to the northward of the river Sutlej.†

"Art. 2. The Rajah will never maintain in the territory *which he occupies* [occupied by him and his dependents]‡ on the left

* In the preamble of the ratified treaty it runs: "By Rajah Runjeet Singh on his own part, and by the agency of Charles Theophilus Metcalfe, Esquire, on the part of the British Government."

† In the original draft of the treaty in Mr. Edmonstone's handwriting, there is this addition to the first article; "And on the other hand the Rajah renounces all claims to sovereignty over the Sikh chiefs to the southward of that river, and all right of interference in their concerns." But this passage was subsequently erased; it was of too general a character; for the Rajah, as the next article intimates, still held certain tracts of territory, acquired before the arrival of the mission, on the left or southern bank of the Sutlej.

‡ The words in brackets were inserted by Metcalfe in the place of those printed in italics.

bank of the river Sutlej more troops than are necessary for the internal duties of that territory, nor commit or suffer any encroachments on the possessions or rights of the chiefs in its vicinity.

"Art. 3. In the event of a violation of any of the preceding articles, or of a departure from the rules of friendship [on the part of either state],* this treaty shall be considered to be null and void.

"Art. 4. This treaty, consisting of four articles, having been settled and concluded at [ ], on the [ ] day of [ ],† Mr. C. T. Metcalfe has delivered to the Rajah of Lahore a copy of the same in English and Persian, under his seal and signature, and the Rajah has delivered another copy of the same under his seal and signature, and Mr. C. T. Metcalfe engages to procure, within the space of two months, a copy of the same duly ratified by the Right Honourable the Governor-General in Council, on the receipt of which by the Rajah the present treaty shall be deemed complete and binding on both parties, and the copy of it now delivered to the Rajah shall be returned.

"N. B. EDMONSTONE,
"Chief Secretary."

On the receipt of this draft, all his demands having by this time having been complied with, Metcalfe informed the Rajah that he was prepared to conclude a treaty of general amity with him. Runjeet received the announcement with undisguised delight. The treaty, he said, would silence and shame those who had been endeavouring to persuade him that the British Government entertained hostile designs against the Sikh territories. There was no room now for any further chicanery. Runjeet had nothing to gain by delay; so, on the 25th of April, 1809, this treaty was concluded at Umritsur; the blanks in the descriptive title being filled up with the name of Runjeet Singh himself.

* These words were inserted by Metcalfe at the request of the suspicious Rajah. It is remarkable that Cunningham, in his history of the Sikhs, gives the treaty, as ratified, without Metcalfe's insertions, which Government approved and adopted.

† At Umritsur, on the 25th of February.

The business of the mission was now fully accomplished;* so Metcalfe prepared to return to the British provinces. "I have this day," he wrote on the 2nd of May, made my first march from Umritsur towards the British territories, having finally taken leave of Runjeet Singh. The departure of the mission took place with every essential mark of attention and respect on the part of the Rajah. He visited me on the 28th ultimo, and received an entertainment at my tents preparatory to our separation. I visited him on the 30th, accompanied by the gentlemen attached to the mission, and took leave publicly with the usual ceremonies. Both these meetings were convivial and pleasant; and the Rajah's behaviour was particularly friendly and agreeable. At his particular request I remained yesterday at Umritsur, and saw him once more in a private interview, at which his conversation

* It may be mentioned here that Government had originally intended that the advanced detachment should be withdrawn from the banks of the Sutlej. But on the earnest representations both of Metcalfe and Ochterlony the occupation of Loodhianah was continued, and from that time it became a frontier post. It may be doubted, however, whether this would have happened but for an accidental circumstance which caused Government to delay the withdrawal of the troops. Writing to Metcalfe privately on the 28th of May, Mr. Edmonstone says: "We have heard of the defeat of the King of Cabul's army in Cashmere, and anticipated Mr. Elphinstone's awkward situation. You will learn from Mr. Seton what has been done at Peshawur, and what has been ordered. This is an unfortunate turn of affairs, but the advantages of the mission will not have been entirely lost. I have written officially to head-quarters about leaving the detachment at Loodhianah until Elphinstone shall have passed, as its presence may possibly countenance his journey through the Punjaub; although I should think the Commander-in-Chief would not remove the post until he heard of the ratification of the treaty, notwithstanding the intimation contained in my last letter that the conclusion of the treaty would afford a favourable opportunity for the removal of the detachment."—[*MS. Correspondence.*]

was principally composed of expressions of anxiety for the permanent maintenance of friendship between the two states."

At this time Runjeet Singh was in the very flush and vigour of life. He lived for thirty years afterwards; but the treaty which he and Metcalfe signed at Umritsur was never violated during his supremacy in the Punjaub either by the English or the Sikhs. For a little while doubts and misgivings on either side may have overshadowed the relations subsisting between them; but confidence was soon established, and Runjeet learned to respect the nation which could send forth such representatives as the youthful Envoy, who had measured himself with him so bravely and so adroitly during the six months spent at his court. It is hard to say in how great a degree the long peace, which was maintained between two warlike and extending states in provocatory proximity to each other, is to be attributed to the firmness and address so conspicuous in the dealings of young Metcalfe with the wily and unscrupulous ruler of the Sikhs. But it would be impossible to read this account of the first mission to Lahore, imperfectly as it sets forth all its incidents,* without appreciating the difficulties with which he had to contend, and

* The contents of this chapter are derived from a vast mass of correspondence, which might have filled some volumes, principally Metcalfe's narrative letters, by no means diffusely written—and although this chapter has extended to a length which is disproportionate to the space of time over which the history extends, I have been compelled to exclude much which would have illustrated both the difficulties of Metcalfe's position, the address with which he encountered them, and the strange character and conduct of the man who, perhaps of all the princes and chiefs of India, made the name most familiar to English ears. It was during these six memorable months that Metcalfe's reputation was made. This was, indeed, the turning-point of his career. He went afterwards straight on to fame and fortune. And the biographer can hardly, therefore, lay too great a stress on such a passage of his life.

the consummate ability with which he overcame them. He had numbered at this time but twenty-three years. Yet the dreams of the Eton cloisters were already realised. He had "prescribed terms;" he had "concluded a peace."* What would he have accomplished at this stage of his career if he had returned to England, and entered "Lord Grenville's office?"

It need hardly be added, that Metcalfe's conduct at Lahore was approved and applauded by his employers. He was sustained and encouraged throughout by the praises of the Supreme Government, conveyed to him in the letters of the Chief Secretary; and he said that he was abundantly rewarded. In private and public letters alike, his zeal and ability were warmly commended. One sample of each will suffice. Writing privately to Metcalfe on the 27th of December, Mr. Edmonstone said, "I can add nothing material to the expressions already conveyed to you in an official form of the favourable sentiments which Government entertains of your general conduct in a situation perhaps as delicate, difficult, and responsible as any public agent was ever placed in. I can assure you that Government is perfectly satisfied of the difficulties and embarrassments which encompassed you, and admits that the course of conduct which you pursued was countenanced by the spirit of your instructions . . . . Upon the whole, your mind may enjoy all the satisfaction—a satisfaction which you, indeed, must amply merit, that can arise from the conviction that Government entertains the highest opinion of your zeal, ability, judgment, and exertions." And when the work was done and the treaty was exchanged, these commendations took official shape, and, taking a retrospect of all the past circumstances of the mission, the same high functionary thus finally announced to the departing Envoy the admira-

* See *ante*, page 8.

tion with which the Supreme Government contemplated his entire conduct: "During the course of your arduous ministry at the Court of Lahore, the Governor-General in Council has repeatedly had occasion to record his testimony of your zeal, ability, and address in the execution of the duties committed to your charge. His Lordship in Council, however, deems it an obligation of justice, at the close of your mission, generally to declare the high sense which he entertains of the distinguished merit of your services and exertions in a situation of more than ordinary importance, difficulty and responsibility, to convey to you the assurance of his high approbation, and to signify to you that the general tenor of your conduct in the arduous negotiations in which you have been engaged has established a peculiar claim to public applause, respect, and esteem."

CHAPTER IX.

[1809—1811]

TRANSITION YEARS.

Approbation of Lord Minto—Metcalfe's Visit to the Presidency—Meeting with his Brother—Appointment to the Deputy-Secretaryship—Voyage to Madras—Return to Calcutta—Appointment to the Residency at Scindiah's Court—Letters from Lord Minto—Translation to the Delhi Residency—The Foundation of Charles Metcalfe's Fortune.

THE admiration which Charles Metcalfe's conduct at the Sikh Court had excited in the breast of the Governor-General was not now to be suffered to expend itself in a few stereotyped phrases of official commendation. It was not a mere formal demonstration; it was a living reality, and was likely to become an abiding one. Lord Minto desired to know the man who had done such great things for his government. He was interested in the personal character of the young statesman, and was eager to communicate with him face to face. So it happened that Metcalfe had scarcely reached his old home at Delhi, when a private letter from the chief secretary came with the intimation that the Governor-General desired to see him at the Presidency. "I am authorised to inform you," wrote Mr. Edmonstone, "that you are perfectly at liberty to proceed to Calcutta. The Governor-General, indeed, is desirous of being personally acquainted with you, and of having an opportunity of conversing with you on the affairs in which you have been so long and arduously engaged. But it would be proper that you should apply officially for leave to come to the Presidency. You need not, however, await the answer. This intimation you may consider as sufficient authority. Favour me with a line of application on your receipt of this, and set off as soon as it may suit your convenience."* Little time was lost after the receipt of this letter; Metcalfe was soon upon his way to Calcutta. There were others whom he desired to see there beside the noble lord at the head of the Government. Theophilus Metcalfe, with his wife and little daughter, had come round from China to Calcutta in the early part of the year, for the benefit of Mrs. Metcalfe's health, and Charles was eager now to embrace his brother and sister and make the acquaintance of his little niece. Public and private considerations, therefore, both urged him to make all speed to the Presidency. He had reached Delhi on his return from the Punjaub on the 6th of June. The 8th of July found him in Calcutta.

But before the journey had been accomplished Lord Minto had ceased to disturb himself about the countries lying between the banks of the Sutlej and the base of the Hindoo-Koosh. Dangers more pressing and more palpable than any that had been looked for in the direction of Central Asia, were now threatening the British-Indian Government from the southern part of the Indian peninsula. The coast army was in a state of feverish excitement — almost, indeed, upon the borders of absolute rebellion. It was not a revolt of the soldiers, but of the officers of the Madras army. The abolition of certain privileges by which the higher grades of the service had been long suffered to enrich themselves, had caused great dissatisfaction, which subsequent circumstances had

* *MS. Correspondence, Calcutta, May* 28, 1809.

aggravated; until the civil and military authorities were in a state of open and violent antagonism The power of the Governor, Sir George Barlow, was set at naught; seditious meetings were held: inflammatory resolutions were passed; and the entire Government of the Presidency, under the convulsions that had arisen, seemed to be hovering upon the extreme verge of dissolution.

In this state of affairs it appeared to Lord Minto that his presence upon the scene of these disturbances was necessary to their extinction. So he determined at once to proceed to Madras. But he did not forget Charles Metcalfe, whom he had invited to visit him in Calcutta. It occurred to the Governor-General that he could not, upon this painful expedition to the coast, take with him any one more likely to be of service to him than the sometime Envoy to Lahore. So, on the 15th of July, the Chief Secretary wrote to Metcalfe that the Governor-General in Council had been "pleased to appoint him Deputy-Secretary to the Right Honourable the Governor-General during his lordship's absence from the Presidency."*

After a brief sojourn in Calcutta, rendered interesting to him by the presence of Theophilus and his family, Charles Metcalfe, accompanying Mr. Edmonstone, left the Presidency on the 5th of August, to proceed down the river to join his ship. On the 9th, the Governor-General embarked. The voyage from Calcutta to Madras occupies a week or a month, according to the season. In the month of August, when a vessel bound for the southern coast meets the south-west monsoon in the Bay of Bengal, the passage is seldom made under the latter period of time. So it was not until the 11th of September that, after a tedious, zig-zag voyage, rendered comfortless by

* His salary was fixed at 2,000 rupees a month—the same amount that he had drawn on the Lahore Mission.

continual rain and baffling winds, Lord Minto was enabled to announce his arrival at Madras.

Of this visit to the Southern Presidency the records are but scanty. The ministerial capacity in which Charles Metcalfe acted at this time afforded no opportunities for independent action, and the incidents of the Madras disturbances of 1809 scarcely belong to the career of the Bengal civilian. His residence on the coast was not distasteful to him. "You know Madras well," he wrote to his aunt, Mrs. Monson, on the 13th of November. "In some respects I like it better than Calcutta." He appears to have spent some time in Mr. Cassamaijor's house,* and to have greatly enjoyed the society of a family that has never been wanting in amiable and attractive members. At the close of the year he visited Mysore;† and at the commencement of 1810, having returned to Madras, he received the afflicting intelligence of the death of his sister-in-law, to whom he was sincerely attached. "Poor Theophilus," he wrote on the 10th of February from the Ameerbaugh, where he was residing with the Governor-General, "has lost his darling wife, who was really one of the most sensible, the most amiable, the most virtuous of women. I received accounts of this afflicting event about a month ago. Theophilus goes home with his sweet little daughter, and will be with you almost as soon as this letter." There was no more

* Mr. Cassamaijor was at this time a member of the Madras Council.

† He went there, I believe, to visit his old friend Arthur Cole. I have before me a letter from Lord Minto to Metcalfe, dated "Madras, December 14, 1809," and endorsed, "Answered from Mysore, December, 1809." In this letter the Governor-General says: "I hope you have by this time afforded another proof of your diplomatic powers by making my peace with Mr. Cole, and that he will not have proved implacable in the hands of one who gained the tender affections of Runjeet Singh."

observable, as there was no more beautiful trait in Charles Metcalfe's character, from very early boyhood to the close of his career, than the depth of his sympathies—

> "He could afford to suffer
> With those whom he saw suffer."

And when he wrote strongly of the afflictions of others, it was because he felt them strongly himself.

On the 12th of May, Lord Minto held a farewell levee at the Ameerbaugh, and afterwards crossed the surf, with his suite, on his way to the *Modeste* frigate, which was to convey him to Calcutta.* The monsoon was now all in his favour, and after a pleasant passage of a week's duration, he ascended the steps of the Chandpaul Ghat, the chief landing-place of Calcutta, and was welcomed back by the members of council and the chief officers of the staff. A very few days after this, Charles Metcalfe left Calcutta by dawk, on his way to Banda, whence he was to take the shortest route to Scindiah's camp. He had been appointed to act as Resident at the Court of Dowlut Rao Scindiah, in the place of Mr. Græme Mercer, who had signified his wish to be relieved from the duties of his office, in order that he might proceed to England by the first ship of the ensuing season.

It was with no great elation of spirit that Metcalfe travelled northward to join his appointment. And there was nothing in the environments of the Residency to give him pleasure after his arrival. It is true that he had not now, as ten years before, to pitch his camp upon a plain, sickly with the foul odour of decaying corpses. The court had recently been removed from Oujein to Gwalior; and the times were as pacific as they are ever

* It would appear, however, from a memorandum in a private account-book which I have chanced upon since this was written, that Metcalfe left Madras on the 8th, and reached Calcutta on the 15th of May."

wont to be in native states, where domestic anarchy is so often the succedaneum for foreign war. Whether it were that there was nothing in the state of public affairs to evoke his energies, or whether there were any personal circumstances which rendered his situation disagreeable to him, I do not distinctly know; but he spoke of it with evident distaste in his letters to his family, and all his after references to it were in the same strain.*

But this second residence at Scindiah's court was not destined to be of long continuance. At the commencement of the following year (1811) an opportunity, of which Lord Minto was eager to avail himself, occurred for the translation of Charles Metcalfe to the Delhi Residency. A Governor was to be found for Prince of Wales' Island, and the appointment was offered to Mr. Seton. In anticipation of his acceptance of it, the Governor-General wrote the following letter, in a style of pleasant familiarity more complimentary to the recipient than if it had been couched in language of the most laboured panegyric:

LORD MINTO TO MR METCALFE.

"*Calcutta, February* 20, 1811.

"MY DEAR SIR,—You may possibly have already heard, although it is yet in the Secret Department, that an offer has been made to Mr. Seton of the government of Prince of Wales' Island; and although it might be thought that he would consider his present situation the most eligible of the two, I have some reasons for supposing that he will be inclined to accept the proposal. In that event, I shall with (or without) your consent, name you to the Residency of Delhi. I know your martial genius and your love

* Of the eight or nine months which Metcalfe spent at Scindiah's Court in 1810-11, the records are remarkably scanty in comparison with those which illustrate all the antecedent and all the subsequent epochs of his life. The deficiency is, however, of but slight importance; for he was then merely in a transition-state, and nothing occurred which had any noticeable influence either upon his character or his career.

of camps; but besides that inclination must yield to duty, this change will appear to fall in not inopportunely with some information and some sentiments conveyed in your letter to me of the 3rd instant. If you ask my reasons for so extraordinary a choice, I can only say that, notwithstanding your entire ignorance of everything connected with the business of Delhi—a city which, I believe, you never saw; and with Cis and Trans-Sutlejean affairs, of which you can have only read; and notwithstanding your equal deficiency in all other more general qualifications, I cannot find a better name in the list of the Company's servants; and hope, therefore, for your indulgence on the occasion.

"I fancy that you must have given me a sly bite, for I am going campaigning myself, and expect to embark about the 3rd or 4th of March for Java, touching at Madras, where I hope to get on board the *Modeste*. It is so difficult to anticipate the important, but delicate points likely to arise in the prosecution of this enterprise, and it would be so impossible to decide them satisfactorily without information, which cannot be obtained at a distance, that I am satisfied I should acquit myself imperfectly of this duty, if I did not approach, or rather convey myself to the very scene of action. My absence cannot be shorter than six months, and may be somewhat more. . . .

"Believe me ever, my dear sir,

"Most sincerely and affectionately yours,

"MINTO."

After the lapse of a few days, in the interval of which Mr. Seton's answer had been received, Lord Minto wrote again to Charles Metcalfe on the subject of the Delhi Residency, in a graver and more business-like style:

LORD MINTO TO CHARLES METCALFE.

"*Calcutta, February* 26, 1811.

"MY DEAR SIR,—I have received Mr. Seton's answer. He accepts the government of Prince of Wales' Island *with the proviso* that the appointment is to be considered temporary, and that he shall be at liberty to return to Delhi when the particular emergency which now invites him to the eastward shall have passed away. That emergency is the proposed conquest of the Dutch settlements in Java. But I conceive the services of Mr. Seton at Prince of Wales' Island will continue to be very important some time after the object has been accomplished at Java; for, considering the great distance of Calcutta, I confess I should wish, that whoever is charged with the administration of our new territories, should have the benefit of communicating intermediately with Mr. Seton, and obtaining such advice as his on the many novel and delicate affairs likely to arise in the first period of our connection with a new and extensive country. I should, therefore, conjecture, that he may be absent from Delhi at least one year. I dwell upon these circumstances, as you will perceive that they affect your situation, and that your appointment to Delhi cannot be depended upon as so permanent as I understood it was likely to be at the date of my last letter. I trust, however, that you will feel no disinclination to accept it under the circumstances which I have described. I am anxious that the temporary nature of the arrangement should be known to the parties alone who are concerned—I mean to Mr. Seton, and the few whose new appointments must be understood by themselves to be temporary. I propose that, in the event of Mr. Seton's return to Delhi, you should resume your present mission; that your successor (Richard Strachey) should return to the Foreign Settlements, and so on; with the condition, however, that if anything more eligible than your present office should open during the interval, it shall be reserved for you, if no particular obstacle should stand in the way.

"As I propose to sail on the 7th of March, if possible, and your answer to this letter cannot be received at Calcutta so soon, I shall leave your appointment at Delhi behind me, to be published when your acceptance arrives. It will be absolute, as you collect from this letter, in form; and nothing conditional or provisional will appear upon the face of it. If Mr. Seton should return, it will be time enough to explain the particulars which attended your appointment.

"I have now to thank you, my dear sir, for your friendly felicitations on the reduction of the French Islands; and being assured, as I am, of their sincerity, I hope you will believe that your kind concern in these events and in any influence they may have upon my credit is, next to the public benefit, one of the greatest and most sensible pleasures I experience on the occasion.

"Believe me ever, my dear sir,

"Sincerely and affectionately yours,

"MINTO."

The offer was accepted. But the acceptance had been already assumed; and before Metcalfe's answer was received, sidering the great distance of Calcutta, I confess I should wish, that whoever is charged with the administration of our new territories, should have the benefit of communicating intermediately with Mr. Seton, and obtaining such advice as his on the many novel and delicate affairs likely to arise in the first period of our connection with a new and extensive country. I should, therefore, conjecture, that he may be absent from Delhi at least one year. I dwell upon these circumstances, as you will perceive that they affect your situation, and that your appointment to Delhi cannot be depended upon as so permanent as I understood it was likely to be at the date of my last letter. I trust, however, that you will feel no disinclination to accept it under the circumstances which I have described. I am anxious that the temporary nature of the arrangement should be known to the parties alone who are concerned—I mean to Mr. Seton, and the few whose new appointments must be understood by themselves to be temporary. I propose that, in the event of Mr. Seton's return to Delhi, you should resume your present mission; that your successor (Richard Strachey) should return to the Foreign Settlements, and so on; with the condition, however, that if anything more eligible than your present office should open during the interval, it shall be reserved for you, if no particular obstacle should stand in the way.

"As I propose to sail on the 7th of March, if possible, and your answer to this letter cannot be received at Calcutta so soon, I shall leave your appointment at Delhi behind me, to be published when your acceptance arrives. It will be absolute, as you collect from this letter, in form; and nothing conditional or provisional will appear upon the face of it. If Mr. Seton should return, it will be time enough to explain the particulars which attended your appointment.

"I have now to thank you, my dear sir, for your friendly felicitations on the reduction of the French Islands; and being assured, as I am, of their sincerity, I hope you will believe that your kind concern in these events and in any influence they may have upon my credit is, next to the public benefit, one of the greatest and most sensible pleasures I experience on the occasion.

"Believe me ever, my dear sir,

"Sincerely and affectionately yours,

"MINTO."

The offer was accepted. But the acceptance had been already assumed; and before Metcalfe's answer was received, men at some period of their lives make these wise resolutions; but few have constancy to keep them. From this time, however, Charles Metcalfe kept, I believe, without intermission, a minute account of his receipts and disbursements.* He was the most liberal and most generous of men —but he died in possession of a fortune which would have creditably sustained the peerage he had won.

At the beginning of 1810, when he had just completed his twenty-fifth year, he wrote on one of the first pages of a new account-book—"I commence this account with a determination to lay by, henceforth for ever, a sum equal to 100*l.* per mensem, to lay the foundation of a fortune. I have 2,000 rupees per mensem. I find by calculation, that my expenses are at present 1,200 rupees per mensem,* and I mean to save 800 = 100*l.*" The system which he adopted was a very simple and intelligible one; and it is curious to trace its working. "It is my intention," he wrote, "at the end of every month to enter a report on the result displayed by the accounts of that month, in order that I may see how far the plan I have laid down for myself succeeds. Now, therefore, I proceed to the financial report for the month of February. The amount expended in this month is as follows. . . . . But before I note it down, I will lay down an outline of my plan for the examination of the result of each month. I take first the amount of my salary, which is at present 2,000 rupees. From this I deduct the amount of all expenses that I am aware of having incurred. From the balance then left I deduct 100*l.*, or 800 rupees, to form a fund which is to

* To account for this expenditure, which is by no means inconsiderable when it is remembered that Charles Metcalfe was a single man, and a member, I presume, of Lord Minto's family at the time, I should mention what he himself has recorded, that he had left "an establishment of servants at Calcutta and another at Delhi." He had been unwilling that his dependents should suffer by his absence, and still retained many of them in his pay.

make my fortune, and which I will term the 'accumulating fund.' The amount which remains after these deductions is to form a fund for contingent expenses, which I will call the 'contingent fund.' If the contingent fund increases, and is more than equal to meet all the demands that may come upon it, then I may consider my finances to be in a very prosperous state; and when it is safe to do so, I may apply the surplus of the contingent fund as an increase to the accumulating fund. On the other hand, if the contingent fund should be unequal to meet the demands upon it, then I must of necessity draw upon the accumulating fund, and my scheme will have failed."

For the first two or three months the result was satisfactory. He regularly set aside the stipulated 100*l.* for the accumulating fund, and at the end of March he found that he had 289 sicca rupees, or something more than 100*l.* in the contingent fund. So he wrote in his account-book, under date April 1—"The account for March presents a favourable prospect of the practicability of the scheme which I have laid down for myself." It was so encouraging, indeed, that a few days afterwards he sent off 200 rupees for the purchase of tickets in the Calcutta Lottery.* Those were days when most men entertained hopes of growing rich *per saltum* through the agency of these Presidency lotteries, and some had so much faith in them that they dispensed altogether with the slower process of hoarding money. It was on account of this purchase that Metcalfe was now obliged to record that the April results were not as favourable as those of March. "The account for April," he wrote, "though not so favourable as that of March, still shows a progressive increase both in the accumulating

* "*April* 12.—Wrote to Calcutta for two tickets in the lottery to be drawn in July. The damage will be 200 rupees." I do not observe in the July memoranda any entrance under the head of *lottery* on the receipt side of the account.

and contingent funds. But heavy expenses are coming on in May, the prospect of which is alarming." In this month of May he passed from Madras to Calcutta, and he had extraordinary expenses to meet at both places. The system had not been sufficiently long in operation—the contingent fund was not sufficiently large—to bear such a drain upon it. So at the end of the month, having found that nothing had been added to the accumulating fund, and that there was a deficiency of 106 rupees on the contingent fund, he wrote in his memorandum-book—"The plan with which I set out at the beginning of the year has thus been shown to have failed, and a deficit has arisen to the amount above stated."

In thus declaring the failure of his scheme he was a little too candid. The result was not to be fairly estimated after an experiment of only a few months. One extraordinary item, entered in this month of May, was sufficient to cover the entire deficit. It is an item at which he had no need to blush, although it disturbed, for a time, his financial projects, and impelled him to record that he had failed—"*Subscription for the benefit of Dr. Reid's family*, 1,000 *rupees*." In those days it was no uncommon thing for some well-known and highly-esteemed member of society, carried off suddenly by one of the diseases of the country, to leave a wife and family behind him in a state of utter destitution. Nor was it an uncommon thing for the friends and acquaintances of the deceased—and many who were neither friends nor acquaintances—to raise a subscription for the benefit of his family sufficient to send them to England, and to keep them from want for all the rest of their days. It was to one of these subscriptions that Charles Metcalfe had now subscribed 1,000 rupees. If he had not subscribed it he could have added the monthly 100*l.* to his accumulating fund, and retained a small balance in the contingent one.

But the failure—if it were one—was soon redeemed. He had scarcely recorded it when he discovered that he was richer than he had supposed. He received his account-current from his agents, and it appeared from the state of it that he could make good the deficit of which he had spoken, and set his system at work again. At the commencement of the mercantile year there was a balance in his favour, which, after deducting the amounts belonging to his accumulating fund, and the payments he had since made on the contingent account, still left him for present purposes more than 15,000 rupees. "This last remainder," he wrote, "I shall at present throw into the contingent fund, but when my accounts (with the Government) come to be settled, I expect that it will be all absorbed." There was money owing to him on the other side, and as all that he wanted was a little floating capital, his system was soon again in successful operation. Month after month he added 100*l.* to his accumulating fund; and at the end of the year, with 1,200*l.* to his credit on this account, he had a balance of 2,000 rupees in the contingent fund to commence the year without misgivings.* From this time he went on steadily, adding to his savings—sometimes spending more than the amount of his salary, but never more than his income. Money brought high interest in those days, and the accumulating fund soon became productive.

I need not pursue any further the history of Charles Metcalfe's accumulations. I purposed only to show how he set about the work; and the little which I have exhibited of his system is not without both interest and instruction.

* It had at one time reached 5,000 rupees. But his salary at Scindiah's Court was less by 500 rupees a month than it had been at Lahore and Madras. In the December account, too, there were some extraordinary disbursements. Among others, "Paid at Madras—remainder of subscription to a masquerade given in January last, 1,500 rupees."

There is one remark, however, which ought to be made in this place, for it is necessary to the right understanding of the fine character which I am attempting to illustrate. Even at this early period of his career, when his accumulations were but scanty, he was a ready lender to men less fortunate or less prudent than himself. There are many still living—and many have passed away—who have tasted largely of Charles Metcalfe's open-handed kindliness; and some who owe all their success in life to his seasonable intervention in their behalf. As he grew older, he did not grow more worldly-wise. But it was an abiding source of consolation to him, that although now and then his generosity may have been misplaced, it fell for the most part on good soil, and fructified in gratitude, if not in reformation.*

* In the entries of the year 1810 there is the sum of 2,711 rupees (about 300*l.*) lent to Lieutenant C——. The name, with characteristic delicacy, is only thus initialised in the account-book. At the end of the year Metcalfe wrote: "Cash lent or advanced is hereafter to be put down as 'an inefficient balance, and not as a disbursement. The money lent, therefore, as per August and November, 1810, accounts, to Lieutenant C——, is now to be brought into an 'inefficient fund.'" As years advanced, the inefficient fund amounted to some thousands of pounds.

CHAPTER X.

[1811—1814.]

THE DELHI RESIDENCY.

Duties of the Resident—Metcalfe's Opinions of his Position—Letters to Mrs. Monson—Appointed Permanently to the Residency—Drawbacks and Annoyances—The Royal Family of Delhi—Removal of Metcalfe's Assistants—Letter from Lord Minto—Expenses of the Residency—Censures of the Court of Directors—Metcalfe's Defence—Administration of the Delhi Territory.

So Charles Metcalfe, now at the age of twenty-six, found himself the incumbent of an appointment coveted by the oldest officers of both services—an appointment which, in respect of its importance, its responsibility, and its distinction, was not exceeded by any other in India below the seats at the Council-boards of Government. The duties of the Delhi Resident were onerous and complex. The residents at other courts were simply diplomatists. They were bound to confine themselves to the political duties of their situation, and to refrain from all interference with the internal administration of the country in which they resided. But the Delhi Resident was at once a diplomatist and an administrator. It was his duty not only to superintend the affairs of the pensioned Mogul and his family, but to manage the political relations of the British Government with a wide expanse of country studded with petty principalities, ignorant alike of their duties and their interests, and often in their ignorance vexatious in the extreme. It was his duty, too, to superintend the internal government of all the Delhi territory—to preside over the machinery of the revenue collection and the administration of justice, and to promote by all possible means the development of the resources of the country and the industry and happiness of the people. He addressed himself to his work with a brave resolution. He might, perhaps, have taken deeper interest in it, if he had been more certain of his tenure of office—if he had believed that he would remain to see the results of his activity—but he could not have laboured more zealously or more diligently in his vocation. The return of Mr. Seton to Delhi was always probable; sometimes it seemed almost certain. And there was something dispiriting in this. For the longer Charles Metcalfe sojourned at the imperial city, the more attached he grew to the place and to the people, whilst the residency at Scindiah's Court, to which he would have returned, had no attractions for him. But whatever might be the event, his professional success was now an established fact; and only death could interpose itself between him and the great goal of fame and fortune.

He had social duties to perform as well as those of diplomacy and administration. The Resident was a great man—he had a court of his own, and a large monthly allowance from Government to support it in a state of becoming splendour. He kept open house. He had what was called a "Family"—all the officers attached to the Residency, with their wives and children, were members of it. In the Resident's house all passing travellers of rank found ready entertainment. Hospitality here put on its best apparel. The new Delhi Resident was just the man to carry himself bravely as the representative of the British nation at an Eastern court. His liberality was of the best kind. It was Charles Metcalfe's nature to give freely; he was bountiful without ostentation, and no man ever left his house without carrying with him a grateful recollection of the kindliness and the geniality of his host, and cherishing it as one of those pleasant memories which he would not willingly let die.

But it may be doubted whether Charles Metcalfe was happy at this time. He was naturally of a cheerful disposition, and he had too much mental occupation to dwell long or frequently upon the necessary drawbacks of his situation. But there were times when he thought that for even his brilliant position he had paid somewhat too dearly; and when he took up his pen to discourse with some member of his distant family, the old clouds which had gathered over him during the first years of his Indian residence began to overshadow him again, and he spoke doubtfully of the apparent advantages of his present, and the promises of his future life. In the following letter to his aunt he dwells feelingly upon the darker side of even the most successful Indian career. His cousin, William Monson,* had been intended for the Indian Civil Service, but he was an only child, and his mother, with a wise discretion which it will be seen Charles Metcalfe highly commended, subsequently determined to detain him at home:

CHARLES METCALFE TO THE HON. MRS. MONSON.

"*Delhi*† *Residency, September* 10, 1811.

"MY DEAREST AUNT,—I have had the pleasure of receiving your letter of January 7. So far am I from condemning you for resigning William's intended appointment to this country, that I decidedly think you have done that which is best calculated to promote his happiness and your own, by keeping him at home.

* The present Lord Monson, to whom I am indebted for these letters and much other valuable assistance rendered to me in the course of my preparation of this Memoir.

† I have substituted the more familiar orthography for Metcalfe's unvarying "Dihlee."

My father, I conclude, will blame you; for he thinks nothing equal to an appointment to this country. I confess that my ideas are different. Why should you make yourself and William miserable by parting never perhaps to meet again? Why doom him to transportation from everything dear to him? What is there in India to recompense for such sufferings? Fortunes, as you justly observe, are not made rapidly. Take my situation. I have been more than eleven years from England; and it will be certainly more than eleven years before I can return. In these twenty-two or twenty-four years the best part of my life will have passed away—that part in which all my feelings will have been most alive to the different sensations of happiness and misery arising out of different circumstances. I left my father and mother just as I became acquainted with them as a man. I have not once had their cheering smile to encourage my labours in my profession. When I return, should they both be alive—which I pray to God that they may be—I shall, indeed, have the happiness of attending on their declining years; but, alas! how much cause shall I have to lament that I was doomed by my fate not to see them from the days of boyhood to those of their extreme old age? But suppose that they should not be alive, and when one considers that my father must live to be eighty to allow me to see him again, it is enough to make one tremble, though I still hope. Suppose, I say, that they should not be alive, what will then be my situation? The thought is too horrible to dwell upon. See my sisters. I left them children, I shall find them old women—married, perhaps, into families which will not care one farthing about me, and whose habits it will not suit me to associate with. Take the worst, and what a melancholy situation I may be in when I return to England! Where will be my connections, my friendships, and even my acquaintance? Unknown in society, and even shunned as being an Indian, I certainly will never push my way into the society of fine lords and ladies, who may turn up their noses and think me highly honoured by being in their presence.

"Neither will I ever fall back and take up my post in the ranks of Indian society. I recollect what it was, and know what it is, and that society will not suit me. I shall not be able to afford to spend all my income on dinners and balls, houses, coaches, and servants. Money was made for better uses, and, by God's grace, I hope to apply mine to some of them. A dull, solitary life, is the one that I shall, most likely, taking all chances, be obliged to pursue. And what shall I have gained by making so many sacrifices? Money—and not more, perhaps, than I might have gained (I allow not probably) by a profession in England. And it must be remembered, that I have been uncommonly fortunate in my present profession. So you see, my dear aunt, I think you perfectly right. Do not suppose from the above, that I am unhappy or discontented. I have long since reconciled myself to my fate, and am contented and as happy as one far from his friends can be. I do not allow unpleasant thoughts to enter my mind, and if I do not enjoy what is beyond my reach—the inexpressible pleasure of family society—I at least am always cheerful, and never unhappy. My father did what he thought best for me; and it is satisfactory to me to reflect, that my career in India, except as to fortune, must have answered his expectations. It has been successful beyond any merits, that I am aware of, in myself. I hold now, as Resident at Delhi, a situation which I consider without exception in every respect the highest in the country beneath the members of Government; and I do not wish to quit this situation until I quit India.

"I hope to lay by at the rate of 3,000*l.* per annum, which in twelve or fifteen years ought to be enough to enable me to live at home in the plain manner in which I mean to live as an old bachelor; for, you must know, that I have no thought of *ever* marrying, as I shall never have money enough for it, unless I consent, which I will not do, to spend the whole of it on what is termed *living.* In that case, I should be poor in the midst of thousands. Then only can I consider myself rich when I have the command of money to gratify such inclinations as may arise. . . . .

"I am ever, my dear aunt,

"Your attached nephew,

"C. T. METCALFE."

FROM THE SAME TO THE SAME.

"*Delhi Residency, November* 16, 1811.

"MY DEAR AUNT,—From circumstances which are likely to last as long as I remain at Delhi, I am now so overloaded with business that I never can get rid of it before nine o'clock at night. This will account to you for my not writing oftener. I am obliged to let my family dine without me in order to write this; but the pleasure of communicating with you is not to be lost. . . . . R—— has some idea of going to England, but I do not conceive that it will be fulfilled. An old Indian takes a long time to determine to quit his emoluments, and put his foot on board a ship for

England. Many is the Indian who dies of staying 'one year longer' in the country, like the gentleman on whose tombstone is inscribed,

'Here lies Mr. Wandermere,
Who was to have gone home next year.'

I hope that this will be neither R——'s case nor mine. . . . . .

"I am likely to return to Scindiah's camp, for Mr. Seton threatens to return to Delhi. He is now Governor of Prince of Wales' Island; but he accepted that appointment on condition, that if he should not like to keep it, he might return to Delhi. In his last letter to me, he announces his intention of availing himself of that condition; and I shall be obliged to turn out for him, to my great regret. I shall be no loser in a pecuniary way; but I consider the Residency at Delhi infinitely superior to that in Scindiah's camp.

"I expect, or rather hope, that Theophilus will marry before he quits England. He is calculated for marriage, and requires it, I think. For my part, I shall never marry. My principal reason for thinking that *I positively* shall never marry, is the difficulty of two dispositions uniting so exactly as to produce that universal harmony which is requisite to form the perfect happiness that is indispensable to make the married state desirable. But little do I know what is to befall me. . . . . .

"Ever most affectionately yours,
"C. T. Metcalfe."

A few more passages from letters written to the same much-respected correspondent during the first years of his residence at Delhi—passages illustrative of the feelings with which he regarded his position in India may be given in this place. They show how little he had ceased to yearn after home—how little time had impaired the strength of his domestic affections:

". . . . . . . To-morrow will be Christmas-day, when all friends meet at home. I have a party of fifty to dine with me, among whom I cannot reckon one real friend. What a blank it is to live in such a society! I have lately been overwhelmed with visitors—Sir George and Lady Nugent,* Colonel and Lady Char-

* Sir George Nugent was the new Commander-in-Chief.

lotte Murray, and twenty others of the same party, have been my guests for eight or ten days. They are gone. I found them all very pleasant. But I often wish that I had some cottage to retire to, where I might live in obscurity and uninterrupted solitude for a time. I feel myself out of my element in attempting to support the appearance which attaches to the situation I hold."—[*Delhi, December* 24, 1812.]

". . . . . . Tom * is arrived. . . . . Poor fellow! He has a long time before him; but, perhaps, not longer than I have. It is not improbable that I may remain eighteen or twenty years more. . . . . . I cannot say that I approve of the plan of sending children out to India for all their lives. There is no other service in which a man does not see his friends sometimes. Here it is perpetual banishment.* There was a good reason for sending sons to India when fortunes were made rapidly, and they returned home. But if a man is to slave all his life, he had better do so, in my opinion, in his own country, where he may enjoy the society of his friends, which I call enjoying life. . . . . Do not suppose that I am discontented, and make myself unhappy. It is my fate, and I am reconciled to it. The time may come, if ever I am able to set myself down at home with a comfortable fortune, when I shall confess that my destiny was a favourable one, and shall be able to look back to past annoyances with composure. But can anything be a recompense to me in this world for not seeing my dear and honoured father, from the days of my boyhood to the day of his death—and, perhaps, the same with regard to my mother? I think not—decidedly not. At present, notwithstanding my uncommon good fortune, I am not convinced that it is conducive to a man's happiness to send him to seek his fortune in India."—[*Delhi, March* 6, 1813.]

". . . . I cannot describe to you how much I am worked. And if I could, there would be no pleasure either to you or me in the detail. I will, therefore, pass over that for awhile, and endeavour to forget my plagues. Tom arrived here on the 18th.† I am very much pleased with him, and think him a superior young man.

---

* His younger brother, Thomas Theophilus Metcalfe, who had come out to India in the Company's Civil Service.

† The younger Metcalfe, by the spontaneous kindness of Lord Minto, had been appointed an Assistant to the Delhi Resident.

I will answer for his doing well. He distinguished himself very much in College, and got out by his own exertions in less than four months. Here he and I are together; and here we shall remain for many and many a long year, consoling each other as well as we can for the absence of all other friends. . . . . I shall see you, I hope, in eighteen years!"—[*Delhi, November* 2, 1813.]

". . . . It is very kind in you to wish me home; and I assure you that I wish myself at home most ardently. Nevertheless, as the sacrifices which a man must make who comes to India have been made for the most part already, I do not mean to return to England to struggle with poverty, or to be forced to draw tight my purse-strings. The sacrifice that I have made I consider great. The recompense that I propose to myself is to have a competency, not merely for my own expenses, but to enable me to assist others without reluctance or restraint. My own expenses may, I think, be trifling. I believe that I should have more pleasure in spending only 500*l.* per annum, than I should have in squandering 5,000*l.* in the same way. But to put extreme economy out of the question, allow 1,500*l.* or 2,000*l.* for my own expenses. You know better than I do what a single man ought to live upon creditably, without attempting to vie with people of large fortunes. Tell me what you think requisite for the support of a bachelor in a decent, comfortable manner. Add to that what would be requisite to procure a seat in Parliament. Add to that a sum to enable me to make presents freely to my friends, and to assist the distressed, and to contribute to public charities. Let me know the sum total, and I will make my arrangements accordingly. . . . . I am become very unsociable and morose, and feel myself getting more so every day. I lead a vexatious and joyless life; and it is only the hope of home at last that keeps me alive and merry. That thought cheers me; though writing to any of you always makes me sad."—[*Shalimar, Delhi, March* 20, 1814.]

From passages such as these, glimpses may be caught of the inner life of the Delhi Resident. Stripped of his externals, the *burra sahib*, or great lord of the imperial city, was but a solitary exile, continually disquieted by thoughts of home. But he lived with the harness on his back, and incessant occupation preserved him from despondency or depression. He had now become Resident indeed. The anticipations of his return to Scindiah's court, which he had expressed in one of his letters to his aunt, were not to be realised. At the commencement of September, 1812, Mr. Seton entered the Hooghly river, on his return from Prince of Wales' Island, full of the thought of revisiting Delhi. But a letter from Lord Minto, announcing that he had been appointed provisionally a member of Council, met him at Diamond Harbour. Two vacancies were about to occur at the council-board. Mr. Lumsden and Mr. Colebrooke had both nearly served for the appointed five years of office. To the first of these vacancies that ripe statesman, Mr. Edmonstone, who had long been little less than the Supreme Government itself, stood nominated by the Court of Directors. For the second, the choice lay between Mr. Tucker and Mr. Seton; but after some discussion at the India House, the latter had been eventually appointed; and the intelligence had arrived just in time to greet him as he entered the river on his return to Bengal.

Scarcely had Seton landed, when he wrote to his old assistant to apprise him of what was a matter to him of such vital importance. But he had been anticipated by some of the denizens of Government-house, who, a week before, had despatched the glad tidings to the Acting-Resident. The intelligence, which was in some measure unexpected, filled both Seton and Metcalfe with joy. To the former, moreover, it was an inexpressible relief. "In addition to considerations of a domestic character," he wrote to his old assistant, "I trust I have a due sense of others of a less selfish kind, which render the situation gratifying in the extreme; and you, my dear Metcalfe, will, I am persuaded, give me credit for the delight with which I indulge the reflection that the arrangement will necessarily fix you at Delhi. I really cannot express to you how awkward and distressed I felt every time that the idea came across me that I could not return to Delhi without being the means of your quitting that station. In vain did I try to reconcile my mind to it by turning to the 'flattering unction' of its being necessary, in consequence of the state of my domestic concerns. All would not do. I still felt the awkwardness arising from the embarrassing reflection that I must either sacrifice the pressing claims of my family, or interfere with the views of my friend—and of such a friend! The present arrangement has, among many other desirable points, the advantage of tranquillizing this painful struggle." The May fleet which arrived in October brought out the official announcement of Seton's appointment; so the old Delhi Resident remained in Calcutta; Metcalfe was confirmed in the appointment which he had now held on a precarious tenure for a year and a half; and Richard Strachey succeeded in the same manner to the Residency at Scindiah's court.

And thus was removed one of the great drawbacks of Charles Metcalfe's position at Delhi during the earlier period of his incumbency; but there were still, as he said in his letters to his aunt, many vexations and annoyances. Among the troubles of the residency, not the least were those which arose out of the folly of the Mogul, and the wickedness of his family and dependents. The generous respect for the fallen fortunes of the imperial house, which had moved the British Government to leave to the pageant king independent jurisdiction within the walls of the palace, had long been bearing bitter fruit. There were things done within the precincts of that vast privileged asylum, and duly reported to the Resident, in violation of all laws human and divine. The crimes which were thus committed, sometimes behind the sanctity of the *purdah*, greatly disquieted Metcalfe, for it was difficult either to prevent their commission, or to deal with them when they were committed. One day it was reported to him by the officer in command of the palace guard, whose duty it was to take cognisance of all that passed within the limits of the imperial residence, that two of the young princes had been playing the parts of common robbers—oiling their naked persons, then rushing with drawn swords among the startled inmates of the zenana, and forcibly carrying off their property. Another time it was announced to him that one of these princes had murdered a woman in the palace, either by beating her to death or by compelling her to swallow opium. Again tidings came to him that one of the ladies of the Emperor's establishment had murdered a female infant. Then it was reported to the Resident that the imperial quarters had been rendered a general receptacle for stolen goods and sequestered property. Then a knotty question arose as to whether the slave-trade, having been prohibited in the city of Delhi, should be allowed to survive in the palace. Then it appeared that the Emperor himself, after sundry intrigues at Calcutta, was intriguing with the Newab-Wuzeer of Oude, through the agency of his favourite son, the Prince Jehanguire, who, on the pretext of attending a marriage festival, had gone to Lucknow, from Allahabad, where he was a state prisoner, to beseech the Newab to intercede with the British Government for the augmentation of his father's stipend.

Since Charles Metcalfe had made his first obeisance at the court of the Mogul, the old blind Emperor, Shah Allum, had been gathered to his fathers: and now Akbar Shah, his son, reigned in his stead. The infirmities of the deceased monarch had not been without their uses. His wants had been comparatively few, and he had grown penurious at the close of his career. When he died it appeared that he had hoarded up some lakhs of rupees; so his successor found himself with a supply of unappropriated cash in his treasury which he might call undividedly his own. But the new king, being neither blind nor penurious, complained that the stipend allowed by the British Government was insufficient for the wants of such a family as he was bound to maintain. The inmates of the imperial palace constituted a considerable population in themselves. There were members of the royal family belonging to several generations, including even the connections of Shah Allum's predecessor; and liberal as were the allowances granted by the British Government, they barely sufficed to support, in comfort and respectability, a royal family of such inordinate dimensions. The condition, indeed, of these wretched people moved the generous sympathies of Lord Minto. Something of a promise had been made to the Mogul, that when the financial condition of the British Government would admit of greater liberality, an addition would be made to the imperial stipend. So, in the summer of 1809, the Governor-General was induced to review the whole question, and in an elaborate minute, partly written by Mr. Edmonstone, partly by himself, declared his intention of augmenting the allowances of the Shah, and indicated the most advantageous method of doing it. The increased amount was still below that which the Mogul had declared to be necessary for the support of his household; but the savings of Shah Allum for some time made good the deficiency, and kept the royal pensioner quiet. No sooner, however, was this reserve-fund exhausted, than he began to bestir himself to obtain a further augmentation of what he called his "tribute," and to this end instructed his favourite son, in whose behalf he had long desired to set aside the rights of the heir-apparent, to obtain the ear of the Newab-Wuzeer of Oude, and to induce him to further his claims. The letter of the Shah* fell into the hands of Colonel Baillie, the Resident at Lucknow, who recommended that thenceforth the prince should be "subjected to those salutary retraints, under the influence and authority of the Resident, which would seem indispensable to the future guidance of his conduct, and cannot be easily applied under any other authority."†

Indeed, it was necessary to exercise no little salutary restraint over the movements of the Shah and his favourite son. The idea which the former had encouraged of setting aside the rightful succession in favour of the latter had been temporarily resisted by the British Government; but it was doubtful, whether it had been wholly abandoned. A little time before the detection of these Lucknow intrigues—that is, in the spring of 1811, soon after Metcalfe's assumption of office—the Mogul had been partly the agent, partly the victim, of another intrigue at Calcutta. This business was known in the official language of the times as the Mission of Prawn Kishen. The secret history of this mission is diverting in the extreme. Two wily natives—the one a Hindoo, the other a Mussulman, headed by a Moollah, or Mahomedan priest—persuaded the Shah that they could do great things for him at Calcutta, especially in respect of the succession of Prince Jehanguire, through the agency of the Chief-Justice, Sir Henry Russell, from whom a letter, addressed

* The exordium of the King's letter sets forth the state of the case as given in the text:

"My beloved son, the light of my eyes and delight of my soul, may the Almighty increase your years! After prayers for the prolongation of your life, be it known to you that in consequence of the great increase of necessary expenditure, the money which was left in the treasury at the demise of his late Majesty has all been removed and expended. The tribute allowed by the English is totally inadequate to defray my expenses, and there seems no prospect of an increase, nor of the satisfactory adjustment of any other matter depending," &c. &c.

† *Col. Baillie to Mr. Edmonstone, March* 8, 1813.—[*MS. Records.*]

to his Majesty, was produced. The weakness of the King caught at the imposture. The cunning knaves were sent as wakeels* to Calcutta, whilst the expounder of the Koran remained behind in the imperial city to consummate the fraud. They did their work with considerable address, and for some time, by means of a series of amusing fabrications, contrived to live upon the credulity of their master. There was no falsehood—there was no forgery—which these sharpers hesitated to utter or commit. They wrote astonishing accounts of their reception by "Lord Russell," and despatched letters to the King in the name of that high functionary. They declared that they had waited on him immediately on their arrival at Calcutta; that on receiving an account of his Majesty's situation he had "wrung his hands with grief;" and, on reading the King's letter he had bitten his lips, and assured the Envoy that he had caused the Governor-General to write a letter to the Nizam (Metcalfe), saying, "I have sent you that you should honour his Majesty, not that you should distress him. If, another time, I hear of your offending his Majesty, you may expect to be punished. . . . . Be tranquil, for the business of the heir-apparentcy, and of the removal of the Nizam, shall soon be effected, and the other matters. also, will be easily accomplished." Having thus assured the King that all his representations had been favourably received, they told him, in a subsequent letter,† that they were "off for London" with the Governor-

* A *wakeel* is an agent, or attorney. In this work the word, which will probably be of frequent occurrence, generally signifies a diplomatic agent.

† The letter in which this is stated is highly amusing. They had told the King before that Mr. Elphinstone had been sent a prisoner to England, and now they related the circumstances of his acquittal:

"His lordship (Lord Russell) has ordered us both to accompany Mr. Seton and his Excellency the Governor-General to London—

General and the old Delhi Resident, and requested his Majesty to pay their wages to a friend, whom they named, in their absence. Lord Minto and Mr. Seton were just at that time embarking for the Eastern Archipelago; and the knaves taking advantage of a circumstance, the outline of which might obtain notoriety even at Delhi, assured the King that they were going to England, and that his humble servants were going with them. The lying Moollah protested that the story was correct, that the imperial wakeels had sailed with the Governor-General, and that all his Majesty's wishes would be speedily fulfilled.

In due course the fraud was discovered. The letters from Calcutta, in which such great things had been promised, were placed in Metcalfe's hands. The Shah expressed unbounded contrition, but it was doubtful whether he did not grieve over the failure of his mission rather than over his own misconduct in attempting to carry on an underhand intrigue; and Metcalfe, therefore, took the opportunity of counselling his Majesty to "relinquish that torment of his life, the worrying desire to effect impracticable changes." He was not without a hope at

so, God willing, off we go to London, by the way of Bombay. We hope in your Majesty's gracious kindness to allow Gora Chund to join us in this quarter, for from the smallness of our wages we can with difficulty make our subsistence if asunder. We trust in your Majesty's bounty for increase of our wages. It has been our bad fortune, and the cause of disappointment, that such has not taken place as yet to the present day. We leave Kevel Ram with the aforesaid gentleman (Lord Russell); Mr. Elphinstone having been accused of partiality to the French was obliged to go to London. There before the King he said, 'I am in no fault, but have been accused through spite because when in Delhi I reviled Mr. Seton on account of his disrespect to the royal family. I am in no fault.' He was accordingly acquitted. We set off with Seton and the Newab Governor on the 18th of March. We beg that our wages be paid to the Moulavee from month to month, who of course will get it conveyed to us."—[*MS. Records.*]

the time that the advice which he offered would have due effect upon the Shah, and dissuade him from launching into any further profitless intrigues. But baffled in the direction of Calcutta, he soon began to consider whether he might not push his diplomacy with better success at Lucknow. There was, indeed, an under-current of intrigue continually flowing out of the palace; and, although it could hardly at any time become dangerous in its effects, it was likely to become inconvenient, and was, therefore, to be restrained. Preposterous visions of a great future revival were indulged by these decayed princes. The more the generous sympathy of the British Government sought to cover their actual humiliation with outward marks of courtesy and respect, the more they dreamt of recovering the substantialities of their by-gone greatnesss. "The King," wrote Lord Minto, in the minute to which I have alluded, "bent on his unattainable purpose, but destitute of power to attempt it openly, and too feeble even to avow it, stoops to every little artifice, engages in every petty intrigue, and is drawn into all the oblique and disingenuous courses which the ladies of his palace, or councillors equally feminine, can suggest and recommend to him. An opening is furnished for such practices by the liberal courtesy with which the exterior observances due to the real sovereignty of his ancestors are, most properly, extended to his nominal title; and under cover of the formal homage, which a tenderness for his personal feelings alone prompts us to render him, he seeks to advance a silent and gradual claim to the substantial attributes of greatness."*

That these wild imaginations would be fostered by the excessive kindness and consideration of Mr. Seton, Metcalfe had always predicted. And now he found that the noble failing of his friend had greatly increased his own

* *Minute of Lord Minto, June 6, 1809.*—[*MS. Records.*]

difficulties—that the evils he had foreseen had actually come to pass. It was now his duty, therefore—a duty forced upon him no less by his own rooted convictions than by the recorded instructions of the Supreme Government—to do all that could be done without any indelicate and vexatious interference in the domestic affairs of the royal household, to baffle all these petty intrigues, and disperse all these idle aspirations. It was his policy, whilst exercising firm control in all matters of essential importance, to abstain from meddling with petty details connected with the interior arrangements of the palace. But nothing was more difficult than this. He could not turn a deaf ear to the reports of robbery and murder which came to him from that great sty of pollution; and yet he could not deal with offences so committed as he would with crimes, more immediately under his jurisdiction, committed in the open city. Even the truth struggled out but dimly from the murky recesses of the palace. Sometimes little things were magnified and mystified into gigantic shadows, which dissolved at the touch of judicial inquiry. At others, it was not to be doubted that terrible realities were altogether obscured and lost among the swarming labyrinths of that great building. All these things greatly disquieted Metcalfe; for the evil was a tremendous one and so difficult to reach.

There were other vexations and annoyances to disquiet him at this time. Among these was one which inconveniently affected the efficiency of his administration. The "Assistants," upon whose co-adjutancy Metcalfe chiefly relied at this time for the due administration of the revenue of the Delhi territory, were Mr. William Fraser and Mr. Gardner. But it happened, as it often happens in such cases, that their efficiency in this particular office became the signal for their removal to another; and Metcalfe was suddenly deprived of their aid. This "spoliation of the Delhi Residency," as Mr. Seton subsequently called it, was done with the best intentions by Lord Minto, who, appreciating their services, was anxious to reward them, and so removed them to the Judicial Department.* But the Resident complained, and not without reason, of being thus stripped of his auxiliaries; and Seton, to whom the letter of complaint was addressed, gave it to Lord Minto one evening at the tea-table. "More complaints, my lord, and legitimate ones too," he said, "from my excellent friend Metcalfe." "Knowing them to be such," replied Lord Minto, "I am almost afraid to read them, more especially as I have not yet been able to write to him the explanatory letter which I have so long had in contemplation."† "He, however," continued Seton, reporting these circumstances to his friend, "did read the letter, and with great interest—I might almost say distress and embarrassment—distress on your account and embarrassment on his own. Yet, though really annoyed at reflecting on the havoc made at the Residency, he could not help laughing aloud at your humorous picture of your distress, concluding with 'kings, vakeels, Sikhs, Patans, and old women.'" And, writing again soon afterwards with reference to the same subject, the member of council said, "If I did not know you to be greatly above all vanity, I might perhaps offer you some consolation by repeating what Lord Minto said upon the occasion with reference to your being in yourself a host (his words were *Ipse agmen*), and consequently

* This, after a lapse of forty years, still remains one of the gravest defects of the Indian Civil Service system. Men are removed, for the sake of promotion, from one department to another, just at the very time when the experience gained in the old office is likely to be turned to profitable account.

† This letter was afterwards written. The elaborate character of the explanation, and the kindly spirit which pervaded it, made up for the tardiness of its appearance.

admirably qualified to do with less aid than most men—to enlighten even when 'shorn of your beams.'"

But that which most disquieted Charles Metcalfe during the earlier years of his residency at Delhi was a circumstance connected, not with the diplomatic, not with the administrative, but with the social side of his multiform office. It was his duty, as has been already hinted, to keep up a certain state at Delhi, as the representative of the British Government at the court of the Mogul. To a public functionary in such a situation the entertainment of a certain, or rather uncertain number of persons every week was a business rather than a pleasure. He had to feast scores of people, of whom he knew little, and for whom he cared nothing; and to live in crowds, where he would fain have been alone. His house was a sort of huge caravansary, from which no one was turned away, but every one carried off something. For purposes of current hospitality, a liberal monthly allowance was granted by Government,* and Metcalfe was not a man to grudge its expenditure to the last sixpence. But it happened that when he joined the Delhi Residency, it was in a poor state of equipment. It was sadly wanting in all the necessary appointments of plate and furniture. Hospitality was impracticable with such means, and the external dignity of the Government could not be becomingly maintained. It was Metcalfe's duty, therefore, as he conceived, to make

* The gross allowances attached to the office had been diminished on the departure of Mr. Seton, who had drawn a consolidated allowance of 8,052 rupees a month—being 2,859 rupees salary, with 5,193 rupees Resident's charges. By a resolution of the Governor-General in Council, February 27, 1811, it was declared that this measure had been adopted on grounds principally of a personal nature with respect to Mr. Seton, and decreed that the allowances of the Delhi Residency should be placed on their former footing. For further information on this subject, see the close of Chapter XII.

certain purchases of public property at the public expense. Of these purchases, the Supreme Government tacitly approved, and the disbursements were formally admitted. But when the accounts went home to the Court of Directors, that body disapproved of the expenditure, and severely rebuked Metcalfe. "The conduct of the Delhi Resident," they wrote to the Governor-General in Council, "in incurring charges of so enormous a magnitude as those referred to in the papers before us, without having received, or even applied for, the previous sanction of Government, is in every view unjustifiable. The charges are reported by the civil auditor to be unprecedented in amount, and we are surprised to find these irregularities in the Resident's proceedings passed over without any mark of displeasure or reprehension." And having commented upon the several items of the charge, they proceeded to say —"We consider the whole disbursements to have been incurred under circumstances so directly in opposition to the regulations of which Mr. Metcalfe could not have been ignorant, and in a spirit of such profuse extravagance, that we cannot possibly sanction any part of them without holding out to our servants in general an example of the most dangerous tendency, as it amounts to no less than an assumed right to disburse the property of the Company at the discretion of the individuals divested of all wholesome control. We shall accordingly consider the whole of this disbursement as having been made unwarrantably, and under the personal responsibility of the Resident, and so accordingly direct that he be peremptorily required to pay into your treasury the whole amount of the said sum of 48,119rs. 6a. 5p., and that the property purchased thus irregularly be considered as belonging to the Resident, and not as constituting any part of the Company's dead-stock."*

* General letter to Bengal, Sept. 30, 1814.—[*MS. Records.*]

This was, doubtless, a severe rebuke. But as in India they throw up before their doors and windows well-watered screens of fragrant grass, through which the fiery winds of the hot season pass cooled and tempered, so the Governor-General was careful that the scorching blast of the Court's economical indignation should reach Metcalfe only through one of these *tatties*, softened and moderated, and rendered endurable by cooling qualifications of his own. "Although the Governor-General," wrote the Political Secretary, John Adam, in an official communication to the Delhi Resident, "has deemed it proper, as an act of obedience to the positive instructions of the Court, to communicate their order to you, yet as his lordship sees grounds for believing that the Honourable Court will take a more favourable view of the question on reconsideration, I am desired to inform you that the orders will not be enforced until the further directions of the Honourable Court may be received in reply to the proposed reference."* And at the same time John Adam wrote privately to Metcalfe, telling him that the Government intended to resist "the encroaching spirit of the Court of Directors," of which he was "destined to be the victim."†

But, in spite of the protection thrown over him by the Supreme Government, the censures of the Court of Directors wounded Metcalfe to the quick. It is the fate of most men, some time or other in the course of their lives, to be suspected and accused of those very offences which they are least capable of committing. In spite of the mollifying influences of the Secretary's official letter, the rebuke of the court was severely felt. "I have the disgrace and mortification," wrote Metcalfe to Mr. Adam, "to acknowledge the

* Secretary to Government to Resident at Delhi, July 15, 1815.—[*MS. Records.*]

† John Adam to Charles Metcalfe, July 19, 1815.—[*MS. Correspondence.*]

receipt of your despatch, conveying to me the censure of the Honourable the Court of Directors, expressed in the most unqualified terms. "It is the severe censure," he added, after thanking the Governor-General for his unsolicited kindness, "contained in the orders of the Court, which I feel most acutely, far more so than the pecuniary injury which it is proposed to inflict. My life and everything that I have are at the disposal of the Honourable Company; but my character I wish to carry unsullied to the grave."*

* It is right that I should give the substance of the defence, though the letter is too long for quotation in its integrity:

"When I arrived as Resident at Delhi," he wrote, "there was not a single article of public property at the Residency in the way of furniture for the house or equipment for the table. I could not make up the deficiency by any brought with me, because the equipment of the Residency which I had quitted was public property, and remained for the use of my successor, though much of it had been paid for out of my monthly allowances. That some furniture for the Residency house and some equipment for the Residency table were necessary, will, I hope, be admitted. It is obvious that a house is useless without furniture, and that a table cannot be kept without equipment. I take it for granted, therefore, that some furniture and some equipment were unquestionably indispensable." Assuming this, he said, two questions arose, one as to the responsibility—the other as to amount. Both had been submitted to the Supreme Government. It was competent for them to pass a decision; and if they had decided in either case against Metcalfe, he would cheerfully have abided by the decision. He argued that as the Residencies at Scindiah's Court, Nagpore, Poonah, Hyderabad, and Mysore possessed property charged to the public account, he was justified in assuming that the Delhi Residency might be brought into the same category, and admitted to the same privileges. But he declared that at the same time he had purchased the property on his own responsibility, and left it to the Government to determine whether it should be a public or a private charge. As Government had decided that it was the former, he reasoned conclusively that the censure, if any, should not be cast upon him, but upon the Government which had admitted the charge.

He then entered into an elaborate and triumphant defence of his conduct, and concluded by saying—"Knowing that I have always served the Company with devoted zeal and indefatigable labour; knowing that I am ready every day to lay down my life in their service; knowing that in the case which has brought down such heavy disapprobation on me, I was far from deserving censure, it is with a feeling stronger than grief that I find myself selected for public disgrace. In whatever spirit my conduct may be judged—whatever return my services may receive, I shall continue, as long as I serve the Company, to serve with unabated zeal and entire devotion. Unfounded censure cannot depress me, neither shall it diminish my faithful exertions. Highly as I prize the approbation of the Honourable the Court of Directors, if I have the misfortune not to obtain it, the approbation of my own conscience will support me; and I shall not sink under censure, however severe, when I feel that it is not merited, and see that it arises from error." It was indeed, as he said, the censure that stung him. The intended punishment was nothing. He was willing to abide by any arrangement for the disposal of the Residency property.* It was not in the

* In a subsequent letter he submitted to the Government the following three modes of settling the question:

"First—Let the orders of the Honourable Court be literally fulfilled. Let me pay into the treasury all the extra expenses passed by Government during my Residency on account of plate, furniture, and equipment, and let all the property purchased by me of these descriptions belong to me. Secondly—Let my allowances be put on a footing with those of my predecessor retrospectively to the day of my appointment, and let me repay to the Honourable Company all the extra expense incurred by me in the equipment of the Residency. Let the equipment of the Residency be my own property as in the time of my predecessors. Third—Let the expenses of the Residency under my predecessor, extra as well as established, be added together for the whole period of his incumbency. Let the same operation take place with regard to nature of the man to haggle with Government on a question of rupees. His whole life was a denial of the injurious supposition hinted in the Court's letter. In after years, when the increase of his fortune enabled him to manifest an increased liberality in all his dealings, he was continually taking upon himself charges which ought more properly to have been borne by the State—continually expending his private fortune upon public objects. It is not improbable that the circumstance here narrated gave a new and sustained impulse to his natural liberality; that, mindful of past vexations, he may have determined at any sacrifice to avoid the possibility of their recurrence, and so have fallen into an extreme of liberality which, noble as it is in itself, is not altogether, in respect of its operation upon others, free from certain inconveniences and objections.

But annoyances and vexations, such as have been briefly touched upon in this chapter, are inseparable from high station, whether in the East or in the West; and there were, on the other side, great compensations. Of these the chief was the knowledge that, under his administration, the industrial resources of the Delhi territory were being plenteously developed, and the prosperity of the people greatly increased. At the period of which I am now speaking—the years 1814-15—it was less, perhaps, from the contemplation of what had been done than from the thought of what might be done, under his auspices, on such a field of beneficent action, that he derived solace under the depressing influences of all public and private

the expenses of the Residency under me for a period of similar extent. Let me pay the difference if it be against me, and let the equipment of the Residency be my property as it was my predecessors'. I am heartily willing," he added, "to abide by any of those arrangements. If I suffer, I shall suffer by my own proposition."

vexations. He saw, indeed, many great defects in the system under which the affairs of our newly-acquired provinces were administered, and he was eager to introduce reforms which he knew would contribute to the happiness of our subjects. When, therefore, he reported that under the excellent management of Fraser and Gardner—for he was not one who sought to monopolise to himself the credit which rightfully belonged in part to his coadjutors—the revenues of the Delhi territory had greatly increased, and that new breadths of land were being brought under cultivation, he did not disguise from himself, or seek to disguise from Government, the fact that the landed settlement of the Delhi territory was on an unsatisfactory footing, and that justice demanded its entire revision. From a comprehensive report before me, written in 1815, I purpose to make some extracts, illustrative of Charles Metcalfe's views at this time of some important questions of domestic government. We have hitherto seen him principally as a diplomatist. Before passing on to other busy scenes of political strife and military action, let us regard him, for a little while, as an administrator, and see how liberal and large-minded were his views at a time when liberality and large-mindedness, in matters of Indian administration, were rarer qualities than they are in the present more enlightened times.

In this report, after mention had been made of the progressively increasing revenues of the Delhi territory—revenues which had risen between the years 1807-8 and 1813-1814 from four lakhs to fifteen lakhs of rupees, and it had been shown that the increase had been mainly an increase in the landed revenue, allusion was made to the *Abkarree*, or spirit tax, and it was shown that the last year of the statement exhibited a considerable decline. This was accounted for by the fact that the men who farmed this part of the revenue had, in the preceding year, bidden too high for the privilege. And if it were not so, humanely argued Metcalfe, there would be nothing to regret:

"A diminution of this branch of revenue is not much to be regretted. There is no danger of a permanent or serious loss as long as people drink spirituous liquors; and any decrease of revenue proceeding from a diminution of consumption would be a cause of joy rather than of regret."

It was, however, to the larger subject of the landed revenue that this report mainly referred. But before the writer passed on to the consideration of it in all its length and breadth, he paused to speak of the advantages of Canal irrigation, and to urge the completion of the Delhi Canal:

"I cannot refrain," he says, "from taking advantage of this opportunity to bring again to the notice of the Governor-General the subject of the Delhi Canal. This subject has engaged the attention of Government for many years; and all the information relating to it that can be furnished from this place has already been submitted. . . . . It is supposed that the produce of the canal would, in a very short time, repay the expense of bringing it into order; and it is certain that the restoration of this beneficial work would be productive of a great increase of revenue to Government, and a great increase of comfort, wealth, and health to the inhabitants of the territory and city of Delhi."

Then he entered on the great domain of land-revenue, and after discussing the much-vexed question of right in the soil, he thus proceeded to advocate the claims of the village zumeendars:

"Admitting that the Government has the property of the soil, the question is, as the Government cannot occupy the land, and as the land requires resident proprietors, who are the people that, next to the Government, may be supposed to have the best right? It is here that the paramount claim of the village zumeendars may be justly, and it is to be hoped, indisputably contended for. What men can have greater rights than those whose ancestors have occupied the same lands and habitations from time immemorial;

who live on the soil entirely, and cultivate it at their own expense and by their own labour; who receive it by hereditary succession or by purchase; who leave it to their children, or, if reduced by necessity, sell it or mortgage it; or if they choose, transfer it by gift during their lives? These rights are exercised by the zumeendars, and have been exercised for centuries. If they be not sufficient to constitute undoubted property, they are surely sufficient to confer a paramount claim. . . . . Notwithstanding the numerous revolutions which have taken place in this part of India, the rights of the village zumeendars have generally been held sacred, more sacred, it seems to me, than any other property; and though numerous sorts of oppressions have been devised, it does not appear that any oppressor, generally speaking, has presumed to interfere with these rights. It is probable that expediency has operated to secure them, as much, at least, as justice; but be the cause what it may, it appears to me that the most clear and most distinct rights held in this part of India are those of the village zumeendars."*

Having thus contended that our engagements ought to be made with this class of proprietors, he proceeded to

* An interesting illustration of the importance attached to these rights, even by the owners of principalities, which is given in this report, may not inexpediently be cited in this place:

"To show the value," wrote Metcalfe, "set on those rights, and the respectable estimation in which they are held, I may mention that Koom Raj Singh, great uncle of the Rajah of Bulumgurh, and sole manager of all the Bulumgurh lands, pointed out to me once, as I was riding with him, a single small village in the territory under his management, of which he boasted, with evident exultation, that he was the zumeendar, having purchased the zumeendaree from the original zumeendars. What made it of consequence to him to purchase this petty zumeendaree of a single village? or why did he exult at this acquired right? Why, he knew that the Raj of Bulumgurh would descend to a distinct branch of the family, his regency would in due time expire, the family might be degraded from its high rank in some future revolution, its territories might be seized, its raj might be lost; but he flattered himself, confidently, that under any circumstances this zumeendaree, purchased with his own money, would descend as a perpetual right to his family, untouched and undisturbed by any explain the nature of the settlement which it would be desirable to make. The evil consequences of short settlements had already manifested themselves, and Metcalfe was eager to persuade the Government to grant long ones in their stead. "Settlements," he wrote, "should be made for periods of ten, twenty, thirty, forty, fifty, or a hundred years—the longer, perhaps, the better. At all events, the periods should be sufficiently long to admit of considerable profit being made by the cultivators from their own labour and enterprise." "This," he added, "is the very essence of the system." Its advantages lie upon the surface. "In exchange for this insecurity, it is in the power of Government to confer security. Instead of wealth lawlessly acquired by opposition to the Government, and hastily spent to avoid plunder, we may confer the power of acquiring solid, legitimate, and lasting wealth, which shall be cherished, applauded, and upheld by the Government; which shall be a source of consequence in the eyes of the people, and of flattering distinction on the part of the rulers. Then, instead of dissatisfied and disaffected landholders truly complaining that we have injured them by diminishing their consequence and their profits, we may expect to have landholders bound to us by the strongest ties of self-interest, and acknowledging, from irresistible conviction, the incomparable benefits of our rule."

He then proceeded to explain in what manner under these settlements, the revenue was to be collected. "Every village is inhabited, wholly or partially, by zumeendars,

future Governor or Government. It must seem strange to the inhabitants of India, who so much respect the zumeendaree rights, that the British Government, which professes to consult justice in all its actions, should apparently undervalue rights which have been respected by the most despotic and the most lawless governments."

or possessory proprietors of the land. These are the persons with whom the settlement ought to be made; but as the number of them is generally too great for the transaction of business, a certain number of mokuddums, or head men, being in general the men of the greatest property and influence in the village, act on the part of the village, agree to terms, sign engagements, and transact negotiations. The village is bound by their acts. The mokuddums having concluded the settlement with the officers of Government, are charged with the duty of collecting the revenue in the village."

On the good effects of such a system as this, Metcalfe descanted with no common earnestness. He wrote as one whose whole soul was in the cause. He showed how wealth would be accumulated—how security would engender providence—how a spirit of independence would be acquired—how commerce and education would be promoted—how the people would be elevated in the social scale, and rise to a height of moral and intellectual grandeur never attained by them before. It was nothing, he argued, that by so raising them, we might teach them in time to emancipate themselves from our yoke. In spite of all such considerations as this, our duty, he said, was clear:

"There may be those who would argue that it is injudicious to establish a system which, by exciting a free and independent character, may possibly lead, at a future period, to dangerous consequences. . . . . But supposing the remote possibility of these evil consequences, that would not be a sufficient reason for withholding any advantage from our subjects. Similar objections have been made against our attempting to promote the education of our native subjects; but how unworthy it would be of a liberal Government to give weight to such objections. The world is governed by an irresistible Power, which giveth and taketh away dominion; and vain would be the impotent prudence of men against the operations of its Almighty influence. All that rulers can do is to merit dominion by promoting the happiness of those under them. If we perform our duty in this respect, the gratitude of India and the admiration of the world will accompany our name throughout all ages, whatever may be the revolutions of Futurity; but if we withhold blessings from our subjects from a selfish apprehension of possible danger at a remote period, we shall merit that reverse which time has possibly in store for us, and shall fall with the mingled hatred and contempt—the hisses and execrations of mankind."

If this had been written yesterday, there would have been nothing noticeable in it; but forty years ago such language was not often to be found in the despatches of our Indian functionaries. Charles Metcalfe, indeed, was much in advance of his contemporaries. There were few of his brethren, I fear, at this time, in whose breasts such liberal utterances as these would have awakened sympathetic echoes. The system of land-revenue which he then desired to introduce into the Delhi territory became substantially, after a lapse of many years, the system which regulated the entire settlement of the North-Western Provinces. The long obscured rights of the village zumeendars were acknowledged; and there is room to hope that many of the predictions of the young Delhi Resident may yet be realized, under the salutary influence of the system which he advocated with so much warmth.

One more illustration of Charles Metcalfe's early liberality may be derived from the same source. At this time there were few evils, real or supposed, which the members of the Indian Civil Service generally regarded with so much dread and abhorrence as the free admission of European settlers into the interior of the country. Their exclusiveness revolted at the thought of such an intrusion; and they could see nothing but oppression of the people and danger to the state in such an innovation. But Metcalfe, even at this early period, was guilty of the heresy not only of desiring, but officially recommending that independent Europeans should be invited to bring their capital, their enterprise, and skill, freely into the British territories.

"I am aware," he wrote, "that nothing that I can say on this subject would have any weight. I am also sensible that in expressing such opinions, I may be deemed guilty of presumption; but on an occasion like the present, I conceive myself bound to recommend whatever promises to be beneficial, with reference to the subject of this report; and, therefore, I recommend the free admission of British subjects to settle in India under laws and regulations suited to the state of the country, and unlimited liberty to acquire property by lawful means, as the surest mode of adding to the resources and increasing the strength of our Asiatic Empire."

It was no small thing, even with the aid of able and indefatigable assistants, to carry on the civil administration of the extensive districts under the superintendence of the Delhi Resident. But Metcalfe was not one to shrink from any amount of labour. To his civil duties he devoted himself with an assiduity which alarmed many of his friends. Among others, Ochterlony, who maintained a close and affectionate correspondence with him, wrote to Metcalfe, in the autumn of 1813, saying: "You will not be long Resident of Delhi, if you pursue your present course; and I cannot but think that a fair representation of your multifarious and miscellaneous duties would exempt you from all but the intrigues of the Palace and the general political duties, which I do most sincerely believe to be quite sufficient for any one mind that was ever created."

CHAPTER XI.

[1813—1818.]

THE POLITICS OF UPPER INDIA.

Metcalfe's Political Duties—Conduct of the Bhurtpore Rajah—Macherry and Jyepore—Indications of general Inquietude—Lord Moira's Tour in the Upper Provinces—The Nepaul War—Metcalfe's Opinions—Meeting with the Governor-General—Offer of a Secretaryship—Letters on the Subject to Mr. Jenkins—The Secretaryship declined—Death of Metcalfe's Parents.

To the "general political duties" of which Ochterlony spoke—duties which greatly occupied the thoughts and employed the energies of the Delhi Resident—it is now time to advert. On the frontier of his territory were a number of native principalities, our relations with which were under his superintendence; and, although he interfered with them no more than was essential for our security, it was necessary to keep upon all of them a watchful eye, and upon some a restraining hand. It was not likely that the rulers of these states, who were as regardless of what was due to others as they were ignorant of what was really beneficial to themselves, should have continually possessed themselves in peace, and consistently reciprocated the good faith and the good feeling which was shown towards them by the paramount power. Mistrustful of the good intentions of the British Government, and unscrupulous in their dealings with one another, it was frequently Metcalfe's duty at this time to turn his thoughts from the great work of domestic improvement to the less gratifying duty of controlling the erratic propensities of some neighbouring chief.

At the Delhi Residency, as the head-quarters of diplomacy in Upper India, there was always a cluster of "wakeels," or agents representing the interests of various princes and chiefs in the states contiguous to our own. Some of these were the agents of petty sovereigns—others of predatory chiefs—whose empire was yet to be acquired. But all had business to transact with the Resident—all had questions to put and demands to make. And the less recognised the position of the master, the more preposterous, in all probability, were the proposals of his servant. It was no uncommon thing for one of these "wakeels" to ask Metcalfe's permission for his master to attack some neighbouring state on his own account, or to be employed in the same work of aggression on the part of the British Government. And when these overtures were civilly declined, the agent would sometimes naïvely beseech the Resident to tell him whom he might attack.

But there were more difficult questions than these demanding solution. Among the earliest of our allies, who excited the watchfulness of Metcalfe during his residence at Delhi, was our old enemy of Bhurtpore. After a lapse of eight years, during which the conduct of the British Government towards him had been uniformly friendly and considerate, he now, in 1813, became suspicious of our designs, and peremptorily signified his intention no longer to suffer a British wakeel to reside at his court. He had committed many excesses on our frontier; he had destroyed our villages; he had murdered our people; he had carried off our property. But instead of chastising him for these offences, we had sent an accredited agent to his court, to be the channel of our representations to the Rajah, and thus, it was hoped, to keep him in check. But what was the result? "The petty-chief," as Metcalfe wrote, "after using ineffectually his endeavours to prevent the approach of this friendly agent to his capital, tries by ill treatment to compel his employers to recall him; does not permit him to take up his residence at his court, nor to exercise his functions, nor even to enter the walls of the capital without special permission, and a special guard, but keeps him and his people outside of the town, encamped on the plain, in a state of restraint, and, moreover, persists in this unfriendly course of proceeding, though invited to a more amicable behaviour in the most conciliatory language; and though warned that a continuance of such insulting conduct must inevitably give offence to the British Government."

The minute from which these extracts were taken is a long and elaborate one; full of characteristic energy and determination, clearly and forcibly expressed. It should never be forgotten by the reader, whose experiences are those only of European life, that the minutes of the Indian statesman, in the history of his career, take the place of the orations which, under free governments in the western world, are delivered to senatorial assemblies. The Indian statesman is not stirred by the excitement of popular applause; his utterances do not reach the ears of hundreds of auditors, and are only in rare instances subsequently reflected by the press, and dwelt upon by thousands of readers. He writes, in the solitude of his own chamber, under many depressing influences, knowing that what he writes is to count its readers by units; but writing nevertheless with his whole heart in his work, earnestly and enthusiastically, and often with a power of expression which in oral discourse would charm a popular assembly. There may be dull writers in India, as there are dull speakers in England; but there are many exceptions, whom it would be easy to enumerate; and the name of Charles

Metcalfe in such an enumeration would be one of the foremost in the list.

In his minute on Bhurtpore the writer dwelt earnestly on the great forbearance which, throughout many years, had been shown towards the offending state, and he contrasted the course which we had adopted, in this instance, with that which had been followed towards a neighbouring principality—the Rajpoot state of Jyepore. Partly in illustration of Metcalfe's style—partly because I shall come presently to speak of our dealings with Jyepore—the following passage is given. In such brief, pregnant, antithetical sentences Metcalfe always rejoiced:

> "It is curious," he wrote, "in adverting to the events of past days, to observe how our policy has operated in favour of Bhurtpore. We formed alliances about the same period with the states of Bhurtpore and Jyepore. Both states on the same occasion were false to their alliances, but in different degrees. Bhurtpore joined and fought with our enemy Holkar. Jyepore only hesitated to fulfil its engagement with us. The one which committed the most venial fault has suffered; the other, which sinned against us more heinously, has been befriended. With Jyepore we kept on terms during the war with Holkar, and made use of its troops against him; but after the war we abandoned it to its fate, and the country has since been overrun by the armies of Holkar and other freebooters. Bhurtpore we had to fight as the ally of Holkar, and we have ever since protected it against all enemies. Jyepore has been sinking every day since we dissolved the alliance with that stat , and is now nearly annihilated. Bhurtpore has been growing in wealth, power, and consequence under our protection. Jyepore is now at our feet, begging for protection and alliance. Bhurtpore refuses to admit our agent to reside at his court."

That there was a clear *casus belli* was never doubted. Metcalfe recommended that the British Government should dissolve its alliance with the Bhurtpore Rajah, and send an overwhelming force against his stronghold. He did not counsel the slow process of a regular siege. For some time past we had been unfortunate in our regular sieges.

The experiences of the Mahratta war indicated that they were not seldom unsuccessful. Instead, therefore, of attempting to breach Bhurtpore, he recommended that we should carry it by *escalade.* Well acquainted as he was with the peculiar construction of the place, and cognisant with the circumstances, both of attack and defence, which had resulted in our former inglorious failure, he pointed out, with great precision and distinctness, the causes of our past disasters, and indicated the best means of avoiding them. He was convinced that Bhurtpore would fall beneath a *coup de main.* He believed that we wanted nothing more than the stout heart and the cold steel. He lived to see the English ensign waving over Bhurtpore; but the stronghold was carried by another process.

He waited more than ten years to see the realization of his hopes. The Government of India were not at this time prepared to undertake a war against Bhurtpore. The Java expedition had diminished our available resources in respect both of money and of men. So our resentment was expressed only by the dismissal of the Bhurtpore agent from Delhi, whilst another and a higher representative of the offended Rajah was permitted to remain at the court of Calcutta. The intention of Government was officially announced to Metcalfe, whilst Mr. Seton, who, it will be remembered, had taken his seat in the Supreme Council, wrote privately to his old assistant to say they were deterred from making war, under so great provocation, not by any want of will, but by a lamentable want of means.*

* "How sadly you have been annoyed by that weak, ungrateful man, the Rajah of Bhurtpore. We may say with truth, '*If we could, we would!*' He has given us repeated cause of offence; and did the state of our army and our finances (now very low) admit of our meeting the probable consequences of an open rupture, we would of course hold very plain language. But as that is now out of the question, we must avoid showing our teeth—that is, we

In the meanwhile, the Jyepore state seemed to be at its last gasp. Unprotected by the paramount power, and helpless in itself, it lay at the mercy of all its unscrupulous neighbours, and all the predatory chiefs who were continually looking out for some undefended quarter against which to direct their attacks. That great Rohilla freebooter, Ameer Khan, whose acquaintance Metcalfe had made during the war with Holkar, and whose subsequent career had been one of unbridled excess, was pursuing his course of spoliation wherever the weakness of others tempted him to let loose his banditti; and, another soldier of fortune, Shah Khan, was emulating the Rohilla in deeds of unscrupulous daring. The notorious weakness of Jyepore had long excited the cupidity of the former chief, who in 1811 ravaged the country and reduced the unhappy prince to a state of feebleness and prostration. which bordered closely upon dissolution. But there were other trials still in store for him. Scarcely had Ameer Khan quitted the Jyepore territory, when the Rajah of Macherry,*

must, whilst we evince to him that we are dissatisfied with his conduct, take care not to appear too angry—because if we did, we might lead him to suppose that we would fain go to war with him at once, if we could, and that conclusion would give rise to another, viz., that we are too weak to have recourse to the *ultima ratio regum*? On this ground it is that we must, whilst manifesting our displeasure, preserve our tranquillity; and to borrow an expression from the *Agreeable Surprise*, take care 'not to give him room to suppose his serene highness (the Governor-General) is in a passion.' This will explain to you our motive for not doing more than insist upon the Rajah's withdrawing his wakeel from Delhi. Since he will not agree to receive an accredited agent from you, it is but fair that you should dismiss his agent from yours. There were, however, powerful objections to our going still further by dismissing his wakeel, who had hitherto been stationed at Calcutta—or declaring the alliance dissolved."—[*Seton to Metcalfe, June* 21, 1813.]

* Macherry is a state bordering upon Bhurtpore.

known as the Rao Rajah, entered it with an invading army, and in the year 1812 took possession of the two forts of Doobbee and Sikrawa with the territories adjacent to them. This was an outrage which, although Jyepore was not under the protection of the British, was to be remonstrated against and resisted; and Metcalfe accordingly, through the Rajah's wakeels, called upon him to make restitution. In spite, however, of the Delhi Resident's repeated requests, the usurper remained obdurate. All through the year of his acquisition, and all through the following year, he remained in possession of the tracts of country he had snatched from his neighbour.* It was time, therefore, that decided steps should be taken to obtain restitution, so Metcalfe counselled a display of military force; and in the meanwhile addressed to the Rajah the following spirited letter of warning and remonstrance:

MR. METCALFE TO THE RAO RAJAH.

"From your want of attention to my repeated requisitions for the restoration of Doobbee and Sikrawa to their lawful owner, the Rajah of Jyepore, I am led to conclude that it is not your intention to restore those places.

"If you have no regard for justice; if you think it right in the sight of God to seize the property of another without cause of

* "He had," says Colonel Sutherland, "so long remained in security, that he had forgotten the danger of involving himself with his neighbours, and thought the British Government would not arm against him in support of the interests of Jyepore. He was, too, supposed to have collected a treasure of nearly half a million sterling. It became a question whether in this state of affairs we should withdraw from the terms of our alliance with the Rao Rajah, and allow Jyepore to avenge its own wrongs, bringing on Ulwar (Macherry) all the evils of an invasion from the forces of that state, those of Ameer Khan, Shah Khan, and other leaders of predatory bands, or whether we should ourselves assemble an army to punish the Rao Rajah."

offence; if you see no difference between the friendship and enmity of the British Government; if you see no good in its friendship and no danger in its enmity; if you prefer the retaining of Doobbee and Sikrawa to the continuance of the friendship of the British Government, and think that you can retain those places in spite of the British Government; if you prefer war with the British Government to the restoration of those places; if you feel yourself strong, and fancy the British Government weak; if you think that success will attend you in war,—then all I can say will be unavailing. What will be, will be.

"But if you believe that the British Government does possess any power; if you are aware that its anger is to be feared; if you know that it adheres to a determination once formed,—then I conjure you to pay attention to your true interests. Do not, I implore you, suffer designing men to mislead you. They are plotting your ruin, and will rejoice at your destruction.

"Do not imagine from the moderation which has been shown that this point can ever be conceded to you. That is impossible. The British Government has a sincere regard for you, and therefore has not yet proceeded to forcible measures, in the hope that you may be persuaded by advice and remonstrance to do what is necessary in justice to the Rajah of Jyepore. But if you do not restore Doobbee and Sikrawa, sooner or later measures of another nature will be necessary, and then repentance will be vain.

"Never, never, never, will the British Government cease to demand the restoration of Doobbee and Sikrawa to the Rajah of Jyepore; and if to accomplish that purpose war be unavoidable, however much it will regret the necessity of hostilities, still it will not fail to do its utmost to compel you to perform that indispensable act of justice.

"Take your choice. Choose between the friendship and the anger of the British Government, and tell me plainly what you are determined to do.

"I perform the duty of a friend in giving you warning. If you should be ruined by not following my advice, you will not have to blame me. I have given you notice. Remember what I say."

Such remonstrances, such warnings as these, were thrown away upon the Rajah. Earnestly, therefore, Metcalfe recommended Government to authorize the employment of a military force to compel the recusant chief to make an unconditional surrender of the places he had conquered, and to pay the expenses of assembling our troops. Lord Moira had by this time entered upon the government of India. The tone in which Metcalfe wrote on the subject to his friend John Adam, then Political Secretary, pleased the new Governor-General, to whom the Delhi letters were confidentially submitted, and impressed him with a high opinion of the moral and intellectual qualities of the Resident.* The authority which Metcalfe sought was granted to him. A military force was assembled; a demonstration was made. The British troops advanced within a march of the capital; and then the Rajah yielded to our demands. The places which he had usurped were restored to their legitimate owners; and he was compelled to open his treasury to repay us for the expenses we had incurred in bringing him thus tardily to reason.

Viewed by themselves, these were but small matters,

* "I could not refuse myself the satisfaction of communicating your letters confidentially to Lord Moira, who entered fully and cordially into the spirit and tendency of your reasoning, and is disposed to go the full length of all your views in the event of the early submission of the Rao Rajah not disarming us. He considers your letter to contain a very able view of the affairs to which it refers, and not less just than able. It is his opinion that the mere submission of a power, which has forced you into an expensive and hazardous appeal to arms, even though accompanied by the cession of the objects in dispute, to be insufficient for the interests of a state (I use his own words)—that there should be infliction to deter others from imposing upon us a similar embarrassing necessity, and other observations to the same effect. If we actually engage in war, then I have very little doubt that he will be disposed to make the Rajah smart for his conduct. The instructions of the 1st authorize you to reduce him to unconditional submission in the case supposed. To-day I shall send you an answer to your last despatch, conveying authority to enforce payment of the expense of assembling the troops, even if he should surrender before the sword is drawn."—[*John Adam to Charles Metcalfe, November* 15, 1813.]

scarcely deserving of the space which I have bestowed upon them, in such a memoir as this. But they were parts of a great aggregate of evil—examples of the confused and embarrassing state of our relations with the numerous petty states of Central India, resulting from those great peace measures of 1806, which Metcalfe at the time criticised with so much severity and censured with so much warmth. It appeared to him now that we were beginning to reap the difficulties and perplexities we had sown; and that a general adjustment of our relations with these states was imperatively demanded for the security of our position and the establishment of a permanent peace. We were now, indeed, on the threshold of great events. It was plainly foreseen that some vast political changes were at hand; and there was not a statesman of high repute between the banks of the Jumna and the western coast who was not eager for the settlement of which I have spoken, even though it should be preceded by a great and burdensome war. The crisis, indeed, was close upon us. Compromises and concessions could not much longer retard its approach.

The most peaceful rulers who ever governed our Indian Empire have left to their successors a sad heritage of political convulsion, military strife, and financial embarrassment. The greatest wars which have taxed the wisdom of our Indian statesmen and the energies of our Indian armies have been undertaken by the successors of Lord Teignmouth, Lord Minto, and Lord William Bentinck. It seems as though in the Eastern world the moderation of our rulers could bear only the bitter fruit of war and conquest—that forbearance in one year were but the antecedent of compulsory violence and aggression in another—that the most steadfast resolution to go so far and no farther, formed, in all honesty and all wisdom, by the least ambitious of our statesmen, could only pave the way to new victories and new additions of territory to an empire already "overgrown."

When in the autumn of 1813 Lord Minto sailed from India, the country, as he believed, was lapped in universal repose. But scarcely had Lord Moira seated himself in the vacant chair, when it seemed to him that war was inevitable. Mutterings of distant hostility reached him from many quarters, and stirred the heart of the old soldier as with the sound of a trumpet. He did not long remain inactive at the Presidency. His associates in the Supreme Government dissented from the views of the Governor-General, and strife between them was speedily engendered. In the autumn of 1814 Lord Moira turned his back upon the Presidency; and then the war became a war of minutes. Into the merits of this controversy I am not called upon to enter. It is sufficient to state the fact, that the greater part of the long administration, on which this narrative has now entered, was disturbed by continual hostilities with neighbouring states. The first of these was a war with Nepaul. The depredations committed by the Goorkhas on our borders—the continual insecurity of our frontier which the conduct of these hardy mountaineers entailed upon us—called for a display of military force. Preparations were made for the coercion of our offending neighbours; and the commencement of the ensuing cold season—the cold season of 1814-15—saw our armies again in motion.

The events of the Goorkha war are not connected with the biography of Charles Metcalfe by any other link than that of the correspondence which he carried on with many of the chief actors in it—with Ochterlony, with Jasper Nicolls, with the young Engineer Lawtie, with his old assistant Gardner, now employed in a political capacity on the Nepaul frontier, and with others, who contributed more or less to the ultimate success of our operations. The correspondence was not a cheering one. For some time it treated mainly of misfortune. The war opened with a disastrous failure at Kalunga, where the gallant Gillespie, attempting to carry a strong fortress without breaching, was shot through the heart at the head of his men. Ochterlony, aided, as in his generous candour the veteran ever delighted to acknowledge, by the brave-hearted, quick-witted subaltern Lawtie, achieved some partial successes; but he did not think that he was strong enough to follow them up; he had never been able to perceive the wisdom of the war, and had little taste for the service on which he was employed.* Marley and Wood failed miserably. Nicolls did better things, and laid the foundation of an honourable fame. But, looking at the whole, the outset of the war was calamitous and discreditable; and Metcalfe, disappointed by repeated tidings of failure and disaster, began to think that the beginning of the end had arrived, and that our Indian Empire would soon be shaken to the base. It was his opinion that a grand cardinal error had been committed in not effecting the settlement of Central India before entering upon this Goorkha campaign. It was his opinion, also, that we were too prone to under-rate the strength and despise the resources of our enemies; that our failures generally resulted from over-confidence; that we were far too prone to fling ourselves, without ordinary caution, upon the strongholds of our enemies; and that

* On his first appointment to command a division of the army in the field, Ochterlony wrote to Metcalfe: "A new sort of service, my dear friend! I have not the least objection to a proper vindication of the national honour, and, if necessary, an attack on the heart of their empire, Catamandoo, or some of the members in this quarter; but to set off with the idea of overthrowing a long-established Government, and for such an unprofitable purpose, appears to me the most Quixotic and the most impolitic measure we have ever attempted—setting aside all physical difficulties."—[*August* 25, 1814. *M.S. Correspondence.*]

inasmuch as our tenure of India was dependent upon the assertion of our military superiority in the field, and that as on several recent occasions this superiority had been assumed rather than demonstrated, our very position in India was threatened by the recurrence of such failures. There were remedies for this he believed at our command, and it was our duty to resort to them. What they were he was eager to indicate—and, in a paper which he forwarded to Lord Moira, in November, 1814, he emphatically set them forth. He was a civilian; but he was no novice in the art of war; he had lived much in the camp; he had seen much of military operations; he had observed our failures, as he had our successes, and traced both to their source. It was no presumption in him, therefore, to write on military questions, as affected by local circumstances in Upper India, even for the guidance of so ripe a soldier as the man then at the head of affairs.

At this time, (holding the offices both of Governor-General and Commander-in-Chief, Lord Moira,) attended by a numerous suite, was progressing through the upper provinces of Hindostan. Among other arrangements, was one, which was to bring the Delhi Resident, accompanied by the "wakeels" of the different native courts within his diplomatic circle, to the vice-regal camp at Moradabad. But early in November there was a conjuncture of circumstances, which rendered Metcalfe's detention at the imperial city a very probable state-necessity, so he despatched to his friend John Adam, Political Secretary, his paper on the conduct of the war, to be submitted to the Governor-General. "I transmit," he wrote, "the accompanying, for submission to Lord Moira, with some trepidation; because I am not sure that his Lordship will approve of my intruding my thoughts on his notice, on a subject not perhaps within the bounds of my official duty; nevertheless, I transmit it under a conviction, probably erroneous, but working powerfully in my mind, that the subject demands early consideration in the point of view in which I have stated it—in which point of view it may not for some time be seen unless brought to notice. His Lordship may deem my opinions absurd, and my conduct in thrusting those opinions upon him presumptuous, but he will, I trust, bestow an indulgent consideration on the motive by which I am actuated; and pardon a presumption which proceeds solely from anxiety for the public welfare."

In the paper thus submitted to the Governor-General, Metcalfe, after alluding to the recent disaster at Kalunga, proceeded to declare his opinion that we held India only by the sword, that the overawing weapon was being blunted in our hands, and that our tenure of the country was precarious. He had begun already to broach those theories which, emphatically propounded at a later period, were said to be little in accordance with the general sound sense and equable temper of the man, but which are now regarded as signs only of his unexampled prescience:—

"Every successive failure of this description is more disastrous, on account of its influence on the stability of our power than on account either of the lamentable fall of brave men, or the temporary derangement of the plans of Government, much as both of these effects are to be deplored.

"The present opportunity is taken for attempting to bring this subject to notice, in the hope that the recollection of the circumstances of our recent disaster may procure some attention to opinions, which cannot derive any weight from their owner, which would probably be disregarded in a time of peace, and might appear ridiculous in a career of uninterrupted victory. These opinions were first excited by personal observations in the field, and have been strengthened by attention to subsequent events. . . . .

"Whatever delusions may prevail in England respecting the security to be derived from the affections of our Indian subjects, and a character for moderation and forbearance with foreign native states, it will probably be admitted in India, that our power depends solely on our military superiority. Yet there is reason to apprehend that our comparative superiority is in some measure diminished in consequence of a general increase of discipline, experience, skill, and confidence, on the part of the military of India.")

Having laid down these general propositions, he proceeded to declare that there was, as there still is, in our armies, a dangerous tendency to under-rate the strength of our enemies. Metcalfe had seen something of this in the Mahratta war. He was familiar with the language of the camp. He knew that it was the fashion to speak slightingly of both the courage and the prowess of our enemies. He knew that men who accepted with caution these disparaging estimates were called "croakers;" that it was considered, indeed, something almost ignominious to question our ability to crush all opposition at a blow. And, knowing this, he felt at the outset of what promised to be a long and harassing campaign that there was nothing more to be guarded against than this over-weening confidence in our gallantry, our resources, and our fortune:—

"It is desirable, in the first instance, that the favourable reports received beforehand relative to the weakness of an enemy's fortresses and the inefficiency of his troops should be listened to with caution. Men of sanguine dispositions give favourable reports, and anticipate unqualified victories, without reflecting on the possibility of difficulties and the chances of failure, because it is in their nature to do so. Other men, not sanguine, are generally very loth to express an unfavourable opinion. There is always the chance of success. Encouraging intelligence is always the more agreeable; and men do not like to subject themselves to the reproach of being alarmists. We are apt to despise our opponents, till from defeat we acquire an opposite sensation. Before we come to the contest, their powers of resistance are ridiculed. Their forts are said to be contemptible, and their arms are described to be useless. Yet we find on the trial, that with these useless weapons in their contemptible forts they can deal about death among their assailants, and stand to their defences, notwithstanding the skill and bravery of our army. If we were not misled beforehand by a flattering persuasion of the facility of conquest, we should take greater pains to secure it."

These pregnant truths are truths equally to be regarded now, after the lapse of forty years of conquest, not unchequered by repeated disaster. It were well that a warning voice, again and again proclaiming them, should be lifted up at the outset of every new campaign.

After speaking in detail of past disasters, of some of which, as our great miscarriage at Bhurtpore, he had personal cognizance, he proceeded to express a very strong conviction that we had failed in all our sieges to turn our ordnance to the best account—that if we were to bring into the field powerful mortar-batteries, with good stores of shells, and try the effect of a brisk and long-continued vertical fire upon the besieged places, they would, if not evacuated by the enemy, be easily carried by assault :—

"We have on our side," he said, "the science of Europe, and we ought to bring it into play. Economy in this department is ruinous. We ought to be lavish of the contents of our arsenals, and saving of the lives of our men. We ought to make defence impracticable and hopeless. We ought to overpower resistance by the vastness of our means. There is a branch of equipment in sieges which might be made of more use than it is at present to the great annoyance of the enemy, and frequently to its total expulsion. A great number of mortars and an abundant supply of shells should be attached to every besieging army. There are many situations in which, from the natural difficulties of the position, an assault cannot take place without considerable hazard of failure. In such cases, an incessant shower of shells, day and night, might make the place too warm for the garrison, and obviate the necessity of a storm. There are other occasions in which it may be desirable to avoid the delay of all the operations of a siege. And on such occasions bombarding day and night might accomplish the object in a short time. There are some situations for which the mode of operation is peculiarly suitable—for instance, the small hill forts of the Goorkhas appear to be of this description; and had Kalunga been bombarded day and night for as many days as we were before it prior to our attempt to storm it, it is probable that we should not now have to lament our disastrous failure at that place, and the loss of our gallant general and his brave companions in death."

These practical considerations Metcalfe supported by adducing several instances of the success of shelling derived from the recent annals of Indian warfare. On some occasions he admitted that it might be expedient "for the speedy accomplishment of a great object to risk a hazardous assault." The capture of Alighur by a *coup de main* at the very commencement of the Mahratta war, had tended, in no small measure, to secure the success of all our subsequent operations. Metcalfe had been of opinion only a little while before this paper was written, that if we again undertook to besiege Bhurtpore, it would be expedient to attempt to carry it by a *coup de main*. But these were exceptional cases; and the writer continued to dwell upon the expediency of following the more cautious mode of operation. One thing, at all events, was certain. If war were to be made, it was expedient to make it with full consideration, and with sufficient means. We were at this time on the threshold of some momentous enterprises. The Indian army did not seem, as then constituted, to be competent to the successful performance of the great work that lay before it. So Metcalfe did not hesitate to denounce the thrifty policy of the Home Government, and to call for an augmentation of the army.

"The writer of these remarks," he said, in conclusion, "does not shrink from briefly stating his opinion, that an increase of our army is highly expedient, and, perhaps, absolutely necessary for our existence in India; and that we ought to govern our policy by different considerations from those which regulate the orders of the Government at home. Our power on India rests upon our military superiority. It has no foundation in the affections of our subjects. It cannot derive support from the good will or good faith of our neighbours. It can only be upheld by our military prowess, and that policy is best suited to our situation in India which tends in the greatest degree to increase our military power by all means consistent with justice.")

Looking at our recent disasters at Kalunga with the eye of a true soldier—the eye of one who had once been what old Sir Theophilus used to call the "nurse of King's officers"—Metcalfe, in this paper, hit the blot to a nicety, and suggested the true remedy. His recommendations were justified by the result. After another failure, rendered memorable by something even more lamentable than the death of the gallant Gillespie, the effect of a bombardment was tried. Never was anything more completely successful. Our mortars and howitzers did terrible execution among the defiant garrison of Kalunga. In a little while the air was tainted by the decaying bodies of heaps of men destroyed by our murderous shells, and all resistance was at an end. Out of the six hundred defenders of the place only seventy escaped. The fortress was speedily demolished; and soon passing travellers related that not one stone was left upon another.

The general opinions officially expressed in the concluding passages of the memorandum had found utterance a few days before in a private letter to Metcalfe's old friend Richard Jenkins, then Resident at Nagpore, whom he had not seen for many years, but whom he still affectionately remembered. Jenkins, who, now become a mature statesman, shared with Elphinstone and Metcalfe the honours of the highest diplomatic triumvirate in the country, had drawn up an elaborate paper on our alliances with the states in the direction of the Berar country and the Nerbudda territories; and a copy of it had been sent to the Delhi Resident, who read it with delight, and returned it with the following letter to the writer—a letter in which Metcalfe thus expounded his general views of the extent to which it behoved the British Government to adhere to, or depart from, their system of non-interference :—

"We require, by-the-by, an increase of revenue to enable us to maintain an increase of the army, rendered necessary to all appearance by the extension of our connections, as well as the great extent of our frontier. I do not know, however, that an increase of the army is in contemplation, or that the necessity is admitted by those who are to judge; I only speak my own sentiments on this point. It is curious to observe how frequently we are compelled by policy to deviate from our *fixed* principles. I remember the time when the advancement of our influence on the Sutlej was reprobated even by Lord Wellesley as too great an extension of our views. Subsequently proposals to that effect were repeatedly rejected, until my mission to Lahore, which produced at least the benefit of an arrangement that has been attended with the best effects; though, when I went on that mission, it was not in contemplation to protect the chiefs between the Sutlej and the Jumna, other plans being in contemplation for the conciliation of Runjeet Singh, whom at that time it was impossible to conciliate. Our subsequent interference in favour of Nagpore against Meer Khan was another deviation from our system, and a very wise one. I only regret that we did not take advantage of the opportunity to make the Rajah purchase our permanent protection on our own terms. Various arrangements since have shown other deviations from our system; and it only remains to renounce a system from which we are always compelled to deviate. Our power in India is so strangely constituted that, unless we take advantage of all fair opportunities to increase our strength, we may meet some day with unexpected reverses, and have our power shaken to its centre, if not overturned. It is doubtful, I think, how long we shall preserve our wonderful empire in India; but the best chance of preserving it must arise from our making ourselves strong by all just means; not from an absurd system which would affect to look on with indifference at the increasing strength of others, and to trust for our existence to the unattainable character of unambitious amiable innocence and forbearance. Are you acquainted with the plans of Government regarding Nepaul? If not, I can send you some information regarding them."

Such opinions as are here expressed were not distasteful at head-quarters. The paper which Metcalfe forwarded to

Lord Moira was favourably received;* and it was soon responded to by an invitation to the writer to visit the Governor-General's camp. "As the immediate urgency," wrote John Adam, on the 21st of November, "for your remaining at Delhi has diminished, Lord Moira has desired me to say that he will be happy if you can meet him at Moradabad, where he expects to arrive in ten days from this date. . . . . His lordship is of opinion that as you are yourself to come to Moradabad, it will be more convenient to bring your host of native visitors to that station, or near it, than to postpone them till his arrival at Kurnaul, as proposed in Swinton's letter to you." This business of the reception was, indeed, an important one. The near approach of the vice-regal camp had thrown not only the royal family of Delhi, but the whole circle of native diplomatists, into a state of excitement; and arrangements were now to be made both for the reception of his Majesty's delegates and the crowd of lesser wakeels, and for a deputation of British functionaries to the imperial court.†

* On the first receipt of the paper, John Adam had written to Metcalfe that there was little doubt of his lordship's approbation. "The indispensable measure," he said, "of augmenting the military force is, I fear, not to be expected. With respect to the mode of conducting operations against fortified places, his lordship's judgment had long since adopted a conclusion corresponding to yours; and the utmost care has been taken not only to furnish the forces destined to act against the Nepaulese with an ample equipment of mortars, howitzers, and shells, but to enjoin in the most positive manner the use of them to the utmost. The neglect of this order at Kalunga it is too late to discuss, and must ever be lamented."—[*John Adam to Charles Metcalfe, November* 20, 1814. *M.S. Correspondence.*]

† Some grave questions of no very easy solution, arising out of the windy dignity of the poor puppet of Delhi, had suggested themselves to the authorities at head-quarters. It was not improbable that the Mogul, considering rather what he, or his

"I am going immediately to meet his lordship at Moradabad," wrote Metcalfe to Jenkins on the 24th of November. By the end of the month he was in the vice-regal camp. The ceremonies, of which he was then master, were soon over, and more serious business was in hand.

There were many important questions to be put to the Delhi Resident—much information to be sought which only he could satisfactorily afford:—what effect our recent disasters had upon the people of the Delhi territory and the adjacent country, and on the minds of the dependent chiefs and independent princes of Hindostan—what would be their influence on the mind of Runjeet Singh—what steps should be taken to counteract such influence—what course of conduct ought to be pursued towards Bhurtpore—whether, and under what circumstances, the Governor-General should have a personal interview with the King of

ancestors, had been, than what he was, would refuse to pay to the Governor-General such compliments as the Governor-General was willing to pay to him. This especially in the matter of nuzzurs or presents of homage—the interchange of which Lord Moira considered desirable to avoid even with the King—but he intimated that he would not object to it, if required, "or to any other indispensable forms, under a conviction that they cannot be misconstrued into demonstrations of homage on his own part." "His lordship," added Mr. Adam, "will also expect that if his deputation present nuzzurs to the King, his Majesty's deputation will present nuzzurs to the Governor-General, and in all respects perform the same or corresponding ceremonies." The apprehensions here glanced at were justified by the result. Metcalfe could not persuade the unhappy King that, if he were to meet the Governor-General at all, it was incumbent upon him to meet his lordship as an equal. The Shah still required that some acknowledgment of his superiority should be shown; so the Governor-General declined the interview. "Have the goodness, therefore," wrote the Chief Secretary to Metcalfe, after the former had left the camp of the Governor-General, "with your accustomed diplomatic ability, to reconcile the King to the impracticability of a meeting."

Delhi—whether the power of granting native titles should be left in the hands of the imperial puppet, or assumed by the British Government—whether an agent from Shah Soojah, the fugitive King of Caubul, should be received in the vice-regal camp, and, lastly, what was the general political and military condition of the upper provinces of India with reference to the defence of our frontier and the expediency of consolidating our power in the interior of India? For the solution of all these questions, the Governor-General and his ministers looked eagerly to Metcalfe's arrival in camp.*

At Lord Moira's head-quarters were many able men. Civilians of high repute and soldiers of large experience and sound judgment clustered around him. It happened that the chief of these were Charles Metcalfe's friends—Charles Ricketts, John Adam, and George Swinton, the chief ministerial functionaries, and George Fagan, the Adjutant-General, all knew and esteemed Metcalfe—nay, they loved him; and now they eagerly welcomed among them one whose public character and personal qualities were equally valued by them. They had all spoken of him to Lord Moira in language of becoming admiration. To the Governor-General, indeed, who had often heard, and on perusing the despatches of the Delhi Resident had echoed his praises, Metcalfe was presented as no stranger. He was received at once into the councils of the vice-regal camp. Such an accession of strength in such a juncture was welcome in the extreme.

For the juncture was one which, in the eyes of Lord Moira and his staff, demanded the exercise of all the talent that could be pressed into their service. The Goorkhas, who were defying us from their hill-forts; the Pindarrees, who were ravaging our frontiers; the Mahratta princes,

* "Memorandum of points for discussion with Mr. Metcalfe," drawn up by Mr. John Adam.—[*MS. Records.*]

who, sheltered by the name of ally, were looking eagerly for a favourable opportunity to assail us—were not the only enemies whose skill and courage at this time disquieted the Governor-General. There was a contest raging between the head-quarters' camp and the council-chamber of Calcutta; and the Pindarrees of Leadenhall-street, with their restrictions and retrenchments, were assailing the rear of the Governor-General. Mr. Edmonstone was then Vice-President of the Council. Mr. Seton and Mr. Dowdeswell were his associates in the Government. The current business of the administration was in the hands of those three gentlemen; and though the power of war-making and peace-making belonged to the Governor-General, the councillors had still the means of conducting an opposition which, however futile for the time, might, backed by the Court of Directors and the Board of Control, eventually be successful, and was, at all events, embarrassing and annoying.

Edmonstone was a host in himself. He had immense experience, a sound head, a ready pen, and a reputation second to none in India. It was with deep sorrow that he arrayed himself against the Governor-General; but what he believed to be his duty he was not one to shrink from doing, and he recorded his opinions with the calm confidence of one never doubting the goodness of his cause, but deploring the necessity of asserting it. Lord Moira respected his opponent; as did all the ministerial officers in his camp—but he was not on that account less anxious to refute him. He saw the necessity of having able men at his elbow to expound his opinions and to give effect to his projects; and he soon saw that Metcalfe was one who would enter with his whole soul into the views of the Governor-General, making light of those very difficulties which were being continually paraded before him by his antagonists of the Calcutta Council. The longer Metcalfe remained in the camp of the Governor-General, the more plainly it appeared that his policy was identical with that which Lord Moira was inclined to favour. Indeed, the boldness and decision with which Metcalfe declared his opinions, seemed to fix and rivet those of the Governor-General and disperse all doubts and misgivings. It was pleasing to the old soldier to be thus supported by one of India's younger statesmen; and all the ministerial officers by whom he was surrounded delighted in the thought that they had obtained the assistance of so thorough-going and efficient an ally.

Invited to declare his opinions freely, Metcalfe not only delivered them, without reservation, in oral discourse, but fully expounded them in elaborate minutes. In one written in December, 1814, in the Governor-General's camp, he laid down a detailed plan for the settlement of Central India, prefaced by a series of general propositions, declaring that everything must give place to the necessity of maintaining an overwhelming military establishment.* But it was apparent to him that now that we had once embarked in the Nepaul war, nothing else could be done until we extricated ourselves from it with honour. The dangers it had entailed upon us, he said, were great; for England could not fail with impunity, and we were now surrounded with enemies all eager to take advantage of our discomfiture:† "There is Runjeet Singh," he wrote

* More detailed mention of this paper will be found in the following chapter.

† That Metcalfe, at this time, was not inclined to under-rate the extent of our failures, or the danger which they brought upon us, may be gathered from some passages in a letter written to Mr. Jenkins about this time (Jan. 15, 1815). In this letter the writer says: "We have met with an enemy who shows decidedly greater bravery and greater steadiness than our troops possess; and it is impossible to say what may be the end of such a reverse of the order of things. In some instances our troops, European and

in a paper given to Lord Moira, in January, 1815, "looking eagerly on from the north-west. There is Meer Khan within a few marches of the Delhi and Agra frontiers. There are Scindiah and the Rajah of Nagpore settling whether they shall attack us or not; and thus virtually menacing our frontier from Agra down to Cuttack. There are the Pindarrees ready to pour themselves into every defenceless country. Had the operations of our campaign against the Goorkhas been decidedly successful, the war would have increased our reputation and power; and so far from encouraging any hostile designs of other powers, would have deterred all enemies from such designs. But when our numerous enemies see us entangled and embarrassed in an unsuccessful war, it is hardly to be expected that they will refrain from taking advantage of such a favourable opportunity, unless they be overawed by suitable arrangements and proportionate exertions on our part."

Under such circumstances Metcalfe argued that it was desirable to conclude peace with Nepaul as soon as a blow could be struck at the Goorkha power—such a blow as would relieve us of all apprehensions of their again inviting a contest with the British. This, he said, could only be done by commencing operations upon a much larger scale

native, have been repulsed by inferior numbers with sticks and stones. In others, our troops have been charged by the enemy sword in hand, and driven for miles like a flock of sheep. In a late instance of complete rout, we lost more muskets by a great number than there were killed, wounded, and missing. In short I, who have always thought our power in India precarious, cannot help thinking that our downfall has already commenced. Our power rested solely on our military superiority. With respect to one enemy, that is gone. In this war, dreadful to say, we have had numbers on our side, and skill and bravery on the side of our enemy. We have had the inhabitants of the country disposed to favour us, and yet overawed, notwithstanding our presence and partial success, by the character of our enemy."

than had been previously instituted. "Let every effort," he said, "be made to open the next campaign with an overwhelming force. And, finally, let every opportunity be embraced for concluding an honourable peace, since it is only by a ruinous expense and unprecedented exertions that entire success is to be expected in a continuance of the war." No better recommendation than this could have been offered. But how was it to be carried into effect? Metcalfe declared that the crisis was a great one; and that it was incumbent on the Government to make extraordinary exertions to bring an overwhelming force into the field. "Reinforcements of Europeans and natives," he said, "should be brought to as great an amount as can be obtained from the other Presidencies. European regiments should be called from our other colonies, even from England. Every exertion," he continued, "that would be made in times of imminent peril ought to be made now to ward off a peril which appears to be not improbable." "We never had," said Metcalfe, "an enemy to contend with in India so formidable as our present enemy. None other ever displayed so much bravery in action or so much system, skill, and conduct, so much prudent caution, and so much well-timed confidence. None other ever possessed a country so easily defended and so difficult to the invader, and so detrimental to the peculiar advantages which we should otherwise have over our enemy. All these considerations demand serious attention. Let us resolve to evince to this bold enemy that we have the means of crushing him. If we cannot secure an opportunity of defeating his assembled army in the field, let us show him that we can collect a force against which opposition would be fruitless. Let us show him that our resources are not confined to local means; and that if a small army be not sufficient to revenge our wrongs, the British nation can send us an overpowering one."

The truth of these propositions was acknowledged, and the suggestions put forth were "approved" by the Governor-General. Indeed, what in this paper was so emphatically propounded, had already been submitted, in another shape, to Lord Moira, and had elicited his approbation. Many were the papers which, at this and a little later period, Metcalfe drew up for the guidance of the Governor-General,* and very much that he then wrote

* A catalogue of these papers is given in the following extract from a letter written to Mr. Jenkins in May, 1816:

"Many thanks," wrote Metcalfe, "for your permission to see your letter on the political state of India. I shall apply to Close for it. Elphinstone told me it was admirable. I would with the greatest pleasure send you mine, though I fear the very reverse of admirable; and it requires a little detail to explain why I cannot. I happened to be the first in the field in writing on this subject. After the first failure at Kalunga, I thought the opportunity a good one for procuring attention to opinions strongly impressed on my mind, which I knew would be unpopular, and I volunteered a paper to Lord Moira on the causes of our numerous failures of late years, beginning with that of Bhurtpore, and on the necessity of adopting measures to ensure success. This was answered by a call to head-quarters. Immediately after my arrival there, I gave in a paper on the measures to be pursued in consequence of the state of affairs at that period. This was soon followed by another, containing a view of the political state of India, or, as Adam called it, De Rebus Omnibus, and recommending the settlement of Central India, the suppression of all predatory powers, the protection of all weak powers, the acquisition of as much territory and revenue as the chances of just war might throw into our hands, and, in short, the establishment of our supreme influence over the whole country within the Sutlej and Indus. This was followed by another paper on the progress of the Goorkha war—next by one on an alliance with Jyepore—then one on our military policy and establishments—then another on the settlement of Central India—with several intermediate ones which I do not accurately recollect. The whole would form a large volume—but they were all written in such haste, that of the greater part I have no record, the drafts having been sent from my hand to the principal private secretary, and never returned, and of the few foul drafts which remain in my was embodied in substance, and sometimes in his very words, in the minutes of the head of the Government. He spent about a month—including the Christmas and New Year of 1814-15—in the camp of the Governor-General, making himself all this time very useful and very agreeable, and leaving a blank behind him when he went. His separation, however, from his friends of the Governor-General's Staff was not of a very long continuance. The pride of the poor Mogul, who insisted upon the acknowledgment of his superiority over the British Viceroy, prevented, as has been seen, Lord Moira's visit to Delhi; but a deputation, consisting of the principal officers of his public and private staff, was to proceed, soon after Metcalfe's departure, to the court of the pageant-king; and, at the same time, Lady Loudoun,* with a considerable retinue, was to visit the imperial city. When, therefore, Metcalfe returned to Delhi, it was his pleasing duty to make preparations for the reception of his friends, and to reciprocate the hospitalities he had received.

How, for some little time after this, Metcalfe was compelled to play the part of master of the ceremonies—to introduce the British deputation to the Mogul Emperor—to attend Lady Loudoun—to manage the meeting of the Countess with the Begum Sumroo, and to superintend the introduction of her Highness to the Governor-General,

possession I have taken no care, not thinking them worth the perusal of any one except the person for whose information they were written, and on whose want of information I presumed to give value to the matter, notwithstanding the faults of the composition. If, however, I can ever put my hand on any, I will send them with all their faults on their heads. Success to your negotiation. Wish the same to mine, for I am about to commence one with Jyepore. Sooner or later, if not very soon, we must undertake the subjugation of all India."

* The lady of the Governor-General—a countess in her own right.

need not be told in detail. Before the month of January had worn to a close, Metcalfe was again in the Governor-General's camp, and again in council with his ministers. Throughout a considerable part of February he remained at head-quarters, and the longer he remained the more strongly was Lord Moira impressed with the conviction that in the great battle which he was about to fight for the settlement of Central India, both with his colleagues in the local Government and with the Home authorities, it would be expedient to have at his elbow a man who so well understood the whole subject, and who was prepared with such an array of arguments in defence of the policy which was favoured at head-quarters.

But how was this to be accomplished consistently with existing arrangements? How was Metcalfe to be removed from Delhi to a seat worthy of his acceptance in the Secretariat? There were changes in that winter of 1814-15 evolving themselves, which seemed to afford facilities for such an arrangement as might bring the Delhi Resident to the vice-regal court. Mr. Tucker, who had filled long and worthily the office of Financial Secretary, had been promoted to the Chief Secretaryship, and soon afterwards announced his intention of proceeding upon leave to sea, and subsequently, as the event proved, to England. This movement caused a vacancy in the Secretariat which it was necessary to fill. Mr. Dowdeswell, who had been Chief Secretary, had succeeded to the Supreme Council; Mr. Charles Ricketts was now Chief and Private Secretary; Mr. Butterworth Bayley was Judicial Secretary; Mr. Adam was Political Secretary; Mr. Swinton was Persian Secretary. But the Financial Secretaryship, which Mr. Tucker had held before his promotion, was still vacant. It was proposed, therefore, to Metcalfe, that he should, in the first instance, enter upon this office, with the reversion of the Private Secretaryship on the expected retirement of Mr. Ricketts. The proposal was a perplexing one. All through the spring and summer of 1815 this great personal question continued from time to time to distract his mind. He clung with peculiar fondness to the Delhi Residency; he knew that he was useful there; but it was probable that a larger sphere of usefulness might be opened out to him by his transfer to the Secretariat—and the Secretariat was ever regarded as the high road to the Supreme Council. What his doubts and distractions were in this perplexity, may be gathered from the following letters to Mr. Jenkins, on whom the Governor-General intended to bestow the Delhi Residency if Metcalfe should vacate it:

CHARLES METCALFE TO RICHARD JENKINS.

[*Without date—received on the* 16*th of June*, 1815.]

"MY DEAR JENKINS,— . . . . . [*Confidential.*]—I was in attendance on Lord Moira during a considerable part of December, January, and February. He expressed a desire to have me at the Presidency. As the only visible mode of effecting this purpose, he offered me the succession to the Financial Secretaryship, about to be vacated, it was supposed, by Tucker's resignation. The flattering manner in which the proposal was made, deprived me of the resolution requisite firmly to reject, and I almost pledged myself to accept it. I have, however, many doubts as to the propriety of the change, and am inclined to retract. These doubts I have expressed in the proper quarter, and I think it probable that the arrangement will not take place. I will not detain you with a detail of the *pros* and *cons* which divide my mind on the question, but proceed to inform you that it was in contemplation, when I was at head-quarters, to make you the Resident at Delhi. I do not know how you would like this; and if you would not like it, you must be prepared to object to it in the event of its being proposed to you. If you wish for any information respecting this Residency to determine your choice, send me your questions, and I will give you full and faithful intelligence. My removal, however, is very uncertain, and will probably not take place, for I am more attached to Delhi in consequence of the apprehension of quitting it, than I ever was before. What would you think of my impudence if I were to set up for a Financial Secretary? I should be glad to have your opinion. I do not like to quit the line in which I have served all my life, for one in which I must be incompetent. I am afraid, too, of being detained longer in the country by the proposed change. But I promised not to trouble you with this detail. God bless you.

"Yours affectionately,

"C. T. METCALFE."

THE SAME TO THE SAME.

"*August* 26, 1816.

"MY DEAR JENKINS,—I have determined to remain at Delhi, and am glad that I have. Lord Moira has on every occasion been most kind to me, and I shall ever be grateful to him. It was proposed to me to take the Financial and Revenue Secretaryship now, with the assurance of the Private Secretaryship in addition on Ricketts's resignation, which the latter pledged himself to give in in December, 1816. Had the latter situation been vacant now, and offered to me together with the other, I could not have refused them. But it is as well as it is. I have discovered that I am more attached to Delhi and the inhabitants of the territory under me than I formerly supposed myself to be. I found, when my removal was probable, that I should quit with great reluctance scenes to which I had become attached by habit, and a people for whose welfare I had several plans unaccomplished. I am well pleased to find myself secured in my own habits, and at liberty to devote myself to the interest of my subjects. I declined the Financial Secretaryship on the ground that it would retard my return to England; and the promise of the Private Secretaryship, from disinclination to bind down Lord Moira and Ricketts. It is now understood that there is no obligation on Lord Moira's part to renew any similar proposal at a future period, nor on mine to accept it, if renewed. The same reasons which induced me to rejoice now at my staying at Delhi, make me wish that I may not hereafter receive any temptation to quit it. One great advantage which I feel at Delhi is, that I shall always there be independent of a seat in Council; that is, that I shall not care a straw if I do not obtain one. Had I accepted a secretaryship in Calcutta, I must have turned my views to Council, and should, in all probability, have been disappointed. I took leave of Lord Moira on the 21st at Futtehghur, and am now on my way to Delhi. I have written this short report of my proceedings for your early information. The necessity of any reply to your questions concerning Delhi is obviated by my continuance at that place. I will not, therefore, trouble you with the details which otherwise I should have sent you, unless you require them with a view to any future contingency. Accept my cordial thanks for the friendly and affectionate contents of your last letter. I shall write to you again soon. I have some communications to make respecting the politics of head-quarters. The Goorkha war is still pending; at least, peace is not concluded, nor can we agree on the preliminaries as yet.

"Believe me ever yours most affectionately,

"C. T. Metcalfe."

But the idea of attaching Metcalfe permanently to the Secretariat was not abandoned at head-quarters, even after the Governor-General had retired to Calcutta.* As the year wore on to a close, the pressure of public business still suggested the expediency of securing the services of one so well acquainted with all departments, and so peculiarly qualified to assist the councils of Government in those great political affairs connected with the settlement

* An effort had been made to persuade Metcalfe to return with the Governor-General's camp to Calcutta. "The 15th of August," wrote the Private Secretary to him, "is still the time fixed for his lordship's departure, and allowing a day or two for delay, I reckon upon the 20th as the day. This, I trust, will square with your plans, and on many accounts we hope that you will be able to take a run with us to Calcutta. . . . . Your presence there would be useful—indeed, the only *ready* means, perhaps, of enabling you finally to determine about accepting a secretaryship or remaining at Delhi." There were other inducements, too, to tempt him to the Presidency, for Theophilus Metcalfe had come round to Calcutta about some important business connected with the factory and the tea-trade—but the Delhi Resident resisted them all. He proceeded soon after the receipt of Ricketts's letter to the camp of the Governor-General at Futtehghur, and after declining the offer of an appointment in the Secretariat, took leave of Lord Moira (as indicated in the above letter to Mr. Jenkins) and returned to Delhi.

of Central India which were fast beginning to absorb every other consideration. It was difficult to make the necessary arrangement. Mr. Ricketts, on whom it seemed mainly to depend, was well inclined to make considerable sacrifices for its accomplishment, but Lord Moira demurred to the plan which his Private Secretary proposed. What the arrangement was, and the powerful considerations which induced him to make it, may be gathered from the following passage in one of Mr. Ricketts's private letters to Metcalfe:

"At this juncture a second campaign against the Goorkhas was probable—the proposed concession to them was resisted by Lord Moira—the affair of Trimbackjee was in a most critical state—the disturbance at Hyderabad was not quelled—the Mahratta confederacy was in agitation—the Pindarrees were in motion—Ameer Khan was overwhelming the Rajpoot states—troops were required to overawe Scindiah—Baillie was tottering at Lucknow—Raffles was to be removed from Java—many financial discussions were on the *tapis* both as relating to the war expenses and to resources for the future, which required a final adjustment between the territorial and commercial accounts, subjects on which all good folks differed—that the orders of the Court of Directors respecting a reduction of the army remained yet to be considered—that the reports of his lordship, in the military, revenue, and judicial departments, were to be completed, and might excite much discussion—that a necessity was imposed upon his lordship of entering into a full review of our political situation and relations, in which the attack made by his colleagues was to be rebutted, their mistaken notions were to be exposed, and the measures to be produced for our security were to be explained—that most questions of any importance in each department of the Government had been left open for his lordship's decision—that feuds betweeen the bishop (who is a high priest) and the kirk remained to be adjusted, and that, in short, so many difficulties and embarrassments presented themselves on every side, that I despaired of his lordship getting over the whole with any kind of satisfaction to himself without the aid of you, my friend!—Adam was a host certainly in himself; but he was already overwhelmed with business; Bayley could only attend to pending judicial questions; no aid from Trant in finance was to be expected;

and I knew that, however well disposed, my talents were very limited, and wholly unequal to the duties with which I was threatened. My plans, consequently, for inducing you to come to Calcutta were as follows:—Mr. Thomson talked of going home in January, and I proposed, therefore, that you should be appointed Territorial Secretary, and that you should divide with me the allowance of Private Secretary on Mr. T.'s departure. This was approved by his lordship; but Mr. T. changed his mind. I then requested that I might be allowed to resign my situation of P. P.* Secretary in your favour. To this, however, his lordship would not assent; and, lastly, I was induced from various causes to beg his lordship to accept my resignation of the situation, now that I had accomplished with your assistance all the reports and papers which he was so anxious to have ready for transmission to the secret committee by the *William Pitt.* Lord Moira, I conceived, would not refuse compliance with my wishes, and I moreover conceived that he would then feel at liberty to place you in a post which you were so eminently well qualified to fill. His lordship, however, requested me to withdraw my application. This has been done for the present; you consequently are not coming to Calcutta, nor am I, which at one time was not improbable, going to Java."†

But the failure of Mr. Ricketts's honourable efforts was not much to be deplored. The time, indeed, was fast approaching when it would be in the power of Charles Metcalfe to render more essential services to the State in Upper India than at the Presidency. The settlement of Central India was about to be commenced, and in this great work the Delhi Resident was to take no unimportant part.

The consideration of this great subject, and the narration of the personal incidents connected with it in the career of Charles Metcalfe, must be reserved for another chapter. But before passing on to these grave political affairs, the writer must pause to touch upon some points of less historical, but, perhaps, not less biographical

* Principal Private Secretary.

† Calcutta, December 19, 1815.

importance. It is curious, in running through the immense wilderness of correspondence which Metcalfe carefully preserved, to see how many and great, at this time, in addition to the claims of public duty, were the demands of private friendship upon his time and attention. The commissions which were entrusted to him were numerons and varied; and he found time to execute them all. It was not only that the kindliness of his heart, his eagerness to give pleasure might always be relied upon; but that there were requests made to him which only he, perhaps, could satisfactorily fulfil—which only he had a power commensurate with the will to accomplish. Thus Mountstuart Elphinstone wrote to him from Poonah, asking him to exert himself to obtain for his friend Mr. Erskine a complete copy of Baber's autobiography, and an authentic portrait of the Emperor.* Malcolm applied

* "Mr. Erskine, at Bombay," wrote Elphinstone, "is employed in translating the commentaries of the Emperor Baber, from a Persian translation of that work, which is certainly the most curious and interesting I ever met with in an Asiatic language. There are, however, several gaps in the translation he has got, and a complete copy in Turkish, which I brought from Peshawur, was lost in consequence of poor Leyden's death, so that Mr. Erskine's translation must remain incomplete, unless you can get us a complete copy of the translation at Delhi. The august representative of the house of Timour must assuredly possess the commentaries of the most illustrious of his ancestors, and the founder of his empire. But if his Majesty should not be able to put his hand on the work, some of the literati at Delhi will probably be able to produce it." A copy of the work was found; but, unhappily, it had the same deficiencies as that in Mr. Erskine's possession. Elphinstone, therefore, requested Metcalfe to obtain for him a Turkish copy from Peshawur. An authentic portrait of Baber was also required, and Metcalfe, his characteristic good-nature stimulated by his literary zeal, immediately instituted the necessary inquiries, and found what was sought. Mr. Erskine's charming translation of Baber's Commentaries is well known to English readers—to some through the book itself, to others through Jeffrey's review of

to him to obtain information relative to the career of the great Bengal banker, Omichund, after the destroying fraud that had been practised upon him by Lord Clive. Ochterlony* wrote to him to prepare a monument, and to write an inscription to the memory of that poor young Lawtie, of the Engineers, killed by his brave exertions in the Nepaul war, to which so much of our first successes were nobly attributed by his chief. Nicolls† commissioned him to procure an ornamental sabre, to be publicly presented to a native officer who had distinguished himself in the same war. Edmonstone, in consequence of a reference from England, besought him to obtain information relative to the matrimonial connections formed between the Mogul princes and the daughters of the Rajpoot Rajahs.‡ Sir William Rumbold besought

it, published among his collected Essays. A posthumous work, embracing an elaborate history of some of the princes of the house of Timour—a work of great ability and research—appeared whilst the first edition of this work was passing through the press.

* "In every letter," wrote Ochterlony, "written to you, I have intended to make a very particular request, which I have ever neglected or forgotten before the conclusion. It is that you will get a slab of marble, and on it cut an inscription of your own composition for the tomb of our lamented Lawtie, at Ruttunghur. Few will read it; but I do not wish an European visitor to pass without knowing that the spot contains the remains of one so deservedly valued and lamented."

† The late Sir Jasper Nicolls, who wrote: "My object in troubling you now is to beg that you will purchase and transmit to me, *viâ* Moradabad, a sabre not exceeding in value 400 rupees, which I have obtained Lord Moira's consent to give to a jemadar of the 4th N.I., who conducted himself with great intrepidity on the 25th ultimo. The blade, if possible, should be good, but it ought to be ornamental also; it should please the eye long after the *éclat* of the action has worn off. I shall present it on the theatre of his valour, and in public."

‡ Metcalfe's answer to this application is worth more than the space that it will take: "I had the pleasure of receiving your

him to despatch a wet-nurse to Cawnpore. John Adam commissioned him to buy for Lady Hood some of the finest garnets to be found in Delhi. Mr. Richardson wrote to him "at the girls' desire" for "three Solimanee necklaces, bracelets, &c., and also three lapis-lazuli necklaces, bracelets, &c., and any other little trinkets, or Hindostanee ornaments, or costume that you think they would like." Added to applications of this varied and interesting character was a never-failing succession of requests for pecuniary assistance, for the most part from military officers, to whom he made advances, with or without any kind of security, often knowing that the loan would prove, as he intended it to be, a gift to the petitioner.

letter of the 9th a few minutes before a visit from the Joudpore Wakeel, a most respectable and well-informed old man, and I availed myself of the opportunity to apply to him for a solution of the question referred to you from England. He says that it was first proposed to the Rajpoot Rajahs to form a connection with the imperial family by taking in marriage imperial princesses; but that this proposal was rejected, as such a communication would have polluted the blood of the Rajahs' families, and would have been utter abomination for ever; that they were glad to effect their escape from so alarming a danger by sacrificing their own daughters, who were considered as dead from the time of their connection with the emperors; that after the ice had been once broken by the formation of a connection of this kind, it came to be considered a custom, and ceased to be objectionable; that a connection with the emperors was thought desirable for political purposes, and that the rivalship of the Rajahs of Jyepore and Joudpore made both occasionally press forward with their daughters, each being jealous when such a connection was formed by the other. Nevertheless that the daughters were considered as dead and gone, though their posthumous influence was an object of desire to their fathers. This is the mode in which the Joudpore wakeel attempts to solve the question. I shall make further inquiries, and have the happiness of making you acquainted with the result."—[*May* 25, 1814.]

But there were letters, very different from any of these, received during the years of his residence at Delhi—letters which inflicted upon him an acuteness of pain which may, in some measure, perhaps, be duly estimated by those who have dwelt upon the passages relating to his parents in the letters which he addressed to his aunt. In the course of the year 1814 he received intelligence of the death of his father. And two years afterwards the sad tidings of his mother's death also reached him.* This is almost a condition of Indian exile. It is a grievous trial which few escape—to lay up fame and fortune and to see those with whom we would share their blessings pass away from our reach. How deeply Metcalfe felt these heavy blows may be gathered from his letters to his friends. "The loss of my mother," he wrote to Richard Jenkins, in May, 1816, "has made all my prospects dismal: and I cannot now look even to a return to England with any pleasure. The purest happiness that I have enjoyed in life is buried in the grave with both my parents; and I have really, at present, no object to live for. The thought of returning to my parents was my stimulus in everything. This affliction has also affected my correspondence of all kinds. But enough of this. You will, I am sure, excuse me, and believe that nothing can alter my attachment or the delight and pride I feel in the possession of your friendship." Indeed, it seemed, as one

* Intelligence of Lady Metcalfe's death was received in India in March, 1816. Both events were unexpected—especially the latter. Lady Metcalfe died on the 9th of September, 1815, at the house of some friends in Dorsetshire, to whom she was paying a visit. She had just been talking to her son-in-law, Lord Ashbrook, about returning home, when she suddenly expired, "without uttering a word or a sigh." Mr. George Saunders communicated the melancholy intelligence to Captain Fergusson, at Delhi, whom he requested to prepare Metcalfe for the receipt of the sad tidings.

by one the links which bound him to England were broken, the firmness with which he clung to his Indian attachments increased. From this time he fell back for support upon the associations of exile, and solaced himself with the friendships within his reach.

It was with little regret, therefore, that about this time he received an intimation that the Court of Directors, among other retrenchments, had reduced the expenses of the Delhi Residency,* by curtailing the Resident's allowances. "The cuttings here," he wrote to Mr. Jenkins, "are 2,000 rupees a month from the public allowance. This I have allowed to take effect, as I considered opposition vain. Reductions were also ordered in the number of assistants and the office establishment. These I have opposed, as they do not affect me personally. The reduction of my allowances will keep me in India all my life, as I do not see how I can reduce my expenses." But, as though he could not altogether abandon the thought of some day returning to his native land, he added, "I shall, therefore, be the more inclined to accept any situation, should any such be offered, which, by enabling me to live like a retired individual on some small means, may present a hope of some day returning to England."

At the close of the year 1815 Charles Metcalfe received another visit from his brother Theophilus, who had come round to Calcutta upon business connected with the financial affairs of the Canton Factory. The visit was a solace to both brothers. "I look forward," wrote the elder brother from Benares, "to a delightful month with

* The expenses of all the Residencies had been reduced; but whilst other retrenchments were ordered to take immediate effect, the case of the Delhi Residency had been treated as an exceptional one, and Metcalfe had been ordered, as a preliminary measure, to report upon the expenses of his office before any reductions were carried out.

you, such as I have not passed for some time; and, alas! have but little prospect of seeing a relative for years to come." They met then at Delhi for the last time. Theophilus Metcalfe did not live to see the completion of these twelve years.

CHAPTER XII.

[1815—1818.]

THE SETTLEMENT OF CENTRAL INDIA.

Peace with the Goorkhas—Relations with the States of Central India—Scindiah, Holkar, and the Rajah of Berar—The Pindarrees—Ameer Khan and the Patans—The Rajpoot States—Metcalfe's Plans for the Settlement of Central India—Adopted by Lord Hastings—Opposition of the Home Authorities—Change of Policy—Correspondence of Metcalfe with Lord Moira—The Governor-General takes the Field—Suppression of the Pindarrees—Metcalfe's Treaties with the Rajpoot Princes.

"HURRAH! peace with the Goorkhas!" wrote Secretary Ricketts from Calcutta to Metcalfe, at Delhi, on the 9th of December, 1815. The intelligence was most welcome. A great object had now been accomplished. But there was a greater before us to which the pacification of Nepaul had in some measure cleared the way. One obstacle at least to the settlement of Central India had been removed. It had been always Metcalfe's opinion that our operations against the Goorkhas should have been postponed until arrangements had been effected for the establishment of permanent tranquillity throughout all the Central Indian States; but the war having been commenced, he argued that we should conclude it, by a manifestation of overwhelming strength, with the utmost practicable despatch; and then, having in the meanwhile increased, by every possible means, our military resources, enter with confidence upon the arrangements which the unsettled condition of Central India so imperatively demanded.

Whatever may have been the policy—or the necessity—in 1806, of the sudden winding-up of our political relations in the interior of Hindostan, it is not to be doubted that the precipitate adjustment of affairs, rendered necessary by the embarrassed state of our finances, caused a vast heritage of stirring work to descend to a future Government. It is very true that no statesman is justified in saddling posterity with political convulsions and pecuniary distresses. But it is equally true that no statesman is justified in inflicting a positive injury upon his own generation, with the hope of averting a conjectural evil from a future one. But the truest statesmanship is that which seizes upon the exact point at which conjectural evils are about to become positive ones, when they have passed altogether beyond the stage of possible prevention, and to delay their extinction is only to nurture their growth. Now, in 1815-16, we had certainly reached an epoch of our career at which any continued reliance upon the efficacy of those principles of non-interference, which had so long regulated our political conduct in the East, would have been suicidal in the extreme. Disorder and confusion were paramount over the whole length and breadth of Central India. The entire country was rent by internal strife. The strong were preying upon the weak. The supremacy of Might was alone recognised. There was altogether a state of lawlessness and disorganization such as it is difficult for those, who square their notions by the rule and plummet of European civilization, adequately to conceive.

To describe, with satisfactory detail, the chaotic state of things that had arisen during the ten years which had elapsed since Charles Metcalfe, on the banks of the Beeas, met Holkar and Ameer Khan in the camp of the former, would demand an amount of space that cannot consistently be afforded to it in such a memoir as this. It was a condition of things that no wise or benevolent statesman could long suffer to exist. Immense bands of Pindarrees were overrunning and ravaging the lands. Certain Patan chiefs, little better than Pindarrees, with large bodies of retainers, were overawing the peaceful states of Rajpootana. And our nominal allies, the substantive Mahratta states, were in a condition of scarcely disguised hostility towards us. Not only did the security of our Indian empire, but the larger interests of common humanity, demand that an effort should be made by the paramount power to restore tranquillity to the distracted country. The duty of the British Government in this conjuncture stood out clearly before Metcalfe's eyes. It was with no misgiving—with no hesitation that he fully declared his opinions to the Governor-General; and propounded a scheme for the settlement of Central India, which Lord Moira was not slow to adopt. The length of the document in which his views were submitted forbids its entire insertion; but its importance demands that I should set forth some of its more pregnant passages.

And the better to follow his arguments, and to understand all the bearings of the great question, it should first be seen in what manner he classified the different states of Central India:—

"That part of India which is not occupied by the British Government and its allies, is divided among powers who may be classed under the following different descriptions:—

"1. Substantive states, ardently desiring our overthrow, and ambitious to aggrandise themselves; who for the gratification of either propensity, would not scruple to have recourse to any measures, and who have armies in their service capable of being converted at a moment's warning into instruments of destruction to our provinces. Against these powers we must always be on our guard;

and the frontiers exposed to them can never be considered to be in safety unless defended by our armies. We may be assured that these powers only want an encouraging opportunity to strike a blow at our existence.

"2. Military powers not substantive states, but more dangerous, perhaps, than these states; being less tangible and having less to lose, living by plunder and devastation—the enemies of all regular governments, more especially hostile in spirit to us, and capable of overrunning and ruining our provinces if we gave them the opportunity, by neglecting our defence. Against these, therefore, we must be equally guarded as against the states of the first class.

"3. Petty states, who are subject to the continual plunder and oppression of the two former classes, who in consequence look up to us for protection, and are therefore well-disposed towards us. From these we have nothing to apprehend. These it is our interest to uphold and protect.

"To the *first* class belong Scindiah, Holkar, and the Rajah of Nagpore (Berar).

"Of these three, Scindiah is now the most powerful, and the one most employed in aggrandising himself.

"The power of Holkar, if considered as unconnected with that of Meer Khan, is very much reduced. That of Nagpore seems to be, too, on the decline. But all three are hostile towards us, and in heart confederated against us; and never will be otherwise until they be forced by the oppression of each other, or of other powers, to throw themselves into our arms for protection.

"The *second* class of powers consists of the Pindarrees, Meer Khan, Mahomed Shah Khan, and generally all predatory leaders. Of these the Pindarrees are the most mischievous. Meer Khan and Mahomed Shah Khan may be considered in a double character, as servants of Holkar and as independent chieftains. These powers, and all others that exist by upsetting peaceful states and disturbing the general tranquillity, must be considered as enemies, since they either act as such, or force us to take the same defensive precautions against them as if they were in declared hostility.

"In the *third* class may be included Jyepore, Joudpore, Oudipore, Bekaneer, Jessulmere, Kotah, Boondee, Kerowlee, and the other petty states on the frontier of Guzerat, and, generally, all states who are subject to the oppression of the military and predatory powers."

Having thus shown with what we had to deal, he proceeded in a few pithy sentences to declare how it was desirable to deal with them :—

"With regard to all the great military states and all the predatory powers, it is clearly our interest to annihilate them or to reduce them to a state of weakness, subjection, and dependence. This observation refers to all the powers of the first and second classes above described. And with regard to the weak and harmless and well-disposed petty states, though it is not so indispensably necessary for our vital interests that we should support them, yet it is a just and proper object of wise and liberal policy."

It was Metcalfe's opinion at this time that the annihilation of all the substantive states of Central India would be advantageous to the British Government, and he was not without a belief that circumstances would arise to justify such a measure. But he was not yet prepared to recommend it. They had been guilty of no overt acts of hostility; and we had no pretext for drawing the sword against them. But the forcible suppression of the Pindarrees was, on the other hand, a measure that called for immediate execution. Forbearance and moderation in such a case would only have been sinful and cruel. The reduction of these lawless bands was, indeed, the first object of our policy. Nothing could be done until it was accomplished :—

"The first object," said Metcalfe, "to which our attention ought to be directed, is the reduction of the power of the Pindarrees. Not only does this predatory power at all times menace the tranquillity of our territories, and force us to adopt extensive measures of precautionary defence, but has actually invaded our dominions and ravaged our richest provinces, and perpetually threatens a repetition of this outrage and devastation. It is impossible to distinguish between the different bodies of these freebooters. The whole of them are the enemies of all states, and they have all been engaged in ravaging either our own provinces or those of our allies. As long as this power exists, we cannot undertake any political or military operations without the apprehension of having our provinces laid waste by bands of plunderers. And from the increase of the power of these freebooters which has actually taken place in the last few years, we may judge to what an incalculable extent the evil may proceed if it be allowed to continue to exist. We ought to recollect that the Pindarree is now what the Mahratta power was in the decline of the Mogul empire of India. Let us take warning, and save the British empire from the downfall which its predecessor sustained, chiefly from the hands of the predecessors of the Pindarrees."

Speaking then of the difficulty of striking a vigorous blow at a power so meteoric and intangible, Metcalfe then proceeded to say:—

"As the destruction of the power of the Pindarrees is the first object of our policy, so is it also, perhaps, the most difficult to be accomplished. The seat of their power is in their camps. It is less tangible than the power of any established state, which must fall with the loss of its dominions. The Pindarrees may be dispersed, and they will gather again. They may be defeated over and over again, without loss of reputation or power, since neither the one nor the other depends on victory in the field. They must be pursued wherever they take refuge; they must be dispersed wherever they assemble. We must not pause until they be annihilated as a power. Even the Pindarree power is in some degree tangible. The Pindarrees have lands and forts, where they keep their families; and the loss of their possessions and the capture of their families would tend greatly, no doubt, to destroy their power."

After speaking of the offensive and defensive preparations which it would be necessary to make for the suppression of these predatory bands, and dwelling upon the advantages to be derived from the success of our measures, Metcalfe proceeded to speculate on the probability of deriving assistance from other substantive states of Central India:—

"Every endeavour," he said, "will be advisable to persuade other powers to take part in the contest. Scindiah, Holkar, and the Rajah of Berar, may be invited at the proper time to join a confederacy for the destruction of the Pindarrees. If they accede, and join with cordiality, the object may be gained with greater facility; and the circumstance of acting in union with the British Government for one common interest might lay the foundation of a general confederacy of the established states of India with the British Government as the acknowledged head. But this is an arrangement, perhaps, more to be desired than expected."

If this confederacy were not arranged, it was argued that the British Government could at least demand the neutrality of the States, with the right of a free passage through their territories; and if this were refused, they could only be treated as open enemies :—

"If Scindiah, Holkar, and the Rajah of Berar," continued Metcalfe, "neither co-operate nor remain neutral—in other words, if all or any of these powers oppose or obstruct our operations against the Pindarrees, we have no choice but to consider all powers so opposing us as our enemies, and to attack them accordingly. The war, in this case, would require greater exertions, but would also be attended with better prospects of solid advantage. The territories of Scindiah, Holkar, or the Rajah of Berar, would afford a recompense for the expenses of the war, and an increase of resources for the payment of additional force."

Having again repeated that the absolute extermination of the Pindarrees by a series of vigorous offensive measures was the first step towards the settlement of Central India, Metcalfe proceeded to consider what should be our bearing towards the military states, as a question distinct from that of their movements for or against the Pindarrees :—

"Let us now examine what should be our policy towards Scindiah, Holkar, and the Rajah of Berar, without any reference to the Pindarrees. As long as these powers adhere to the spirit of the treaties which we have with them respectively, and act towards us in a friendly and inoffensive manner, we have no right, it is needless to mention, to deviate from the spirit of existing engagements, however desirable a deviation may occasionally be. We must act towards them with friendship and a liberal regard for their rights and pretensions. But we ought never to forget, that as long as these, or any of these, powers are military, ambitious, and unprincipled, it is our interest to overthrow them, or bring them under our influence; and every opportunity should be taken to pursue a policy tending to one of these results when it can be done consistently with good faith and justice. In the event of a war with all or any of these powers, it is our interest to secure the greatest possible acquisition of territory, in order that we may maintain the greatest possible amount of force."

In these suggestions, Metcalfe contended that there was no spirit of aggrandisement; the only object being to secure the safety of our possessions and the general tranquillity of the country:—

"In these proposals there is no ambition or wish for aggrandisement beyond what is necessary or desirable for our safety and strength. If the British Government were secure in their present predicament, it might confine its attention to its own internal prosperity, without involving itself in the dissensions and distractions of other states. But we must tranquillize the centre of India, in order to acquire strength in our external boundaries sufficient for the security of our Indian empire."

Having considered the course of policy to be pursued towards the substantive states of India and the Pindarree freebooters, Metcalfe adverted to those powers which occupied intermediate ground between them—which partook of some of the substantive attributes of the one, and were distinguished also by the predatory habits of the other:—

"The military powers of Ameer Khan and Mahomed Shah Khan, remain to be spoken of. The existence of such powers is incompatible with the preservation of the tranquillity of India, and they must be destroyed by dispersion or attack before that great object can be secured. Such armies might be dispersed by making a provision for the chiefs and afterwards disbanding their troops; but unless measures be taken at the same time to prevent the rise of other powers of the same description, new armies will rise up under new leaders, and we shall have the expense of supporting the old chiefs, without doing away the evil. But the destruction of the Pindarrees and the other arrangements proposed, will necessarily effect the reduction of the remaining predatory powers."

Having thus considered the policy to be pursued towards hostile states, he glanced at the condition of those friendly principalities which it was desirable to take under our protection.

"These," he said, "should be systematically taken under protection whenever they seek it, and whenever our engagements with other powers leave us at liberty to grant it, and other considerations of an urgent nature do not interfere to prevent such an arrangement. By taking the petty states under our protection, we prevent the aggrandisement of the great military powers, and the growth of the predatory powers which feed on the weaker states. We at the same time secure the political attachment and dependence of established governments, and the extension and confirmation of our own power and supremacy. . . . . These states should be made to purchase our protection; and whenever the circumstances of the party will admit of it, a tribute should be demanded sufficient to pay for some increase of our military establishment, an object which should never be lost sight of in any of our political arrangements in the present state of India."

It was true that our engagements with Scindiah and Holkar prevented us from forming alliances with some of these petty states,* but it was recommended that we should take advantage of any rupture that might free us from these engagements; and such a contingency seemed not very remote.

Special mention was then made of Jyepore:

"The state of Jyepore has long sought our protection, and we are not restrained by any engagements with other powers from affording it. An alliance, however, with Jyepore would necessarily annoy Scindiah and Holkar, and would deprive Meer Khan, Mahomed Shah Khan, and other freebooters, of their chief resource. The state of Jyepore could afford to pay a considerable tribute, especially when tranquillity and protection shall have restored the prosperity of the country. An alliance with Jyepore has been objected to as an insulated measure, under the belief of its inefficiency. Although an alliance with Jyepore be effected singly—and a general alliance with the Rajpoot states is impracticable consistently with good faith—nevertheless the alliance should not be considered an insulated measure, but one of a

* Joudpore, Oudipore, Kotah, &c.

system which can only be accomplished by degrees. We must not expect that a number of states will come forward to seek our alliance exactly at the moment most convenient to our views. If we do not afford our protection when it is solicited, we must expect that it may be rejected when we proffer it. If we refuse now to conclude an alliance with Jyepore, it may happen that Jyepore will be reluctant to conclude one at the precise period when we deem it advantageous for ourselves.* If we adopt the system of protecting the weak states, we must put it in practice gradually, by taking under our protection such of them as are aware of the benefit of it, and we must make some temporary sacrifice for the sake of the advancement of the system."

The result of these alliances, Metcalfe argued, would be great, for they would place us, either by the generation of an immediate crisis, or by sowing the seeds of slow decay among the Mahratta states, in possession of the whole expanse of Central India:

"The formation, as suggested, of these alliances would confine the military and predatory powers of India within narrow limits. They must then either devour each other or waste away, or attack us. In the latter event we ought to have made ourselves strong enough to conquer them all, and annex the whole of these territories to the British dominions. In that case, by one great exertion, the tranquillity of India might be established on a permanent footing, and our supremacy would be complete. In either of the other cases the same end will eventually be gained in a more progressive manner."

Such was the plan for the settlement of Central India which Metcalfe presented to the Governor-General. But how was so comprehensive a scheme of policy to be carried out? It was anticipated that our measures for the suppression of the Pindarrees would very probably embroil us with all the Mahratta states; but, so far from shrinking back alarmed at the contemplation of such a contingency, Metcalfe regarded it as an element of extreme

* In how remarkable a manner these anticipations were verified by the result will presently appear.

hopefulness in the great scheme which opened out before him. He felt, indeed, that it was absolutely necessary for the permanent tranquillisation of Central India, not only that the Pindarrees should be rooted out, but that the substantive states should be curtailed of their power, and reduced to a condition of subjection that would prevent them from ever again exciting our fears. The war with the Pindarrees might be followed by a war with the Mahrattas. It was incumbent upon us, said Metcalfe, to be provided for this. But how were we to undertake the prosecution of a scheme of policy demanding a display of such immense resources? To this it was replied, that everything must give way to one paramount consideration —that the maintenance of an efficient military establishment must be the first care of the Government, and that to accomplish this we must increase our revenue by every possible means:

"The following," said Metcalfe, "would appear to be the system which we ought to adopt for the security and confirmation of our dominion in India:—

"1st. To make it the main object of all the acts of our Government to have the most efficient army that we can possibly maintain, not merely for internal control or the defence of our frontier, but also for those services in the field which our army is perpetually called on to perform on emergencies when we have not time to increase it in sufficient strength.

"2nd. If our resources should, at any time, be unequal to the maintenance of an ample force, not to cripple our strength by attempts to reduce our force within the limits of fixed resources at the imminent peril of our dominion; but to endeavour to raise our resources to meet the demands on us for force.*

* Elsewhere the writer says: "If an increase in the existing branches of revenue in our own dominions prove sufficient for the maintenance of such armies as we require, so much the better. If not, we ought to draw forth new resources; and if these be impracticable within our own dominions, we must look to increase of territory by conquest over our enemies in the interior of India.

"3rd. To enlarge our territories in the interior of India on every occasion of war as much as possible consistently with justice and policy, moderation to our enemies, and due attention to our allies.

"4th. To apply the net revenues of conquered countries to the maintenance of additional force, and the acquisition of additional force to the achievement of new conquests, on just occasions—thus growing in size and increasing in strength as we proceed, until we can with safety determine to confine ourselves within fixed limits, and abjure all further conquests.

"5th. To enter on no wars from views of aggrandisement without just cause; to respect with the most liberal attention the rights, interests, feelings, and prejudices of all powers; and to cultivate with those who are willing the most sincere and cordial friendship."

These propositions Charles Metcalfe supported in a manner which, doubtless, would have thrown his old friend and correspondent, Sherer, the financier, into a state of considerable alarm—especially if it had been imparted to him with what favour the Delhi Resident's arguments were received in the tent of the Governor-General. But it must ever be considered that we were on the eve of a great crisis, which in the estimation of some of the ablest statesmen in India, demanded a departure from ordinary rules of procedure. Let us settle the country first, cried Metcalfe; and then practise economy:

"The error," he said, "seems to belong to the Government at home, which has been resolved to make everything bend to a desire to keep down the expenses—as if our expenses could be regulated at our pleasure; as if we could control events so as to render them subservient exclusively to economical and commercial views! The most effectual remedy would be—and a most necessary one it is—to reverse the system of Government, and to make views of economy and retrenchment secondary to those of safety and

---

There is no doubt that opportunities will arise for effecting such conquests, for with the utmost moderation and justice upon our part, misunderstandings and wars in the course of time will be occasionally unavoidable."

power. Let us first adopt measures for the security and strength of our dominion, and afterwards look to a surplus of revenue. If retrenchments be necessary, let them be made anywhere rather than in that branch of our expenditure which is necessary for our existence. Let us cherish our military establishments above all others, for on them our power entirely depends."

The answer of the financier, doubtless, was, that it is impossible to cherish our military establishments without money—that money has been emphatically called the sinews of war—and that without money, though we may talk of war, we cannot make it. To this, however, Metcalfe replied:

"It is in vain to say that our commercial and financial arrangements do not admit of an increase of force—commerce and finance will soon be destroyed if we have not at all times an army sufficient for the exigencies of our situation. If it were a question whether our military establishments, or any other, should be sacrificed, there could be no doubt that any other establishment must be sacrificed, because our military establishment is the most necessary for our existence. But it is to be hoped that this will never be a question. Let us preserve all our establishments, and make them contribute to the support of each other; but it is necessary to guard with peculiar care the efficiency of our armies. Let us not adopt the absurd notion that commerce and finance can thrive by the neglect and reduction of the vital sources of our strength and existence. As well might we expect to give vigour to the limbs by chopping at the heart."

To this the financier would reply, that if military establishments be necessary for the protection of revenue, it is equally true that revenue is necessary to the support of military establishments, or in a word, that armies are of no use if we cannot pay them—nay, that unpaid armies are worse than useless, for they may become dangerous enemies. Our own guns have been shotted ere now in anticipation of the rising of our unpaid sepoys. Metcalfe, however, anticipated the objection:

"It may be said, that we must, of necessity, confine our expenses within our resources. Nothing can be more true than this—that our power cannot last long, if our expenses exceed our resources. So far all are doubtless agreed. The difference between the system prescribed by the Government at home and that which it is here proposed to recommend, is this:—the former—not avowedly or wilfully, it is hoped, but, nevertheless, actually in its operations, attempts to restrain our military expenses within fixed limits, without regard to our safety. The latter would attend to our safety as the first consideration, and endeavour to make our resources meet our necessary expenditure. The inevitable consequence of the former, if persevered in, must be ruin; we may form better hopes of the latter."

Having said this, the writer proceeded to state his opinion that if our revenue be not sufficient for the payment of our troops, we must augment it:

"If," he said, "the present state of our resources be inadequate to the provision of force sufficient for our safety, we must seek to raise them by extraordinary means. It is true that resources are not always procurable at will, but we must not acknowledge that we cannot raise sufficient resources from our immense empire, unless we be prepared also to admit that we cannot keep the country. When additional resources become necessary, they must be raised, and means must be had recourse to which in ordinary times might be deemed objectionable. There ought to be, and surely must be, ways and means of raising additional revenue from the vast territories under our dominions. A native Government, equally strong in other respects, would extract much more from the extensive empire which we possess without injuring the prosperity of the country. For instance, a duty on the transport of grain would be levied by a native Government, and would probably be exceedingly productive. The proposal will no doubt be objected to. It is not agreeable to European prejudices; but a duty on traffic in grain—the principal trade of most parts of the country—is a source of revenue under every native Government, and, whether a good or bad source of revenue, it is the only one which promises to be abundantly productive. It is not intended here to enter into any discussion on the expediency or otherwise of such a duty. All that is meant to contend for is, that instead of indulging in the vain hope of promoting our prosperity by the reduction of our establishments, we ought to search for additional sources of revenue."

He then proceeded to argue, that in proportion as it was difficult to derive increased revenues from our existing territories, "the necessity of an increase of territory becomes more apparent:"

"Any acquisition of territory in the centre of India would contract the extent of frontier to be defended, or approximate the connections between the forces of Bengal and those of the other Presidencies, or give a surplus of revenue available for the payment of a military force, without the chance of involving us in any embarrassments beyond those to which we are already exposed. So far, therefore, from contemplating an increase of territory as an evil to be avoided, we ought to desire it, wherever it can be justly obtained, as the source of safety and power."

But on whatsoever side of the controversy between the soldiers and the financiers reason and justice might array themselves, it is certain that for some time the home authorities, as represented no less by the King's ministers than by the Court of Directors, took the financial view of the great question, and determined that war and diplomacy should remain in abeyance. The Secret Committee sent out positive instructions against interference with existing arrangements, and directed that "the system which was consolidated at the close of the last Mahratta war should be maintained with as little change as could be avoided." And soon afterwards, a great man having succeeded to the India Board,* the same mysterious authority wrote again, in 1816, "We are unwilling to incur the risk of a general war for the uncertain purpose of exterminating the Pindarrees. Extended political and military combinations we cannot at the present time sanction or approve. Any attempt," it was added, "at this moment to establish a new system of policy, tending to a wider diffusion of our power, must necessarily interfere with those economical

* George Canning. See documents quoted in Professor Wilson's continuation of Mill's "History of India."

relations which it is more than ever incumbent on us to recommend as indispensable to the maintenance of our present ascendency."

The Governor-General was ripe for action; but the decided tone of the home authorities necessarily compelled him to pause before he put into execution the great measures on which he had determined when Metcalfe was in his camp. The opposition which he had encountered from the members of Council had in some measure given way under a pressure of circumstances, if not under a pressure of arguments. He had returned to Calcutta in the autumn of 1815, carrying with him in his portfolio an elaborate minute on the settlement of Central India, to be laid before the Council immediately on his arrival. This minute was drawn up by Mr. Ricketts, principally from memoranda furnished by Metcalfe. Some parts of it, indeed, were written in Metcalfe's own words; all parts contained his arguments.* But it was little likely that the bold schemes of the Up-country Council would find

* See letter of Mr. Ricketts to Mr. Metcalfe. "By this dawk I have forwarded to you the outline of a proposed minute to be laid before the Council by his lordship on his arrival in Calcutta. It has been seen by Lord Moira, by Adam, and by Fagan; and will meet your approbation generally, as the sentiments and plan are your own—nay, the wording yours in many parts, as taken from the admirable notes with which you furnished his lordship. Still, the whole will require correction, and which I beg of you to undertake without any scruples." And again, in another letter, "You know the value which Lord Moira attaches to your suggestions—you know also the importance to Lord Moira of defending with sound arguments a point of this nature, which, though of vital consequence to the interests of the Indian Government, will be opposed, I fear, by the Council and by the Court of Directors. As a friend of his lordship, you will feel every anxiety to aid in so good a cause, and I cannot prove my friendship better than by entrusting the labouring oar in the struggle to your able management."—*Camp, Futteghur, July and August,* 1815.—*MS. Correspondence.*]

ready acceptance at Calcutta. In the "Chapter of Accidents," however, there was much written down in their favour. The audacity of the Pindarrees was increasing under the fostering influence of continued impunity, and it was clear that we could not much longer abstain from taking decided measures for the suppression of these reckless marauders, without danger to ourselves, and cruelty to our subjects. Ameer Khan and his Patan levies were making further encroachments on the weak Rajpoot States, and there were indications of a spirit of increased hostility discernible at Scindiah's Court. In this conjuncture, Lord Moira's associates at the Council Board began somewhat to relax in that rigid maintenance of the principles of non-interference which had distinguished their recent proceedings; and a reluctant assent to the proposed movement for the suppression of the Pindarrees was wrung from the Home Government. Somewhat enlarging the scheme sanctioned in Leadenhall-street, Lord Moira now determined to take the field with an overwhelming army for the extirpation of these destructive marauders. It was determined that, at the commencement of the cold season of 1817, war to the knife should be declared againt these people, as common enemies of mankind. No neutrality on the part of the Mahratta States was to be permitted. They were to be called upon to co-operate with us against the Pindarrees; and perhaps the expectation entertained that some previous reluctance, or some subsequent infidelity, would embroil us with the substantive states in such a manner as to enable us to make certain new distribution of their territory, was not, in some quarters, much unlike a hope.

It was hard to say, when we should once have taken the field and commenced operations, who would not come within the scope of the chastisement we were preparing for the Pindarrees. There were symptoms in many quarters of that restlessness, born of suspicion, which is soon developed into open hostility at a native court. In the meanwhile, preparations on a large scale were being made for the coming campaign; and our statesmen were busying themselves with the tangled skein of politics which the aspect of affairs in Central India presented to them. First to clear away one difficulty, then another; to simplify their diplomacy as much as they could, was the great primal object of their endeavours. One great point was to detach Ameer Khan from the confederacy of predatory chiefs. On this subject Lord Moira wrote to the Delhi Resident early in May:

LORD MOIRA TO MR. METCALFE.

"*Barrackpore*, *May* 5, 1817.

"MY DEAR SIR,—Bustle in any one quarter of this country is so likely to excite the speculations and spur the activity of individuals in other parts, that the state of things at Poonah may influence districts nearer to you. Hence it may be wise, if it can be done without affectation, to waken a little the hopes of Ameer Khan. An appearance of wishing to know precisely the territory to which he looks, with obscure hints that there may be soon a course of measures favourable to his views, might be likely to keep him right. Endeavours, I am persuaded, are earnestly exerted to secure his aid in a grand co-operation of predatory powers; and his declining to enrol himself in such a combination would operate much to keep the others quiet. The coming to a point would be easily evaded by you on the plea that I was shortly expected in the Upper Country. That visit I shall undoubtedly make, though I shall not think it necessary to be at Cawnpore till near the opening of the cool season. . . . .

"Adieu, my dear sir.

"I have the honour to be, sincerely,

"Your faithful, humble servant,

"MOIRA."

To this question of the detachment of Ameer Khan from the great predatory confederacy, Metcalfe directed his thoughts. In a review of the state of affairs, forwarded, soon after the receipt of this letter, to the Governor-General, he thus expressed his opinion of the course to be pursued towards Ameer Khan:

"To Meer Khan we might offer a guarantee in perpetuity, for himself and his heirs, of the territories which he at present holds from Holkar, yielding from nine to twelve lakhs per annum.

"Some provision is necessary to induce and enable him to quit his present course of life, and it is proper that it should consist of the same territories which have hitherto supported him as a pest to the peaceable part of India.

"We might require of him to disband his predatory army, to dispose of his artillery to us at a fair valuation, and to reside quietly and inoffensively on the territories assigned to him under the protection of the British Government, with only such a force as might be necessary for the collection of his revenues.

"Meer Khan would, perhaps, require from us a large sum of money, under the pretence of having to pay up his troops before discharging them; but we shall require all our money for other purposes.

"He would also, probably, ask for a grant of territory in our dominions; but it is to be hoped that we need not make such a sacrifice in his favour.

"Should he not accept the terms we offer him, he must abide by the consequences of our determination to put down all predatory powers, without having any provision secured to him."

On the great chart of diplomacy now to be unfolded, the conduct of negotiations with Holkar, with Ameer Khan, and with the Rajpoot states, was assigned to Metcalfe. Our bearing towards these principalities had been much encumbered by our treaty with Scindiah. But in the autumn of 1817, as the Governor-General was proceeding towards the scene of his intended operations, he came to the resolution, which had for some time been taking root in his mind, to ignore these embarrassing obligations, and to enter into treaties for the protection of Oudipore and the other forbidden states. On this subject the Governor-General—Lord Moira no longer, for he had been created, for his services, Marquis of

Hastings—wrote from Cawnpore, at the beginning of October:

LORD HASTINGS TO MR. METCALFE.

"*Cawnpore, October* 5, 1817.

"MY DEAR SIR,—You will have formal instructions sent to you on the point; but you cannot too soon learn my sentiments respecting Oudipore. It has been notified to Scindiah that from late occurrences I consider the treaties existing between us as virtually dissolved—that I am ready to renew our relations, with the confirmation of all his former advantages; but that I must claim and exercise the right of entering into engagements with any states whose position may afford me a security against the re-establishment of the power of the Pindarrees, when they shall be once dispersed. That there might be no ambiguity, I have specified the Rajpoot states. Now, the desirable effect would be to have Jyepore, Oudipore, and Joudpore concur in one general arrangement to be taken under British protection. The same subsidiary fine would then do for all three, and the full expenses of it would be easily met by these states. The attempt to bring them into this agreement should be made before such a shock is given to the predatory associations, as may make the Rajpoots feel tolerably secure against future molestation.

"Scindiah has assented to the progress of the British troops from Boorhanpore to the Nerbudda, and is full of professions of his good disposition; but we do not trust him too far. The troops here, both European and native, are in high health, though there is dreadful sickness down the river. At Chaprah, the burials have been threescore to fourscore in a day. The Bhurtpore Rajah has spontaneously sent 400 horse. I have the honour, my dear sir, to remain, with great regard,

"Your faithful and obedient servant,

"HASTINGS."

Metcalfe now saw clearly his work before him; and in a little while he was in the very midst of its performance. It was attended with no such stormy proceedings as beset the paths of Elphinstone, Jenkins, and Close at their respective Mahratta courts. His negotiations with Ameer Khan were brought to a favourable issue. On the 9th of November, the agent of the Rohilla chief signed at

Delhi, on behalf of his master, a treaty, by which he stipulated to disband his Patan levies, and to restore all the territories which he had wrested from the Rajpoots. On the part of the British Government, it was stipulated that a sum of money should be paid to him, to enable him to disburse the arrears of pay due to his followers, and that the lands which he had held under Holkar, as the price of his military support, should thenceforth be secured to him under British guarantee.*

But to conclude a treaty with a native chief is one thing; to render it binding upon him is another. Great doubts were entertained whether Ameer Khan would be true to his engagements. And a question of very difficult solution arose after the signing of the treaty—a question whether it were more expedient to disband Ameer Khan's levies, or to keep them together under his command until the end of the war. On Ochterlony, who commanded a division of the grand army posted in the Delhi territory, and who had diplomatic powers in the Rajpootana country, devolved the duty of giving effect to the arrangements involved in the treaty with Ameer Khan. Conceiving a higher opinion of the sincerity of that chief than Metcalfe had ever entertained, he was anxious to keep the Patan levies together, and was not without a hope that

* Colonel Sutherland, one of Metcalfe's warmest admirers, in his "Sketch of the Native States of India," calls this treaty one of "rather doubtful character;" but does not enter upon any more minute criticism. Sir David Ochterlony, writing to Metcalfe, put the transaction in its true light, when he said, "Excepting the convenience of the measure, I am not convinced of the propriety of detaching this chief from his nominal master, and giving him a large portion of country not our own, before we have had the least communication with his principal on his past conduct, the grounds of our displeasure, or our wishes or determinations respecting his future conduct." That future conduct, however, soon quieted our scruples, and imparted to the treaty with Ameer Khan a sort of *ex post facto* justice.

they might be advantageously employed against our enemies.* Metcalfe believed him to be the dupe of the Rohilla; but Lord Hastings trusted in the sincerity of Ameer Khan,† and was anxious to encourage it by hopes of future reward. What he might have done, had the war progressed differently, it is hard to say; but he soon saw that it was his true policy to assume friendship, if he did not feel it, and at least to comport himself as a faithful ally.

Whilst thus detaching Ameer Khan from the great confederacy, it was Metcalfe's business, at the same time, to spread over the different Rajpoot principalities the net-work of diplomacy which had long been designed for them. As soon as it had been finally determined to take the field for the suppression of the Pindarrees, Metcalfe had addressed a circular letter to all the chiefs of Rajpootana, inviting them to send agents to Delhi for the purpose of concluding such engagements with the British Government as would ensure for them, throughout the coming struggle, the protection of the paramount power.‡ The requisition was promptly obeyed. The first who sent his representative to Metcalfe's Durbar was Zalim Singh, of Kotah. Zalim Singh had been the first chief with whom, when a boy on his way to Scindiah's Camp, he had inter-

* "If I had two lakhs of rupees," wrote the General, "of my own, I should not hesitate to give it to Meer Khan, so completely has he assured me of his sincerity."

† "If he will depend on me," wrote Lord Hastings to Ochterlony, "the narrow condition of the treaty shall not be the measure of his reward."

‡ "The conditions were simply, that any tribute demandable under a fixed agreement with a Mahratta or Patan chief should be paid directly to the British treasury, leaving us to account for it to the party to whom it might be due; and that our protection should be afforded on the usual condition of abstaining from the contraction of any new relations with other powers, and submitting to our arbitration of external disputes."—[*Prinsep's History*, vol. ii.]

changed diplomatic amenities;* and Kotah had been the subject of the first state-paper which he had drawn up for the use of Government.† Then the princes of Joudpore and Oudipore, long-suffering victims of Mahratta and Patan oppression, sent in their adhesion to the great scheme of alliance. Next, Boondee, Bekaneer, Jessulmere, and other lesser states, sent their agents to the British Durbar, to conclude engagements with the paramount power. And, lastly, came Jyepore, which ought to have been first to allow itself to be saved by our intervention. It happened that, when the time came, this state did not wish to be saved, and talked largely about saving itself. Our negotiations with Ameer Khan had somewhat embarrassed our proceedings towards the Rajpoot states; and now Jyepore was obviously endeavouring to take advantage of our complicated relations, and, as Ochterlony said, to play us off against Ameer Khan. There were curious alternations of presumption and alarm discernible in the conduct of the Jyeporeans; and it was hard to say whether the wavering policy they pursued was dictated by apprehensions of our designs, or a studied effort to overreach us. The example of the other states was, however, followed at last, and on the 2nd of April the long-talked-of treaty with Jyepore was formally signed.

Two great objects had thus been gained by our diplomacy. We had rendered Ameer Khan harmless, and we had brought the Rajpoot States under our protection. In the mean while, equal success was waiting on our arms. The Pindarrees were scattered and destroyed. Holkar, who had joined the enemy,‡ was disastrously beaten in a

* See *ante*, pages 55, 56.

† *Ante*, page 82. Zalim Singh was not the nominal, but the virtual ruler of Kotah.

‡ Metcalfe, it has been shown, had always been of opinion that Holkar's strong disinclination to place himself under the protection

pitched battle. The Peishwah was a prisoner in our camp. The Rajah of Berar was a miserable fugitive. Scindiah was hanging upon our skirts, a reluctant ally; feeble as a friend, but, at least, harmless as an enemy. The condition of things which Metcalfe had so long desired had now arrived. We had suppressed the Pindarree power; we had obtained the right to make new treaties with the substantive states, to enforce a new distribution of territory, to consolidate our own empire, and to secure the permanent tranquillity of Central India. The death-blow, indeed, was now given to the Mahrattas. The Poonah territories were bodily absorbed into our own dominions. Berar, after the amputation of a considerable limb, was placed, during the minority of a new ruler nominated by us, under the administration of the British Resident. Holkar, convinced of his true interests, alike by our power and our moderation, was brought, after certain cessions of territory and tribute, including the Jagheers we had transferred to Ameer Khan, under British protection; whilst the latter chief became a peaceful administrator and a firm ally to the end of his life. Central India was really settled by these great military and diplomatic operations, and peace and security established where before had been incessant strife and continual alarm.

But the period of Metcalfe's residence at Delhi was now drawing to a close. The question of the secretaryship, which had agitated him a few years before, was now to be revived. On the 9th of October, 1818, John Adam wrote, at the request of Lord Hastings, saying, that as Mr. Ricketts had determined to proceed to England in the

of the British, was not to be overcome so long as there was a hope of his obtaining, by other means, a more independent position. The confederacy now established against us seemed to encourage these hopes, so he threw himself into the arms of the enemy.

following January, the Private Secretaryship would then be vacant, and that as the Political Secretaryship would then also be vacant,* the Governor-General hoped that Metcalfe would be induced to accept the conjoint offices. The flattering offer was not refused. Not, however, without some misgivings, did Metcalfe, on the 23rd of October, reply that he was at the service of the Governor-General, and that he would at once make his arrangements to deliver over the charge of the Delhi Residency to his successor.

But who was to be his successor? The solution of the question greatly perplexed the Calcutta Council. After much consideration, it was determined to entrust the military and political duties to Sir David Ochterlony, and to place the civil administration of the district in the hands of a Commissioner or a Board.† "It is not to be expected," wrote John Adam, "of Ochterlony, or of any

* By the elevation of Mr. Adam to a seat in council. In another letter that gentleman wrote: "I am working hard to impose upon you nothing that I can do myself. I sincerely hope that you will like your new employment. I do, from long habit, in spite of the toil and occasional vexation that belong to all employments. I am sure you will find yourself happy in Calcutta, where so many will rejoice to see you established. I cannot tell you the comfort I feel at the department passing into such hands."

† The details of the arrangement consequent on Metcalfe's transfer to Calcutta are sketched out in the following passage of a letter from John Adam, dated November 16, 1818:—"You will receive by this post authority to make over charge of the Residency to Ochterlony, whom Lord Hastings has resolved to appoint to succeed you. He is to command the third division, and to manage the affairs of Jyepore and Ameer Khan, Kerowly, Kishenagur, and generally of the Eastern Rajpoot states; and to take charge of Joudpore, Oudipore, Kotah, and Boondee. The extension of political and military duty thus to be assigned to Ochterlony, will make it necessary to relieve him entirely, or nearly so, from the administration of the territory of Delhi. The outline of the plan proposed is to appoint a civil officer, with high powers, judicial and revenue, distinct from the political authority."

other man, that he should go through the Herculean labours that you have sustained." "The political and military duties," he added in another letter, "will be abundant occupation for any one man; and the internal administration has now become so large a concern, as to make it very expedient to place it on the proposed footing on your being withdrawn."

It is hard to say whether the arrangement for the succession were more pleasing to Ochterlony or to Metcalfe. Throughout long years—years which had brought fame and honour to the old soldier—he had smarted under a sense of the injury that had been inflicted upon him, in 1805, by his removal from the Delhi Residency. And when the rumours first reached him, that he was to succeed Metcalfe, he could not bring himself to believe in their truth. "I cannot help thinking," he wrote, "that Sir George Barlow's infliction is to pursue me through life." He had long been eager to recover his lost position. He cared not where the situation might be—what the emoluments of office, as long as he were styled "Resident" again.* When, therefore, Metcalfe, eager to convey the

* How strong this feeling was, may be gathered from the following touching passage, in a letter written to Metcalfe, in January, 1818:—"In twelve days," wrote Ochterlony, "I shall complete my sixtieth year; and in that long period have never but once had just ground to complain of ill-fortune or ill-usage; but that once, though it has led me to unexpected fame and honour, has, for nearly twelve years, preyed upon my spirits; and all I have since gained appears no recompense for a removal which stamped me with those who knew me best, and loved me most, as ignorant and incompetent, and with the world in general, venal and culpable. A feeling which I cannot describe, but which is quite distinct from the love of ease and the advantages of a Residency, makes me wish for that situation. I would not care where; the name alone seems as if it would wash out a stain—but if that is denied, I shall be happier at Kurnal than anywhere—for there, or near it, are, or will be at no distant date, I trust, assembled all those whom I love

glad tidings to his friend, was the first to communicate to him that his appointment to the Delhi Residency had really been determined by the Governor-General, the delighted veteran, who at threescore was as eager and enthusiastic as a boy, wrote back that his correspondent was not to "expect much sense or connection in a letter written in a tumult of joy and exultation." He was eager, in carrying out all the subordinate arrangements attendant on the change, to be guided by the wishes and suggestions of his friend. "To whose recommendations," he asked, "can I more earnestly wish to attend than to those of the child of my affection? If I do not speak of other motives, it is not because I am insensible that others exist; but because I flatter myself that none can be more acceptable to you than the forcible one implied in a parental love."*

The time for Metcalfe's departure had now come. He was deeply attached to Delhi, and he could not quit the place or its society without many a throb of regret. He was much beloved by the people of all races. His benevolence, his hospitality, his pure unselfishness, his strict integrity, had endeared him alike to natives and to Europeans. As the day of his departure approached, the latter held a public meeting and voted him a farewell address.† It was the first of a long line of similar testimonials of public admiration, which were now to pursue him, from different parts of the world, almost to the very day of his death.

He went, regretting and regretted—but he knew that as

with paternal affection; and there, like a patriarch, I wish to live in the greatest enjoyment this life can bestow—the society of those I love, and who, I believe, return it with sincere and fond affection."

* *Sir D. Ochterlony to Mr. Metcalfe, November* 24, 1818.—*MS.*

† The address, and Metcalfe's reply to it, will be found in the Appendix.

Resident at Delhi he had not been an unprofitable servant. Twelve years afterwards, referring to this period of his career, he thus summed up the benefits which, under his administration of the Delhi territory, had been conferred upon the people:*

"It may be as well to mention a few facts, as characteristic of the spirit in which the former administration at Delhi was conducted, and the discretionary power of the superior authority exercised. Capital punishment was generally and almost wholly abstained from, and I believe without any bad effect. Corporal punishment was discouraged, and finally abolished. Swords and other implements of intestine warfare, to which the people were prone, were turned into ploughshares; not figuratively alone, but literally also, villages being made to give up their arms, which were returned to them in the shape of implements of agriculture. Suttees were prohibited. The rights of Government were better maintained than in other provinces, by not being subjected to the irreversible decisions of its judicial servants, when there were no certain laws for their guidance and control.

"The rights of the people were better preserved, by the maintenance of the village constitutions, and by avoiding those pernicious sales of lands for arrears of revenue, which in other provinces have tended so much to destroy the hereditary rights of the mass of the agricultural community. In consequence there has been no necessity in the Delhi territory for those extraordinary remedies which have been deemed expedient elsewhere, both to recover the rights of Government, and to restore those of the people.

"When it comes to be decided whether the Delhi territory has on the whole been better or worse governed than the provinces

---

* Although in Chapter X. I have treated at some length of Metcalfe's civil administration, I had intended to say more in this place about what some years afterwards was described as the "Delhi System," and which was severely criticised by a very able member of the Bengal Civil Service, but the length to which this chapter has already extended, and some doubt as to whether the discussion would be interesting to the general reader, have warned me to desist. Some passages, however, from Metcalfe's defence of the system are given in the Appendix.

under the regulations, the question, it is to be hoped, will be determined by impartial judges, free from prejudice and passion."

How deeply Metcalfe's departure from Delhi was felt by the inhabitants may be gathered from the following extracts from letters written to him by Sir David Ochterlony :—

"If you had known how much and how generally your departure would have been mourned, you never could have left Delhi; but your humility never gave you a just idea of your value, and I shall have much to do, much to change in my habits and temper, and much to perform, before I shall be able to reconcile the palace, the city, or the European society, to the great loss they have sustained. I appreciate their feelings justly, and if there is in it a spark of envy or jealousy, I hope it will only produce a flame of emulation to imitate your virtues. . . . ."

"I enclose a Razee Nameh. Were you to receive one from all whose inclination would prompt it, I should have transmissions from the whole city. You have no idea of the attachment they felt for you. It cannot be doubted when expressed to me, for they do not usually deal in those articles to a present incumbent when speaking of a predecessor."

A few months afterwards, his old assistant, Mr. Wilder, wrote to him from Ajmere, saying—

"Several people from Delhi have come here since you went away; and it would really do your heart good to hear them speak of the impression of love and respect you have left behind. I never thought before that the natives possessed such feelings; but I do believe that the sorrow they express for your departure is sincere, and that it will never be effaced."

CHAPTER XIII.

[1819—1820.]

THE SECRETARYSHIP.

Constitution of the Supreme Government—The Secretariat—Duties of the Political Secretary—The Private Secretary—Metcalfe and Lord Hastings—Irksomeness of the Situation—Correspondence with Sir John Malcolm—Contemplated Removal to Central India—Correspondence with Mr. Henry Russell—The Hyderabad Residency.

So Charles Metcalfe again revisited Calcutta, and entered upon the duties of the Private Secretaryship. After an interval of a few days, the higher office of Political Secretary was vacated by the elevation of the old incumbent to a seat in council, and the some-time Resident at Delhi launched manfully into the ministerial duties of Government—a worthy successor of Edmonstone and Adam.*

The colleagues of Lord Hastings in the administration were at this time Mr. James Stuart and Mr. John Adam.

* Sir John Malcolm, who had the highest possible opinion of Adam, wrote to Metcalfe, December 30, 1818:—"I am glad, both on your own account and that of the public, that you are gone to Calcutta. I think you in every way an adequate successor to John Adam. I could say more to no man." And not long afterwards Mr. Edmonstone wrote to him:—"Highly as your abilities and services at Delhi were to be appreciated, still I confess that I am happy to learn that my department—the department in which I laboured for so many years, and to which I must chiefly attribute my success in India—had devolved upon one so peculiarly capable of fulfilling the duties as yourself."

Metcalfe's old friend and comrade, Butterworth Bayley, was Chief Secretary; Mr. Holt Mackenzie had charge of the revenue and judicial business; and Mr. Swinton was Persian Secretary. So far, therefore, as personal associations could render his position at this time a pleasant one, he had everything to make it so in the characters of the men with whom he was brought into official intercourse.

No one who has observed the frequency with which the names of Edmonstone and Adam have occurred in the preceding chapters of this memoir, can be altogether ignorant of the duties of a political secretary. With the extension of our Indian empire these duties had necessarily increased. The office is one which has been held in succession by the most eminent men who have adorned the service of the company. It demands the possession of extensive local knowledge and experience, and profound political sagacity. Although ostensibly only an executive officer, the secretary is the adviser of the Governor-General, and, in most instances, the rough-hewer of his measures. The amount of his actual power is necessarily determined by the personal character and qualifications of the Governor-General. But the immense extent and diversity of the business to be discharged by the Government being well considered, it is obvious that no statesman at the head of it, whatever may be his genius, his knowledge, and his activity, can shape or even originate all the measures for which he is responsible. A weak man will become, perhaps, the tool of his secretaries, and leave the Government of the country entirely in their hands; but such weakness is strength in comparison with that of the Governor-General who thinks that he can govern India *without* the aid of his secretaries. Great men, like Cornwallis and Wellesley, steer a middle course. They govern India for themselves, but not by themselves. They use their secretaries; they are not used by them. They know the full value of their Barlows and Edmonstones; but they do not surrender themselves to be tools in their hands. Lord Wellesley was a man of consummate ability, of brave resolution, and of infinite self-reliance; but it is not too much to say, that he would have been shorn of half his strength if Mr. Edmonstone had not been continually at his elbow.

Of the influence of the political secretary in the councils of the state, Metcalfe had seen enough of the ministerial arrangements of three successive Governments to acquire a very clear perception. But he was not one to usurp power not legitimately his own, or to dogmatise where it was his duty to suggest. He had the highest possible respect for constituted authority; and he did his duty without exceeding it.* Moreover, the circumstances of the Indian Government of 1819-20 were not of a nature to place any large amount of power in the hands of a political secretary, even if he had been inclined to exercise it. Metcalfe had, in fact, been more powerful when only a volunteer in the camp of the Governor-General. He then really shaped the great measures which were now completed, or which only required a few final strokes from the artificer's hand to render them complete.

That with regard to these final measures for the settlement of Central India he sometimes differed from the highest authorities, and had opinions of his own apart from those which he was called upon to enunciate as the organ of Government, may be gathered from the following

* Some years afterwards, when he had himself become a member of the Supreme Council, Metcalfe complained of this usurpation of the secretaries, said that they often gave their opinions very arrogantly and dogmatically in Council, and that they not seldom caballed with the Governor-General against the members of Council, and contrived to get all the patronage into their own hands.—See some further remarks on Metcalfe's respect for constituted authority in Chapter XV.

letter to Mr. Jenkins. It is an important commentary on the events described in the last chapter, and illustrates the general views of the writer on the great question of interference with the native states :—

CHARLES METCALFE TO RICHARD JENKINS.

"*Calcutta, July* 5, 1820.

"My dear Jenkins,—Both at Delhi and here I have for many years been complaining that public business does not leave me any time for private correspondence; and from giving way to this feeling, I have lost the interchange of ideas with several valuable friends; I may say with yourself, for our communications have been rare; and certainly with Elphinstone, a most delightful correspondent, with whom I have now little or no intercourse of that kind. I often think that the fault is more my own than that of my business, though at Delhi the work in my time was certainly overwhelming; and here I cannot say that I find leisure for what I wish. Be the cause real or fancied, I have for a long time been anxious in vain to give you my own sentiments distinct from those of Government, given through the channel of their secretary on part of your late letters, in which I think my own sentiments came nearer than those of Government to yours. I must, however, go some way back. I have always regretted that, after the conquest of the Nagpore country, we elevated any new rajah to the Musnud. As soon as I heard of the breaking out of the Peishwah and Appa Sahib, I wrote to Adam, urging him with my feeble voice that we should take the territories of both, and unite them to the British dominions. Malcolm and others seemed to take up and advocate a scheme of setting up a Mahomedan interest in opposition to the Hindoos, or more especially the Mahrattas. It appeared to me that the time was past for our trusting to any balance of power for our support; that the setting up of Mahomedan powers was in itself objectionable, and that our true policy was to secure as much country as possible for ourselves; and to announce ourselves avowedly as the master of all the powers of India. I abhor making wars, and meddling with other states for the sake of our aggrandisement—but war thrust upon us, or unavoidably entered into, should, if practicable, be turned to profit by the acquisition of new resources to pay additional forces to defend what we have, and extend our possessions in future unavoidable wars. With these sentiments, I rejoiced at Lord Hastings' decision regarding the Peishwah's territories, and regretted that which he came to respecting the Nagpore country. I cannot concur in Malcolm's apprehensions of extending our direct rule too rapidly. The sooner the better if done justly. Next to making the Nagpore country our own, the system at present in force there seems to me to be best; and I wish that it were permanently established. Next to permanence, if that cannot be, I would have the longest possible period; and its continuance even for three years, as proposed by you, is better than its immediate transfer. When I say, 'proposed by you,' I mean, proposed in despair of obtaining more. I most entirely agree with you in the sentiment, that we should not set bounds to our interference if we interfere at all; and that if we do interfere, it ought to be with good effect. If possible, I would leave all native states to their own government, without interference. But we are always dragged in somehow, and then it is difficult to say what should be done. The worst plan of all, I think, is to keep in a minister against the will of the prince, and to support the man without regard to his measures. Yet this is the mode we have generally slidden into; and as it has been adopted by wiser heads than mine, it is probably right, or unavoidable. I would prefer leaving the minister to the choice of the prince, and interfering only as to measures; insisting on the exclusion of the man if his measures were incorrigibly bad, but still leaving the choice of a successor to the Prince. I am not sure how this scheme would answer. I do not think that it has ever been attempted. But I would certainly give it a trial if I were at a Court where interference were necessary, and I were not fettered by previous engagements to a particular minister.

"I think you will say, 'Ohe! jam satis est'—so I will conclude with a line or two respecting my own present plans.* . . . .

"Yours most sincerely and affectionately,

"C. T. METCALFE."

There was little at this time in the posture of political affairs to evoke Metcalfe's energies—little that demanded an application of the skill of the master-workman. But there was much to be done. For the most part it was detail work of no great importance—the routine business of the political secretary's office—with nothing bracing or inspi-

* The conclusion of this letter will be found at p. 355.

rifing in it.* His days were given up to official drudgery, and his evenings to society. "Mornings and days," he wrote to a friend at this time, "I have been at work, and as hard as possible; and every night and all night, at least to a late hour, I have been at all sorts of gay parties. I have been raking terribly, and know not when it will stop; for to confess the truth, I find I rather like it. But I hope the hot weather will check it, for though I do not dislike it, I cannot approve what is so contrary to all my notions of what is wholesome for body and mind."

There were, however, occasional diversities of social enjoyment, rising above the ordinary level of Calcutta gaiety, which Charles Metcalfe regarded with more genuine appreciation. There were now and then banquets given by himself or his friends, redolent of pleasant reminiscences of ancient days, when he built up airy castles in the cloisters of Eton, or laid the foundations of more substantial ones in Lord Wellesley's office. Charles Lushington brought together at his table a goodly assemblage of the old "Howe boys," when the sayings and doings of their old lord and master were pleasantly discussed; and Metcalfe himself gave an Eton dinner whereto all the Etonians at the Presidency were bidden. And well remembered in after days was the joyous festival at which *Floreat Etona* was drunk with all the honours; and Metcalfe's honoured friend and correspondent, Dr. Goodall, was toasted in a manner which showed how the good old man was still

* Doubtless, however, there were some compensations in the midst of all this thankless routine work. It must have been, for example, with no common satisfaction that, as the organ of the Supreme Government, he wrote a public letter to his friend Mountstuart Elphinstone, congratulating him on his elevation to the Government of Bombay. The autograph draft of this letter is almost the only document drawn up by Metcalfe during his tenure of office as Political Secretary, which he preserved among his private papers.

respected and beloved. Into such festivities as these, Metcalfe entered with becoming geniality, and was sure to be the life of the party,

I have spoken of the airy castles of Metcalfe's early days. He was always a castle-builder. And now the Political Secretary differed not at all from the eager schoolboy in the Eton cloisters, or the "little stormer" in Lord Lake's camp. His position at the Presidency had brought him again into familiar correspondence with his old friend and teacher, John Malcolm, who now wrote to him from Mhow: "I recognise in all your letters the unaltered Charles Metcalfe with whom I used to pace the tent at Muttra and build castles; our expenditure on which was neither subject to the laws of estimate nor the rules of audit." Miles, counted by the hundreds, now lay between them; but they could still build castles together. There was one magnificent edifice which at this time they were intent upon constructing—but it took fifteen years to convert the airy fiction into a substantial fact.

With such dreams of a brilliant future Metcalfe was wont to solace himself amidst the discontents of a dreary present. Before he had been a year in Calcutta, he had grown weary of the place and of the office. There were many reasons for this; but none which it is very easy to explain. His services were greatly appreciated by Lord Hastings. There were seldom any differences between them on points of vital importance. Both in principle and in practice they seemed to agree. The Governor-General was continually commending the executive aptitude of his Secretary; and when he had altered any of Metcalfe's drafts, always apologised or explained in such a manner as to give a complimentary turn to such assertions of superiority. His undeviating kindness was, indeed, thankfully acknowledged. Metcalfe was not only Political Secretary, he was Private Secretary at the same time; and, therefore, though he did not reside in Government House, he was one of the "family." It does not appear that in this capacity any derogatory duties were entailed upon him—that in any sense he was converted into a lacquey. Six years before, Lord Moira had arrived in India with very magnificent ideas of vice-regal state, and had drawn up a schedule of the various duties of the household, by which the Private Secretary was degraded into a sort of chamberlain, or *maître d'hôtel.* But he had arrived with a "Private Secretary" in his train, appointed under rather peculiar circumstances, who was, perhaps, not ill-suited to the kind of work that had been assigned to him; and a "Principal Private Secretary" was appointed as the Governor-General's confidential assistant in matters of a more public nature. But before Metcalfe's assumption of office, the Governor-General's ideas of vice-regal proprieties had toned down, and the Household Secretary had returned to England. There was now but one Private Secretary, and his functions were mainly of a public character. The duties as a member of the family were few; and if he were occasionally requested to invite some distinguished stranger to take up his quarters in Government House; or if he were instructed to issue orders about court mourning; or if some delegated members of society solicited him to request the honour of the Governor-General's and Lady Hastings' attendance at a bachelors' ball, or other public entertainment, these were small matters of business which no man of sense would conceive himself to be humiliated by executing. Lord Hastings was an old courtier; and Metcalfe had every reason to be satisfied with the personal courtesy and urbanity of his lordship. But for all this, he was not contented with his position. The husk may have been pleasant to look upon; but there was something rotten in the kernel.

What it was does not very plainly appear. Perhaps the

causes of Metcalfe's discontent may be found partly in the environments of his position, and partly in his own personal character. As a ministerial officer, he may have been sometimes compelled outwardly to participate in arrangements of which he could not inwardly approve. A high-minded, conscientious man may see too much for his peace of mind of the occult machinery of Government—of the working of all its secret springs, and hidden wheels, and mysterious contrivances. Metcalfe was too near to Government House; or, perhaps, he was not near enough. He had a natural taste for kingship. It pleased him best to be his own master. He had, for many years, been habituated to independent command. At Delhi he had been lord paramount—without a rival. At Calcutta he was one of many—a minister among ministers. It is not strange, therefore, that he should have found his new situation irksome to him. None of his friends, when they heard of his disappointment, expressed any surprise. Three of the ablest and most distinguished men in India—Malcolm, Elphinstone, and Jenkins—wrote to him that it was just what they expected.

It was whilst in this frame of mind—eager to escape from what seemed to him both the grave of his independence and the grave of his fame—unwilling to drowse, by imperceptible degrees, into a member of Council, and to close his career whilst yet in the heyday of his intellectual vigour, that the letters of John Malcolm came opportunely to give a new direction to his ambition, and to stimulate his energies by again exciting his hopes. The almost superhuman activity of that great soldier-statesman had found in Central India free scope for exercise; but on this great field of labour he seems to have expended himself in unrequited service. Believing that he was neglected by his employers, he had determined to return to England, either to regain the position which he was said to have lost, or to lay down the wand of office for ever. He desired to see a worthy successor enthroned in his place, and he felt in his inmost heart that there was none so worthy as Metcalfe. His old pupil had written to him that the Secretaryship had become distasteful to him; and now Malcolm wrote with all that genuine earnestness which was so refreshing an ingredient in his character, urging the dissatisfied minister to come to Central India, and not to quit it until the territories committed to his charge had grown into an independent Government:

"I have this moment," he wrote on the 19th of February, 1820, "received your letter of the 30th ultimo. I can enter fully into your feelings, and can only wish, if it is determined to place this situation upon a proper scale (which I deem quite indispensable for the general peace of the country), that you should be my successor. It is a station worthy of your talents and ambition. Talk over the work that has been done and is to be done with Caulfield, who understands the whole scheme; and you will be convinced that there would be more than embarrassment—that there would be danger, in depriving this province of one head to whom all looked, and who was competent to act for Government in cases of emergency. I can have no idea that the nature and extent of my political duties are fully understood. They comprise not merely general control, but in many cases minute interference with every large state and petty chief from Serorissi east to Dungerpore west—from the Satporah Hills to the Mahindra Pass north and south. They include the keeping of the peace, by orders, requests, arbitrations and decisions among the numerous Nabobs, Rajahs, Rogues, and Ryots of this extensive space, who are united in no sentiment but one—a common respect and deference for the representative of the British Government. On him their continuance at peace with each other depends. When I reflect on the elements of which this mass is composed, I can hardly trust the charm by which they are kept in concord; but weaken that, and you have years of confusion. . . . . Had I been near you, the King of Delhi should have been dissuaded from becoming an executive officer and resigning power to jostle for influence. But you acted from high motives, and should not be dissatisfied with yourself. Delhi has had you long enough. It is bad that men of your stamp should in any way stagnate or become too local. . . . . If they offer it (the Central-Indian appointment) on proper terms, accept it; come up in November, and let us be one month together. I may leave you a Governor-General's Agent or Commissioner; but depend upon it that ere long you would be a Lieutenant-Governor. These are changes which will force themselves; and I shall give Adam my sentiments confidentially on this point."

To a man of Charles Metcalfe's temperament there was something very spirit-stirring in such an appeal as this. And it did not come singly to stimulate his ambition. A few days after the receipt of this letter from Malcolm, another came from Mr. Marjoribanks, who had political charge of the districts bordering on the Nerbudda River, urging him to obtain permission of the Government for the immediate resignation of his charge. It was Malcolm's theory that more good was likely to result from the combination than from the division of offices of political control; inasmuch as that the latter necessarily induced the enforcement of different systems of policy, and the prosecution of different modes of procedure. He argued, and with much show of reason on his side, that this seeming want of unity in our councils did much to weaken our influence with the chiefs and people of India; and declared that on that account one man might often do what many would fail to accomplish. Taking this view of the case, he contended that it would be advantageous in the extreme to consolidate all the different residencies and agencies in Central and Upper India into one great political charge, eventually to be placed under an officer with the title of Lieutenant-Governor. And he saw in Metcalfe a man well qualified to assume charge of such an office.

This great idea fired Metcalfe's ambition. In the junction of the two extensive tracts of territory over which Malcolm and Marjoribanks had held political control, he saw the commencement of this consolidation, which was to lead to such great results. So he determined at once to take counsel with John Adam on this momentous subject. Adam entered at once into the idea; admitted the advantages of the plan; and on the following day, having in the meanwhile received from Malcolm himself a sketch of his great project, he wrote to Metcalfe, saying:

"A part of the enclosed is so much to the purpose of our conversation yesterday, that I must ask you to read it. Further reflection confirms my conviction of the advantage of the plan we talked of yesterday, and this letter of Malcolm's would serve as a ground for making the proposition to Lord Hastings at the proper time. I am satisfied that it ought to be done, independently of Marjoribanks' final decision, though if his charge could be combined with the other, it would be more worthy of your powers, and more advantageous to the public interests. I cannot wonder at your preferring such a situation to your present one, even if the latter had better answered your expectations."

To have found in John Adam a cordial auxiliary was a great point gained. The opinion of such a man fortified Metcalfe in his resolution to address Lord Hastings on the subject. But when he sat down to write a letter to the Governor-General—a letter which was, in effect, a solicitation to be relieved from the privileged situation of his lordship's confidential adviser—he felt the difficulty and delicacy of the task. The object, however, was a great one; and the thought of it sustained him to the end. At the foot of John Adam's letter he had written roughly in pencil—"*The union of Malcolm's charge and Marjoribanks' would be grand indeed; and make me King of the East and the West!*" And now this kingship in prospect carried him through all the delicate distresses of the following letter:*

MR. METCALFE TO LORD HASTINGS.

"MY LORD,—I am not sure that your lordship will think me in my right senses in what I am about to submit; but I am, never-

* I have transcribed the letter from a rough pencil draft in Metcalfe's handwriting, a little confused as respects the collocation of the paragraphs. It is without date in the original, but it was written at the beginning of April, 1820.

theless tempted to proceed, by a well-founded assurance that it will meet with indulgent consideration.

"The apparent determination of Mr. Marjoribanks not to be induced by any consideration to retain his situation, and the intention of Sir John Malcolm to return to England at the end of the year, seem to leave unoccupied an important field of public service.

"The union of the duties of these situations would obviate in a great degree the objection, on the score of expense, that might otherwise exist against the permanent continuance of Sir John Malcolm's political office, which is stated by him to be desirable.

"That union would, at the same time, hold forth the prospect of a noble station, combining high political and administrative functions.

"And the view which I take of the importance of such an office, if it were instituted, makes me ambitious to fill it, if such an arrangement should meet with your lordship's approbation.

"Your lordship will at one glance determine whether or not this general notion is likely to have your sanction. If it be, I can hereafter trouble your lordship with details, which it would be a waste of time to intrude upon you at present.

"Your lordship will, perhaps, be surprised that, after relinquishing such a situation as the residency of Delhi for the office which I have now the honour to hold, I should think of quitting the latter for any other situation whatever.

"When I reflect on the respectability, emoluments, luxury, comforts, and presumed prospects of my present situation—on the honour of holding a place so near your lordship's person, combined with the enjoyment of continual intercourse with your lordship, and on the happiness conferred by your invariable kindness, I cannot satisfy myself that I act wisely in seeking to be deprived of so many advantages in order to undertake arduous duties of fearful responsibility.

"It is very possible, I think, that if your lordship should indulge my wishes, I may hereafter repent of them; but at present I am under the influence of the following considerations:—

"After a sufficient experience, I feel that the duties of the Secretary's office are not so congenial to me as those which I have heretofore performed. I see reasons to doubt my qualifications for this line of service. I think that many persons might be found who would fill the office more efficiently; and I fancy that I could serve your lordship better in a situation such as I have described, nearly resembling that which I formerly held.

"If the Residency at Delhi on its former footing were vacant, the strong local attachments which I have at that place would induce me to entreat your lordship to restore to me my former office. But that ground is occupied; and neither would your lordship agree to my return were I to make the proposition; nor would I wish it, or willingly consent to it, at the expense of my friend Sir David Ochterlony.

"The situation which I have suggested would have duties similar in nature to those of the Residency of Delhi—nearly as extensive, if not more so; and, perhaps, from the circumstances of the present moment, more important.

"It may appear that the duties at which I aim are too extensive, and that those of Sir John Malcolm's office alone would be ample for any one man to undertake. In anticipation of this possible objection, I beg leave to remark, that if Sir John Malcolm's situation alone were to be provided for, perhaps a more economical arrangement than that herein proposed might be devised by transferring his duties to the Resident at Indore, and fixing a subordinate agent at Holkar's court; that the discharge of the territorial duties of Mr. Marjoribanks' office is to me a fascinating part of the plan which I have suggested; and that, admitting the principle that my duties should be those of general control and management, and that I should not be loaded with detail, I should not think the united charge of the two offices beyond the power of an ordinary man, with the able aid which already exists in all parts of that field.

"If your lordship should doubt the expediency of retaining Sir John Malcolm's political office, or should wish to confer it on any other person, or should desire still to persuade Mr. Marjoribanks to resume his station on the Nerbudda, or should have any other arrangement in contemplation for that territory, I hope that your lordship will not allow my wishes to interfere with your intentions. As above observed, I am too proud of my present situation to seek any arrangement accompanied by the uncomfortable consciousness of having intruded myself on your lordship's indulgence.

"I beg your lordship not to consider what I have submitted as a formal application, but rather as a representation of what is floating in my mind, communicated with unreserved confidence, inspired by your lordship's kindness. Distrusting my own judgment, I have communicated on the subject with Mr. Adam, who seems to think the scheme very feasible and recommendable.

"If my notion should meet generally with your lordship's approbation, it would not necessarily press for immediate decision. As far as my own wishes and convenience would be concerned, I should prefer the postponement of the arrangement to the proper time for relieving Sir John Malcolm—I presume about November, when I could proceed by dawk to the Saugor and Nerbudda territories, and onward to Mhow. The duties of the Saugor and Nerbudda territories might intermediately be carried on by Mr. Molony and Mr. Maddock, in correspondence with Government; and, in this interval, all the arrangements for the future management of those districts respectively under my general control might be matured and established. But with regard to the time of my departure, as well as upon every other point, I should, of course, be ready to obey with alacrity your lordship's commands.

"Your lordship will perceive that I have considered only myself in this proposition; but I trust that you will not misapprehend my motives for doing so. Had I the vanity to suppose that your lordship would have any preference either for retaining me here, or employing me elsewhere, I should consider myself bound by every duty to suppress my own inclinations, and think only of your lordship's pleasure; but believing that your lordship will not have any bias on the subject, except what may arise on the one hand from your disposition to do an act of kindness, or on the other from doubts of the public utility of forming such a situation, and of my competency to fill it, I have thought myself at liberty to submit my ideas with reference to myself alone.

"My simple proposition has led me to trouble your lordship with a tedious explanation; and yet I must conclude, still under the fear that I have not adequately explained my feelings—especially those of respectful attachment and gratitude which your lordship's undeviating kindness has inspired, and which must ever bind me to your lordship—lest I should encroach too much on your lordship's time.

"I have the honour to be,

"Your lordship's obedient servant,

"C. T. Metcalfe."

On the 5th of April, Lord Hastings, writing to Metcalfe, primarily on another topic, said: "We will discuss the subject of your private letter when we meet. But I would not delay saying, that I did not startle at it." The project, indeed, was favourably received by the Governor-General, and before the end of the month Metcalfe wrote to his friend Richard Jenkins, saying it was designed that the scheme should take effect; and asking what was the best way of getting to Mhow in November or December?* But, little more than two months afterwards, he wrote again to the same correspondent, saying: "I have given up the idea of succeeding Malcolm and erecting my standard on the Nerbudda, in order to go to another field, not so extensive, but more compact and more comfortable, and offering a prospect of greater leisure. It is a bad sign, I fear, that for these reasons I think it preferable. I look upon it as a sort of retirement for the rest of my service in India. I have seen enough of the Secretaryship to know that the respectability and satisfaction of those stations depend upon circumstances beyond one's own control; and though, under some circumstances, I should prefer my present situation to any other, I shall quit it without any desire of ever returning to it, and without much wish of ever having a seat in Council—were it not for the name of the thing I might say without *any* wish. This state of feeling I have gained by coming to Calcutta; and it is fortunate that it is so, for I have no chance whatever of a seat in Council at any time."†

* "I have disclosed," wrote Metcalfe, "the scheme I communicated to you to Lord Hastings, and it is at present designed that it shall take effect. If so, the Nerbudda territories will come under me—a bad substitute, I fear, for you; but we shall act, I trust, on the same principles. What will be the best way of getting speedily to Mhow in November or December? Though I am not to see you so soon as I hoped, we shall meet, I trust, at Nagpore before the end of the year. At least I shall embrace the first opportunity of renewing old days with you. What time would it take to get to Nagpore and thence to Mhow?"—[*Charles Metcalfe to Richard Jenkins, April 28th*, 1820.]

† *MS. Correspondence, July* 5, 1820.—He had written, a few days before, to the same effect, to Malcolm, who wrote in reply: "The only part of your letter of the 29th ultimo that I did not

The other field—more compact—more comfortable—offering prospect of greater leisure—was the field of Hyderabad in the Deccan. The Residency was then occupied by Mr. Henry Russell. In the month of April that gentleman had written to Metcalfe that he purposed to remain at Hyderabad until the commencement of the following year, and that he earnestly hoped his correspondent would be his successor. The two gentlemen were on terms of intimate friendship and familiarity. They were connected, indeed, by marriage. Mr. Russell was a first cousin of Theophilus Metcalfe's wife. The thought of handing over his office to such a man as Charles Metcalfe afforded him, both upon public and on private grounds, the liveliest satisfaction; and even when such a transfer seemed to be remote, he spoke in glowing terms of the situation. "I always thought," he said, "that you would regret the change from Delhi to Calcutta. It can hardly be long before you are placed in Council; but if this should not be the case, and you should continue desirous of returning to your own line, I should be delighted to deliver this Residency into your hands. You will find an excellent house completely furnished; a beautiful country; one of the finest climates in India, and, when the business which now presses has been disposed

like, was that the plan of your succeeding me was given up. If it has been abandoned in consequence of an arrangement that is better for you, I shall rejoice on your account, but not for Malwa, because for all that good work of which I think I have laid the foundation you were precisely the successor I wished, and the man under whom my tucavées, potails, zemindars, thakoors, newabs, rajahs, and maharajahs would have flourished; but I shall hope the station will yet tempt you, and depend upon my word it will become great in your hands, and work its way, in spite of all routine-mongers, to that consequence it must have before its duties can be efficiently and satisfactorily performed."—[*John Malcolm to Charles Metcalfe, July* 22, 1822.]

of, abundance of leisure to follow your personal pursuits. My original intention was to go home at the end of this year, having made a sort of promise to my father to be with him by the time he is seventy, which he will be in August twelvemonth. These measures of reform will detain me; but by the end of next year matters will be so completely set agoing in their new train, that I shall certainly go then."

But at this time the great Central-Indian project held possession of Metcalfe's mind. In reply to Henry Russell's letter, he communicated an outline of the plan. Still the Hyderabad Resident did not despair of inducing Metcalfe to become his successor. He had an insuperable array of arguments to adduce in favour of the appointment in the Deccan. He was able, too, to announce that his reformatory measures had been so far initiated, that he might with confidence quit his office at the end of the current year. But there was one condition necessary to this. It was essential that he should be able to rely on the succession of one sure to enter into his views and advance his plans of reform. The letter was an enticing and a convincing one. On more accounts than one, it calls for insertion:—

MR. HENRY RUSSELL TO MR. CHARLES METCALFE.

"*Hyderabad, May* 26, 1820.

"MY DEAR METCALFE,—The project mentioned in your letter of the 10th inst. has made an alteration in my views; or rather it has done away the alteration I had before made in them, and restored them to what they originally were. Until lately, my plan always was to go home at the end of this year; and nothing could have induced me to think of staying longer but the wish of not only carrying the reform of the Nizam's affairs into complete effect, but also of placing it on so firm a footing as to prevent a clumsy successor from injuring the work, or a hostile or illiberal one from depriving me, after I am gone, of that share of credit to which I may be justly entitled. Now everything that experience and local knowledge enable me to do better than another person will have been done by the end of this year. The foundation has already been substantially laid. The Minister knows as distinctly as I do what is to be done, and by what means it must be accomplished. The reduction of establishments has been arranged, and is in progress; our interference and the objects and effects of it are known and felt throughout the country; and by the end of the revenue year, in September, all the Talookdars will have been chosen and appointed, and the necessary new engagements framed and executed between them and the Government. In short, the whole of the new system has been discussed and matured, and put in action. In the course of the year, therefore, my first wish will have been accomplished; and the second will be effectually secured, if, at the end of it, I can deliver the Residency into such hands as yours. In point of magnitude, your situation in Malwa will certainly be superior to this Residency; but you may do as much real good, and acquire as much real importance, here as you could do there. The office now proposed for you will be made great by adding many things together; at Hyderabad it will be compact and considerable in itself, and will afford, for several years to come, an ample field for the exertions of a man of talents and benevolence. As to personal convenience, there can be no comparison. In Malwa you will have no time to yourself, and you will either be wandering about the country, which is always irksome when it is perpetual, or you will have to build and furnish a house, at the expense of certainly not less than a lakh of rupees, out of your private fortune. At Hyderabad, after the first six months, when you have looked thoroughly into everything, you will find, compared with what you have been accustomed to, little to give you trouble: at least half your time will be at your own disposal; and you will step at once, without care or expense, into a house completely furnished, and provided with every accommodation. Upon the point of honour, surely you need give yourself no concern. Colonel Wm. Kirkpatrick was appointed from your present office to the Residency at Poona; and even if there were no precedent of that kind, you might be content to measure with Sancho's rule—wherever you sit will be the head of the table. You say yourself that you think you should prefer Hyderabad to Malwa, if you had your choice of the two at the same time. My principal fear, therefore, is lest you should suppose that, by coming into this arrangement now, you would be consulting your own inclinations in the smallest degree at my expense. But a man may be trusted to judge for his own happiness. Be assured that there is quite as much of selfishness in my proposal as you could possibly desire. No galley-slave ever laid down his oar with greater joy than I shall feel at laying down this Residency, whenever I can do so with justice to myself, and with a conviction that I leave the public interests in the hands of an able and upright successor. As it was, it was a sacrifice, and a great one too, for me to resolve on staying so long; and I know that if you succeed Malcolm this year, you will be engaging in plans and measures which will effectually prevent your coming to Hyderabad hereafter. If, therefore, you can be prevailed upon to think the arrangement agreeable to yourself, and do not foresee any serious obstacle in the way of its accomplishment, you can at once intimate to Lord Hastings my wish to retire, and propose to him to nominate you my successor. As I should like to leave Hyderabad in November, so as to be ready to embark at Madras or Bombay, by the first ships that sail after Christmas, it is desirable that no time should be lost in doing whatever you may be resolved upon. My end would of course be defeated unless you were to secure the appointment for yourself at the same time that you announce my intention of vacating it. Indeed, I would not resign after all, if I found that any other person was intended for my place.

"Believe me ever, my dear Metcalfe,

"Most sincerely yours,

"H. RUSSELL."

This letter had the desired effect. The great Central-Indian kingship had begun by this time to appear before Metcalfe as something vague and illusory. The charmings of John Malcolm were already losing their power over his mind. Perhaps Lord Hastings had begun to relax in the adhesion which he had given in to the scheme of consolidating the Malwa and Nerbudda agencies. There may have been other circumstances tending to shake his faith in the advantages or the practicability of the plan which had once so strongly laid hold of his mind. Or Henry Russell's letter may have done the work, without aid from any other quarter. Metcalfe, it has been seen, declared that the promise of greater leisure was irresistibly attractive. He said it was "a bad sign" that such considerations should have had so much weight with him. But in this he was mistaken.* Good or bad, he accepted Russell's offer; and the Hyderabad Resident wrote eagerly to him, on the 4th of July: "I am delighted to find by your letter that my arguments have prevailed with you. You will have made me the happiest man out of India; and I shall be disappointed if, at Hyderabad, you are not one of the happiest men in it. I shall now quit my station without a wish ungratified. It is very desirable that I should deliver the Residency immediately into your hands. . . . . If anything should unfortunately occur to prevent your coming here, the very object of my retiring would be defeated; and much as I should lament the necessity, I should nevertheless feel myself compelled to remain until I had consolidated the reform, even at the sacrifice of all the projects of happiness which your concurrence in my proposal has enabled me to entertain."

The Hyderabad Resident, however, was not to be disappointed. Metcalfe had made up his mind to proceed to the court of the Nizam; and the proposed arrangement was at once sanctioned by Government. As the cold season approached, the Political Secretary began to make his arrangements for the transfer of his office to Mr. Swinton, who was to succeed him; and by the beginning of November everything was in readiness for Metcalfe's

* The great want of our European functionaries in India is want of leisure. The great impediment to their efficiency is, that they have too much to do. Many first-rate men, with the power and with the inclination to initiate and to carry out great schemes of amelioration, which would confer incalculable benefit on the people, are necessitated to expend themselves in the detail-work of mere routine. Metcalfe was often painfully conscious of this. What an Indian functionary calls leisure, is exemption from a stringent necessity to perform a certain amount of work within a certain space of time, and to expend all the available hours of the day in the current duties of his office. Metcalfe's desired leisure was leisure to do good—not leisure to play at billiards, or to hunt hogs.

departure. He had many friends in Calcutta, who deeply lamented his going; and now that he was about to leave them, they desired to evince their sense of his worth, both as an officer of the Government and a member of society, by giving him a public entertainment; but the notoriety of such a proceeding had no attraction for him, and he desired that the manifestation of the kind feelings of his friends should assume a more private character. A dinner, however, was given to him by a large party of his friends, and it was at least sufficiently public to form a topic of commendatory discourse in the public journals of the day.

He parted from Lord Hastings with expressions of earnest good-will on either side. "And now, my dear sir, for yourself," wrote the Governor-General to him, after touching on matters of public concern, "let me assure you that I have been duly sensible of your kind and cordial attachment; and that it is with earnest prayers for your welfare that I wish you all possible prosperity and comfort. We shall not meet again in India, and the chances for it in Europe must, considering my age, be small; but I shall rejoice in hearing from you, and you will believe that I remain yours faithfully, HASTINGS."

CHAPTER XIV.

[1820—1821.]

THE HYDERABAD RESIDENCY.

Hyderabad—Its Government—The Administration of Meer Allum—His Death—Elevation of Mooneer-ool-Moolk—Chundoo-Lall—Captain Sydenham and Mr. Russell—Intrigues of the Minister—Misgovernment of the Country—The Nizam's Contingent—The House of William Palmer and Co.—Loans to the Nizam—State of the Country—Projected Reforms—Metcalfe's Appointment to the Residency—His Inauguration—Remedial Measures—Improvement of the Country.

HYDERABAD is the chief city of that tract of country known as the Deccan, which half-way down the great Indian peninsula stretches almost from the eastern to the western coast—from the borders of Candeish to the banks of the Kistnah. This country was of old time held under the Mogul emperors by a Soubahdar, or Viceroy, known as the Nizam.* After the decay of the empire, this fine principality would doubtless in due course have fallen to the Mahrattas, but for the support it derived from its close connection with the British Government. The Hyderabad state was one of our oldest, and outwardly at least, our most faithful allies. The extent and position of its territories rendered it a matter of vital importance that we should maintain the integrity of the country, and secure the independence of the government. Hyderabad was, indeed, a necessary barrier against foreign invasion at a time when

* The Nizam is properly the manager, or administrator of the state; but the nomenclature is scarcely known among the people of the Deccan.

the unscrupulous aggressiveness of the Mahrattas suggested the necessity of zealously preserving every means of external defence.

In spite of the mutations of time, at the period of which I am now writing, the fiction of dependence on the Mogul sovereign was still maintained. The ruler of the Deccan was still the Nizam, though his titular master was a pensioner at Delhi. On the death of an Oriental potentate there is generally a scramble for the vacant throne. In 1803, Sekundur Shah, supported by the British Government, had succeeded against all competitors in seating himself upon the *musnud* of Hyderabad. But he was a man of slender intellect and little principle; and, like all the tribe of Eastern princes, capricious in the extreme. Much as he was indebted to the British Government, he felt neither gratitude towards, nor confidence in, his supporters. He was jealous of our influence—restless under our supervision—and easily wrought upon as he was by evil advisers, he might, perhaps, have been roused into overt opposition, if he had possessed energy sufficient for so manly a demonstration. But instead of this, he abandoned himself to the delights of the zenana, and contented himself with petty intrigues against the Government which had made him the ruler of a great principality, and had power to reduce him to as poor a pageant as the "Great Mogul," who was wearing out his life in vain repinings and vainer intrigues in the imperial city.

That in such a frame of mind the Nizam should have found creatures to minister to his pleasures and to foment his discontents, is so much a matter of course that it need hardly be stated. Foremost among these parasites and evil counsellors was one Mohiput Ram, a Hindoo noble, who exerted himself, and with considerable success, to counteract the good influence of the responsible Minister, and eventually to supplant him in the direction of affairs. This Minister was Meer Allum, an old servant of the state, who had been employed to negotiate the treaties with the British Government—who in the war with Tippoo Sultan had commanded with great credit the auxiliary troops of the Nizam—who knew, therefore, and respected the power of his Christian allies. In 1804 he had been appointed, at our suggestion, to take charge of the administration of Hyderabad. But the evil influence of Mohiput Ram soon reduced the authority of the Minister to a name; and when, in 1806, Captain Sydenham took charge of the Residency, he found that the wily Hindoo was on the very point of effecting the deposition of the Minister, and setting himself up in his place.

But there was one thing yet to be done; and Mohiput Ram did not despair of doing it. This one thing was the propitiation of the new Resident. It was felt that unless the good offices of the representative of the British Government could be secured, all his schemes would fall to the ground, just at the very point of accomplishment. So he made his dispositions to secure the favour of the Resident, with a promptitude and an energy worthy of a better cause. Before Captain Sydenham had reached Hyderabad—when he was yet, indeed, some thirty miles from the capital—a confidential agent of Mohiput Ram stopped his palanquin in the middle of the night, and, with a complimentary message from his master, presented the English gentleman with a dress of honour, and a tray of costly jewels. It need not be said that these presents were rejected. But soon after Sydenham's arrival at Hyderabad, Mohiput Ram attempted to open a private correspondence with the Resident, declared his devotion to the interests of the British Government, and thinking perhaps that he had not bidden high enough on the former occasion, attempted to "stimulate his proposal by the offer of four lakhs of rupees."*

At this time Mohiput Ram exercised unbounded influence over the mind of the Nizam. This it was the policy of Sydenham to counteract. "Without exercising any direct or offensive interference," he said, "I thought I was justified in trying what effect the fair undisguised support of the Minister would produce on the state of parties at this court; and the consequences of such a procedure exceeded my most sanguine expectations. The influence of Mohiput Ram was checked; the Minister was roused to an exertion of his talents; and the Nizam became gradually disposed to more liberal sentiments."† The Minister, now reconciled to his master, recovered his health and his spirits, which had before languished; and public business, which had fallen greatly into arrears, was now energetically discharged. But much of it was done by Meer Allum's financial assistant—a man of unquestionable

* *Captain Sydenham to Mr. Edmonstone, September* 8, 1806.—[*MS. Correspondence.*] I have narrated this anecdote less for the purpose of illustrating the anterior history of the Hyderabad administration, than of showing the kind of temptations to which the Resident at a native court was always exposed. Nor were the Residents the only men in authority who were thus beset. I have heard a story somewhat similar to the one in the text, illustrative of the honourable career of Mr. N. B. Edmonstone. It is related that when he was Chief Secretary, a wealthy native endeavoured, as Captain Sydenham says, to "stimulate a proposal" he had made to Government, by offering Mr. Edmonstone 30,000 rupees (or 3,000*l.*), and was, of course, indignantly dismissed. For some time after this the native was greatly depressed in spirit, and was continually reproaching himself. "Fool that I was," he repeated, "to offer a gentleman of his rank 30,000 rupees. I should have offered him three lakhs (30,000*l.*), and then I should have got it." He could not understand that the one offer would have shared the same fate as the other.

† *Captain Sydenham to Mr. Edmonstone, September* 8, 1806.—[*MS. Correspondence.*]

vigour of understanding, and activity of habits—a Hindoo, named Chundoo-Lall, who superintended the internal administration, and more especially the revenue business of the principality, with an indefatigable perseverance which called forth the warm commendations of the Resident.

The time, indeed, was fast approaching when this man was to take a more conspicuous part in the administration of the country. Meer Allum, now far advanced in years, was little able to sustain the pressure of public business, and it is probable that, but for the assistance of Chundoo-Lall, he would have been incompetent to the discharge of his duties. For some time, indeed, the chief business of the administration had been performed by the latter, when, at the close of 1808, Meer Allum was seized with mortal sickness and died. The question of succession was a most important one, in all respects, to the British Government. The Nizam, weak and incapable, even below, in intellectual acquirements, the average of Oriental princes, required the guardianship of a sagacious and experienced statesman, and it was necessary for the interests of the British Government that the guardian selected should be friendly towards our alliance, and eager by good offices and wise conduct to cement it. It would be out of place to narrate the long-protracted negotiations which then ensued between the British Resident and the Nizam. Each had his favourite candidate; and the appointment was not finally adjusted without the lapse of half a year of discussion and intrigue. At last, a compromise was effected. The nominee of the Nizam, by name Mooneer-ool-Moolk, was appointed to the office of Prime Minister, but it was arranged that the actual administration should remain in the hands of the deputy, Chundoo-Lall, whose good feeling towards the British Government the Resident never doubted. The two men had previously entertained but little friendship towards each other; but they fell amicably into the proposed arrangement, embraced over it as brothers, and from that time were completely reconciled.*

On the 14th of June, 1809, Captain Sydenham reported that he had at length brought his negotiations to a close. "I am satisfied," he said, writing privately to the Chief Secretary, "that the arrangement which has been concluded is, on the whole, the most eligible that could have been adopted. There can be little doubt that Mooneer-ool-Moolk is well assured of the necessity of cultivating and improving the good opinion and confidence of the British Government, and the stipulations under which he will be admitted to the office, will secure the continuance of that system which first established, and will continue to maintain, the predominant influence of the British Government in this part of India."† But sanguine as were the expectations thus expressed, Sydenham was compelled ere long to acknowledge that the ostensible Minister, jealous of British influence, endeavoured secretly to counteract it; and that the country was miserably misgoverned. Less than a year after the establishment of the new Ministry he wrote his farewell despatch to Government. About to vacate the Residency, he declared that he had little hope of any salutary impression being made on Mooneer-ool-Moolk, and that he considered the disorders of the Nizam's Government to be "too deeply rooted, and too widely extended, to admit of any remedy short of placing the administration of the country under the control of the Resident."

On the departure of Captain Sydenham, in the summer of 1810, the responsible business of the Residency devolved temporarily on Mr. Charles Russell, whose brother, Mr. Henry Russell, a civilian, had been appointed to the office.

* *Private Correspondence of Captain Sydenham and Mr. Edmonstone, MS.*

† *Captain Sydenham to Mr. Edmonstone.*—[*MS. Correspondence.*]

On the arrival of the new Resident, new intrigues were set on foot. Mooneer-ool-Moolk hoped to find Mr. Russell more tractable than his predecessor. But the civilian set his face no less resolutely than the soldier against all attempts on the part of the nominal Minister to usurp an authority which did not belong to him; and he so far succeeded, that the details of internal administration were carried on by Chundoo-Lall with little interruption from his titular chief. But the influence of the latter over the indolent and imbecile Nizam was often exerted for evil; and his intrigues, if not dangerous, were inconvenient and embarrassing to the Resident. For this there seemed to be no remedy but the removal of the Minister; and that remedy might be worse than the disease. "The only measure," wrote Mr. Edmonstone privately to Mr. Henry Russell, "that could be adopted is obviously the expulsion of Mooneer-ool-Moolk from office, and for this extreme proceeding Government is not prepared." "Never, to be sure," he added, "was there such a Government since the world began, and what can be done to remedy its present state would baffle any politician but a French one, who would no doubt propose to take the said Government under the protecting care and superintendence of its ally."* The fact is, that there was nothing to be done. Mr. Russell was of opinion that the removal of Mooneer-ool-Moolk would only open the door for the entrance of worse evils. There were weighty reasons against the elevation of Chundoo-Lall to the ostensible head of the administration, and it was nearly certain that if any man of rank and influence were to take the place of the old Minister, he would soon be in a state of violent antagonism with the deputy. "And if," said Mr. Russell, "Chundoo-Lall is to have an opponent in his colleague, he cannot have a better

* *Mr. Edmonstone to Mr. Russell, April* 12, 1812.—[*MS. Correspondence.*]

one than Mooneer-ool-Moolk, who is both a coward and a fool." *

An abler man than Mr. Henry Russell has seldom gone out to India. He seems to have seen clearly, from the first, the wrongs under which the unhappy country was groaning. He declared, in one of his earliest despatches to Government, that it was "in so lamentable a condition that it could not long continue to endure the extortions which were practised upon it by the avarice and rapacity of its governors." † He was, indeed, continually describing, in language so vigorous and eloquent that it is a pleasure to read his despatches, the diseases which were eating into the State and making the whole one mass of corruption. But it may be doubted whether his talents were of the kind best suited to the work that lay before him. He said, years afterwards, that he did not make the disorders which had so long been destroying the Hyderabad State, but found them there ready-made—a heritage from his predecessor. He found them; and it is but right to say that he desired and endeavoured to remove them.

It was the natural tendency of such a state of things to grow from bad to worse—to find in the lowest deep a lower deep of misery; a confusion worse confounded. "I was for seven years," said one most competent to speak on such a subject, and sure to offer impartial testimony,‡ "a witness of the afflictions in which the reign of Chundoo-Lall in the Hyderabad Provinces involved this unhappy country." The whole system of administration was rotten to the very core—it was a great congeries of diseases. Nothing seemed to flourish there except corruption. Every man was bent on enriching himself at the expense of his neighbour. No one cared for the people, no one cared for

* *Mr. Russell to Mr. Edmonstone, May* 6, 1812.

† *Mr. Russell to Government, May* 21, 1811.

‡ The late Colonel John Sutherland.

the State. Everything had its price in Hyderabad. If a man wanted a place, he counted out his money to buy it. If a man wanted justice, he bade for it, as for any other marketable commodity. Every public officer in every department of the State was accessible to a bribe. But there were worse things even than these. The revenue was farmed out to greedy contractors, who made immense profits by underletting the lands to smaller farmers, who sent their tax-gatherers into the country to wring the last farthing from the cultivators, until their oppressions could no longer be endured; and then the wretched people were dragooned into submission, and the required payments extorted from them at the bayonet's point or the sabre's edge. Such mighty wrong-doing as this bore abundantly the accustomed fruit. A peaceful and industrial population was converted into rebels and bandits. Neither life nor property was secure. On the high road, and in open day, it was safe to travel only under the protection of a military escort. There was nothing left, indeed, but the name of government. All the rest was lawlessness and confusion.

But this was not Mr. Russell's fault. "I protest," he wrote some years afterwards to the Court of Directors, "against being held in the most remote degree responsible for the disorders of a Government with which not only I was not empowered to interfere, but with which I was prohibited from interfering. It was a fundamental rule of our policy, repeatedly insisted upon in the orders both of your Honourable Court and of your Governments in India, to abstain from all interference in the internal concerns of our native allies. I was employed at Hyderabad from first to last for upwards of twenty years, and I affirm that during the whole of that time no influence or interference was exercised by the Resident in the domestic affairs of the Nizam's government. In questions of foreign policy, in measures affecting the safety of the Government, and generally in matters in which our own interests, or the common interests of the alliance were involved, we always did and always must exercise that influence which essentially belongs to the relative condition of a protected and protecting State. But in the management of his country, the collection and distribution of his revenues, the control of his local officers, and the command, payment, and employment of his whole army, with the exception of that part to which English officers were attached, no influence whatever was exercised by the Resident; and the Nizam's government was as much an independent state as if the alliance with us had not existed."*

But the exception here indicated was one of grave importance. Whilst Henry Russell occupied the Residency, that "part of the army to which English officers were attached" was growing, under his fostering hands, into formidable dimensions. The history of the Nizam's force is one which it would take long to narrate. At the close of the last century it was disciplined by French officers; but the war with Tippoo cemented a close friendship between the English and the Nizam; and as English interests became paramount at Hyderabad, our ally was induced to disband his French battalions, and to organise a new force in its place. Little by little the connection of Englishmen with the Nizam's army increased during the early years of the present century. It was permitted—perhaps it may be said that it was encouraged—whilst Kirkpatrick and Sydenham represented British interests at the court of the Nizam. Among the first who took service under the Hyderabad state was Mr. William

* Letter to the Court of Directors relative to Hyderabad affairs, by Henry Russell, late Resident at Hyderbad. London, 1824.

Palmer, a gentleman not of pure European blood,* but of good courage and excellent abilities, who rendered considerable service to the state by supplying, when at a distance from Hyderabad, information to the British Resident relative to the outlying districts and the neighbouring native states, and who was sometimes employed to negotiate with the rebellious subjects of the Nizam. But the army, in spite of the few European officers who were connected with it, was at this time lamentably inefficient; and on one memorable occasion, in 1808, suffered itself to be disgracefully defeated by a rebel force under Mohiput Ram.† Mr. Palmer was informed, on credible authority,

* He was son of General Palmer, and brother of John Palmer, the well-known Calcutta merchant.

† Some idea of what the Nizam's army was at this time may be gathered from the following passage of a letter from Captain Sydenham to Mr. Edmonstone, written in February, 1808:—"Mohiput Ram continued to negotiate with every appearance of sincerity till the 11th of February, when he suddenly changed his tone, threatened the life of Mr. Palmer, marched out his troops from Shahpoor, and joined Mahomed Rezza Khan. Mr. Palmer obtained with great difficulty permission to leave Shahpoor. On the morning of the 12th, Mohiput Ram and Mahomed Rezza engaged the Nizam's troops under Nizamut Jung and Mr. Gordon. The Nizam's cavalry behaved with the most shameful cowardice, and fled at the commencement of the action. The infantry, under Mr. Gordon, showed great resolution and spirit, drove the enemy back, took their guns, and would have gained the day, if they had been supported by the cavalry. But being deserted by the cavalry, they were soon surrounded. A general panic seized them. All the exertions of Mr. Gordon and Mr. Palmer were insufficient to rally them; and they were completely destroyed by superior numbers of horse and foot. Mr. Palmer luckily escaped, but Mr. Gordon was wounded and taken prisoner. From the concurring testimony of many accounts, I am afraid that Mr. Gordon was cruelly butchered. Mr. Bertie Burgh and a Mr. Bellair were killed. Mr. Pearson was wounded and taken. His subsequent fate is uncertain. The other Mr. Burgh escaped. Of 1,300 infantry that entered the action, not more than 300 have been

after this affair, that "there was not a jemadar of horse but was disaffected to our interests." * It may have been treachery rather than cowardice, which made the cavalry fly like sheep before the battalions of Mohiput Ram.

One thing, however, was certain. The few European officers who were attached to the Nizam's army in 1808 seemed to be only there to be butchered. It was advisable, indeed, that over the Hyderabad levies there should be efficient European control; or that they should be left to their native officers. When Mr. Russell joined the Residency, this subject in no small measure occupied his thoughts. Perhaps he thought too much of it. Perhaps he made the Nizam's Contingent too much of a plaything. At all events, whilst Henry Russell occupied the Residency, the Contingent became, in all essential respects, a British force, paid in some manner or other, directly or indirectly, from the treasury of the Nizam. This matter of the payment of the troops was one which led to very grave results. It did not always happen that there was money in the treasury to pay them. On one occasion, in 1812, the unpaid troops mutinied, tied their commanding officer to a gun, and threatened to blow him away if their arrears were not discharged.† Money was sent from the Residency, and for a time the mutiny was quelled. But it was obvious to Mr. Russell that something must be done, both to keep the Contingent in an efficient state, and to

able to effect their retreat, and many of them were wounded. The Nizam's cavalry, after this shameful retreat, gradually collected at a place about thirty miles from Shahpoor, and are slowly returning to Hyderabad."—[*MS. Correspondence.*]

* *Mr. Palmer to Captain Sydenham, March* 18, 1808.—[*MS. Correspondence.*]

† "Calcutta Review," vol. xi., article "Nizam's Contingent," in which ample details connected with the history of this force will be found.

secure its loyalty. "Nobody, I presume," he said afterwards, "will dispute that if the troops were to be maintained at all, it was necessary to provide for their being regularly paid."

But how was this provision to be made? The arrangements which Mr. Russell had instituted to secure the efficiency of the Nizam's Contingent had greatly increased the costliness of the force. Such an army, disciplined and commanded by English officers, could only be maintained at a cost altogether incommensurate with the means of discharging it. The Hyderabad State, distressed and embarrassed, ever forestalling its revenues, was not in a condition to secure regularity of payment to such a force. It is not to be doubted that the reorganization of the Contingent had greatly increased the burdens of an already overburdened state. The English commandant of the Russell Brigade, so baptized in honour of the Resident, received from the Nizam 5,000*l.* a year as his own salary; and other officers were paid in proportion.* Employment in the Nizam's service was generally coveted by the officers both of the King's and the Company's army. The Resident was importuned with applications for these comfortable staff appointments, and large sums passed annually into the pockets of our own people. That the efficiency of the Contingent was greatly increased, that it became, indeed, an admirable body of disciplined troops of all arms, is not to be doubted. But it is equally unquestionable that it increased the burdens of the state in a manner for which any advantages accruing from the enhanced efficiency of the Contingent could never sufficiently compensate.

* The writer of the paper on the Nizam's Contingent says, that as job followed job, and other superfluous offices were made, it became a proverbial expression current in Hyderabad, that, "Poor Nizzy pays for all!"

From such a Government as that of the Nizam—a Government of shifts and expedients, whose system of finance was little more than the great system of hand-to-mouth, the regular payment of the troops was clearly not to be expected. But in such a matter as this the interposition of the Resident was justified, if not demanded. So Mr. Russell made an arrangement for the payment of the troops, of which it is necessary to speak somewhat in detail. Mr. William Palmer, of whom mention has been made, had quitted the military service of the Nizam to enter into commercial transactions, and had established a house of business at Hyderabad known as the firm of William Palmer and Co. This firm, by a series of successful operations with which I am not particularly acquainted, had become the possessors or the depositories of a large amount of capital, and were in a position to make considerable advances of money to the Nizam. As they had the power, so they had the inclination, to enter into large transactions with the embarrassed Government of Hyderabad. All legal impediments were removed by the sanction of the Governor-General—a sanction granted without inquiry into the particulars of the proposed transaction—and it was arranged that the house of business should undertake to advance a certain sum of money—first, for the payment of one portion of the troops, then of another, and that certain assignments of revenue should be made by the state for the security of the lenders. The advances were to the extent of 20,000*l.* a month. The assignments were of the annual value of 300,000*l.* The interest payable by the Nizam was 25 per cent. These arrangements were made under the sanction of the Resident. There was no express guarantee for the protection of William Palmer and Co., but it was understood, both by the lenders and the borrowers, that the Resident endorsed the transaction.

The troops were now punctually paid; but the financial embarrassments of the Nizam were increased by the arrangement, and the people were plunged into a lower deep of suffering than any that had overwhelmed them before. The disorders of the Nizam's Government had, indeed, become intolerable; and Mr. Russell was eager to apply a remedy to the evils which stared him so reproachfully in the face. It was plain to him that the connection of the Nizam with the British Government had been one of the chief sources of the decrepitude of Hyderabad. But, he argued with a force of truth not to be withstood, "if we owe the foundation of our empire in this country to the weakness in which we found the native princes, we ought not to complain of the evil which that weakness necessarily produces. If we have reaped the benefit we must submit to witness the inconveniences which are its inseparable attendants." "And," he added, if it be true that a part of the mischief has arisen from the predominance of our power, it is for that reason the more incumbent on us that we should endeavour to employ the remedy."* But what was the remedy to be? The Nizam was to be left to the uncontrolled administration of his own provinces; how then could we ameliorate that which we were not to be permitted to touch? There was to be, if such were possible, intervention without interference. We were to shape the administrative measures of the Nizam without appearing to have anything to do with them. We were to be everything and nothing at the same time. "I suggested," says Mr. Russell, "as the leading features of a plan of reform, that whatever control our Government might resolve to exercise, should be applied through the medium of advice and influence, and not by direct exertion of authority; that we should enlarge the sphere rather than increase the degree of our interference; exerting the same

* *Mr. Russell to Government, November* 24, 1819.

influence in correcting the abuses of the internal administration that we already applied to objects immediately connected with our own interests; that we should improve and direct the implements of the country, and not introduce agents or regulations of our own."

Instructions* to this effect were drafted by Metcalfe, as Political Secretary, emphatically sanctioned by Lord Hastings, and forwarded to Mr. Russell. They met with the entire concurrence of the Resident. "The instructions about reform," he wrote privately to Metcalfe, "are everything I could desire. If I had drafted them myself, I could not have made them more entirely consonant to my own views and wishes. The result, I trust, will answer the expectations of Government. I have had a great deal of discussion with Chundoo-Lall, whom I believe to be as willing as he is able to discharge his part of the duty. A manifest change has already taken place in the tone and character of the internal administration. Complaints are received and grievances are redressed, and justice is expeditiously and gratuitously administered by a new tribunal erected by Chundoo-Lall for the purpose. Reduction of expenses and remission of revenue are the next great objects, and at these we are hard at work."† There was no doubt of Mr. Russell's sincerity. His letters abundantly show that these reforms lay very near to his heart.

Throughout the greater part of the year 1820, he was sedulously employed in giving them effect. But the reign of the Resident was now nearly at an end. He could only

* These instructions, in a few words, were "To authorise him to interfere with his advice and influence for the benefit of the Nizam's Government, to improve its revenues, reduce its expenses, and ameliorate its system of administration. Chundoo-Lall to be supported."—[*MS. Memorandum by Charles Metcalfe.*]

† *Henry Russell to Charles Metcalfe, March* 21, 1820.—[*MS. Correspondence.*]

initiate the reforms which were so necessary to the prosperity of the country. But with this he was content. He had such strong faith in his successor, that he knew the good work would be carried on vigorously and successfully after his departure.

Such, hurriedly traced in dim outline, was the condition of things in Hyderabad when, in the second week of November, accompanied by Lieut. Hugh Barnett, who was appointed Second Assistant to the Resident, Mr. Richard Wells, of the civil service, who was Third Assistant, and Captain Mackenzie, who was appointed to the Nizam's cavalry, Charles Metcalfe embarked on board the *Hattrass*, which was to convey him to Masulipatam, on his way to Hyderabad.* He was not sorry to quit the seat of Government; but there was a new and untried world before him at Hyderabad; and as he was departing, intelligence reached him which caused some temporary regret that he had made his election to proceed to the court of the Nizam. Mr. Monckton, who was at that time Resident at Lucknow, had announced his intention of proceeding to England, and Sir David Ochterlony had declared his willingness to be transferred to that court, in order that Metcalfe might return to his old post at Delhi. To the latter, who had many pleasant recollections of the years he had spent in the imperial city, and had often regretted his departure from it, this arrangement, as far as his personal feelings were concerned, would have been very gratifying—but he had now gone too far to recede; the course of his duty lay in the direction of Hyderabad—so he went straight on, sending back no vain regrets, but fixing all his thoughts upon the future.

* He had another very amusing travelling companion, too, in the shape of "Spence's Anecdotes," then newly arrived in Calcutta, which a friend had sent him to beguile the tedium of the voyage.

On the 10th of November, Metcalfe and his friends embarked from Calcutta, and coasting down the Bay of Bengal, anchored, on the 16th, in Masulipatam Roads. The state of the weather did not suffer him to land before the 18th; and on the following day he proceeded by dawk to Hyderabad. There he found Mr. Russell awaiting him. He found, too, that the place was in an unusual state of social excitement. The race-week was commencing, and there were dinners, and balls, and suppers—race-ordinaries and lotteries, in which he was expected to take a part. But he was eager to commence business; and how it was commenced may be gathered from the notes which he made at the time:

MEMORANDA FOR JOURNAL.

[1820—1821.]

"Saturday, the 25th, having been fixed upon for my presentation to the Nizam, the Ministers Mooneer-ool-Moolk and Rajah Chundoo-Lall came to the Residency in the morning, about ten o'clock, according to custom, to pay their compliments to me, and invite me to wait on the Nizam. They remained some time at the Residency, and during their stay produced a note from the Nizam, of which the following is a near translation:—

"'Mooneer-ool-Moolk Bahadoor and Maharajah Chundoo-Lall will go to-morrow to Sahib Jung Bahadoor's (Mr. Russell's) residence. Let the pending negotiation regarding taking and giving between the above-mentioned Bahadoors be settled, in order that there may not be any injury after the departure of that gentleman. This matter is at the responsibility of the talookdars and Abbas Allu Khan.'

"If I were to explain this note myself, I should conceive it to allude to the pending unsettled negotiation regarding the Partition treaty, and to be dictated by an apprehension that a new Resident might come forward with new demands, or might urge those already discussed and declined. It was, however, urged by the Ministers as having a more general meaning, and as proceeding from a fear lest matters formerly settled should be ripped open for fresh discussion. Friendly assurances were given, without hesitation, on this point; but it was pointedly impressed on them that these assurances had no reference to the pending treaty, which, being avowedly unsettled, was fully open to discussion and negotiation. The Ministers took leave of us, and went to the palace with their suite. They had been numerously and respectably attended. Not long after, Mr. Russell and myself, attended by the gentlemen of the Residency, and others who wished to see the Nizam, proceeded to the palace; where, after being met in the usual manner by the Ministers, we were received by the Nizam. He was, it is said, unusually affable and talkative—though he did not certainly talk much. To what this might be attributed—I mean his uncommon affability—I cannot pretend to say. After remaining with him about a quarter of an hour, we received our leave, and came away. The gentlemen who were introduced, presented nuzzurs; which struck me as an unusual practice, never having heard of such at any native court except the king's. The style of the durbar, and the dresses of the court, were plain; the palace itself not grand."

"On Sunday, the 26th, went to church. Afterwards returned the visit of the commanding officer, Colonel Boles, who, with the staff, had called on me on the 23rd. Was received in the cantonments with salutes, and had a guard of the company of the 50th N.I. drawn up for me at the commanding officer's. I had heard much of the overdoing of these matters at Hyderabad; and was therefore prepared for all the honours I received. The sermon at church was about Aurungzeb, Lord Chesterfield, and Mr. Fox, to the text of 'Vanity of vanities, all is vanity.'

"On the 26th November paid my first visit to the minister, Mooneer-ool-Moolk, and dined with him. He has a splendid house, fitted up at great cost, and with some taste. He gave us an excellent dinner, and conducted his entertainment in very good style. I am not in favour of dining with people who cannot or will not dine with us; and only went on this occasion because I did not choose to make difficulties regarding what had been customary under my predecessors; especially as I had not received charge of the Residency and was in a manner under the guidance of Mr. Russell, who accompanied me, as did also all the gentlemen of the Residency, including his party and mine.

"Rajah Chundoo-Lall joined us after dinner, and we got home about half-past ten, having been entertained with a nautch. Mooneer-ool-Moolk's manners are good. Two of his sons are fine boys. Chundoo-Lall's manners are also good.

"This morning, the 28th, after breakfast, the officers of the cantonments of Sekunderabad and Bolaurum came to the Residency to be introduced to me. A fine body of officers. I find that our society is likely to consist of 130 or 140 persons, including ladies.

"On the evening after our visit to the principal, but nominal, minister, Mooneer-ool-Moolk, we paid a similar one to the deputy, but real, minister, Chundoo-Lall. The house and the entertainment were not less splendid than on the preceding occasion; indeed, the profusion of costly ornamental furniture exceeded everything I had ever before seen. In addition to a dinner, nautch, and brilliant illumination, equal to those at Mooneer-ool-Moolk's, we had at Chundoo-Lall's a display of fireworks and gaslights.

"On the 30th, Russell explained to me the several forms of accounts relating to the Residency; and on the 1st of December, delivered over charge of the office.

"13th December.—Sent Mr. Sotheby to Rajah Chundoo-Lall to propose the gift of sixteen lakhs of rupees, for the purposes desired by the Governor-General.* Mr. Sotheby reported, on his return,

---

* This requires explanation. As one of the consequences of the great events touched upon in Chapter XII., and the partition of territory which they had involved, a new treaty with the Nizam had become necessary. This treaty, the terms of which had been chiefly arranged by Mr. Russell, was still unconcluded when Metcalfe proceeded to Hyderabad. The opportunity was considered by the statesmen of Calcutta a good one for the extraction of a bonus of money from the Nizam; and it was suggested, therefore, that an article should be introduced into the treaty, pledging his highness to manifest his sense of all our kindness to him by a gratuity of sixteen lakhs of rupees (160,000*l.*) for the improvement of the city of Calcutta. Who was the originator of this suggestion I do not know; but Metcalfe went to Hyderabad, carrying with him, in Lord Hastings' handwriting, the following draft of the proposed article:—

"His highness the Nizam, contemplating the great benefits which he has reaped from the late military operations, in the security of his dominions, and in the advantages accruing to his revenue, is anxious to manifest his sense of such a boon by a gratuitous contribution. In this view his highness desires that he may be allowed to furnish sixteen lakhs of rupees (payable at the rate of four lakhs yearly till the amount be completed) for public purposes connected with the city of Calcutta or its vicinity within the twenty-four pergunnahs; on the condition that the sum shall

that the rajah agreed to the proposal. It remains to be seen whether the consent of the Nizam will be obtained or not. Mr. Sotheby also put in train the settlement of the little difficulties which have arisen out of the abolition of exemption of duties on articles proceeding to the markets of our cantonments, &c."

"Subsequently to the 13th, I again sent Mr. Sotheby to Rajah Chundoo-Lall on the subject of the sixteen lakhs. The Rajah did not start any difficulty on the subject, but proposed that I should report the matter to Calcutta as settled, and engaged on his part to procure the consent of the Nizam, after the arrival of the ratification from Government. To this I objected, and sent Mr. Sotheby again to explain that the Nizam's consent must be obtained before I could report the matter as settled. It should have been mentioned that at the second interview of Mr. Sotheby, the agreement about the sixteen lakhs was added, in the terms prescribed by Lord Hastings, as an eleventh article to the ten before settled by Mr. Russell.

"On the day after Mr. Sotheby's third mission, the Rajah reported to me that the Nizam had cheerfully assented to the arrangement, and expressed his gratification that the matter was so settled. I sent a report on the subject to Calcutta, which will be found on the records.*

---

be applied in such portions and for such objects as the Governor-General in Council may direct."

Well might it be said that "Nizzy pays for all," when he was called upon to contribute 100,000*l.* towards the tanks and aqueducts and lamp-posts of Calcutta.

* In another memorandum of an intended interview with the Minister, Metcalfe says: "MEM.—The sixteen lakhs.—To tell the Minister that I have reported to Government upon this subject; and that I am sure the Governor-General will be much gratified by the handsome conduct of the Nizam's Government; but that I have also some reason to think that the donation will be declined, which I shall be glad of, for the financial interests of the State." And he was right. The donation was declined. On this very 13th of December, Lord Hastings was writing to Metcalfe that the Home Government would not give their sanction to such a dubious measure. "We have received," wrote the Governor-General, "from the Secret Committee a positive injunction not to urge the Nizam to a contribution of sixteen lakhs of rupees. Therefore

"Some days after this a horrible outrage was committed by some Arabs in the service of Shums-ool-Omra. An Arab had been killed in a drunken fray. The Arabs, the next day, went in a body to the house of a Dukhanee chief, of whose party they supposed the killer to be, to demand that he should be delivered up to them. It appears that the chief offered to send him to the Minister, if he could be pointed out; but, from the outrageous conduct of the Arabs, the discussion ended in the death of the chief and some others. The Minister reported the circumstances to me, announcing his intention to punish the guilty. In reply, I urged him to persevere in this intention, for the credit of the Nizam's Government and the protection of the people. The matter ended in two Arabs being shot by their own brethren, after a sort of trial by jury, and twenty-five being banished. Some people say that the men executed were not the real offenders, but mere slaves, executed by the Arabs to appease public opinion. The more general account is, that they were the principal actors in the outrage—one having been the murderer of the Dukhanee chief, and the other the person who instigated the Arabs to remain at the house when they were willing to come away peaceably. The result is not quite satisfactory. The Government should have carried on the investigation, and inflicted the punishment. As it is, the business has been slurred over, having been left to the Arabs, many of whom were the offenders."

"On Christmas-day gave a dinner, ball, and supper, to the society of Hyderabad, Sekunderabad, and Bolaurum."

Of the general state of the Nizam's country, Metcalfe soon began to derive from passing events some painful experience. Letters came in from officers of the Nizam's Contingent employed in the provinces exhibiting the unsettled state of the country, and the lawless condition of the people:

---

you must drop that object entirely, and cancel any procedure that may have taken place respecting it. The Court's instruction proceeds on the erroneous intimations previously transmitted to some of its members from Calcutta. It all turns upon the inconsistency of exacting from the resources of the State such a sum when we represent its finances to be embarrassed in such a degree as to require the aid of a British house of agency."—[*MS. Correspondence.*]

"A letter received from Lieutenant Sutherland," he wrote in his journal, "dated 24th December, 1820, reporting an attack made by him on a party of plunderers, headed by a person named Solinga, which had taken possession of the village of Soolyali, in the Talooka of Moory, and Pergunnah of Odgeer. Solinga, it appears, is a known character, who has for some time been in rebellion against the local authorities. Lieutenant Sutherland having decoyed a considerable number of this party into the plain, before the fort, which is only sixty yards square, charged and cut them to pieces. A number of matchlock men who came out to their assistance, were also charged and sabred by Lieutenant Sutherland's detachment, consisting of 170 horse, which had only four men and six horses wounded in the affair. Solinga has evacuated Soolyali, and fortified himself in Gozegaon.

"Another letter from Lieutenant Sutherland before Gozegaon, requesting a reinforcement of the companies of infantry from Hyderabad, which has been despatched. Information received of the cholera having attacked the detachment which was sent as a reinforcement to Lieutenant Sutherland."

Every day brought the new Resident some fresh proof of the deeply-seated disorders of the Nizam's country, and the necessity of immediate interference in the concerns of a territory so rent and distracted by internal convulsion. But it was necessary that, in the first instance, Metcalfe should obtain the confidence of the Nizam and his Ministers, and obtain from the latter, or rather from Chundoo-Lall, a true state of the financial condition of the country. The following memoranda for his journal give a brief account of his interviews with these authorities, and a slight sketch of the measures which he purposed to recommend for the reform of existing abuses:

"*Memoranda for Communications to Rajah Chundoo-Lall.*

"To require a statement of revenue and expenditure, from which to judge of their relative extent and the financial prospects of the Government.

"To require a statement of Khalsa lands, revenues, and management, whether under farmers or collectors, or any other class of managers.

"To require a statement of lands in Jagheer, Jaidad, &c.

"To require a statement of Jagheerdars of troops supported by Jaidad, and of personal Jagheers to commanders.

"To require a statement of pensioners, with the revenues or claims on account of which pensions have been granted.

"To explain that information on all these points is required as a necessary foundation for improvement.

"The statements of these things, which no doubt already exist, will be preferable to others which it may take trouble to prepare.

"To inquire about the late outrage of the Arabs, and the measures pursued for redress.

"To urge the Minister to discontinue on his own part, and to procure the discontinuance on the part of Mooneer-ool-Moolk, of all clandestine allowances to servants, &c., at the Residency. The same with regard to fruits, dinners, &c., &c., sent to the Residency, which come in such quantities as to give them the appearance of regular supplies instead of being merely complimentary.

"To desire the Minister not to give ear to any natives who may pretend to have influence with me, either directly or circuitously, and to inform him that I shall never employ natives in any communication with the Nizam's Government. That ordinary matters will be discussed as at present, by Notes; and all of importance either personally or through one of my assistants.

"Districts towards the Wurda—at present depopulated—the people gone to the Nagpore country. Propose to authorize Lieut. Clark to give them a general guarantee for the enjoyment of their rights free from oppression or extortion; the farmer or manager subsequently to make such particular engagements with them, not violating their general guarantee, as may be expedient."

"On the 17th January I had a private audience of the Nizam, at which no third person was present. My object was to give him confidence as to the views of our Government, and my personal disposition. The manner in which he received and replied to my communications was gratifying; and he seemed to derive pleasure from the meeting. On the whole, I was much satisfied with the result of my visit; though a paltry trick was played in a point of etiquette, unobserved by me at the time, which it was afterwards necessary to notice and rectify.

"On Friday, the 26th, Rajah Chundoo-Lall paid me a visit on business, and remained with me several hours, conversing on the state of the country, and the measures proper to be pursued, on which he spoke very plausibly and sensibly, and promised to give cordial assistance in the work of regeneration and reform. He brought me accounts, which I had called for, of the receipts and charges of the Government; from which, if they can be relied on, it appears that there is a present annual deficit of about ten lakhs. If the deficit do not exceed this amount, I shall not despair of bringing the finances of the Government into proper order in the course of time, either by ameliorations of the revenue, or by reductions of the expenditure, or the joint operation of both. I was much pleased with the disposition shown by the minister at this conference.

"This visit arose out of my declining to go to the Minister on the old footing. It was customary with my predecessor to visit the Minister on business, though the Minister never came to him. This course appearing to me to be derogatory, I have hitherto sent one of my assistants on business to the Minister, instead of going myself. This alone, without any proposition on my part, has been sufficient to bring the matter into a better course; and I shall now, without scruple, visit the Minister on business as he will also come to me.

"I applied to the Minister for accounts of the income and expenditure of the Government. These, after requesting delay for time to prepare them, he brought to me in detail. From these I observe that the annual expenditure exceeds the income, after allowing for the advantages gained by his Highness's share of the conquests of the late war, in the amount of about ten lakhs.

"The measures which appear to me to be most essential in the first instance, and which I shall endeavour to carry into effect with the concurrence of the Nizam's Government, are—1st. The reduction of the expenditure of the Government within its income. 2nd. A general settlement of the land-revenue for a term of five years on the principle of a village settlement, including arrangements with the heads of villages for the introduction of a system of police. 3rd. The superintendence of respectable European officers of the Nizam's service, for the purpose of preventing oppression and breach of faith in the districts in the vicinity of their respective posts."

Having thus made up his mind that the evils under which the country had long been groaning could be removed only by the exercise of efficient European superintendence over the native functionaries employed in the executive duties of the internal administration, Metcalfe at once obtained the sanction of the Nizam's Government to the measures he proposed, and lost no time in setting them on foot. He soon found, indeed, that the leisure which Mr. Russell had promised him, and which at one time he had promised himself, was a mere delusion. "I find my time as much occupied here," he wrote to James Baillie Fraser,* "as at Calcutta or Delhi, though leisure was one of the principal objects for which I came. I am now convinced that want of leisure is a constitutional disease which will stick by me to the grave, and that it does not proceed from excess of business alone." It did not, indeed, proceed so much from excess of business, as from the conscientiousness with which he discharged it. Twenty years afterwards it was said, in another quarter of the globe, that he "worked like a slave;" and one of the shrewdest observers† who ever watched his proceedings, said of him, "How he finds the time is a problem: I know only that he is never in a hurry."

He soon began to make preparations for a tour of personal inspection through the outlying districts. He was not one to satisfy himself with the reports of others—to study the condition of the country at ease in the Residency-house. So, having handed over to his Chief Assistant the duties of the capital and the court, and left instructions‡ for his

* The well-known author of "Travels in Khorassan," the "Kuzzilbash," &c., &c. He was brother of William Fraser, Metcalfe's old assistant.

† Mr. Gibbon Wakefield.

‡ These were very brief, but very distinct. It were worth while to insert them:

"MEM.—In the event of the unexpected demise of the Nizam, his eldest son, Nasir-ool-dowlah, to succeed him. This intention is not to be divulged unless it be necessary to carry it into effect.

"In the event of the death of Mooneer-ool-Moolk, the nomination of a successor to his office should be prevented altogether, or at least postponed to my return.

"In the event of the death of Chundoo-Lall, his duties should guidance in the event of the unexpected demise either of the Nizam or one of his Ministers, the Resident commenced his progress. What was the result of his first visitation may be set forth in his own language. It is clearly described in the following private letter:

MR. CHARLES METCALFE TO MR. GEORGE SWINTON.

"*Camp, Dewalwarra, June* 14, 1821.

"MY DEAR SWINTON,—The more I see of the Nizam's country, the more I am convinced that, without our interposition, it must have gone to utter ruin, and that the measures which have been lately adopted were indispensably necessary for its continued existence as an inhabited territory. As it is, the deterioration has been excessive, and the richest and most easily cultivated soil in the world has been nearly depopulated, chiefly by the oppressions of the Government. It will require tender nursing. The settlements are advancing. The moderate revenue, which it has been found necessary to receive in many instances, has greatly disappointed the Government, which, not convinced by the depopulation of villages in consequence of ruinous extortion, would have persisted in the same unprincipled course until the rest were depopulated also. The loss of revenue, if confidence be established by the settlement, will be but temporary. In some of the settlements on which the assessments for the first year are the lowest, they are doubled and trebled, and in some instances quadrupled and quintrupled in the period, generally five years, for which the settlements are concluded. Such are the productive powers of the soil, that I have no doubt of the propriety of the increase where it occurs to that extent, the assessments for the first year having been made uncommonly low from local circumstances affecting the particular cases. After the conclusion of the settlement, one measure more, and I think only one, will be necessary, and to that I conceive our interference ought to be limited. We must preserve a check on the native officers of the Government, to provide that they do not violate the settlement; otherwise they certainly will, in which case it would be better that it had never been concluded, as it would then, by giving false confidence,

---

be made over to Mooneer-ool-Moolk for the time; and the appointment of a successor to Chundoo-Lall should be postponed till my return."

furnish the means of additional extortion, and would effectually destroy the very foundation of our probable success, which is the reliance put on our faith and guarantee. I therefore propose, with the assent of the Nizam's Government, to employ the assistants of the Residency and some of the best qualified of the Nizam's officers in different divisions of the Nizam's territory, for the purposes of checking oppression and violation of faith on the part of the officers of Government, securing adherence to settlements, taking cognisance of crimes, and looking after the police, especially on the frontiers, on which point I receive continual complaints from the neighbouring Governments. These officers should take no part in the collection of the revenues, nor in the general administration of the country. Neither should the forms of the Nizam's Government be invaded. The officers should not have any peculiar official designation, founded on their duties, lest it should be considered as a partial introduction of our rule; and if at any time, from good schooling or rare goodness, there should be reasonable ground of hope that a district could be managed safely without such a check, I should think it a duty to withdraw the officer from that district, though I have no expectation, I confess, that such is likely to be the case. In order to save expense to the Nizam's Government, the number of divisions should be small—six or seven in all. This would make each of them very extensive, but not, I hope, too much so for the performance of the duty. They ought to be continually in motion (the officers, I mean), and the Resident ought to be frequently in motion also, to observe the state of the several divisions. I hope that this measure will be approved, for on it all my hopes of successful reform in the Nizam's country are built. Without it they will fall to the ground. It appears to me to be the only way of preserving the Nizam's Government in all its parts entire, with the addition of the check of European integrity, which can at any time be removed without damaging any other part of the edifice, if at any time it can be dispensed with. If the Nizam's officers were allowed to go on without some such check, it would soon end, I think, in our being compelled to take the country entirely into our own hands. As most of the officers so employed would be already in the receipt of pay in the Nizam's service, the Nizam's Government would only have to make such an addition as might be thought suitable to the increased importance and labour of their duties. The allowances of the superintendents in the Nagpore territory, or of the assistants in the Delhi territory, might be taken as a model, and, after calculating what the gentlemen so employed already receive, either as officers in the Nizam's service, or assistants to the Resident, or agent at Aurungabad (for the latter, I think, is pointed out by his local situation as one of them, if he would like the duties), the difference might be made up from the Nizam's Government, which would be the cheapest way for him in which the business could be done.

"I mentioned, I think, in an official despatch that ninety villages had been re-peopled in one district. Since then the number has increased to 300, and this must now be within the mark, for it is a period of two months since I received the report. Two days ago I received intelligence of the settlement of forty-five waste and deserted villages in another district, which will be re-peopled on the assurance of this settlement. Some of the original cultivators have returned from so great a distance as Bombay, and the rest are returning from the several countries to which they had emigrated. I mention this as the result of confidence in European character and interference. Were these to be entirely withdrawn, the country would either revert to its former state of galloping consumption, or its progress to dissolution would be accelerated even more rapidly by the violence of reaction. I have troubled you with a long letter, but the fate of millions hangs on the result.

"Yours most sincerely,

"C. T. Metcalfe.

"I shall be at Ellichpoor to-morrow, and at Aurungabad in the beginning of July."

This first excursion in the Hyderabad country greatly strengthened Metcalfe's previous convictions that only by the active intervention of British authority could he hope to mitigate such deeply-seated disorders as he saw everywhere around him. "The country," he wrote officially to Government, "through which I have passed in my tour commenced in April, has everywhere exhibited the most striking features of decay and depopulation; and completely evinced the necessity of the interposition of the influence of our Government for the prevention of utter ruin." Under this conviction he set bravely to work; and before the close of the year was able thus to report the first success of his measures :—

"I am now on my return to Hyderabad, after witnessing the accomplishment almost to completion of the primary objects which called me to the northern parts of the Nizam's dominions. The settlement and limitation of the land revenue for terms of years have been effected for the most part in the districts north of the Godavery, and throughout a considerable portion of the western frontier southward of that river. The gentlemen employed in this undertaking in different divisions of the territory—namely, my assistant, Mr. R. Wells, and Major Seyer and Captain J. Sutherland of the Nizam's service, performed the duties assigned to them with the greatest zeal, ability, and judgment. . . . The measure carried into effect by these gentlemen throughout a considerable extent of the Nizam's dominions, promises the most favourable result. It has been received by the cultivator with manifest satisfaction, clouded only by a dread that the systematic bad faith of the Nizam's Government may render nugatory the benefits of the arrangement. It has had the ostensible support and co-operation of the Government, without which it could not have succeeded."

But it was apparent to Metcalfe that this support was only ostensible. The sufferings of the many had been so profitable to the few—the rapacity of the Minister and his underlings had so long been glutted—that this wholesome restraint upon their greed was irksome to them, and they secretly endeavoured to baffle measures which outwardly they were compelled to support. All this Metcalfe saw plainly; but it only stimulated his energies and roused him to greater vigilance. The success of these great ameliorative efforts, perseveringly and consistently persisted in by the Resident, is a great fact not to be questioned. "No sooner had Government," writes one who saw the effect of these measures with his own eyes,* "commenced the good work of inquiring into the rights of the people, thought of redressing their grievances, and fixed the extent

* The late Colonel (then Captain) J. Sutherland.

of their own demands on them, than the country was restored to comparative tranquillity. Men began to feel secure of reaping a return proportioned to their exertions, and industry took the place of rapine and sloth." In fact, the work of regeneration had commenced. There was hope still for Hyderabad.

The system under the operation of which Metcalfe looked for these good results has been sufficiently explained in his letter to Mr. Swinton. It was a system of pure native agency under European superintendence. The superintendents did not interfere in the executive details, but exercised a presiding influence over the general administration both of revenue and justice. Under this system, those village settlements which Metcalfe had found so beneficial to the people in the Delhi territories, were introduced, and with excellent results. That during the period of Metcalfe's residence in the Deccan the inhabitants of the Hyderabad provinces were rescued from much oppression—that the rights of the agriculturists were more clearly defined—that extortion was checked—and justice rendered something better than a mockery is not to be denied. He did not labour in vain. His best reward was in the increased happiness of the people—but the commendations of the Government, ever so dear to him, were not withheld.* It was said afterwards, when there was an object in the distortion of the truth, that Metcalfe had been guilty of improper interference in the internal affairs of the Nizam's Government. Bnt the system was not his system. He found it in

* Lord Hastings wrote to him in April, 1821: "Let me take the opportunity, my dear sir, of saying to you how gratifying the prospects are which you hold forth respecting the improvements in cultivation and comfort of the Nizam's territories. I feel keenly the duty of rendering our influence so beneficial, and I thank you sincerely for the generous energy with which you prosecute the purpose."—[*MS. Correspondence.*]

operation. He only gave it greater and more beneficial effect.

But there were those whose interest it was to misrepresent, if they could not nullify his measures. And he had need of all his resolution. It was with a clear insight into the difficulties which beset Metcalfe's ameliorative progress that his old friend and master, Sir John Malcolm, wrote to him at this time the following high-toned words of encouragement:—

"Every step you take to ameliorate the condition of the country will be misrepresented by fellows, who have objects as incompatible with public virtue and good government, as darkness is with light. That these men should be allowed to speak or write, upon subjects such as you discuss and manage, is deplorable. But the fact is so; and though the circumstances in which you are placed require all your firmness, recollect at the same time they call for all your caution and prudence, and, above all, for great temper and patience. These qualities I should never ask you to exercise in any extraordinary degree for selfish views. Were your personal interests alone at stake, I know you might give way to the spirit of an offended gentleman and a high public officer. But you have a more momentous duty to perform. You have to fight the good fight, and to stand with the resolute but calm feelings such a cause must inspire against all species of attacks that artful and sordid men can make, or that weak and prejudiced men can support. . . . . I am quite confident in your ultimate triumph, though I expect that you will have great vexation and annoyance."*

These were prophetic utterances—the vexation and annoyance were close at hand, and the ultimate triumph was not far behind.

* *MS. Correspondence.*

CHAPTER XV.

[1820—1825.]

"THE PLUNDER OF THE NIZAM."

Finances of the Nizam—Residency Expenses—William Palmer and Co.—The Sixty-lakh Loan—Influence of the House—Sir William Rumbold—Metcalfe's Friendship for the Partners—Proposed Financial Arrangement—Correspondence with Lord Hastings—Intrigues of the House—The Governor-General and Mr. Adam—Further Revelations—Reconciliation with the Governor-General—Discussions in England.

WHILST, under Metcalfe's instructions and superintendence, the subordinate officers upon whom he relied were pushing forward, with good success, these ameliorative measures, the Resident himself was diligently inquiring into the financial circumstances of the Nizam, and tracing the causes of that chronic state of embarrassment which had so grievous an effect on the prosperity of the country. It had been his first care, on entering upon his new duties, to see that the Residency itself was entirely free from the reproach of increasing the unprofitable expenditure of the Nizam; and at one of his first interviews with Chundoo-Lall he had, as I have shown, "urged the Minister to discontinue on his own part, and to procure the discontinuance on the part of Mooneer-ool-Moolk, of all clandestine allowances to servants, &c., at the Residency; the same with regard to fruits, dinners, &c., &c., sent to the Residency, which came in such quantities as to give them the appearance of regular supplies, instead of being merely complimentary." And he especially "desired the Minister not to give ear to any natives who might pretend to have influence with him; and informed him (Chundoo-Lall) that he should never employ natives in any communications with the Nizam's Government—that ordinary matters would be discussed by notes—and all of importance, either personally or through one of his assistants."* He saw clearly the importance of putting a check at once upon every description of back-stairs influence, and preventing the Nizam or his Ministers from being fleeced by the fathomless cunning of the native underlings of the Residency. He was averse, too, to any of those convenient arrangements which, by transferring the expenses of certain parts of our own establishment to the treasury of the Nizam, lightened our own burdens at the cost of our ally; and wherever he scented a job he was resolute to suppress it.

But of all the sources of the financial embarrassments of the Nizam, that which in Metcalfe's eyes seemed to call most obtrusively for the consideration and intervention of the British Resident, was the connection of the Hyderabad Government with the great mercantile house of William Palmer and Co. It seemed to him that the State was lying prostrate and helpless at the feet of the English money-lenders. In the preceding chapter mention has been made of the manner in which the Hyderabad Government first became the debtors of the house, and of the extent of their obligations. Since those loans had been contracted, a new arrangement had been entered into between the two parties, with the avowed object of a gradual liquidation of the liabilities of the Nizam. A readjustment of the business, however, had become expedient upon other grounds. In spite of the immense payments of interest, the claims of William Palmer and Co. on the Hyderabad Government were increasing;

* *Memoranda for Journal by C. T. Metcalfe, ante page 385.*

and the members of the house were not without a hope that, by placing the transaction altogether on a new footing, seemingly more advantageous to the Nizam, a guarantee might be obtained from the British-Indian Government for the repayment of the entire advance. In the course of the year 1820 the loan was negotiated. The amount advanced was sixty lakhs of rupees, or 600,000*l.*, to be paid within six years. For this accommodation the Nizam's Government were to pay interest at the rate of 18 per cent., seemingly a reduction of 7 per cent. on the old advances. But the reduction was no more than a sham. In consideration of the nominal advance the borrowers were to pay a bonus of eight lakhs of rupees. The whole business of the loan Metcalfe subsequently described as "a fiction." There was nothing of reality about it.

Of the terms of this loan the partners of the house were naturally anxious to keep the Government in ignorance. Metcalfe was at this time Political Secretary; and not only did all the official correspondence with Government relative to the sixty-lakh loan pass through his hands, but a considerable burden of private correspondence regarding it was also entailed upon him. One of the members of the house, of whom more particular mention will presently be made, wrote privately to Metcalfe in July, asking him to exert his influence to silence inquiry. "I find," he said, "that there is a discussion in Council about our loan, and that the rate of interest is required. What can the Government care whether the arrangement be more or less beneficial to us, provided it bestows upon the Nizam's Government the great advantages that have been held out? If our loan has the effect of liberating the Minister from all his debts in five or six years, and that in the mean time the revenue is actually increased, surely those who suggest the means of so desirable an arrangement ought to be allowed some advantage. But for us this could never have been settled; and if we made millions by it, the result were the same. No one need object to us."*

This reasoning did not satisfy Metcalfe. Nor was he pleased with the motive given for the secresy—the hope of keeping matters quiet at home. There was truth, however, in the assertion, that "what is very low interest at Hyderabad would sound very high at home." The reader must not measure the exorbitancy of William Palmer's demands according to the Bank of England's rates of discount, even in the midst of an European war, or a great financial crisis attending an unprecedented drain of bullion. In obedience to the requirements of Government, the rate of interest demanded by the house was declared. "But the grant of the bonus"—to use Metcalfe's words—"on the pretended loan was concealed from the British Government in the same spirit of fraudulent deception that characterised the whole transaction. The sanction given by the British Government to this fictitious loan was represented and understood by many to be a guarantee; and the number of European officers who entrusted their property to the house was increased. The house received money at 12 per cent., and lent to the Nizam's Government and to individuals at 25. Their business was almost confined to this traffic, and to the supply of costly articles to the Ministers and others at the Nizam's court, all other branches of their concern being comparatively insignificant. The accumulation of wealth in their books, from the immense interest which they charged, seemed to be boundless, and the actual influx of cash, from the remittances of constituents on the one hand, and the payments of the Nizam's Government on the other, was such as to supply the most wasteful expendi-

* *MS. Correspondence.*

ture on the part of the members of the firm, and was nevertheless overflowing." *

It is no uncommon thing for capitalists to pay one rate of interest on money received, and to charge another on money advanced. There is not a banking or agency house in England or India that does not carry on its business upon this intelligible principle. It was not of this, therefore, that Metcalfe complained. Needy Governments, like needy individuals, must pay for money when they want it. But the new Resident saw with painful distinctness that there were other than commercial considerations involved in these transactions. The question had, indeed, become a political question. The house of William Palmer and Co. had, in fact, usurped the government of Hyderabad. They were fast becoming all-powerful in the state. "Of the power which the house acquired in the Nizam's territories," wrote Metcalfe, some years afterwards, "partly by the actual influence of the partners over the Minister, and partly by their reputed influence with the British Government, no conception can be formed by those who did not witness its operation. The house was armed with the double authority of the British and Mogul Governments; nothing could withstand it. Its power was at its climax when the new Resident appeared on the scene, and its members were making rapid strides towards the entire possession of the revenues of the country." †

How this extraordinary influence was acquired may be briefly stated. It was not merely the influence of a sturdy creditor over a struggling debtor—it was an influence derived from extraneous sources; the growth of an accident. One of the partners of the house was Sir William Rumbold. This gentleman had married a ward of the Governor-General, and had accompanied his lordship to India with

* *Minute of Sir Charles Metcalfe, ut supra.*

† *Minute, ut supra.*

the not very rare or unintelligible design of making as much money as he could. He had passed the age at which the foot can be placed on the lowest step of the ladder of official promotion, and so, with the aid of his friend, he had endeavoured to make for himself a shorter cut to fortune. Metcalfe said of him, that he went out "to make a large and rapid fortune in the style of the old time, by other means than his own personal labour." "He soon found that the British territories did not yield a harvest of the kind which he sought. He therefore visited the courts where British influence was then most predominant, and wealth supposed to flow most freely, in search of it. He included Delhi, Lucknow, Mysore, and Hyderabad, in his extensive progress. Delhi was a barren waste for his purposes. Mysore did not offer any enticing prospect. The choice lay between Lucknow and Hyderabad. There was a scheme for his settling at Lucknow; but either that failed, or the temptations of Hyderabad were more powerful; and this was the place on which he finally pounced. . . . . He was just the man for the concern; and the concern was just the thing for him. He joined it; and brought with him the influence to be derived from the reputed support of the Governor-General."*

It was not possible, indeed, that it should be otherwise. The natives of India, who understand the nature of back-stairs influence as well as any people in the world, could not believe that one, whom they regarded as the son-in-law of the Governor-General, was not a person of prodigious influence and importance, competent to employ the great engine of British authority as he would in the affairs of Hyderabad. The house, indeed, had become so identified in men's minds with the British Government, that even in remote districts, where the cabals of the capital were but little known, it was said that the revenue which they paid

* *Minute, ut supra.*

on account of the lands assigned to William Palmer and Co, was paid into the British treasury. Gradually, indeed, there had grown up in the Deccan a power greater than the Nizam—greater than the British Resident—greater than the Governor-General of India. It was the belief of the Minister that so long as he had the house on his side, the support of the Resident was of comparatively slight importance. To secure this, large sums of money in the shape of annual allowances were paid to members of the firm, or their near relatives. Even the sons of Mr. William Palmer, boys at school in England, grew, under this mighty system of corruption, into stipendiaries of the Nizam. If the stipends were not paid, they were carried to account in the books of the firm at an interest of 25 per cent.; and thus increased the ever-increasing embarrassments of the Nizam, and rendered difficult the regeneration of the country.

The new Resident saw all this, and other things of which I have not yet spoken; and the contemplation of such extortion caused him acutest pain. If he had known in Calcutta all that he subsequently learnt in Hyderabad, no temptations of fame or fortune—of ease or dignity—would have enticed him into that hornet's nest. He was a man of profound sensibility, of a most affectionate nature, very constant in his friendships; one whose chief happiness was derived from his contemplation of the happiness of others. If the principal members of the Hyderabad house had been utter strangers to him, he would still have arrayed himself against them with extreme reluctance; it would still have caused him much personal suffering to incur their resentment by restricting their gains. But it happened that the men, whose career of self-aggrandisement it now become his duty to check, were bound to him, by those very personal ties which, with a man of Charles Metcalfe's gentle, loving nature, are only to be resisted by painful efforts of self-negation. Mr. William Palmer was the brother or one of Metcalfe's oldest friends. An unbroken intimacy of twenty years' duration had greatly endeared John Palmer to him, and he had gone to Hyderabad prepared to love William Palmer for his brother's sake, and had found all his prepossessions strengthened and confirmed by the amiable character of the man himself. To Sir William Rumbold he was bound by a personal friendship of many years. He had first made the acquaintance of this gentleman at Delhi, when, as the bearer of letters of introduction from John Adam and others, Sir William had presented himself to the Resident, and been the recipient of his unfailing hospitality. It happened, either on this first or another visit to Delhi—I do not know—that Rumbold had fallen sick, and had been nursed by Metcalfe at his pleasant residence in the Shalimar gardens as tenderly as though they had been brothers. A year before the new Resident's departure for Hyderabad they had renewed their personal intercourse in Calcutta, and Rumbold had returned to his family to speak gratefully and delightedly of Metcalfe's charming "cordiality of manner—the same as it used to be at Delhi." And when the tidings of his appointment to Hyderabad reached that place, there were no warmer congratulations than those which Metcalfe received from the Rumbolds; unless they were those which came from another partner—his old friend Dr. Lambe.

It need not be said, therefore, that the new Resident went to Hyderabad with no personal prejudices against the principal members of the great banking house. All his prepossessions were in their favour; and it grieved him to the soul now to find himself compelled to do battle against men with whom he would fain have lived in habits of unclouded friendship. "I rejoice," he wrote to John Palmer, "that your health has been perfectly recruited by your late trip. Mine is very good, and I am as happy as any man can reasonably expect to be; I should be perfectly so, were it not for one thing: but you are the last person whom I ought to trouble on this subject, for unconsciously you helped to create the mischief which I deplore. Habits, however, of old confidence will prevail—I allude to the plunder of the Nizam by William Palmer and Co., in league with an unprincipled Minister. I do not object to merchants making good bargains for themselves. But when the resources of the State are sacrificed by a profligate servant, without any regard to the interests of his master, as the purchase of the support of the Governor-General through the influence of an individual, it is bribery in the most horrible degree, and the misery of it will be long felt by this suffering country. Had I known what I now see before I quitted Calcutta, nothing should have induced me to come here. Being here, I must do my duty, and make myself as cheerful as I can be in a very disagreeable predicament." *

That Mr. Secretary Metcalfe must have had some knowledge, even in Calcutta, of the ill effects of the close connection between the house of William Palmer and Co. and the Nizam's Government, is not to be doubted. But until he himself appeared on the scene, he had no just conception of the extent of that evil influence. He knew that in some quarters there was a strong feeling against the house; but he declared that he could not fathom the cause of it. But now that he stood face to face with the gigantic evil and plainly discerned the shape thereof, "the vague sort of apprehension," of which he had before spoken, loomed before him as a palpable reality to be steadfastly encountered. He had not been many weeks settled in the Residency before the conviction forced itself on his mind, that the safety of the Nizam and the dignity of his own

* *Charles Metcalfe to John Palmer, January* 29, 1822. *MS.*—This letter was written in reply to one asking the Resident to procure the appointment of a friend to the Nizam's artillery.

Government could be maintained only by rescuing the former from the gripe of the English money-lenders.

To accomplish this great object, Metcalfe now proposed, in the spring of 1821, to open, in Calcutta, a six-per-cent. loan guaranteed by the British Government, and from the proceeds of this loan to pay off all the Nizam's obligations to Palmer's house, and other creditors. The proposal was made to Government in an official letter; but before he forwarded it to Calcutta, the Resident, with characteristic manliness, communicated his intentions to the members of the firm. It need not be said how unwelcome was the announcement—the announcement of a project for suddenly blocking up that short road to gigantic wealth which had recently been opened out before them. But now that the great danger threatened them, they encountered it with consummate address. Having first of all secured, under the worst of circumstances, a mitigation of the evil, they made a grand effort to ward it off altogether. They represented to Metcalfe that as the sudden liquidation of the loan to the Nizam would inflict a very serious injury on the firm, a certain compensation for the losses they would sustain ought in fairness to be made to them. With an amount of good-nature for which he subsequently reproached himself, he consented, therefore, to introduce into the arrangement a clause conferring on the house an additional gratuity of six lakhs of rupees.* Having accomplished this object—something easy to fall back upon—they made their great *coup* in advance. Metcalfe had consented to delay the despatch of his proposal to Government whilst he discussed it with the members of the firm. "They employed the interval," said Metcalfe, "in communicating with Calcutta to pre-

* Making, with the eight-lakh bonus, fourteen lakhs, or 140,000*l.* (besides interest at eighteen per cent.) to be divided among the partners, as the profits of the sixty-lakh loan.

vent its success, and succeeded in their object." In other words, Sir William Rumbold wrote an urgent appeal to Lord Hastings; and when Metcalfe subsequently despatched his official letter to Calcutta, it never elicited an answer.

But upon the receipt of Sir William's letter, Lord Hastings wrote privately to Metcalfe, reproaching him for not having made some preliminary reference to the Governor-General. "You assume," he said, "that Government will guarantee such a loan. Many points must be settled before I can agree to such a step. Not long ago the expediency of raising a large sum here for the Company at four per cent., in order to pay off a portion of the six per cent. debt, was strongly pressed upon me. I rejected the proposition absolutely, because I thought it a cruel procedure to force upon the bondholders the receipt of their capital when they had no means of employing it."* But if large bonuses and gratuities had been offered to the bondholders, the cruelty would have been less obvious. The House of William Palmer and Co. never contended that the Nizam was not entitled to pay his debts whenever he pleased. On this point Metcalfe replied clearly and emphatically—thus stating the effects on the general prosperity of the Hyderabad country to be anticipated from the liquidation of the debts of the Nizam:

* *Lord Hastings to Mr. Metcalfe, April* 21, 1821.—[*MS. Correspondence.*]—The proposed loan, however, met with the approval of Mr. John Adam and of Sherer, then Accountant-General. "I am much pleased," wrote the former, "with your plan of a loan for the Nizam, and it meets with Sherer's entire approbation. I fear it is not so well relished elsewhere, and will occasion some debate. Tindall has struck out a plan for buying the Peish-cash out at a given number of years' purchase, which seems a good scheme, and will, perhaps, be followed up."—[*Calcutta, May* 23, 1821. *MS.*] See also Minute of Mr. Adam, May 12, 1821, published in the Hyderabad Papers.

"A serious apprehension that the Government will not be able to keep its engagements with W. Palmer and Co., is one of the motives of my anxiety for the reduction of the interest. The Nizam's Government has for a long time struggled on, under pecuniary difficulties, by the aid of extortion, limited only by the want of substance to supply its demands. This has necessarily led to a gradual deterioration of revenue, which was rapidly hastening towards a crisis. The measures now in progress, not only, I trust, will have the effect of checking further decrease—they have also a natural and, I confidently believe, a sure tendency towards improvement and augmentation, and eventually to an incalculable extent. But their first effect will not be to increase the Nizam's revenue. The reform must commence by the Nizam's Government lowering its demand to the amount which the country in its present depopulated state can yield, without entire exhaustion; and I much fear that it may not have the means of fulfilling its engagements to Messrs. W. Palmer and Co., in which case the accumulation of their demand, at its very high rate of interest, will become an insupportable burden to the State.

"Had there been any contract between the Nizam's Government and Messrs. W. Palmer and Co., binding the former, for a certain time, to abandon the right of paying its debts according to its power to do so, all the principles which I profess would have precluded me from proposing any arrangement for its liquidation without their entire concurrence; but though Messrs. W. Palmer and Co. would have maintained that ground, if they could, their honourable regard for veracity induced them to acknowledge repeatedly to me that the Nizam, from his own funds, might justly pay off the whole debt in a day, without their having any right to complain; and all that they could allege against payment in the mode suggested by me was, that they were secured by the Nizam's avarice against payment from his private treasury, and did not expect it from any other quarter."*

But the authority of the Governor-General was insuperable, if his arguments were not; and Metcalfe's proposals were silently rejected. So far, Sir William Rumbold had gained his point; but he had other complaints soon to prefer. The Resident was not a very ductile resident. He was not to be made either a tool or a plaything in

* *MS. Correspondence.*

the hands of the members of the house. So Lord Hastings was assailed with representations to the effect that the frost of Charles Metcalfe's disfavour was nipping the prosperity of William Palmer and Co. Upon this the Governor-General sat down and wrote the following letter to the Resident:

LORD HASTINGS TO MR. METCALFE.

"*Calcutta, August* 27, 1821.

"MY DEAR SIR,—A letter from Sir William Rumbold, which I have received this day, mentions the heavy losses to which the house of W. Palmer and Co. has been subjected through the opinion prevalent in the country of your being hostile to that firm, as well as from a belief current at Hyderabad of your being disposed to work at the removal of Rajah Chundoo-Lall. Any ill-will on your part towards the house of W. Palmer and Co. must necessarily be an idle imagination. And I am sure you will feel no less pain than I do that the appearances whence the Shroffs inferred it have had as much effect as could have flowed from the real existence of an adverse sentiment. I will confess to you that, when you knew how much contest had taken place in Council respecting the mode of relieving the Nizam's affairs, your submitting officially a proposition on that subject without any previous communication with me, seemed a procedure in which I was unaccountably neglected. It was obvious that, should any particular conceptions of policy or duty forbid my adopting your plan, the inevitable consequence would be the renewal of a vexatious controversy, originally brought forward from the view of conveying fallacious impressions to the Court. Such conceptions were much more than possible; they were highly probable. They, in fact, existed. I considered the guarantee, which was the basis of your project, as irreconcilable to just expedience—to the recorded opinion of the Court in a parallel case—and to law; positions which, nevertheless, did not prevent the peevish discussion that was to be anticipated. This, however, is not the important part of the matter. The rumour respecting Rajah Chundoo-Lall, coupled with the depreciatory language which you have used of that Minister, alarms me. I must thence not let a day slip in observing to you that I am personally pledged to the support of that individual. He would not engage in those measures of reform which we pressed upon him, without a special assurance that he should be upheld by the British Government. That promise was notified to him from the Governor-General in Council; and the Rajah, in a becoming reliance upon it, manfully performed his part. Thus bound to protect him, it is incumbent on me to profess that any step tending to render our plighted faith delusive must not only be disavowed, but decisively overruled by this Government.

"I have the honor, my dear Sir, to be, with great esteem,
"Your very obedient and humble servant,
"HASTINGS."

Metcalfe, at this time prosecuting an official tour through the outlying districts, was residing at Aurungabad. There, a little while before the receipt of this letter, he had met, by concerted arrangement, his old friend, Sir John Malcolm, who was then on his road from Central India to Bombay. "I go more than a hundred miles out of my road, and would go three, for three hours' conversation with you," wrote Malcolm. They had not met since, fifteen years before, they had paced together the tent at Muttra, but many letters of mutual support had passed between them; and high and noble, when they met at Aurungabad, was their discourse of the corruption which was eating into the Government of the Nizam, and of the great but dangerous work which lay before the Resident, in the battle which he was beginning to wage against the sinister influences by which he was beset. They differed upon some points—but they were points only of secondary importance. From Malcolm, Charles Metcalfe received the most invigorating support and encouragement. The elder man admired and applauded. "You have to fight," he said, "the good fight, and to stand with the resolute but calm feelings such a cause must inspire against all species of attacks that artful and sordid men can make, or that weak and prejudiced men can support."* But he was an

* *Ante*, page 393.—See also "Life and Correspondence of Sir John Malcolm," in which is a more detailed account of this meeting.

older diplomatist, and he counselled greater caution than Metcalfe was disposed to infuse into his plan of operations. The meeting did good to both. It was no small delight to Metcalfe to converse freely with one who could thoroughly appreciate the manliness of his conduct and glory in his courage. And Malcolm went on his way rejoicing in the thought that he left so much public virtue behind him.

It was soon after this meeting that Metcalfe received the above letter from Lord Hastings. Without a misgiving, he sent back a reply, manly in its tone, vigorous in its diction—altogether worthy of the man. I cannot persuade myself to abridge it:*

MR. METCALFE TO LORD HASTINGS.

"*Aurungabad, September*, 1821.

"MY LORD,—I have had the honour of receiving your lordship's letter of the 27th ult., written in consequence of one addressed to you by Sir William Rumbold. I beg leave to assure your lordship, that I am far from being disposed to work at the removal of Rajah Chundoo-Lall. It is very true that I think ill, in the highest degree, of the spirit of his internal administration; that I groan for the devastation inflicted on the country by his merciless extortions; and that I cannot love his heartless recklessness of the miseries of the people confided to his charge. I mourn also for the reproach attached by public opinion to the British Government, as if it countenanced the criminalities which its support alone has given him the strength to practise; but it has never yet occurred to me as desirable, all circumstances considered, that he should be removed. His removal, and that of his dependents, abstractedly would no doubt be beneficial, because they are altogether an unprincipled set; but there is no man in the country, not one that I know of, who could be recommended as his successor. There is no one, perhaps, who would be more facile in agreeing to those plans of reform, the execution of which is in progress—notwithstanding the underhand counteraction on his part, of which I am sensible—no one who would look up to us

* The transcript is from the original rough draft in Metcalfe's handwriting.

more for support, consequently no one more in our interests—no one who could be personally more conciliating, more obliging, more ready to meet our wishes. Add to this, that he has rendered us essential political services, and is entitled to our thankfulness in such a degree as, though the connection has its disgrace, would most probably attach disgrace also to our abandonment of his cause. Further, I am not sure that his removal would be an easy task, even were I authorized to attempt it; for I think it very probable that the Nizam would apprehend fresh encroachments from the success of the attempt, and set himself to oppose it. Nothing could be more impolitic or more subversive of the improvements in progress and contemplation, than the failure of such an attempt. I mention these things in order to show your lordship that I have very sufficient reasons in my own mind against the formation of the design of which Sir William Rumbold has led your lordship in some degree to credit the existence. But independently of all such considerations, I was aware of your lordship's disposition to support Chundoo-Lall, and would not have attempted anything against him without your previous sanction.

"Respecting the other point mentioned by Sir William Rumbold, my reputed hostility to the firm of W. Palmer and Co., I am at a loss what to say, for I know not whence such an idea can have arisen. Excepting Mr. W. Palmer, the European partners of that firm were my friends before I came to Hyderabad. Mr. W. Palmer's brother, Mr. John Palmer, has been my much esteemed and warm friend for the last twenty years; and Mr. William Palmer himself is one of those men so amiably constituted by nature, that it is impossible to know ever so little of him without feeling one's regard and esteem attracted. There is no family at Hyderabad with which I have so much intercourse as Sir William Rumbold's. Mr. Lambe, one of the partners, accompanied me in his medical capacity as acting surgeon of the Residency during my tour from Hyderabad to this place, and in every respect on the most friendly and confidential footing. Since I came to this place, I have accepted without hesitation as a personal favour from Mr. Hastings Palmer, the head of the branch of the firm established at this place, the loan of a house which I occupied till I could otherwise accommodate myself. I may add, that I have lately given my assent to extraordinary exactions proposed by the Minister for the purpose of meeting the demands of that firm on the Government, which the Minister would not attempt without my concurrence.

All these circumstances, I venture to say, would naturally indicate to the public mind feelings the very reverse of hostile; and I am so unconscious of any appearances that could have justified, in Shroffs or any others, an inference of adverse sentiment, that, notwithstanding the apparent presumption of disputing the accuracy of Sir William Rumbold's apprehension on a point on which he ought to be so well informed, I am much inclined to doubt the existence of such an impression; to ascribe whatever losses the house may have sustained to other causes, and to attribute Sir William Rumbold's persuasion on the subject to artful misrepresentations industriously conveyed to him for purposes distinct from the concerns or interests of the firm.

"I could conscientiously deny the existence, on my part, of a shadow of ill-will; but I might deceive your lordship were I to stop here. I cannot help entertaining sentiments regarding the transactions of that firm, which, as being adverse to their own views of their interests, they might possibly charge to the account of ill-will. Those sentiments have been slow in growth, but strengthen as I see more of the state of affairs in this country. I lament that Messrs. W. Palmer and Co. have grasped at such large profits in their negotiations with the Nizam's Government as place his interests and theirs in direct opposition. I lament that they have succeeded in conveying to your lordship's mind an exaggerated impression of services to the Nizam's Government, which obtains for them on public grounds your lordship's support, in a degree to which they do not seem to others to be entitled—support which for any ordinary mercantile transactions would be wholly unnecessary. I lament that they are so sensible or fanciful of their weakness on every other ground as to be drawing on your lordship's personal favour on every occasion in which they apprehend the most distant approach of danger, extending their sensitiveness to the smallest diminution, from whatever cause, of their immediate profits—thus repeatedly forcing on the public the name of your lordship as the patron of their transactions, whilst these are likened by the world in general to former pecuniary dealings in Oude and the Carnatic. I lament the connection between them and Rajah Chundoo-Lall, because it tends to draw them quite out of their sphere of merchants, and make them political partisans. It is scarcely possible that this can ultimately be beneficial to them. I lament their connection with some of the most profligate and rapacious of the governors of districts, through whom their character, and what is of more consequence, the British name has become involved in detestable acts of oppression, extortion, and atrocity. I lament the power which they exercise in the country through their influence with the Minister; enforcing payment of debts, due to them either originally or by transfer, in an authoritative manner, not becoming their mercantile character; acting with the double force of the Nizam's Government and the British name. I lament the continuance of their loan to the Nizam's Government, because it would be a great relief to its finances to discharge it. I lament the terms of the loan, because I think them exorbitant. I lament the concealment of the actual terms of the loan at the time of the transaction, and the delusive prospect held out by which your lordship was led to conceive it to be so much more advantageous to the Nizam's Government than it really was. I lament the monopoly established in their favour by the sanction and virtual guarantee of the British Government, because it deprives the Nizam's Government of the power of going into the European money-market, where, with the same sanction, it might borrow money at less than half the rate of interest which it pays to Messrs. Palmer and Co. I lament the political influence acquired by the house through the supposed countenance of your lordship to Sir Wm. Rumbold, because it tends to the perversion of political influence for the purposes of private gain. All these things I lament, not only because they are in themselves evils, but because they must in the end injure the firm itself. Individuals of it may snatch a hasty and splendid harvest, if they do not care for aught else, but the firm itself cannot continue to flourish on such a pinnacle, where it becomes an object for all the shafts of envy, hostility, and unjust opposition, as well as just objection.

"It is not impossible that these sentiments might be considered by the members of the firm as indications of ill-will; but I cannot plead guilty to such a sentiment; and I would gladly challenge the production of any appearances whatever that could warrant any notion of its existence. The opinions which I have now expressed are widely different from those which I entertained before I arrived at Hyderabad. If I had thought as I now do regarding the transactions of the firm before I quitted Calcutta, I do not think that I should spontaneously have ventured on my present station; for I might then have foreseen the predicament in which I should be entangled. But having undertaken the trust confided to me by your lordship, and entertaining, as I now do, these sentiments as the results of local observation and conviction, without being sensible of any improper bias, I feel that I am discharging my duty in submitting them to your lordship in this form. Yet, my lord, these sentiments, I am persuaded, will not cause any mischief to the firm of Messrs. W. Palmer and Co. I am, and shall be, their constant advocate for good faith on the part of the Nizam's Government. Even the plan which I submitted for its relief provides a splendid compensation for the firm, and would leave them much larger profits than can possibly have been made in India on any similar venture with equal risk in the same period of time; and if that plan is rejected by your lordship, and the Nizam's Government cannot otherwise find the means of extricating itself, it will remain for me to exhort it to maintain good faith, as far as practicable, with respect to the engagements which exist. Messrs. W. Palmer and Co. have nothing to fear from me, even if I have the power to injure them, which is very doubtful. I rather apprehend, indeed, that I have more to fear from them.

"The spirit of your lordship's letter has filled me with grief and dismay.

"I grieve to find that in an act in which I felt assured that I was performing an imperative duty towards the Government, and more especially towards your lordship, I am judged by your lordship guilty of personal neglect. I despair of removing that impression, for your lordship would not lightly receive it, nor easily forego it. I lament its existence more than I can express, and suffer the saddest disappointment at such a termination of the favourable opinion with which your lordship once honoured me. I am dismayed, because the tone of your lordship's letter implies a loss of confidence, and opens to my view the abyss on the edge of which I stand. My situation peculiarly needs the confidence and support of Government. I have to wage war against oppression, corruption, extortion, and individual interests of all kinds, as opposed to those of the Government. Supported by the confidence of my Government, I have no fear, but without it, I am in a perilous predicament. The duties of my station are more undefined than those of any other. Without power to do anything, everything must be done by influence. Odium cannot fail to be excited by reform. Interests of all kinds will be roused to arms to oppose the success of my invidious undertaking. Why has it prospered hitherto? Why does it now promise to be crowned with ultimate success? Only, my lord, because I am supposed to possess your confidence, because I am supposed to act in furtherance of your designs. Let those suppositions be removed, and my efforts to improve the condition of this oppressed people will be laughed to scorn. Hollow, indeed, is the ground on which I stand, if your lordship is disposed to receive prepossessions of my proceedings and intentions from a gentleman who conceives himself to be interested in their failure. Under such circumstances, simple integrity would not be sufficient to save one from disgrace. One must not only be pure in intention, but faultless in execution; and there must be superadded talents to ensure success, and set at defiance accident and the caprices of fortune, which I am sure are far beyond the scope of my limited capacity. Sir William Rumbold has placed his views on making a rapid fortune chiefly at the expense of the Nizam's Government. He sees, or fancies, that the prosperity of the Nizam's Government must lessen his profits. Nothing is further from my intention than to speak with the least disrespect of Sir William; but it is obvious that he cannot be a disinterested observer of events. He has, in the present instance, prepossessed your lordship with a belief of my entertaining designs against Chundoo-Lall, which I have never entertained. On Sir William Rumbold's information, your lordship has judged it necessary to warn me that any step tending to render our plighted faith delusive will not only be disavowed, but decisively overruled. What must your lordship's opinion have been of me before you would have communicated your pleasure in those terms? But on that I will not presume to dwell. If your lordship has replied to the same effect to Sir William Rumbold, there is every reason to suppose that he will notify the same to Rajah Chundoo-Lall, with whom I shall have the credit of designs which I never entertained, coupled with the belief that those designs have been overruled through the report and influence of Sir William Rumbold. This, and everything like this, must tend to increase the difficulties of my situation; but for such difficulties alone I do not much care. They may be overcome, and I hope to see even Chundoo-Lall himself reformed. My duty towards every one happens to be the same, whether towards your lordship, or the Nizam's Government, or Rajah Chundoo-Lall, or W. Palmer and Co., it is a clear and straightforward course. My eyes are opened to the dangers to which I may be exposed, from the misapprehension and misrepresentation of the self-interested; but I shall still look to your lordship's justice and indulgence as a shield and protection. In all this, what most distresses me is the apparent loss of your lordship's confidence, and that pains me extremely; for I had always relied on its continuance if I merited it, and I am not sensible of ever having deserved it more than in the discharge of the duties which have fallen to my lot at Hyderabad.

"I am, &c., &c.,

"C. T. METCALFE."

After an interval of between two and three months, this noble remonstrance called forth the following reply:

LORD HASTINGS TO MR. METCALFE.

"*Calcutta, December* 9, 1821.

"MY DEAR SIR,—Your answer to my letter respecting Chundoo-Lall ought to have had a reply long ago. But I was seduced by a variety of heavy tasks into procrastination; and once one falters with what is incumbent, delay is sure to creep imperceptibly to a shameful length. I needed not to have deferred taking up my pen, because I had not to follow you through your detail. A very few observations would have sufficed then, as they do now. You err much in supposing that Sir W. Rumbold made to me any representation bearing the character of a complaint. He addressed himself to me respecting a person who had proved unworthy of some services rendered by me. Before he closed his letter, he mentioned, merely in the light of information which would interest me, the losses which had been suffered by their house; and, in accounting for them, he stated the prevalent rumour of your indisposition to Chundoo-Lall, without intimating any degree of speculation whether it was well founded or not. The fact of such a rumour being afloat was immediately connected by me with the disparaging terms in which your despatches spoke of that Minister; and I feared that in your dissatisfaction at not finding in Chundoo-Lall so perfect an instrument as you wished, you had overlooked the deep engagement of this Government to uphold him. You seemed, through keenness in the contemplation of your plans, to have thrown out of view other collateral circumstances; and I might well apprehend that, were you not duly warned, you might place me in an embarrassing dilemma. This explanation of the grounds on which I wrote to you may suggest that you have, under an erroneous impression, applied to Sir W. Rumbold observations which your candour will, on reflection, scarcely approve. Had he obtruded upon me a secret arraignment of your conduct, the procedure would have been mean as well as presumptuous—colours which I am sure will never justly attach to any act of Sir W. Rumbold's. When you hint the supposition of my encouraging a correspondence the tenor of which was to be a course of underhand comments on your official management, you impute to me a disposition the quality of which you have not weighed. In short, what you have written is tinctured throughout with misconception. Let the assurance of such being the fact set me right with you, while you thence equally stand acquitted towards me.

"I have the honour, my dear sir, to remain, with the highest regard and esteem, your faithful and obedient servant,

"HASTINGS."

But other matters, even more painful than these, in connection with the financial transactions of William Palmer's house, were now forcing themselves upon Metcalfe's mind, and greatly disquieting him. Had his proposal for a guaranteed loan been supported by Lord Hastings, it is probable that there would have been little further discussion relative to the proceedings of the Hyderabad house. But the failure of the Resident was the triumph of the firm. The influence of the Palmers and Rumbolds was greatly increased. It was now patent to Chundoo-Lall that the Governor-General was on the side not of the Resident, but of the members of the house. The state of things which then arose was greatly injurious to the interests of the British Government at the Nizam's Court. The power and authority of Metcalfe was fast becoming a nullity. Fortified as he was by so influential an alliance, the Minister exerted himself, and with no common success, to counteract the influence of the Resident. He had not been accustomed to see antagonism between the Residency and the bank. Contrasts were drawn, which in time led to disclosures; and it was soon openly declared that certain officers attached to the Residency in the time of Metcalfe's predecessor, had been, to all intents and purposes, partners in the house.

Some suspicion of this had been vaguely hinted in the early part of the year 1821, and in consequence of the reports current, Palmer and Rumbold had drawn up an affidavit, setting forth that "no public functionary at the head of any public office or department ever had any avowed or direct partnership, directly or indirectly, with us, or any interest in our concerns, which could influence him in countenancing our dealings with the Nizam's Government, or give him any means of deriving any personal advantages from them." And to this, when Metcalfe was making his first tour in the provinces, they had deposed upon oath before his Chief Assistant. With this affidavit, which was forwarded to Lord Hastings, it appears that the Governor-General was satisfied. But the Resident, on his return to the capital, heard much that caused a different impression to fix itself on his mind. Month after month, however, passed away, and Metcalfe exhibited no eagerness to obtrude upon the Governor-General any unwelcome revelations concerning the great money-lending house. "From the beginning of April, 1821," he wrote subsequently, "to the latter end of June, 1822, I awaited the result of my proposition regarding the loan, and did not once renew the mention of their affairs. They pursued their course without impediment or interference upon my part, and I only claimed the right of pursuing mine with respect to the public interests."

But by the period here named—by the month of June, 1822—suspicion in Metcalfe's mind had grown into strong conviction that certain officers of the Residency in the time of his predecessor, *had* been, directly or indirectly, concerned with Palmer's house; that they had either shared in its profits, or been allowed an exorbitant interest on their deposits. The circumstances which had been brought to his notice, were, in the month of May, confidentially communicated to Mr. John Adam, then one of the members of the Supreme Council. The communication both astonished and perplexed him. "I confess to you,"

Adam wrote in reply, "that I feel very uneasy in the possession of your secret." "It would be with the greatest reluctance," he added, "that I should take any step which would injure your predecessor's reputation; but the turn which the discussion has taken, and may still take here, renders the knowledge of this implication a most embarrassing circumstance; and its concealment from Lord Hastings may either lead him to commit himself more deeply than ever in the support of the house, or ultimately expose me to the charge of knowingly permitting him to do so." He then spoke of the affidavit—said that Lord Hastings had caused it to be recorded on the proceedings of the Council—and asked how, with the knowledge which he then possessed, could he suffer such a document "to pass without comment, and leave it to operate in deceiving others as well as Lord Hastings?" He said too, that Lord Hastings was preparing a minute, in which he laid great stress on the disinterested support which the late Resident had given to the house. How then, Adam asked, could he consistently with his duty remain silent? "Still," he said, "that must be my course, while I owe my knowledge only to a confidential communication, which I am not at liberty to use. . . . . It is for you to determine what is to be done, as I have no option but to preserve your confidence until you relieve me from it."*

By one of Metcalfe's nature—brave and generous—such an appeal as this was sure to be responded to with becoming manliness. He was eager to relieve his friend from the embarrassments into which he had thrown him. So he sat down and wrote a long letter to Mr. Adam, more minutely circumstantial than the last. "It is a disclosure," he said, "which I have hitherto avoided, and would still anxiously avoid as most odious, if I could shake from my mind the ever-recurring conviction that my duty demands

* *Calcutta, June* 12, 1822. *M.S. Correspondence.*

it from me as the confidential agent of Government in this quarter." "I avail myself," he continued, "of our long-established friendship to request you to convey to Lord Hastings, in any manner that you may think proper, the substance of the information which I have to relate, trusting that you will support my respectful entreaty to his lordship, that it may be considered strictly as a confidential communication, and not to be made the cause of public injury to the reputation or interests of those whose irregularities it may expose."

The anger of Lord Hastings was, at this time, greatly kindled against the Resident. Chundoo-Lall had been complaining that he was not supported by Metcalfe; and instead of sending his complaints through the proper official channel, he had forwarded them through William Palmer and Co. Firmly, but respectfully, Adam had pointed out, in a private letter, the impropriety of such a proceeding.* But the Governor-General either could not, or would not, see it. "The pronouncing," he said, "from whom the Governor-General shall receive communications is to make a puppet of him; and my past life has not impressed me with any sense of peculiar fitness for that character."† He was determined to receive, through any channel, information against the Resident; and, in spite of Adam's just and spirited defence of his friend,‡ and

* And also in an official shape. His colleagues also in the Government—Mr. Fendall and Mr. Bayley, who had been called to Council on the resignation of Mr. Stuart—were of the same opinion, and expressed it.

† *Lord Hastings to Mr. Adam.*

‡ I am reluctantly compelled to condense into small compass Mr. Adam's correspondence with Lord Hastings, full of interest as it is. The following passage, however, cannot be withheld:—"After what I have said of the effect produced on my own mind by the proceedings of the house, it cannot be, to me at least, matter of surprise that Mr. Metcalfe, viewing the scene more

Swinton's no less spirited remonstrances, was, at one time, so carried away by his feelings, as to meditate the precipitate removal of Metcalfe from Hyderabad.

On receipt of the letter from Metcalfe, entering into all the circumstances of the alleged connection between William Palmer and the members of the old Residency circle, John Adam had determined to withhold it, at all events, until some circumstances should render it incumbent upon him to reveal its contents. The strong feelings which the Governor-General had expressed, and the decided course which he seemed determined to pursue, now compelled the recipient of this painful information to throw away all

nearly, and experiencing more sensibly the ill effects of the system of which they are so prominent a part, should be even still more forcibly prepossessed with opinions unfavourable to the permanence of their connection with the Nizam's Government. To similar causes is to be ascribed his disapprobation of the Minister, whose counteraction of his measures of reform he imputes, and I conceive justly, to the Minister's subserviency to the corrupt system in force, and to the prevailing influence of the house over the whole of the financial arrangements of the state. My knowledge of Mr. Metcalfe's character, founded on an intimate acquaintance of many years, entitles me to say that he is incapable of being swayed by any petty jealousy of his own power and influence. Actuated by a sincere desire to promote the reform of the Nizam's Government, and perceiving in the connection between the Minister and the house maintained by these loans the most powerful counteraction of his measures, he naturally views that connection and the conduct of the parties with dissatisfaction; but I must confess myself incapable of perceiving, either in his language or proceedings, anything inconsistent with the most pure and upright public principles, and conduct untainted with any private prejudice or dislike that he can have carried with him to Hyderabad. Any such feeling against the members of the firm is wholly irreconcilable with probability; and I am equally unable to divine any grounds for supposing that he could cherish a personal ill-will against the Minister, and as little that his censures of that person are connected with any covert design to effect his removal from office."

reserve. The motives which actuated him, and all the circumstances which attended the revelation, are on record under his own hand. The following letter explains them all:*

JOHN ADAM TO CHARLES METCALFE.

"*Calcutta, September* 2, 1822.

"MY DEAR METCALFE,— . . . . From the time when I wrote to you of my intention to withhold the letter for the present, I continued to indulge the hope that its production would not be necessary until the receipt of your despatch of the 29th of July, and almost at the same time of the Minister's letters through the two Palmers. . . . . That despatch appeared to produce a violent irritation, and the warmest expressions of dissatisfaction with your proceedings. . . . .

"It is not necessary to dwell on all the hasty remarks that fell rom Lord Hastings in his passion; but you will perceive an allusion to your recall—a measure which he had said he feared your neglect of his injunctions respecting the reform and the degree of interference in the Nizam's administration would force upon him. These injunctions, on which he dwells so much, seem to be an incidental remark in a minute written on the 27th of May, 1821, on the subject of the loan proposed by you about that time. He then observed, that you had exceeded the line he had prescribed; but he expressly declared that he did not state this in the way of censure, as the necessity of the case might render it unavoidable; and that though he could not sanction it, he would not abruptly interrupt your measures. It being introduced in this incidental manner, and with these and other moderating expressions, doing ample justice to your motives, any discussion of a point which would only have carried us away from the main question seemed unadvisable and unnecessary. . . . .

"The talk about recalling you did not alarm me much on your account; as, if it had been done, it would only have ended in your triumph. But such a proposal must have been resisted by myself and the other members of Government, and would probably have produced an entire breach, and it would have covered Lord

* It should be stated that, with one exception, the passages omitted either relate to circumstances already related, or refer to correspondence the subject of which has been given.

Hastings himself with indelible disgrace. Such a notion is now quite gone by, and of course you will regard it merely as a piece of history, and not as affecting either your feelings or your acts. In that confidence I have mentioned it. . . . .

"We met in Council (on the 22nd of August), but he did not mention the subject of our correspondence, nor did I. The next day we met in the political department, when he laid translations of Chundoo-Lall's letters before the board, and desired they might be circulated. At the same time, he produced the draft of a letter to Chundoo-Lall, and desired that instructions conformable to its tenor should be prepared for you. With some alterations, the draft has since been sent to you, with corresponding instructions. I hope this will draw from you a complete exposure of the intrigue in which it is quite certain the Minister's letter originated. His lordship's eyes seemed now to be opened to the culpability of the house; but still while he was receiving and acting upon papers sent through a channel acknowledged to be impure, and thereby gave colour to their pretensions to a predominant influence, he took no measures founded on your exposure of their practices; but instead of proposing an inquiry, or any other measure, he merely requested me to consider what course of proceeding it would be best to pursue.

"This I of course undertook to do; but when I came to review all that had taken place—the little progress that had been made in counteracting the acts of the house—the unrenounced prejudice against your proceedings, and the coldness with which your information was received, contrasted with the eagerness with which anything from the house or the Minister was acted upon, I began to despair of effecting any good without making him fully acquainted with all I knew; and on the other hand, to feel that I was exposing both you and myself to the charge of keeping back a knowledge of facts, which, just at this time, might turn the scale and rescue Lord Hastings, while it effected a material public benefit. Still, I think I had made some impression, and that though he did not acknowledge that he had been led into a wrong path, that he was nevertheless sensible of it. At this time came your despatch, announcing the visit of Mooneer-ool-Moolk to the Residency, an event which, with its assigned object and consequences, was, I have no doubt, punctually reported through the confederates. This event awakened the feeling which I had hoped was in some degree at least subdued; and my apprehensions of some violent act were revived. Upon the whole, I thought the time was come when the communication could no longer be delayed with justice either to *you* or Lord Hastings; and after pondering the matter well, and going over it again and again with Bayley and Swinton, I determined on sending your letter to his lordship.

"A most material point in the deliberations was the manner in which Lord Hastings would receive the communication. I should have had no hesitation from the beginning in making it, if I had felt assured that he would receive it in confidence; but I feared he would assume a high tone—treat it as an unwarranted aspersion of the house, and the other individuals mentioned—and insist on a public inquiry, and that thus not only the object of the disclosure would be lost, but what you so anxiously deprecated would occur. This fear, however, diminished as matters advanced; and after the admitted strong suspicion of criminality in the house, I thought he would feel the less shock at what remained to be told of others about whom he could not be supposed personally to care. . . . .

"It now remains to tell you the result. My letter was sent the day before council-day; and he sent no answer, but when we met the next morning he took me aside, and returned your letter, and after reproaching me in a good-humoured manner for not imparting it at first, he entered on the subject with the greatest unconcern and ease. He professed to give credit to all that was stated on your own knowledge, and to great part of what you stated on report, but said that he could not help supposing that in some points you had been misinformed, and that on others you had given your belief too readily. He could not reconcile the *clear* and spontaneous affidavit of Mr. W. Palmer and Sir W. Rumbold, and the fact of it being taken by Mr. Sotheby, with the facts stated of the connection of the latter and other members of the Residency, with the House. He said it ought to be sifted; and though he felt all the motives which must make you averse to such a disclosure, he did not see how he could avoid making a public inquiry. He spoke of you without any of that irritable feeling which he had lately evinced; and said that it was plain the knowledge of these circumstances, and the natural unwillingness you felt to bringing them forward, must have thrown an embarrassment over your correspondence with him, for which he now could easily account. Whether this last was meant as an overture to renew correspondence, I cannot say. It is not improbable that he himself may renew it by writing to you.

"In the course of this conference, which lasted a considerable time, I endeavoured to show the solidity of the grounds on which your statements were made, and to remove his conjectural objections. I adverted to the art and care with which the affidavit was drawn up; admitting, however, that if one could get over the weight of evidence against them, it would be better to believe that you had been deceived, than that men could be guilty of such profligate wickedness. I showed him how all the facts could be got at if he chose, by taking up the points stated in your official despatches, without involving the necessity of referring to any private communications; or, what would be better still, how he could, without entering into these questions at all, put an end to all the mischiefs resulting from the influence of the house, by paying off the debt, and putting an end to their connection with the Minister.

"He more than once said that that was indispensable in any event; but I now found, to my great disappointment, that his views did not, as I supposed, extend to an advance or a loan from the public treasury, on the security of the Peshcush, but were limited to making a public loan for the use of the Nizam to such an extent as would be paid (principal and interest) by the Peshcush in a term of ten or twelve years, which he calculated would be about fifty lakhs of rupees. I represented that this would not effect the object of paying off the debt, as what the Minister proposed to raise could not be depended on. I thought this made an impression; and as he admitted the necessity in any event of breaking off the connection between the house and the Minister, he left me to hope that he would not reject the only apparent means of effecting it. He ended by desiring me to show your letter to Fendall and Bayley, and said he should not determine on anything till we could talk over the matter again.

"Through the whole of this conversation there was the utmost calmness and good-humour, without the least appearance of constraint, or endeavour to command himself; and what surprised me more, without any appearance of that shock to his feelings which I thought the letter must have produced. It ended, leaving me under the impression I stated to you in my letter of the 27th ultimo;* though I was, perhaps, more sanguine than I ought to

* To the effect that the communication had raised Metcalfe, and lowered Chundoo-Lall and the "house" in the estimation of Lord Hastings.

have been, and certainly than the result has justified. Next day we renewed the subject, when I am sorry to say I found him still more sturdy. He spoke of an advance from the public treasury as out of the question—repeating, at the same time, that the house must be paid the debts that had been incurred with the knowledge and consent of the British Government, and the connection with the Minister broken off. As to the other debt, now first brought forward, he would not recognise or have anything to do with it.

"I showed him the affidavit, and pointed out the artful manner in which it was drawn. He endeavoured to explain it; but it was easy to show that it was a pure deception. He had expressed dissatisfaction at your having only noticed the Minister's proposition 'obiter,' as he expressed it. I showed from your despatch that you brought it very prominently forward, and reasoned upon it, and pointed out its defects.

"With regard to your letter to me, he still reserved his decision; but, in the course of conversation, he dropped some words about recording it. This, however, without your express permission, I shall not agree to. I showed him the reference in your despatch of the 1st of August to Dr. Currie's name as a partner in the house, and pointed that out as a fair ground of exception to the affidavit, upon which any inquiry he pleased might be founded, without touching on your private communication. At one time he said he thought we must send a commission to inquire into the circumstances of the house, as to their connection with the Minister and the old Residency. This idea had occurred previously to Bayley and myself, as a measure which, if things go to that extremity, you would prefer to being yourself employed in that investigation. I confess I shall not be very sorry if the shameful conduct of all these parties is exposed, provided it flows naturally from the course of the public proceedings; but I will employ every effort to induce Lord Hastings to refrain from acting avowedly on the information in your private letter.

"I have no reason to think yet that he has communicated its contents to anybody; possibly he may to (John) Palmer, but I have no ground for supposing it. I gave it to Fendall, to whom I have a notion a good part of it was no great news. . . . . . . I have written till I have tired myself, and have taken effectual means to tire you. I am about to draw up such a resolution on your late despatches as I think the Government ought to record; and I will give you early intimation of the result. I have not had a line from Lord Hastings on the subject since our last conversation. I am sorry to say he has had another attack of illness.

"Believe me most sincerely yours,

"J. ADAM."

But before this letter could reach Hyderabad, communications had been made to the Resident from other quarters, setting forth the extreme displeasure which Lord Hastings had expressed. Under a sense of the most unmerited disapprobation of the Governor-General—of one who had once been his friend, and whom he had both loved and admired—Metcalfe could not remain without an effort to recover the good opinion which he had thus forfeited. If there was one quality peculiarly foreign to his nature, it was contentiousness. He delighted to live in harmony with all men. He was eminently a lover of peace—eminently of a genial and kindly temperament—with a continual craving after the love and approbation of his fellows. To obtain these he was ready to make any sacrifice but the forfeiture of his self-respect. To any one who had ever been kind to him, Metcalfe clung with affectionate tenacity; and although the Hastings of 1822 was not in his eyes what once had been the Moira of 1815, who had listened to his counsel in the vice-regal camp, and in accordance with it shaped some of the greatest measures ever initiated by an Indian statesman, he could not help remembering the old associations of confidence on the one side, and veneration on the other, which had knit them together. And remembering them, he grieved over their disruption.

Moreover, it was not forgotten that Lord Hastings was the head of the Indian Government—the representative of British power in the East. It mattered not in whose person Authority might be incarnate; Metcalfe had a profound veneration for it—a veneration which made him as willing to render to others as he was to exact for himself what was due to the representative of that authority. As there was nothing sordid or subservient in this on the one side, so there was nothing arrogant or exacting in it on the other. It was, indeed, nothing more than a paramount sense of the claims of the public service. It was this that rendered him very sensitive under official censure, and keenly alive to official praise.* And it was to this, I am inclined to believe, that very much of his success in life may be justly attributed. He was not an usurper himself, and he would not suffer the usurpation of others. As Resident at Hydrabad he would be Resident indeed; but he never forgot the homage which was due to the Resident of all India. He might have loved and respected Lord Hastings much less than he did, but he would still have been grieved to the soul by the censure of the Governor-General. But as it was, in spite of all that had passed, though he had been disappointed, though he had been wronged, he had a grateful recollection of past kindnesses, he still delighted to dwell upon the many really good qualities of the Governor-General, and he was not mistrustful of the effect of an appeal to them.

* Since writing the passage in the text, I have alighted upon a letter written by Metcalfe's old friend, J. W. Sherer, with reference to the discussion on the subject of the Delhi Resident's expenses (*ante*; Chapter X.), which contains a similar view of this peculiarity of Metcalfe's character. "These papers have interested me exceedingly," wrote Sherer, who was a man of high religious principle, "but what has struck me most, and that too with a sort of almost envious admiration, is the very quick and delicate and noble sense of public character manifested in your letters on this occasion. I would that I could see our whole service more and more alive to public praise or censure."

So he sat down and wrote the following characteristic letter:

MR. METCALFE TO LORD HASTINGS.

"*September*, 6, 1822.

"MY LORD,—I have been made acquainted by my friend Mr. Brownrigg with the substance of a most distressing communication which your lordship directed Mr. John Palmer to convey to him. I scarcely need add that it has filled me with grief and consternation.

"I have no hope of obtaining from your lordship a more favourable view of my conduct; but it is due to myself to declare, that I am in no way sensible of having acted as your lordship supposes.

"Up to the time when your lordship withdrew your confidence from me on account of my proceedings regarding Messrs. William Palmer and Co., I had received at your hands numerous and innumerable kindnesses and favours, which, whatever may be your present displeasure, or your future severity, I shall never forget as long as I live. What inducement, then, my lord, could I possibly have had wantonly to excite your lordship's displeasure by disrespectful or neglectful conduct in a situation where your confidence and support were necessary for my respectability, comfort, and efficiency, and where your approbation was indispensable fer my happiness and reputation?

"I am not aware of any step whatever that can have incurred your lordship's displeasure, besides the part which I have taken with regard to the affairs of Messrs. W. Palmer and Co. In that, it has been my fortune to jostle in the path of my public duty with persons who were there pursuing their private gain. If I had abandoned my duty I should have suffered and merited your lordship's contempt.

"If I could obtain an indulgent and confiding hearing, I could show, I think, that duty and gratitude towards your lordship had no small share in the governance of my proceedings; but I have such strong impressions to encounter against me, and for others, that I desist from the effort in utter hopelessness.

"The house of W. Palmer and Co. has not suffered any loss whatever, to the best of my belief, in consequence of any of my proceedings. The only person really injured is myself, who by their fears and misrepresentations have been cruelly deprived of your lordship's good opinion.

"The proposition which I submitted for the discharge of their loan would have left them a clear gratuity of fourteen lakhs upon an advance of about twenty-two lakhs of borrowed money for one year, in addition to more than 18 per cent. interest on sixty lakhs, for the same period. What must be the state of a concern in which such a proposition can be called hostile and injurious, and where the execution of it could be, as it undoubtedly would have been, greatly advantageous for the other party? This is the extent of my primary offence. Since which, they have set themselves in array against me; and have too successfully attacked me in the hold which I before had in your lordship's favour.

"As I am sure that your lordship would not have approved the sacrifice of my public duty for their private interests, I can only conclude that you do not take the same view that I do of the obligations of my station; and it is more than probable that my opinions on this point may be formed on local circumstances, with which your lordship is not at present, and probably never will be, acquainted.

"Permit me once more to assure your lordship that I am not, and never can be, hostile to the firm of W. Palmer and Co. as a mercantile establishment whilst regulated by mercantile principles —that they are in no danger from any doings of mine—that if they were in any danger, I would gladly assist to extricate them if it were in my power—and that I shall always rejoice in their legitimate prosperity.

"But to them as a faction, aiming through presumed influence at the sacrifice of every public principle, purpose, and consideration, for their gain, I am inevitably opposed. I cannot forego my duty in that respect. I cannot compromise the honour of the station in which your lordship has placed me. I must act up to the part which necessarily belongs to my office, subject always to your lordship's correction and commands. I am the local guardian of public interests. They study their own. We are unavoidably in collision. I cannot allow them to trample on the Resident, and reduce him to a state of base subserviency. I should deserve to be despised by all men were I to act so ignominiously.

"If I could see the slightest prospect of success, I would implore your lordship to restore me to your confidence, and grant me your support; and I would engage that no harm should befall Messrs. W. Palmer and Co. therefrom; but with so many predilections arrayed against me in your lordship's warm heart, I despair of making any impression. Mourning and deprecating your displeasure, and ever retaining an unalterable sense of past kindness.

"I have the honour to remain, with the highest respect, your lordship's most obedient, faithful, humble servant,

"C. T. METCALFE."

Lord Hastings had really a warm heart; and this appeal was not wasted upon it. He had been very angry with Metcalfe—perhaps all the more angry for the old friendship which had existed between them. He had been wounded by the recent reserve of his old secretary, who was not one to feign a confidence which he could not feel; but it may be doubted whether he had ever lowered his estimate of Metcalfe's character. The reign of Lord Hastings was now nearly at an end. He was already maturing his arrangements for a speedy return to England, and it would have grieved him to leave behind him any animosities, especially in such a quarter. There was a genuineness in Metcalfe's letter which could not be doubted—there was a manliness in the sorrow it expressed, a dignified gentleness, which, while it courted sympathy, claimed also respect.

It accomplished even more than the writer dared to hope. It elicited from Lord Hastings the following frank explanation of his past conduct, and unreserved communication of his sentiments:

LORD HASTINGS TO MR. METCALFE.

"*Calcutta, September* 27, 1822.

"MY DEAR SIR,—Your letter delivered to me by Mr. Brownrigg has afforded me extraordinary pleasure. It is impossible for me to doubt any professions you make, and I have sincere comfort in the assurance of your cherishing towards me sentiments to which I attach a high value. My doubt of your retaining such dispositions was, however, not lightly indulged. So many circumstances combined to persuade me of your estrangement, that I could not avoid adopting the belief. It was not I alone who remarked a change in your manner before you left Calcutta; for Lady Hastings observed it to me. I am now convinced that it was accidental, and uninstigated by any adverse feeling; but having once received the impression, I necessarily endeavoured to devise what might be the cause of your alteration. The only one that occurred was this—that my repeated statements of the obligation to uphold Chundoo-Lall were considered by you as a shackle on your free agency in the business you had to undertake. As the faith of Government for his support had been plighted to that Minister long before it was contemplated that you should go to Hyderabad, it struck me as unequitable that you should regard with sullenness my sense of an engagement which public pressure had forced us to contract with that individual. You departed, leaving me with that sensation on my mind. The earliest letters from you were full of criminations, sometimes direct, sometimes implied, against Chundoo-Lall. This apparently studied contravention borrowed additional colour from your decidedly disregarding inculcations communicated to you, not verbally alone, but through a letter which I caused you to write to the then Resident, prescribing that he was to sway the Minister by conciliatory advice—not to guide him by mandates. You at once assumed over Chundoo-Lall the very tone of despotic rule which I had laboured to preclude, rousing unavoidably in him occasional displays of vexation, which you construed as indications of systematic purpose to defeat your objects.

"At this juncture a new light broke in upon me. The losses which your demeanour entailed on the firm of W. Palmer and Co., when the Court had so emphatically expressed its desire that the house should not be injured, were inexplicable, but from some collateral consideration. I readily surmised that you imagined the house to be in league with Chundoo-Lall for baffling your measures, and that they looked to be maintained in their opposition through the influence of Sir William Rumbold with me. This you nearly avowed in writing to myself—omitting the thought what must be the despicable debility of my character could I be so unconsciously practised upon, what must be its worthlessness could I secretly counteract my own official representative.

"That such a suspicion had been admitted, wounded me deeply. My mortification was greatly augmented when, without any previous reference to me, you submitted to Council a proposition for furnishing the Nizam's Government with a loan, on a plan which you should have remembered (and I conceived you did remember) I had before rejected, as not being within my legal competency to sanction. I naturally thought this a step taken merely to give me annoyance by reviving those contests which

Mr. Stuart, on an amiable suggestion from home, spun out with such useful perseverance. Here you have the detail of what were my conceptions. From your declaration, I believe that they have been erroneous; and I regret the having yielded to them. At the same time, your reflection may lead you to question whether you might not have been more kindly attentive to me. The frank sense of failings is the best foundation for a steadier course. You solicit my confidence. Let us endeavour to re-establish it mutually; for real reliance is not created by an assertion of its existence. Were it not for my experience that it is not to be produced in the instant, I would offer it to you at once; because I am not sensible of any present reservation, while I have always so highly esteemed and so sincerely liked you, that it is irksome to me to withhold the fullest pledge. There, then, the subject must rest. The Court's last letter gives a constructive license for a guarantee on certain terms. I am thence ready to guarantee a loan on the security of the Peshcush for twelve years. This must furnish an amount which, with what the Minister can produce, must suffice to pay off all other debts, and set these teasing discussions to permanent sleep.

"Believe me, my dear sir, with unfeigned regard,

"Your very obedient and humble servant,

"HASTINGS."

The openness and unreserve—the genuine kindliness, indeed, of this letter, filled Metcalfe with delight. He eagerly grasped the hand of reconciliation which was held out to him. He was anxious, indeed, "to set these teasing discussions to permanent sleep," but he was not sure that this could be accomplished. He could, however, meet the frankness and unreserve of his correspondent with a response equally frank and unreserved:

MR. METCALFE TO LORD HASTINGS.

"MY LORD,—The kindness of your lordship's letter of the 27th ultimo has in a great degree restored to me a happiness of which I had been for a long time entirely bereft; for the apprehension of having lost your lordship's good opinion had, from its commencement, preyed on my mind, and caused incessant uneasiness. Having experienced continual kindness and numerous favours from your lordship, and being sensible that gratitude and attachment were due as well as felt, it was most painful to me to find that I was considered by your lordship as unmindful of these obligations.

"I have been much relieved by your lordship's letter, and again beg leave to renew the solemn assurance of my own unconsciousness on those points on which I have been misapprehended by your lordship, or misrepresented by others.

"With respect to Chundoo-Lall, it would have been highly presumptuous to consider your lordship's policy respecting that Minister as warranting any sullenness or dissatisfaction on my part; and neither before nor since I quitted Calcutta have I entertained any unpleasant *feeling* or thought on that subject. In speaking freely of his character, I have never had any other object in view than to lay it faithfully before your lordship, as a matter of necessary information in the discharge of my duty. In my intercourse with him I have always endeavoured to sway him according to your lordship's intentions by conciliatory advice; and if I have seemed to assume a mandatory tone, it must have appeared from my representations regarding him rather than from my actual communications with him. In these, if such a tone has ever occurred, I assure your lordship that it has been undesignedly and unconsciously—though, for the purpose of checking the spirit of extortion which has heretofore reigned throughout his administration, very urgent but conciliatory remonstrance has undoubtedly been necessary.

"In submitting, in April, 1821, my scheme for the guaranteeing of a loan from the public to the Nizam's Government, on the security of the Peshcush, *I believed it to be* an entirely new proposition, free from the objections which had occurred against a loan directly from the Company, and flattered myself that it might meet with your lordship's approbation. To have made that or any proposition with a view to give your lordship annoyance would have constituted me an ungrateful wretch, totally unworthy of your past or future favour; and I trust that this impression is entirely removed from your lordship's mind.

"To suppose that your lordship's sentiments towards me could alter without any errors on my part, would be unwarrantable. I am sensible, therefore, that however unintentionally, I must have committed faults which it requires your lordship's indulgence to forgive. I confess that I ascribed to Sir William Rumbold a more powerful hold on your lordship's feelings than I can pretend to. I knew that your lordship's attachments were strong. I thought on his particular connection with your lordship. I felt that I had no claim, and that my only ties with your lordship had been kindness on your part and obligation on mine. I believed that Sir William Rumbold was endeavouring to excite unfavourable sentiments regarding my proceedings here; and I retired from the contest, as one of personal feeling, in despair of succeeding against him, reposing, nevertheless, most fully on your lordship's justice for your support in my public capacity. I now sincerely regret that I was not more open with your lordship, and that I did not place greater reliance on the kindness which I had previously enjoyed on all occasions.

"The combination between Messrs. W. Palmer and Co. and Chundoo-Lall, and the proceedings of the latter, under their instigation, as I believe, have brought on very unpleasant representations on my part, of which I deeply lament the necessity, as well as every other discussion regarding their affairs. Viewing their connection with the Nizam's Government as fraught with present and future mischief, I am anxious certainly to see its termination, if this should meet with your lordship's approbation; but my notion has always been, that it might take place without injury to their pecuniary interests, and without any discussion regarding their conduct. I wish, most sincerely, that all such discussions were ended, and unfeignedly regret that they ever commenced. Messrs. W. Palmer and Co. have complained of losses entailed on them by my conduct. I know not how to bring this point to proof, but I feel myself at present warranted in expressing to your lordship my firm belief that they have not sustained any losses whatever in consequence of my behaviour or demeanour.

"I have addressed your lordship with perfect freedom, being assured that it is what your lordship desires, and that I have suffered in your estimation from my former reserve.

"I am, my lord,

"Your lordship's obedient servant,

"C. T. METCALFE."

And thus Lord Hastings and Charles Metcalfe were reconciled; but the "teasing discussions" were not "set to permanent sleep." On the first day of the new year Lord Hastings quitted India; and Mr. John Adam, as senior member of Council, succeeded temporarily to the chief seat in the Government. The debt due to William Palmer and Co. by the Nizam's Government was soon discharged. "This," says Metcalfe, "was effected chiefly by specie remitted from Calcutta to the Resident at Hyderabad. The clandestine bonus and the clandestine allowances to the members of the firm, with the interest accruing on those items, were disallowed. The firm received about eighty lakhs of rupees from the Resident's treasury. . . . . In less than a year after the Nizam's debt was paid, the house became bankrupt; not from any run upon it, but merely from want of funds to meet ordinary demands."*

So the debt was paid; and the house was dead—but still the "teasing discussions" were not "set to permanent sleep." It took many years to set them to sleep. In India they might have been lulled to rest; but they broke out with furious activity in England; and there was a war of words such as has not in the present century, on any other occasion, disturbed the accustomed quiet of the India House. Never, since the days of the great trial of Warren Hastings, had partisanship risen to such a height in the discussion of any Indian question as during the controversy which ensued after the return of Lord Hastings to England, on the affairs of Hyderabad. It was not with reference to the conduct of either of the Residents that these discussions were raised in England, but with reference to the conduct of the late Governor-General. They were forced on the Court of Proprietors by the vehement friendship of Sir John Doyle and Mr. Douglas Kinnaird, who thought that the Company had treated the noble Marquis with consummate ingratitude. To enable the Proprietors to judge whether the Directors had acted becomingly in this matter, a vast mass of papers was

* *Minute in Council, by C. T. Metcalfe, December* 11, 1828.—[*MS. Records.*]

printed,* illustrative of the administration of the late Governor-General. A large folio volume of nearly a thousand pages was devoted to "Papers relating to certain pecuniary transactions of Messrs. William Palmer and Co. with the Government of his Highness the Nizam;" and it was this division of the subject which monopolized nearly all the discussion to itself.

During six long days these Hyderabad debates were continued at the India House with an energy and a perseverance, which nothing but the *vis vivida* of their personality could have sustained. I should have marvelled at the interest which the subject excited, if I had not seen a far more important popular assembly, roused from the languor and inertness into which it had sunk during the discussion of matters affecting the interests of 120 millions of British subjects, by a personal insinuation against the character of a single man. The question debated in the months of February and March, 1824, in the Court of Proprietors, was a question affecting the personal characters of several distinguished men; and so spiced and seasoned, it overcame the general want of appetite for Indian discussions of every kind. The friends of Lord Hastings were on this great occasion ever foremost in the affray. It was their policy to assail Metcalfe's reputation, and they

* On the 3rd of March, 1834, at a Court of Proprietors, it was proposed by Mr. J. Smith, "That there be laid before this Court all such papers and documents respecting the loans made by Palmer and Co., of Hyderabad, to his Highness the Nizam, as may enable this Court to decide on the merits of any claim which the Marquis of Hastings may have on the further liberality of the Company." But another resolution of a more general kind was substituted by the chairman, and carried by the Court—"That there be laid before this Court all correspondence or documents to be found on the public records of this House with regard to the administration of the Marquis of Hastings, which may enable the Court to judge of the propriety of entertaining the question of further remuneration to the late Governor-General."

did it with an impetuosity which nothing could restrain.* Sir William Rumbold was in England, and he had for some time been busily employed among the proprietors of India stock, endeavouring to disseminate opinions hostile to the Hyderabad Resident and his supporters. It was said, indeed, that the party which had made such great efforts to defile Metcalfe's character was less the party of Lord Hastings than of William Palmer and Co., and that the name and credit of his lordship had been used only to cover the ulterior views of the house. But Douglas Kinnaird and Sir John Doyle were the personal friends of Lord Hastings. Their primary object had been to obtain further pecuniary consideration from the Company for the services rendered by the late Governor-General; † and when they found that the course which they pursued had brought obtrusively before the public matters which they had no desire to render notorious, they addressed themselves to the work of defending the reputation of their friend, and assailing all who stood in the way of their

* *Exempli gratiâ;*—Sir John Doyle declared his conviction that Metcalfe was better fitted to be resident in Bedlam than Resident at Hyderabad; and said, "He believed that all the stories about William Palmer and Co. were merely subterfuges invented for the purpose of concealing the attack on the Marquis of Hastings. They were tubs thrown out to the whale, and only calculated to divert attention from Sir C. Metcalfe's real design."—General Thornton made the astonishing declaration, that if Lord Hastings had been guilty of any favouritism, it was not towards Sir William Rumbold, but towards Sir C. Metcalfe.—Mr. Randall Jackson said, "When they compared the characters given to Chundoo-Lall by Sir Charles Metcalfe, before and after the Minister had complained of him, they could not but see that the last character had been dictated by the wounded spirit of an ambitious man who had been foiled in his projects, and who had consequently determined on the destruction of those who had offended his pride and crossed his purpose."

† The Company had already made him a grant of 60,000*l.*

object. Sir William Rumbold's levies were of course with them; and hence the display of force which they made.

But truth and justice prevailed. All the activity—all the strategy—were on the side of Hastings and the house. Metcalfe's cause was left to itself. But it needed no other backing than that which its own merits secured for it. There were friends of Charles Metcalfe in England who were prepared to "qualify" and to take their place in the Court of Proprietors for the express purpose of defending him, if the debates should take a turn unfavourable to his cause. But there was no need of any such demonstrations of friendship. The published papers had told their own story, and it needed not that much should be said in elucidation of them. He was not, however, without able and vigorous defenders in the House—Mr. Poynder, Mr. Carruthers, Mr. Freshfield, Mr. Weeding, Mr. Impey, and others, were all earnest in their applause of the manly conduct of the Resident; and his old friend Mr. Trant, who had been in the same house with him at Eton, who had entered the Company's service contemporaneously with him, who had worked beside him in Lord Wellesley's office, and had been one of the unforgotten fraternity of "Howe Boys," stood up with affectionate enthusiasm to do honour to the noble character of his comrade.* The

* Some passages of Mr. Trant's speech are worthy of quotation:—"His gallant friend (Sir John Doyle) had said that Sir Charles Metcalfe was fitter to be resident in Bedlam than in Hyderabad. Now he need not remind the honourable and gallant officer of what an illustrious person had said, when he was told that General Wolfe was *mad*: 'If he is mad,' said that illustrious individual, 'I wish he would bite some other generals.' . . . He would say it, and he wished it most sincerely, if Sir C. Metcalfe was mad, that the Company had a great many more such mad servants. He congratulated the Company in having such an useful madman in their employ; and he should not be sorry if he

result of the six days' debate was the discomfiture of the Hastings-and-Rumbold party. And Metcalfe's reputation in both countries stood higher than it had ever stood before.*

As I write, more than thirty years have elapsed since these painful discussions were closed; and any further

bit a few of their civil servants. . . . . The gallant general had informed them that he was acquainted with the Marquis of Hastings during a period of forty years' duration. He (Mr. Trant) must look back to a date which would not make him appear a very young man when he called to his recollection his first acquaintance with Sir Charles Metcalfe. They were children together. They were at school together, under the same tutor, Dr. Goodall. . . . . He and Sir Charles Metcalfe went out to India about the same period; they there pursued their studies for some time together, and they entered the Company's service together. . . . . The Company's servants were often placed in very delicate situations, where duty and feeling were opposed to each other. He congratulated the Court on having amongst their servants a man so entirely devoted to the discharge of his duties—a man whom threats could not intimidate, nor promises mislead—a man who realised the picture drawn by Horace:—

'Justum et tenacem propositi virum,
Non civium ardor prava jubentium,
Non vultus instantis tyranni
Mente quatit solidâ.'"

* The resolution, moved by Mr. Kinnaird, was to the effect, that the Court, having taken into consideration the Hyderabad papers, "is of opinion that nothing therein tends to affect, in the slightest degree, the personal character or integrity of the late Governor-General;" but an amendment was proposed by the chairman, substituting the words "is of opinion that there is no ground for imputing corrupt motives to the late Governor-General;" and adding, "at the same time this Court feels called upon to record its approval of the political despatches to the Bengal Government, under dates the 24th of May, 1820; 28th of November, 1821; 9th of April, 1823; and 21st of January, 1824" (despatches reprehensory of the transactions of William Palmer and Co. with the Nizam). The amendment was carried by a majority of 575 to 306.

than is necessary for the illustration of Metcalfe's character, I do not desire to re-open them. That which I have sought to bring prominently forward is the noble effort which the Resident made to stop what he called "the plunder of the Nizam;" to rescue the Hyderabad state from those financial embarrassments which were engulphing it in a sea of ruin. That the pecuniary transactions between William Palmer and Co. and the Nizam, though at the outset they may have afforded some temporary relief to the latter, did eventually work grievously to the detriment of the country, and greatly increase the sufferings of an overburdened people, is not to be doubted. That Metcalfe, in endeavouring to extricate the Nizam's Government from a connection which he knew to be destructive of its best interests, was compelled painfully to wrestle down his personal feelings and to do his duty as a public servant at the sacrifice of long-standing private friendships, and of the ease and comfort of his life, gaining nothing in exchange but the ennobling consciousness of rectitude, I think has been amply demonstrated. Whether the Hyderabad bankers did or did not transgress commercial morality as it is understood in India—whether they were worse or better than other money-lenders—it is not my business more particularly to inquire. The transaction was an immense one, and it became notorious. Neither its immensity nor its notoriety affect its real character; but they bring it within the legitimate domain of history and render it amenable to public inquiry. With the ordinary gains, however unhallowed, of a house of business, Metcalfe had nothing to do; the commercial morality of its partners was nothing to him. But when he found that their transactions with the Nizam's Government were not only embarrassing the state and impoverishing the people, but gradually erecting the partnership into a great political institution more influential than the British representative at the

Court of Hyderabad—when he found, indeed, that William Palmer and Co. were gradually absorbing the revenues and usurping the government of the country—it became a duty, greater than any other, to sever the connection between them, and to rescue the Nizam from the gripe of a creditor so exacting and so oppressive. He did it. And it cost him much to do it. But "the evil tongues and rash judgments" which assailed him, he lived down; and it was not one of the least of his consolations in after days to know, that the example of fearlessness and disinterestedness set by the Hyderabad Resident was not lost upon the younger members of the profession he adorned. It did much, indeed, to stimulate the progressive reform which has brought the Indian Civil Service to its present high state of moral discipline and efficiency.

APPENDIX TO VOL. I.

MISSION TO HOLKAR'S CAMP.

(Page 134.)

TO HIS EXCELLENCY THE RIGHT HON. LORD LAKE,
&c., &c., &c.

Camp, three miles N. W. from Umritsur, January, 1806.

MY LORD,—I have the honour to report the proceedings of the Mission to the camp of Jeswunt Rao Holkar, which your lordship was pleased to commit to my charge.

Having encamped on the night of the 8th instant at Loodhiana, we yesterday morning marched, accompanied by the Wakeel Walaram Seth, to the vicinity of Holkar's camp. Deewan Gunput Rao, Bukhya Hooshaba, and Gholam Khan, with a large retinue, were sent to meet the Mission, and conducted us to the place appointed for our encampment. A salute of fifty guns and repeated discharges of small arms announced our arrival, and a general rejoicing took place throughout the Mahratta army. I am informed that although Holkar had circulated the intelligence of the establishment of amity with the British Government, his followers had not given credit to it, and considered the report to be an expedient adopted with the intention of easing their minds from the state of depression and despair into which they had been cast by repeated defeat, distress, and disaster. The arrival of a friendly mission from your lordship confirmed the rumour of peace, and caused most manifest and universal joy.

It was my wish, in conformity to your lordship's commands, to visit the Chief yesterday, but the importance which was attached by the Durbar to the occasion, and the arrangements for the ceremony, produced a delay. The Brahmins, having consulted, declared this day to be propitious.

Gunput Rao and Chimna Bhao having been sent this morning to conduct us, I proceeded, accompanied by Mr. Macaulay and the officers of the escort, to make the visit.

The procession moved slowly on in order to give time for the arrival of the moment which had been decided to be the most auspicious for the interview. Holkar was attended by all the chiefs and officers of his army, and nothing was omitted which could tend to make the reception of the Mission most formal and honourable.

After the usual salutations, I delivered your lordship's letter and compliments on the establishment of peace. Both were received by Holkar with particular respect. When I expressed, on the part of your lordship, a hope that the friendship which was happily founded would be strengthened and improved, the chief and his principal officers exclaimed with one accord, and with evident pleasure, that by the blessing of God it would increase daily. A conversation ensued, which lasted for some time, on the present happy state of affairs, in the course of which Holkar and his ministers made many professions of sincerity, and expressed the highest satisfaction. On my part, I met their professions with the declaration of perfect belief, and was reciprocal in expressions of happiness. I was highly gratified to observe the extraordinary joy which was visible in the countenance and conduct of the chiefs and the whole Durbar.

I afterwards proceeded to observe, that your lordship marched yesterday from the banks of the Beeah towards the Honourable Company's territories, and inquired when it was the intention of Holkar to march; and on the appearance of some hesitation, I added, that your lordship had been led by the declaration of the wakeels to expect that he would march immediately, and quit the country of the Sikhs; and remarked, that his performance of the promises of his agents would lead to the establishment of perfect confidence in your lordship's mind, and would afford the most satisfactory proof to your lordship, to the Honourable the Governor-General, and to all Hindostan, of his sincerity in the conclusion of amicable engagements with the British Government. Some conversation followed between Jeswunt Rao Holkar, Bhao Bhasker, and me on this subject, in the course of which Holkar and his Minister assured me they had no desire whatever to remain in the country of the Sikhs; that there should be no occasion to doubt their sincerity, and that the march was only delayed for one or two days, in order that it might be made at a propitious time, and that some necessary arrangements might be completed. I continued to urge the necessity of an immediate return to Hindostan, and Holkar finally promised to move on the 13th.

He then made several requests in behalf of persons who, being in the power of the British Government, have aided Holkar against it, which he desired me to communicate to your lordship. The details of these I shall hereafter have the honour of representing. I replied, that I would communicate his requests to your lordship. I added, that your lordship was anxious to improve the good understanding which now exists, and that doubtless, when time had given strength and security to the friendship—of which the foundations were established—the British Government would be forward to meet all his wishes. I did not consider myself authorised to give any positive encouragements from which Holkar might expect the accomplishment of the particular requests which he mentioned. A subsequent conversation with the Wakeel Balaram has convinced me that the Chief introduced the subject at the Durbar for the gratification of the persons interested, but that he is not anxious regarding it; and, among others, he states that Meer Khan is not yet satisfied with the portion of country which Holkar has assigned to him.

After some general conversation, and the delivery of presents to me and the other gentlemen of the Mission, we rose to depart. On taking leave, Holkar addressed himself to me, and in a manner marked by an appearance of uncommon earnestness, assured me that he would adhere to the word which he had given, and would render such services to the Honourable Company as should entitle him to its regard and approbation.

Since my return to our camp, Balaram has been sent to me. He has alleged several causes for the delay which has happened in the march of the Mahratta army. He, however, assures me that the army will march ten kas on the 13th, and that it will make no halt before it reaches the Sutlej. Its route does not seem to be settled.

On a review of the whole behaviour of Jeswunt Rao Holkar towards us, it appears to me to mark strongly his high respect for your lordship, his just sense of the act of confidence and friendship conferred in a mission of English gentlemen to his camp, and his most sincere happiness at the establishment of amicable relations with the British Government. The gladness which was visible in him and his chiefs was not confined to the Durbar; it was manifest in every part of his camp; and the crowds of his followers which thronged the way on our procession to the visit, and our return, testified, in the most lively manner, unbounded joy.

We shall march to-morrow towards your lordship's army.

I hope that I may be allowed to express the thankfulness which I feel towards Mr. Macaulay and Lieutenants Short and Laud for their obliging and cordial assistance in the progress of this Mission.

I have the honour to be, with profound respect,

My lord,

Your lordship's most obedient, humble servant,

C. T. METCALFE.

RESIDENCY ALLOWANCES.

(Page 258.)

[*From a Minute by Sir Charles Metcalfe, written in* 1830.]

"The allowances to Residents, in common parlance misnamed 'table allowance,' was an allowance, not for table alone, but nominally for 'table, attendants, camp equipage, &c.,' and in reality for every expense of a domestic nature that was proper for the support of the Resident's station. The expenditure of this allowance was left entirely to the Resident's discretion; but every honourable man knew that if he did not expend it for the purposes for which it was granted,—that is, if he made any savings from it for his own gain—he would be guilty of a shameful fraud. When, therefore, I am asked whether I invariably and sacredly expended that allowance every month, I should be greatly ashamed of myself if I could not answer the question in the affirmative. I expended the whole of the public allowance for the purposes for which it was granted. I might say more, but the sole object of these remarks being to give an unqualified contradiction to an insinuation against me, it is not necessary to pursue the subject."

THE DELHI SYSTEM.

(Page 338.)

[*From a Minute written by Sir Charles Metcalfe in* 1830.]

"Completeness of control and unity of authority were remarkable parts of the Delhi system of administration, as distinguished from that which prevailed in other provinces. One European officer in each district, at the time in question, had entire control over the subordinate native officers in every branch of administration. One superior European officer had entire control over all the superintendents of districts. His control extended to every part of their duties. When the authority of a board was introduced, the only change that took place in the system of local management was the transfer of control from one to several; the district authorities remained as before. . . . .

"It is far from accurate to assert that the Delhi territory is governed without laws. It might more correctly be said to be governed by the same laws which prevail in the provinces subject to the Bengal regulations; for, although these have not been bodily introduced, their spirit has guided the administration, generally, of the Delhi territory; there are local rules besides. The existing institutions were first established by Mr. Seton, a disciple of the regulations. There are generally the same laws in civil and criminal judicature as in the other provinces. The practice of the courts is assimilated. Whatever improvements take place in the other provinces are naturally adopted in the Delhi territory. It has the benefit of every good regulation, with the advantage of not being subject to those which have been found injurious elsewhere, or which might not be locally suitable. The presence of the King and royal family, and of chiefs possessing sovereign power in their separate territories, but residing much at Delhi, as the head-quarters of political supremacy in that quarter, as well as of many other chiefs, formerly Surdars of the Mahratta armies, settled in Jageers, in the Delhi territory, and of numerous diplomatic agents from native states, seems originally to have pointed out the inexpediency of a literal and inconsiderate enforcement of the Bengal regulations; but so much of the spirit, and practice of these laws has from the beginning, and from time to time, been introduced into the Delhi administration, that probably the addition of what remains would only produce deterioration. Were it not for this apprehension, there would be no great change if the regulations were formally established in the Delhi territory, so modified as not to affect those who ought not to be subjected to their direct operation. . . . .

"With respect to the control exercised by Government, as well as with respect to the introduction of laws, the condition of the Delhi territory has been progressive and not stationary. At first, as in other newly acquired countries having peculiarities to deal with and difficulties to overcome, much was entrusted to the local authority. By degrees, the control of Government has become more minute, and the details of management have been more and more approximated to those which prevail elsewhere; whether, in the latter case, with real advantage or disadvantage, it would unnecessarily open a wide field of discussion were I now to inquire. . . . . . .

"At first, when the revenues were small, not much more than a tenth of what they are now, and when the territory was occupied chiefly by dependent Jageerdars, the administration was exclusively in the hands of the Resident, and the assistants under him had only such power as he chose to entrust to them, subject to such control as he thought it expedient to exercise. The system gave him absolute control, and he was exclusively responsible to Government for the proper management of the territory. The assistants were then necessarily young men, because being only assistants to the Resident, their salaries were too small to tempt older servants to seek the same employment. This may be said to have been the case until 1819, with this difference, that some of the assistants remained long enough to cease to be young; and the allowances of the first, augmented by a commission on customs, had become considerable, owing to increase in that branch of revenue. In 1819, a new arrangement took place. The territory was divided into districts, a principal assistant was put in charge of each district, and a civil commissioner appointed to superintend them. From this time the situation of the assistants in respect to salary has improved, and it is no longer necessary to appoint young men. It is now on that footing, that officers of the same standing with those who are usually judges or collectors would naturally be selected. Their powers are, nevertheless, entirely under the control of the commissioner over them; and if they have any power in any degree independent of such control, it has been produced by the progress made in approximating the Delhi system of management to that which prevails in the provinces subject to the Bengal regulations.

"In contending that the employment of young men is no necessary part of the Delhi system, I wish to guard against the impression that I am opposed to the employment of young men. Under control, they may be employed with advantage in any situation. There is a zeal, an energy, an activity of virtue in young men which often more than compensates for mere age and even experience, too often accompanied by apathy, lethargy, and inertness, the consequences of disease caused by a climate, the fiery ordeal of which few constitutions can stand unimpaired for a number of years. In rejecting the services of men when young, in situations in which they can be efficiently controlled, we may lose the best aid that they can ever bring to the public interests. I take it to be an error in the regulation-system of administration, that young men obtain prescribed powers in which they are not sufficiently controlled, and an advantage of what once was the Delhi system that the control is thoroughly absolute and unquestionable."

METCALFE'S DEPARTURE FROM DELHI—ALLEGED CORRUPTION OF HIS SERVANTS.

CHAPTER XII.—ADDENDUM.

[The following extracts from a minute written by Sir Charles Metcalfe, in November, 1829, contain a narrative of all the circumstances connected with the alleged corruption of his "coachman," Khoda Buksh, and his "moonshee," Hufoozoodeen, at Delhi. It was alleged that the former, who was *not* Metcalfe's coachman, had made a lakh of rupees by selling the cast horses and old carriages of his master, on the occasion of Metcalfe's departure from Delhi; and that the latter had for many years been enriching himself by taking bribes from the natives—in both cases, under the pretext that some advantage was to be derived by the Resident, and reciprocated in favour of the donor. To these statements I have appended, taken from the same minute, the case of Peer Alee, the "Khitmudgar," who accompanied him to Hyderabad, and was also said to have made a large fortune by corrupt practices. These histories are on many accounts interesting and suggestive; but I give them here, principally because the circumstances were somewhat notorious at the time, and I should not like it to appear that I considered them subjects to be avoided. In all the three cases Metcalfe's conduct was irreproachable. But he truly said, that he would be a bold man who, after so long a connection with native courts, would venture to say that none of his servants had ever taken bribes. The moonshee, Hufoozoodeen, is the man of whom mention is made in the earlier chapters of this memoir.]

THE CASE OF KHODA BUKSH.

"Khoda Buksh Beg was the son of a respectable old soldier, who commanded a body of 100 horse attached to the Residency, and used partly in the police of the country, and partly as the Resident's body-guard. The father being worn out by age, the son, as his lieutenant, was the efficient commandant, and as such was in constant attendance on the Resident. I had known him in that capacity for twelve years, during the last seven of which he was in almost daily attendance on me, and accompanied me in my morning and evening exercise, as well as on all occasions of out-of-door state and ceremony. During the whole of my acquaintance with him I had no reason to think otherwise than well of him, until the circumstances about to be related.

"When I was quitting Delhi in the end of 1818, I found myself encumbered with a large stud, consisting in great part of a breeding stud, with which I had amused myself for several years without disposing of the produce. Having accounts to settle, I was desirous of selling this stud to the best advantage. I consulted Khoda Buksh Beg on the subject, who was accustomed to traffic in horses, and he persuaded me that my stud would sell well. Having no practice in such dealings, and no wish to enter into them, I entrusted the sale entirely to him. It went on, to appearance, prosperously, and most of my horses, but not all, were, as I supposed, sold, when one of my servants informed me that there was no fair sale, but that Khoda Buksh Beg had imposed my horses on several persons, and levied considerable sums of money in my name, without any reference to the price of the horses.

"As soon as I received this intelligence, which I ascertained to be true, I recovered all the horses supposed to have been sold, and repaid the several parties the sums received by me as the purchase-money. I ordered the restoration, by Khoda Buksh Beg, of the sums which he had fraudulently obtained and appropriated. He was brought to trial for defrauding those who had been the sufferers by his imposture, and sentenced to imprisonment, with an order that he should not be released until he had disgorged all that he had levied. The discovery of this villany was so close upon the period fixed for my departure from Delhi, that I had scarcely time to take the requisite measures to repair the mischief perpetrated as far as it was in my power to do so."

CASE OF MOONSHEE HUFOOZOODEEN.

"The next assertion connected with my name is that of my moonshee, Hufoozoodeen, having accompanied me to and from Hyderabad, and retired with a fortune of about four lakhs of rupees. Moonshee Hufoozoodeen neither accompanied me to nor from Hyderabad, nor was he with me there at any time, and if he possesses anything that can be termed a fortune it is unknown to me, and I am a great dupe, for he is at this moment in my service on an allowance which I give him solely because I believe that he needs it. . . . . I shall enter more fully into the history of Hufoozoodeen. His father was the moonshee with whom I studied in college, and is still living. I read a little with the son (author, also, of a work used in the college for instruction), who was also a college moonshee after I quitted college. When I was in Lord Lake's army in 1805, I sent for Hufoozoodeen, and entertained him in my service, in which he continued until I was sent on a mission to Lahore in 1808, when he became moonshee of the mission, having previously accompanied me, in 1806, on a mission to Holkar's camp, with which I was charged by Lord Lake, and having also performed public duties under me when I was attached, in 1805, in a political capacity, to a separate division of the army commanded by Major-General Dowdeswell. After the termination of the Lahore mission, Hufoozoodeen was again my private servant until I became Resident at Delhi, in 1811. He was then appointed head moonshee at the Residency, and remained in that office until I quitted the Residency in 1818, when he also resigned his situation.

"Up to this period I had never received any complaint against him, and had no reason to suppose him guilty of any improper act whatever. I had never, however, doubted that a man in his situation was liable to strong temptation, and likely to yield to it. My conduct, therefore, towards him had always been regulated by caution, founded on that general distrust; and when I heard, after quitting Delhi, rumours of his having made money there, I was more sorry than surprised.

"The information was vague, and contained nothing positive or tangible. It, however, induced me to discontinue my connection with him, until the suspicions which it created could be completely removed. I wrote to Mr. Fortescue, who was my successor in the civil administration of the Delhi territory, to request that he would inquire and ascertain what was alleged against the moonshee; he replied that he could discover nothing specific against him; that he bore a good character; and was entirely acquitted of doing anything that the natives considered improper; but that he was supposed to have made money, some said by trade, others by the receipt of presents.

This account did not satisfy me, because, if he had received presents unknown to me, he had acted faithlessly; and I continued to withhold my support, and had no intercourse with him.

"About two years afterwards I again wrote to Mr. Fortescue, who was still at Delhi, with a view to ascertain from him whether a longer residence had furnished him with more distinct information respecting the moonshee's conduct, and I asked specifically whether, making the case his own, he would discharge a moonshee of whom he had the same opinions which the result of his inquiries might have led him to entertain of Hufoozoodeen? His answer on that point was, that he should not discharge him. In other respects, it was much the same as before. I had still doubts as to the propriety of employing Hufoozoodeen, and, in fact, never did employ him either at Hyderabad or during my last Residency at Delhi: but I was not, I confess, without suspicions that I had done him injustice, nor without consequent self-reproach.

"On my last return from Delhi to Calcutta he made his appearance, and seemed to be in reduced and impoverished circumstances. As I had ceased to hold that kind of public employment in which a native moonshee would have temptations to take presents, and as my information respecting Hufoozoodeen was, on the whole, creditable to him, I restored him to my private service, after a separation of nine years.

"This is the history of Hufoozoodeen, into which I have been led by a desire to leave nothing untold respecting a man who is said to have made a fortune of four lakhs at a place where the man never was."

CASE OF PEER ALEE, KHITMUDGAR.

"The Khitmudgar, Peer Alee, alluded to in the marginal extract, accompanied me to Hyderabad. He went with me in the pilot schooner which conveyed me to Masulipatam, and arrived, therefore, long before any of my other servants, who followed by land. I had avoided taking a moonshee, as before mentioned, in order that there might be no corruption; but the Ministers and others at Hyderabad could not refrain from tampering with a single servant that accompanied the new

Resident. In a few months after my arrival, I was informed by one of my assistants that this servant was receiving presents extensively. I requested the same gentleman, the late Mr. R. Wells, to investigate the matter. He did so; and although no specific instance could be established, he satisfied his own mind of the general truth of the imputation. I was sure that his decision was just. I could not make the man disgorge, because nothing was proved, and everything was denied. I discharged him from my service, and sent him out of the Nizam's dominions. Whatever he may have acquired in that way, he has since, I believe, in a great measure, squandered; and he is now living at his home on an allowance from me, which he receives because he was the person who discovered to me the iniquitous proceedings of Khoda Buksh Beg, before noticed."

THE DELHI ADDRESS.

[The following is the Address voted by the British residents of Delhi, to which allusion is made at page 337.]

Dear Sir,—Were we to permit your departure, contemplated by us with deep regret, without expressing the veneration and respect we entertain for your many personal excellences, we should do violence to our own feelings.

On this occasion, well aware as we are of your solicitude to shun the most just and measured commendation, we must entreat your permission to declare our sense of that exalted worth, that candour, and openness of heart which shine in all your words and actions, and which exact the highest esteem of all who have enjoyed the happiness of your society. Closely connected with these traits of character are that condescension to all subordinate to your authority, which rendered business a pleasure to those who transacted it under your guidance, and that judgment, firmness, and rectitude, which gave satisfaction to all whose affairs were confided to your decision.

Whilst, however, we contemplate with unfeigned regret your approaching departure, we should deem ourselves deficient in sentiments of public spirit did the loss we are about to sustain so entirely engross our thoughts that we should neglect the opportunity, which your removal from this Residency to fill an honourable and important office near the person of the Governor-General of India affords us, of soliciting your favourable acceptance of our sincere congratulation on the distinguished choice of his Excellency. This selection, by so able a judge of character and merit as the Marquis of Hastings, is to us a sure indication of the extent and importance of the services which have been rendered to Government by the exertion of your talents and virtues; and we cannot, we think, utter a wish which evinces in us a stronger desire for the prosperity of our Eastern possessions, than that you may long continue to aid the councils of British India.

To give this address, however, a more private and particular application, and to do which we are forcibly called by a recurrence to the regretted occasion of our meeting, we beg to assure you that no period of time can efface the sentiments of friendship and affectionate attachment imprinted on our minds by the urbanity, kindness, and marked attention to private rights and feelings, which we have invariably experienced at your hands; and that we shall feel, to the latest moments of our existence, the deepest interest in every event which may be connected with your welfare, happiness, and fame.

METCALFE'S REPLY.

My dear Friends,—I am at a loss for language to express in adequate terms my sense of the kindness which has led you to give expression to the sentiments conveyed in the communication this day received from you. I shall ever remember with lively gratitude the honour which you have thus conferred upon me; nor is the value of this delightful testimony of your regard lessened in my estimation by the consciousness which I feel that I am indebted to it entirely to your indulgent partiality, which has thrown my faults into oblivion, and exalted the little merit to which I may have any pretensions.

The record of your approbation will ever be a source of pride and exultation to me, and furnish during my future life a strong excitement to laudable exertion, from the anxious desire which it must produce that I may not at any time do discredit to the opinion which you have had the goodness to express.

The thanks I owe you are not confined to the present occasion. The obliging attention, cordiality, and friendship which I have always experienced from you in official as well as social intercourse, have made an indelible impression on me; and though highly sensible of the gracious and condescending favour of the Governor-General in calling me to a situation near his own person, I cannot part without deep regret from a society to which I have so much reason to be warmly attached I trust, however, that our intercourse is only suspended, and that I may have the pleasure of renewing it with most, if not all of you, in some of the various scenes of life in which we may be respectively summoned to take a part. With most hearty wishes for your prosperity and happiness, and a grateful recollection of all your kindness, I shall ever remain,

My dear Sirs,

Your sincere and affectionate friend,

C. T. METCALFE.

END OF VOL. II.

London: Printed by SMITH, ELDER and Co., Little Green Arbour Court.

CPSIA information can be obtained
at www.ICGtesting.com
Printed in the USA
LVHW110025200123
737431LV00007B/384

9 783375 134563